Book Cover Design by B.M. Light

Paperback ISBN: 979-8-9902554-8-7

Ebook ISBN: 979-8-9902554-7-0

Secrets in Miami

Book 2 in the Everyone Has Secrets Series

B.M.Light

Trigger Warnings

Your mental health matters.
In this story, there are mentions of the following:

- Remembered events of rape (not detailed on page), and discussions of the subject.

- Kidnapping.

- Scenes of car accidents due to racing.

If any of these subject matters are concerns for you, please do what's best for you. But I will say, this story is one of trauma and recovery where the bad guys get their due justice. So if that's something you'd like to experience, then please open this book up and dive in.

<u>Dedication</u>

To the ones who are surrounded by their 'found family' and the ones
who are still looking for them.
They're out there, just keep searching.

Chapter One

Taylor

"Babe, are you up? I want to get some pool time to ourselves before Mark and Lexi get here!" Bryan shouts from somewhere downstairs.

"Yes, I'm up." I shout back as I walk out of the bathroom that's attached to my room.

In nothing but my pajamas, which consist of Bryan's large T-shirts and my shorts, I search my dresser for a bathing suit so I can go relax by the pool on this warm July morning. As I pull the suit from the drawer, I begin to think back to what all happened seven months ago.

I found out that Bryan's an FBI agent along with his best friend Mark Stone. They were both working undercover looking for the ones responsible for murdering Bryan's parents when he was a child. It turns out they were the same individuals that my best friend, Alexis Smith, or Lexi for short, and I once looked into during my time as a temporary undercover agent—back when I let curiosity get the best of me and got mixed up in her secret world.

Phil and Daryl. I shiver as their names float through my head. Phil was a crooked FBI agent who sold information overseas to the highest bidder, and Daryl was the muscle he used to take out those who learned of his secrets and tried to stop Phil. They almost succeeded in taking out Bryan seven months ago.

From December to February, I barely lived. All I could focus on was losing my boyfriend from that gunshot wound to his chest. Then, in late February, I found out where Phil and Daryl were hiding, and I struck. Looking back, I know it was stupid to walk into that warehouse on my own, but I *needed* to take them down, no matter what.

I glance down at my right forearm, at the little scar that was left behind from taking a bullet to protect Lexi that day. I find myself smiling because it's that scar that actually brought me back to Bryan.

Turns out, during the months that I thought he was dead, he was very much alive, just waiting on Phil and Daryl to be caught so he could come back to the land of the living. FBI protocol and shit.

Wayne Anderson, the man behind the desk at the FBI, told my mother, Kathy–who works at the same hospital that Bryan was admitted to–she was to keep me in the dark until it was safe for everyone involved. Well, that protocol was tossed out the window when I was admitted to the same floor after I was shot.

When the memory of seeing Bryan for the first time comes to mind, a smile spreads across my lips as I slowly pull my red bikini bottoms up over my hips, then I secure the straps of my top against the back of my neck and at my shoulder blades before making sure everything is in place. A moment later, as I look at my reflection in the full-length mirror that hangs on the back of the door; my smile fades as another memory takes place.

I killed Phil that day. He was the first life I was forced to remove from this earth.

He was making one final attempt on Bryan's life, and I knew there was no way I could physically stop him from choking Bryan to death, so I shot him. Sometimes I can still imagine the blood blooming across Phil's back as the bullet did its lethal damage.

I think that's why Wayne gave us these last five months with no cases. To allow us time to get our heads back in the game, and Bryan has made sure of that.

He's always taking me to Mark's cabin, the one that we never got to fully enjoy because of our first run-in with Phil when he hired goons to run us off the road. Bryan's truck was shot at, and he ended up with a bullet lodged in his shoulder. But thanks to the medical training courtesy of Mom and the fact that I wanted to become a nurse at some point in my life, I was able to help him that day.

Looking back on everything, if someone were to ask me if I would have changed anything, I would look them dead in the eye and tell them no.

Being an agent, whether it be temporary or active like I am now, has brought me closer to Lexi and brought Bryan into my life along with Mark, and I never would have met them otherwise.

I know this path we all are on is not going to be easy, but when is *normal* life easy? I just like to add some spice to my everyday life.

After pulling my mid-shoulder-length chestnut brown hair into a ponytail and making sure I'm happy with my bikini, I make my way downstairs.

When I hit the bottom step, I notice the house is empty. I know Mom's working a shift at the hospital right now, and I think my brother Cody is next door with a friend, which leaves me to wonder where my dad went.

I open the sliding glass door to go out back, and find my dad and Bryan pulling the solar cover off the in-ground pool. I lean against the railing on the porch and watch the two men work, both none the wiser of my presence.

Since we've had this downtime, Bryan started working part-time at my dad's garage as a mechanic. I know Dad gave him hell the first time they met, but I'm glad that the two most important men in my life are getting along now.

Once the solar cover is completely removed, Dad taps Bryan on the back, pointing in my direction before heading inside the house. I smile, knowing I'm finally busted, as Bryan's head snaps up to look at me, his own grin pulling up the corner of his mouth.

As he walks over to me on the patio, he bends down, gathering a handful of pool water to splash onto his broad chest and washboard abs. I watch the water droplets slide down his body, and my cheeks flush when his grin turns into a full-on smirk as he catches me eyeing his form.

"Having a good look there, Annie?" Bryan asks, using the nickname he gave me after we first met as he runs his damp hand through his dark brown hair before flopping onto the lounge so the sun can dry his skin.

The name *Annie* comes from how accurate I am with a gun. You know, like Annie Oakley. And Bryan has seen firsthand how good of a shot I am plenty of times now.

"Always, Babe," I say with a smile. "Working on your tan, huh?"

He picks up his black Ray Ban's off the small glass side table and slips them on. "Well, yeah. I'm not gonna be white as a ghost in the summer, Babe."

"Well, in that case," I begin, as I sit down on the lounge between his legs and lean my back against his stomach and chest. "I'll work on mine too."

"Oh, come on! Now I'll have a huge white spot!" Bryan whines.

"Aw, poor baby."

"Like you always so eloquently say, bite me." Bryan deadpans.

"Don't mind if I do."

I flip over onto my knees, so I'm straddling his lap, and even though I can't see his eyes, I know they widen with anticipation. Leaning forward, I press my lips tenderly to his collarbone. The taste of the pool water blooms on my tongue as I tenderly trail kisses up his neck. When my teeth graze the sun-kissed skin right under his jaw, he rewards me with a low groan that rumbles in his chest.

"Taylor," Bryan warns breathlessly.

"Yes, Bryan?" I ask, with my lips still against his neck.

His hands begin to glide up my exposed back, and I'm thankful for the little coverage that my bikini top gives as his warm, rough hands caress my skin. While he pulls me tighter against him with his left hand, his right hand travels up to the base of my skull, fists the hair at the nape of my neck, and pulls my lips away from his skin. A whine of my own tumbles from my throat, and he chuckles at me.

"The term 'bite me' is meant as a metaphor, not an actual challenge, Annie."

"Really? I guess I missed the memo on that one."

Bryan shakes his head as a smile brightens his features. "You are so bad," he chastises as he guides my head down to press his lips to mine.

I pull away just enough where our lips still brush as I say, "You love it, don't lie."

"I never said I didn't." He says as he pulls us together once more. "I was just stating a fact, Baby." He begins tracing his tongue over the seam of my lips, asking for permission to enter.

I gladly oblige as I thread my fingers through his hair, and a moan of desire escapes my mouth at his touch. As our kiss deepens, I feel him grow hard beneath me, making my core light with need.

Just as I'm about to roll my hips against his for any kind of friction to ease the ache, his right hand slides down my neck and back before coming to rest on my left side, pausing in the middle of my skin.

We pause in our movements, knowing what he's feeling, and I can't help it when my fingers find the scar on his chest. All playfulness and want evaporates from our systems, like water on hot asphalt.

Bryan gently traces the three-inch scar on my side with his thumb, sending goosebumps skittering over my skin. I look from the small circular scar on his chest, my own index finger tracing the circle, before lifting my eyes to his sunglass-covered ones.

I pull the Ray Ban's off so I can look into his green eyes with no restrictions. "Hey, remember what you said before? They're just reminders of what we went through; they mean nothing now." I whisper.

"I know. But it's hard not to think about it sometimes." Bryan says as he drags his hand up my side to caress my forearm before pressing a tender kiss to the flaw staring back at him.

"Well," I taunt as I kiss his chest, right over his scar, before making my way back up his neck and just hovering over his lips. "Why don't you think about me again? Or am I that forgettable?" I tease as I playfully stick out my bottom lip in a pout.

Pulling me against his solid body once more, Bryan crushes our mouths together, pulling my bottom lip between his teeth, which sends a pleasurable shiver down my spine. "You are far from forgettable, Annie."

Just as our lips meet again, I feel someone staring at us. Glancing toward the house, I see Dad in the kitchen window above the sink. Bryan tilts his head backward, so he's looking in the same direction, before letting out a defeated sigh.

"I tell ya, parents really know how to kill the mood."

"Yeah, well, they know we are getting serious about each other, so they are watching us like hawks." I say.

We are being a little more adventurous in our affection towards each other. Kissing one another a little more deeply and teasing jabs like we did just now, but we haven't done anything out of the way. Besides, if we had sex in my parents' house and Mom found out, Bryan would really be dead. The angel of death would cash in on him; she'd make sure of it this time.

"I keep telling them that we aren't doing anything, but they won't let up," I grumble.

"She's just being a mom, and he's being a good dad. Every time I go see Granny, she asks me if I'm being a gentleman to you. If we are doing anything we would regret later. But Grandpa just looks at me and winks." Bryan says with a smile.

"Oh, so he's edging you on while your grandmother is basically telling you not to screw up." I say with a smile.

"He wants me to tell him that we are, but deep down he knows I'm listening to Granny."

"I say keep doing what we're doing unless Mom or Dad actually tells us to stop. We know we're not doing anything, so why change?"

"You got more guts than I do." Bryan chuckles.

"No. It's just they're thinking the worst, and if we stop, they'll think they were right and jump on us." I say as I trace a finger down the middle of his chest. "We just might hold back a little."

"Alright, it's your call," Bryan says with a nod.

I turn back around to lie on Bryan's chest and close my eyes to let the sun warm me. After a few minutes of silence, I hear footsteps in the grass.

"Mark, what are you doing here so soon?" Bryan asks before I can.

"Spending some extra quality time with you." Mark shoots back.

"Smart ass," Bryan says.

"Hey, you better think about who you're talking to, buddy!" Mark snaps with a playful attitude.

"Oh, yeah?" Bryan questions him and gently pushes me off him so he can get to his feet.

I roll my eyes, and I already know that this will be a man-fight. It won't be anything serious, but it will make them both look like a couple of children fighting over something stupid.

"Here we go again." Lexi says with an exasperated sigh as she collapses onto the lounge next to mine.

She rests her right hand on her forehead to shield her eyes from the sun so she can watch our boyfriends make asses out of themselves. I can tell that she is ready to kill him, just like I'm ready to kill Bryan.

"Come on, guys, this is ridiculous," Lexi says.

I look at the two of them, and I size them up. Mark is bigger and a tad taller than Bryan, but he has a little more speed than Mark does, but not by much. I watch as Bryan slowly backs Mark toward the in-ground pool, and I try to keep the smile off my face as Bryan inches him toward the edge.

Once he has Mark where he wants him, he pushes on Mark's chest, making him fall backward into the pool with a shout. I shoot Lexi a quick glance, and she instantly nods her approval at my scheme. I quickly get up, rush over to Bryan, flatten my palms against his back, and push.

"Taylor, what the—" He begins as he has no choice but to belly flop into the water with Mark.

"There, now you both are wet," I say once Bryan breaks the water's surface.

Mark snorts at my comment like the child that he is, but Bryan is too busy looking at me to get my innocent remark.

I stand there, my gaze fixed on his playful green eyes as he swims towards the side of the pool and he runs both of his hands up my legs, making them tremble at his tender caress. Then, with a sly smile blooming on his face, he makes my knees buckle, and I fall forward into the pool.

When I break the surface, I hear Bryan and Mark laughing at me, so I swim behind Bryan and jump on his shoulders, pushing him under the water's surface. After a few seconds, I let him up, and he just stares at me, shocked that I would retaliate like that.

"What, you didn't think I would do something to get back at you? Well, you thought wrong, buddy." I say.

Bryan smiles at me as he shakes his head like a wet dog, making his dark hair spike up in all directions, and I can tell by the look in his eyes that he is going to come for me again. I back up until I hit the edge of the pool and just stand there, looking him in the eye.

"Touch me, I dare you."

"What are you going to do to me if I do?" Bryan asks, his tone dipping to a lower octave.

"You'll never know," I taunt.

He stands in front of me for a few seconds, and I watch him, trying to guess what he's going to do. Then, in one swift movement, he scoops me up in his arms and turns around.

"Bryan, don't you dare—"

He throws me into the middle of the pool, and I sink all the way to the bottom. When my butt touches the floor, I flatten my feet so I can spring back up. Once I clear the water from my face, I glare at him when I see that he and Mark are trying to hide their smiles.

"Lexi! Come on, Babe! Come in and have some fun!" Mark says while still laughing at me.

"Yeah, Lexi, come in here so we can gang up on these guys." I say.

"Fine. You want this, you got it," Lexi grins as she walks over to the side of the pool, jumps in, and immediately goes after Mark.

"Not me, Lexi!" Mark exclaims, and this time it's me who's laughing at him.

Lexi swims up behind him and wraps her arms around Mark's waist, pulling him under and holds him there. I can tell he's trying to get out of her hold, but she's not letting up until *she* wants to.

Finally, he's able to break free and comes up for air. "You almost made me drown!"

"Oh, no, I did not, you big baby. You overreact too much." Lexi says as she splashes him. "You just got had by your girlfriend!"

"She's strong. Sometimes I'm surprised by just how strong she is." Mark says as pride shines in his eyes for his girl, but just under that, I see a darkness flicker in his stare, too. Almost like he's remembering something that makes him equally angry and terrified at the same time.

I don't get to think too much of his reaction when Lexi drags me out of the pool so we can sit in the loungers and let the sun dry us off. The guys join us a minute later, taking a few beach towels and laying them beside us, and we all work on our tans together in comfortable silence.

After about an hour, turning once to work on our backs, we hear the sliding glass door open behind us. I look over my shoulder to find my dad standing in the doorway.

"Taylor, there's a phone call for you."

"Who is it?" I ask, looking from my father, who still has the house phone clutched in his hand, then back to my friends, who are waiting with bated breath to see who's on the other end of the phone.

"It's Wayne." Dad replies stiffly.

Chapter Two

Taylor

I take the phone from my father and slowly start to walk back to my lounge. "Hello?"

"Taylor, hello. Sorry to bother you out of the blue, but I would like for you to come down to the agency and help me out with something," Wayne says, his tone friendly, but all business.

"Okay, I'll get the others and we will be there in thirty."

"No. I just want you to come down."

"Okay, sure, I'll be there in a bit." I say with a touch of confusion in my tone and begin to wonder why he only wants me as I hang up the phone and glance around at my friends, all eager to hear what the exchange was about. "I have to go to the agency for a while. I'll be back as soon as I can."

"What's going on?" Bryan asks as he stands from his beach towel on the ground and walks over to me.

"Wayne didn't tell me. But he said it was only for me, though. So, I guess I'll find out soon." I tell him as I grab for his hand, giving it a reassuring squeeze.

"Just be careful, Babe." Bryan says.

"I will. I'll let you know when I get there and when I'm coming home."

I lean into him, my hand running over his chest as I give him a quick kiss to ease the concern shining in his green eyes. Once I feel him smile against my mouth, I pull back, wave to Mark and Lexi, and go up to my room to get dressed in a pair of jean shorts and a yellow tank top. Once dressed, I grab the keys to my 2009 Ford Focus and leave.

When I arrive at the agency thirty minutes later, I walk up the cream-colored marble stairs to Wayne's office and wait at the threshold of his door for him to get off the phone. I hear him laugh, which is something I have never heard from him. He rubs at his temples like the person on the other end of the line is the biggest pain in his ass, but his amused smile conveys a different story.

Wayne finally looks up when he clocks my movement near his door. He must be close to closing out the call because he motions for me to come in and take a seat. I notice his tan button-down shirt is pressed to perfection and compliments his dark skin tone.

"Sure, Levi. I have a few names in mind to send over to you. You're still in California, right?" He pauses, apparently this Levi person answering on the other end. "Okay. I'll send them over within the hour." Wayne places the receiver into the cradle with a sound click before turning his attention to me. "Sorry about that." Wayne says with an apologetic smile. "Old friend from my army days." He adds while pointing to one of two newspaper clippings he has framed behind his desk.

W. Anderson and L. Chamberlain Bust Local Trafficking Ring.

When my eyes take in the second clipping, I still wonder who this T. Huntington is that helped Wayne find the daughter of the Vice President that went missing several years ago. But I don't ask him about that yet. I have more important things on my mind, like why he asked me to come here...alone.

"It's okay." I flick my wrist to wave him off. "So, what's up?"

"I was hoping you could help us crack a code we found four and a half months ago." Wayne says, and all the humor that was in his tone a moment ago completely vanishes.

"You found something that long ago and you're just now calling me in to look at it?" I ask, furrowing my brow in confusion that he would sit on something for that amount of time.

"Well, we think it would be personal to one of your partners," Wayne says.

"Who?" I ask, but he just looks at me. "Wayne, tell me who it is." I demand, annoyance filling my voice.

"We're not sure," Wayne says, his voice low and serious.

"If you weren't sure, you wouldn't have said to come alone!" I take a breath. "Is it Bryan?" I ask bluntly. Wayne doesn't answer me, but that's all the answer I need from him. "What do you think it is?"

"It's a message from someone, and yes, I believe it's for Bryan, but we can't figure it out. That's why I called you. I hear you're good at breaking codes." Wayne says with a small smile.

"Alright, I'll help. Show me where to go."

"You need to go down to the morgue." Wayne says simply.

"The morgue!" I yell.

"Oh yes, I forgot to mention the code is on two sets of bones."

"Two sets of bones? That just *happened* to slip your mind?!" I shriek. "Where did you find them?"

"The warehouse."

My stomach drops as images of two skeletal bodies, one hanging from the ceiling and another resting on the floor, flood my mind. "You mean they might be Paul and Cindy?" I ask, instantly thinking about the worst.

Wayne nods his head, and I get a sick feeling in my gut. I don't want to keep playing with the dead.

"Misty will take you down. Once you think you have something, let me know. My extension is on the phone; just dial the numbers."

I look back over my shoulder, and Misty stands in the threshold of Wayne's door, black pencil skirt and white button-up blouse all pressed to perfection. She's a little taller than me, but that's because of the three-inch black heels she's wearing, and her hair is a short blonde bob that comes to just the bottom of her earlobes. Misty gives me a bright, nervous smile, and I reluctantly stand to follow her down to the elevator.

Once inside, she presses a button labeled M and swipes her keycard. When the elevator doors close and the car begins to move, I notice that she is looking at me out of the corner of her eye, but when I glance at her, she turns away to look down at her feet. Feeling her nervous energy, I decide to break the odd tension between us with a little small talk.

"So, how long have you been with the agency?" I ask.

Her voice matches her smiley personality, all light and bubbly. "About two years." She pauses and with an exasperated sigh, she turns to me and adds, "I'm sorry if this is inappropriate, but I can't believe that I'm in the same elevator with *the* Taylor Sparks. I heard about the big case you and your partners solved seven months ago." Her voice drops to a somber tone. "I'm just sad it ended the way it did."

"I didn't mean to kill anyone, no matter how much they deserved it, but I had no choice at the time." I say, knowing she's talking about the deaths of Phil and Daryl.

"Don't beat yourself up." Misty says while resting a reassuring hand on my shoulder. "I'm sure you did the best thing you could in the moment."

Once we reach our floor, the elevator doors open, and I am hit with the coolness and stillness of the basement. I take a cleansing breath as I walk out of the elevator, and on my left I see a set of metal double doors with MORGUE written above them in bright, simple silver lettering, but Misty stops short, not following me in.

"Here we are. If you have any problems, Dr. White can help you." Misty says quickly, all friendliness fading when she sees the doors in front of her.

I turn around to thank her, but I hear the ding of the elevator and I know she's already gone.

I wish I could run away too. I hate being in the morgue.

With a sigh, I walk through the double doors and into the belly of the morgue.

"Hello?" I ask the empty room.

Just as I think I'm going to be alone down here, an older man pops out from a room to my left, and I jump at his sudden appearance in front of me. His thinning white hair stands out wildly in a few places on his head while his white doctor's coat swishes around his waist. He looks almost like Doc Martin from those *Back to the Future* movies Dad liked to watch when I was younger.

"Ahh, Agent Sparks. How are you today?"

"I'd be better if I wasn't standing down in a morgue." I say, trying to remove the note of fear in my voice.

"I like you." He grins, but it's a wild expression as he leads me deeper into the room, and I wonder just how sane this dude is. "Now, here are the two skeletons that Wayne wants you to look at. Take your time. If you need anything, let me know."

"Well, what have you done to try and crack that code on the bones?" I ask.

"I have done everything you could think of. I've put them into a GPS. I've tried a phone number, and I've come up with nothing." He says.

"Oh, by the way, in case you haven't figured it out, my name is Dr. White."

"Well, Dr. White, I will try everything I can to crack this." I say as I give him a smile that I hope comes off as friendly and not pleading for him to not try any experiments on me. With his white coat and wild hair, and creepy grin, he looks like a mad scientist.

"Good luck." Dr. White says while leaving to go into his lab.

I grab a pair of blue medical gloves from a box that sits on a table against the far wall before I walk over to the bones, which are sitting on the two metal tables before me. I don't even know where to look to study this code, so I just take it one bone at a time. Skull, vertebrae, ribs, sternum, and so on.

After looking them over for about an hour, I finally find a number sequence on both femurs. The numbers 93273 are supposedly on Paul's bones, and the numbers 25483 7.3 2.3 are on Cindy's. I begin to wonder how else I can start to put them together when Dr. White pops his head back into the room.

"Agent Sparks, I forgot to disclose an important piece of information."

"What is it?" I ask.

"These bones are not real. There is no bone marrow in them at all." Dr. White exclaims.

"Seriously? Why would someone put numbers on fake bones?" I ask.

"To say something to someone. You must figure out this code, Agent Sparks," Dr. White says with urgency.

After a little bit, and when Dr. White leaves the room for the second time, I find that I'm stuck. I haven't been able to make a connection with the numbers at all. I look up at the clock that hangs over the metal double doors, and I realize I've been here for four hours and I am nowhere close to figuring this code out.

"Dr. White!" I call into his lab, and he grunts his acknowledgement. "I'm gonna head out for the night. I'm coming up with nothing so far. I'll be back tomorrow."

"Alright. Have a good night, Agent Sparks."

I just get into my car when my phone beeps with a text message.

Bryan: Hey babe. R u doin' ok?

Me: Yeah. I'm fine. I'm actually leaving now. Be home soon. Luv u. *heart emoji*

When I get home, I find that the house is dark. So, I quietly make my way upstairs and into my room. I don't flick on the light, because I faintly see Bryan's form and he's already asleep in my bed. I smile at his slumbering form as I peel out of my tank and shorts, grab one of his t-shirts again along with a fresh pair of sleep shorts, and head into the bathroom to finish getting ready for bed.

Once I slip underneath the covers, Bryan instantly turns over, acting like the bigger spoon and cradling my back into his chest while his arm drapes over my side and stomach. The last thing I remember before I let sleep take me is his soft kiss behind my ear.

Chapter Three

Taylor

I wake up at five the next morning from those numbers dancing around in my dreams, mocking me with an answer that's just out of reach. Bryan's light snore catches my attention, and when I turn my head to look at him, I am met with his broad, shirtless back. I don't move for a minute, waiting to see if he will somehow feel that I'm awake.

As I listen to the steady rhythm of his breathing, I begin to think about the numbers once again, but they don't give me any answers. I turn over, trying to keep the frustrated sigh locked in my chest as my eyes land on my phone. I keep staring at it and, for some reason, I think back to old-school texting, where you had to press the same button so many times to coordinate to a single letter. My whole body freezes.

What if the numbers represent letters?

I slowly get out of bed and quietly get dressed in the main bathroom, so I don't disturb Bryan. I leave him a note on his nightstand to let him know where I am before I grab my badge from my bedside drawer and quietly leave the house.

When I arrive at the agency, no one questions why I'm here at five-thirty in the morning. I step into the elevator so I can head down to the morgue, scanning my badge like Misty did yesterday, hoping that somehow my ID is logged into the system. I let loose a relieved sigh when the elevator begins to move. Once the doors open a moment later, I go over to the bones and get to work.

I copy the numbers down on a piece of paper, then I look at my phone to see what letter corresponds to each number and begin my decoding process.

After several hours of running every phrase I can think of, I finally break the code.

"We are alive P.E C.E." I say out loud.

I rush over to the black phone that hangs on the wall, pick up the receiver, and dial Wayne's extension to tell him to meet me.

"The code was a message." I tell him as soon as he exits the elevator five minutes later. "On the male set of bones is 'We are', and on the female set is 'Alive P.E C.E'."

"I'll be damned." Wayne says.

"Do you think it's real?" I ask.

"I don't know."

"Why would they send this kind of message?"

"They might not even be alive now. They might have planted those years ago, and no one has ever found them until now. So, until I have more concrete evidence, I would keep this under wraps." Wayne instructs.

"I agree. Bryan doesn't need to be hurt." I say as I shove the paper into the back pocket of my shorts.

"In the meantime, you can go home and tell him and the others that a case may be coming up within the next few days." Wayne tells me with a tight smile. "I'm just ironing out a few more details first."

"Alright. We'll get ready and wait for your call." I say.

As I leave the agency, I start to think about the bones and the code again. If Bryan's parents are alive or were at one point after everyone thought they were murdered, why would they plant them in the warehouse? I'm sure they knew of the possibility that no one would find them.

Besides, I was in that warehouse before Bryan ever came into my life, and I never noticed any skeletons or bodies in there. But I did the night Bryan saved me and got shot back in December. I just hope that no one would have planted them to hurt him. I decide then and there I will get to the bottom of this, no matter the end result. Bryan deserves to know whether his parents are alive or not.

When I pull up to the house thirty minutes later, I notice that his black F-150 is missing from the driveway. So, I unlock the door, and when I'm met with an empty house, I pull out my phone and text Bryan.

Me: Hey babe. I'm home. Where r u?

Bryan: At Mark's place working out

Me: Oh. Well I'm home. And I think I'm gonna take a nap for a while. Don't get into any trouble. *Winky Face emoji*

Bryan: I'll be home soon. And I'm like you, trouble is my middle name. *Winky face with tongue emoji*

Me: Yeah, yeah, I know. *Eye roll emoji*

I lock my phone, kick my shoes off and lie in bed as I wait for Bryan to get home, but in the meantime, I'm thinking about the message again.

Why would they send a coded message like that? Are they trapped somewhere? Or are they scared that Bryan wouldn't want to see them after all these years? I know Bryan would want to see them; he misses them so much, even with the limited memories he has of them. Now, calling them mom and dad right off the bat, maybe not, but still, I know he would want to get to know them again. I just really hope that this ends in a good way and not in a bad one.

I must have fallen asleep because, when I hear my door open, it takes a moment for my eyes to focus on Bryan standing next to the bed with a loving smile on his face.

"Hey there, Annie. When did you get up? You look exhausted."

"Five. I told you in my note I had to get to the agency early this morning."

"Hold that thought, Babe. I'm all sweaty, and I've missed you today, so I want to get cleaned up before I give you a hug."

"Okay. Hurry back." I tell him as I grab his hand, pulling him down so I can give him a quick kiss, and the saltiness of his skin blooms on my tongue.

"Be right back." He says as he goes into the bathroom, takes a quick shower and joins me in bed five minutes later.

"So how'd it go?" Bryan asks as he pulls my chest against his so we can look at one another face to face.

As he holds me close with his hand at the small of my back, I can feel that his body is warm and tense from working out, but it is slowly relaxing from the shower, and with my weight pressed against him.

"Good." I say with a fake cheerfulness that I hope he doesn't see through. I can't let him know that I'm still boggled about that code and what it could mean.

"What did Wayne want?" Bryan asks.

"He...wanted me to teach a shooting class today." I lie.

"And?" Bryan asks.

"I told him yesterday that all the rookies better be there and that this will be a one-time thing." I say. I hate lying to him, but right now, it's best until we have solid proof one way or another.

"Really?"

"Yeah," I begin. "Oh! And just as I was getting ready to leave, Wayne told me he has a case coming up for us." I add, so I can distract Bryan from asking too many more questions.

"He did? Did he say where we're going?" Bryan asks.

"I don't know, he didn't say yet."

"Do you know any more details?"

"Nope," I say. "He said he'd call us in the next few days, but be prepared to leave soon." I say as I close my eyes, leaning into him and placing a gentle kiss on his chest while trying to focus on what's coming for us and going on my first real case as a full-fledged agent.

Chapter Four

Taylor

The next morning, as I'm lying on my stomach, I wake up to the feeling of Bryan's fingers lazily tracing lines down the curve of my spine. I turn my head to the right and I find him staring at me with an easy grin on his face.

"Good morning, beautiful."

"Morning." I reply sleepily, turning over onto my side to face him fully.

His gaze dips to my mouth for a heartbeat before looking back into my eyes, the green hue darkening in a silent request. I smile, and that's all the answer he needs. He pushes me onto my back, the upper half of his body hovering over mine a moment before his lips find the sensitive skin of my neck. As I bend my head to the side, I hook my leg over his hip, my own silent request to have his whole body pressed against me.

He complies with a growl against my skin, and I can't help the low moan that escapes when I feel the weight of his body envelop mine. His lips move up my neck to my jaw before landing on my mouth, kissing me once, twice, before teasing the seam of my lips with his tongue, asking permission to enter.

This is one of the many things I love about this man. He's always asking, either verbally or with his actions. He never does anything I'm not ready for. So with his silent plea, I open my mouth for him, and he dives in. His tongue dances with mine, and he greedily swallows my moans while his hands caress the curve of my waist.

He pulls back enough to let the both of us catch our breath, but I don't let him stay away for long. I lift my head, pressing my mouth to his, and I pull his bottom lip between my teeth, urging him back into my space.

"Annie, you drive me crazy, you know that?" Bryan growls.

I just give him a sultry smile, almost daring him to show me just how crazy I really make him. And he complies instantly. Pushing me back down to the bed and trailing the knuckles of his left hand over the swell of my breast. My breath comes out in quick pants as he grazes my hardened nipple through the fabric of my shirt.

"So damn beautiful, Taylor."

His eyes lock onto mine as if thinking about his next move. I swallow as his right hand continues to caress my breast and watch as he moves his left hand down my belly, and I suddenly know where he wants to be. Part of me screams for him to touch me where the fire burns the most, but it's like my brain is trying to reign in my raging hormones, and before I comprehend what I'm doing, I grab his wrist, halting his movement.

"I'm sorry." I blurt out.

"Don't you dare apologize." Bryan says, his eyes sharp, but not because I'm stopping him from touching me. "I told you before, you have all the power here. If you're not ready yet, that's fine, Baby. I'll wait until you are." He pulls his hand away from the waistband of my shorts and from my breast before grasping the back of my neck, making me look into his loving green eyes. "What can I do to make things better for you?"

I stare into his eyes and I see nothing but love and patience shining back, and I know his words, just like always, are true.

"Kiss me." I request, because in this moment, that's what I want more than anything now.

"I can do that, Annie," Bryan says with a smirk playing on his lips.

His mouth collides with mine, and he threads his fingers through my hair, bending my head where he wants so he can deepen the kiss. As his tongue enters my mouth a second time, my body reacts, saying the hell with my brain, and I hook my left leg over the small of his back.

Without any further coaxing, his hips roll against my aching center, igniting a fire deep in my belly when I feel just how hard he is for me through the fabric of his sleep shorts.

"You're a tease, Taylor Allison Sparks." He growls into my neck as he flexes his hips again, and I can't stop my other leg from moving so that he's now trapped between my legs. "You love torturing me, don't you?" He pants like he's in actual pain.

"Well, I like to torture the both of us then." I say breathlessly.

Bryan then pivots us where he's on his back and I am straddling him, my hands splayed across his bare chest. "You just need to trust yourself, Baby. You have the instincts to know what you want, and you just have to realize that you're safe with me." He picks up my left hand and kisses the pink sapphire promise ring that sits on my ring finger. My heart skips a beat as he looks up at me with hooded eyes. "I will take good care of you, Taylor."

"I know." I say, leaning in to kiss him again. "And I want you, but it just doesn't feel right, right now. I'm sorr–"

I stop short when Bryan nips at my ring finger, and his sharp glare tells me all I need to hear.

"Okay, okay." I say, holding my right hand up in surrender, and he gives me a playful smile. "But I am all for you kissing me senseless."

"Glad to hear that, Baby."

Bryan pulls me down on top of him, and just as his lips touch mine, his phone begins to ring, but he doesn't stop his worship of my mouth.

"It's probably Mark. Let it go to voicemail." Bryan says while his lips brush against mine.

He flips me back over, pulling his shirt that I slept in last night up my body, just stopping short of baring my breasts to him. He again looks at me before making any movements, waiting for my permission.

I tilt my head, urging him to show me his intentions. He slowly leans in, pressing his lips right at the base of my sternum before traveling down the length of my belly, his lips tickling the sensitive skin on my sides. I squirm under his tender touch, and just when I didn't think the sensation could get any better, he throws me for another loop, grazing his teeth over my skin and I can't help it when my back bows off the bed in response.

Bryan chuckles darkly against my skin. "This is what you do to me, Taylor. You drive me to the point of insanity. I only thought it fair to give you a taste of your own medicine."

His words trigger something in my brain like it's finally catching up to the white flags my body is desperately waving for any kind of relief. So I grab his right hand and before I really know what I'm doing, I'm guiding it to my short-clad core. Bryan's gaze snaps to mine for reassurance, and just before his hand cups me between the legs, his damn phone rings again.

"Damn it! No." I whine.

"This better be good." Bryan growls and then snaps into the phone when he answers it, "Hello?" A heartbeat later, his cringe lets me know it's not Mark on the other side. "Yeah, hold on, let me put you on speaker." He does and shows me the caller ID. "Go on, Wayne."

"Hi Taylor." Wayne has the audacity to laugh. "I hope I wasn't interrupting anything."

"Oh no. Not at all." I try to keep the sarcasm out of my tone, but I fail when both men chuckle at me and Bryan rolls his eyes.

"I have a case for you two and for Mark and Lexi. You four will be going to Miami, and your objective is to bust a local drug and illegal street racing ring. You are to report at the airfield in a few hours where you will meet the agents you will be working for, and they will fly you down. Any questions?" Wayne asks.

"No," Bryan and I say in unison.

"Good. Now you let Mark and Lexi know and to pick you up within two hours."

Wayne disconnects the call without another word, and I look at Bryan, all desire from a few minutes ago fading from my body to be replaced with apprehension. "Well, my first real case." I say with a hint of fear filling my voice.

"It's no different from what you have already done. You'll do fine." Bryan says while sitting up on the side of the bed to text Mark. Once the whoosh sound of the message being sent echoes in the air between us, he gets up and starts to look for clothes to pack, and I do the same.

"Hey, Bryan, we need some jean shorts; could you throw a few pairs in the wash?" I ask.

"Already on it." Bryan says.

He takes a few pairs of his jean shorts along with a few pairs of mine, and he goes down to the laundry room. After ten minutes, I finish packing and I look at what I have in my suitcase. There are several different types of tops: tanks, short sleeves, and three-quarter sleeves, all in different colors, especially black. I have a few pairs of cotton shorts and capris to go along with the jean shorts once they are done. For shoes, I have one pair of sandals and a pair of sneakers. I also pack a small toiletry bag with make-up, hair ties, my toothbrush and some perfume.

Once I have everything of mine packed, I just sit on the side of my bed and stare at my two pieces of luggage while trying to prepare myself for the upcoming flight.

Chapter Five

Mark

The sounds of Lexi in the kitchen of my apartment fixing breakfast hits my ears, and the smell of bacon, eggs, sausage and toast fills the air as I walk out of our ensuite bathroom. Just when I'm about to walk out of the bedroom to help her, my phone pings with a text message from Bryan, and I sit on the corner of the bed to read it.

Bryan: Hey man. We have a case finally. We're flying down to Florida. Meet here at Taylor's place in two hours and we'll all go to the airport in your SUV.

Me: Ok man. Sounds good.

Just as I send that message, Lexi walks into the bedroom in nothing but my black t-shirt that comes mid-thigh and two plates resting in the palm of her hand.

"Oh man. Breakfast in bed? Baby, I feel special." I grin.

"I can turn around and walk out of here and put it on the table." Lexi snaps teasingly.

"As much as I'd love to watch you walk away, Baby, I want you here with me so I can take care of you."

She smiles as she hands me my plate of scrambled eggs, sausage links, and toast. "You took *care* of me last night." She says suggestively.

"Apparently not enough if you're already spicy this morning." I say while pulling her free hand to my mouth and playfully nipping at her wrist.

I pick up her fork, then stab the eggs before lifting the utensil to her lips.

"Mark, I can feed myself." Lexi grumbles, but when I edge the fork closer, she reluctantly opens and I ease the food into her mouth.

"I know you can, but you know it's a kink I have."

"Yes. My ever-loving Pleasure Dom," She says while rolling her eyes.

"Damn right." I smirk.

After she's finished off half her plate, I take a breath and tell her about Bryan's text. "Hey, Lex. Bryan messaged me this morning."

She looks at me, her body going still. "What was it about?" She asks slowly.

"Wayne sent the four of us a case."

"That's great!" Lexi exclaims. "You had me worried there for a minute."

"Yeah, well. It's out of town."

Her eyes sharpen at my words. "And it's not in Cali, is it?"

"No, Baby. It's in Florida." I tell her while rubbing her upper arm.

"It's fine. Nothing will happen in Florida." She says, but her words are more for herself than me.

"Alexis." I say, my voice commanding but flowing with safety. She looks at me, her blue eyes glazing over with a touch of fear. "You are safe with me. You know that."

She nods, but then I can see that something snaps in her mind and as she flicks her eyes back down to the gray and white comforter on the bed, her voice is so low that I barely hear it when she whispers, "Remind me."

It breaks my heart that after two years, things still haunt her. But we have our ways to remind her that nothing will ever come as close to that hellish day again.

I gently pick up both plates from the bed and take them over to my long dresser near the door. When I turn back to face her, she's moved to where she's leaning against the headboard, knees tucked against her chest, eyes still locked onto the bed trying to hide the fear in them, but I can tell they are pleading for me to rip the memories away from her mind.

I take a step towards her and drop my black shorts and boxers. My movement must catch her attention because her eyes immediately land on my face before her gaze travels down my body, stopping at my semi-hard erection. I can't stop the chuckle that drifts from my throat when her eyes widen at seeing me.

Obviously, this isn't the first time she's seen me naked; I mean, hell, we made love just last night, but her reaction is the same every single time. I think it's because deep down she knows this is all hers whenever she wants it.

When I step closer to the bed, she drags her gaze up my body again, and when she meets my stare, her breath hitches a little in both panic and anticipation.

"I think it's time that I get to see your perfect body, Baby." I growl as I climb onto the bed to kneel in front of her before gripping the hem of my shirt, slowly tugging it over her head, and tossing it onto the floor where my shorts lie forgotten in the corner.

I stare at her soft and supple body, and under the heat of my gaze, her nipples harden as an involuntary shiver runs through her, and I can't help the smirk that lifts the corner of my mouth.

"Are you cold, Alexis?" She just keeps staring at my mouth, not answering my question. "Well then, let me warm you up."

I lean in, softly pressing a kiss to her lips, and she jumps a bit at the contact. I have to bury the flare of anger that ignites in my chest at her reaction to my touch, but the feeling is in no way directed at her; it will forever and always be towards the son of a bitch who opened this internal wound inside her.

I thread my fingers through her blonde hair as I continue to tenderly kiss her until her muscles relax a bit under my hand. Then, I tease my tongue over the seam of her lips, silently asking for permission to enter, and she immediately opens up to me. I slide my tongue inside, gliding it over hers and her teeth before I bite down on her bottom lip. This seems to finally bring her out of her PTSD episode a little bit, and she caresses the back of my neck with her slender, trembling fingers.

Once I feel her touching me with the slightest bit of intent, I grab her hip with my right hand, pulling her flat onto her back and pressing my knee against her warm center. She softly moans in response, but I can tell it's only an instinctual sound. It's not *her*. I still don't see her present behind her eyes, and that tells me she's still wrestling with memories.

"Alexis, look at me." I demand, pressing my knee closer to her core while flicking her clit with my middle finger.

She cries out, but when she looks at me, I see my Lexi blazing back at me with desire that's warring for space between the fear.

"That's it, Baby. Look at me. Only at me." I praise.

"Mark, please." She begs.

I lean in to kiss her again while I line my now rock-hard shaft at her entrance. "How do you want me to rip those memories away, Sweetheart? Slow and easy, or fast and hard?" I ask as I tease her with my crown.

Lexi grips my back, her fingers grazing over the scar that could have been a killing blow if it was just a hair more to the left.

"Talk to me, Alexis." I growl as I edge into her just enough to feel her inner muscles begin to ripple around me.

"Hard and fast." She pants.

"Then hold on, Baby." I tell her as I pull back to the tip and thrust into her with one move, sinking to the hilt.

Her screams and my grunts echo in the room as I feel the tension, which was caused by those fucking memories that plague her, fade from her body. As I piston in and out of her in the brutal way I know she goes feral for, her head tilts back into the pillow and as the loudest whimper of pleasure rips from her throat, that's when I know I finally have her back with me.

"That's it, Baby. Who does this body belong to?" I grunt as I bottom out inside her.

"Me." She moans.

"Good girl. Who else?" I ask as I drive deeper, hitting her sweet spot that I know makes her see stars.

"You." Lexi pants as she drags her nails down my back and arms while nipping and kissing my neck.

"That's right." Thrust. "I am the *only one* that can touch." Thrust. "Kiss." Thrust. "Devour. Love. Claim." I rut into her with each word. "And sink into this *perfect* body so deeply that you come around me in a fit of fireworks. Isn't that right?" I growl, thrusting one last time inside her perfect body that I swear was made only for me.

"Yes! Yes! Only you, Mark!" Lexi shouts as her orgasm rolls over her.

"I am the one that kills these memories each and every time." I declare as my own release barrels down my spine, filling her to the brim.

Once the aftershocks of our release fade, I slowly pull out of her, and smug satisfaction blooms in my chest from the mess I made of the both of us. But when I look into her shiny cornflower blue eyes, the smugness turns into pure pride that she was able to once again win in this fight against her inner demons.

I reach out and brush a strand of hair away from her face. "Since that's settled, let me get you cleaned up so we can start packing."

"Thank you, Mark." Lexi whispers, still half-dazed, her skin sweaty and pink from her release.

I lift her from the bed bridal style, cradling her to my chest as I walk into our bathroom. "There's nothing to thank me for, Baby. I will forever help you fight your demons until my last breath."

I give her a firm kiss on the lips as I walk into the shower stall so we can clean up, pack our necessities, and get ready for this case.

Chapter Six

Bryan

As I take our jeans into the laundry room, I find myself smiling at Taylor going on her first real case. I know she's scared, but she'll be alright. I mean, she can kick ass and take names just as well as Mark and I can.

"Hey, Bryan. Why are you doing clothes this early in the morning?" Tom asks from the doorway, and I'm thankful for my black shorts to hide the semi hard-on I'm still sporting from our morning make-out session.

"Wayne called us with a case, and we are meeting Mark and Lexi at the airport in two hours, so Taylor is upstairs packing while I do a quick load of laundry." I tell him as I finish putting my jean shorts in the wash and start to check Taylor's pockets for anything, since I know she's always leaving shit in them.

"Oh, okay. I was wondering when Wayne was going to call you all with one." Tom says and I hear the note of fear in his voice, but when his eyes find mine, they shine with a father's protectiveness and I wonder, not for the first time, that if my own father was alive, if he would have the same look on his face whenever I would go out on a case.

"Take care of my daughter, Bryan. I obviously can't be there with you all, so I can't protect her. So I'm leaving that job to you."

"Yes, sir. I'll protect her, don't worry." I say, nodding in understanding.

He leaves with a firm nod as Cody bursts through the front door with Kathy trailing along behind him, carrying in a few bags from the grocery store. As I continue to go through Taylor's jean shorts, I hear Tom tell his wife about our case, and they busy themselves in the kitchen while I work.

Just as I look at the last pair of shorts that Taylor had on yesterday, I find a piece of paper balled up in the back pocket and I toss it to the side before throwing them in the washer, adding a half a cap of Tide, then starting the machine. I roll my eyes and let a small smile play at my lips as I gather up the pieces of paper that I found in all four pairs of her jeans, but just before I throw them all in the trash can near the door; I pause.

One is in her handwriting, and I can tell it's freshly inked to the paper due to the darker tone of the ink as compared to the others in her pocket. I lean against the wall as I unravel the paper, and confusion fills my mind. It's nothing but random numbers with dots between the last four digits. I unfold the paper a little more, and I realize she's cracked whatever code this is.

"We are alive. P.E. C.E." I whisper. "What the hell?"

I wrack my brain, trying to figure out who P.E. and C.E. could be. As I reread the message three more times, it finally clicks into place, and white-hot rage fills my chest so fast that I storm up the steps two at a time and walk to Taylor's bedroom door.

She didn't teach a damn shooting class.

I stand in the threshold of her doorway to find her kneeling on the floor smiling down at three suitcases. One is hers, and the other I notice is filled with my stuff.

How dare she. She knows how I feel about this. About them.

Taylor must feel me staring at her because she looks up at me and I know my body is all hard, tense lines and I'm sure the heated scowl on my face is on damming display, but right now I don't freaking care, I'm too angry right now.

"What's wrong?" Taylor asks carefully.

"What did you say Wayne had you do yesterday?" I ask, even though I already know the answer. I just hope she'll tell me the truth.

"I told you," She begins, rising to her feet and taking a cautious step towards me. "Wayne wanted me to teach a shooting class, so I did."

I scoff, shaking my head as a pained laugh bubbles from my chest. "Then explain this." I challenge as I lift my hand next to my head while holding the paper between my index and middle fingers.

Her eyes widen in shock as she sees the paper, and she takes another step towards me, but my next words that I snap at her have her pausing in her tracks.

"What does this mean, Taylor!?"

"Babe–"

"Don't you babe me. Tell me, damn it. What does it mean?" I seethe.

She takes a breath before she speaks. "Wayne found skeletal remains in the warehouse a little over four months ago. That code was on them, and they couldn't break it at first." She shakes her head with a defeated sigh, and the sound grates on my nerves. "Well, yesterday morning I did, but Bryan, nothing is for sure. We don't even know if this is a real code. It could have been someone messing around."

I shake my head as a humorless laugh trickles up my throat. "You are a damn piece of work, you know that? We broke up the first time because you thought I lied to you! And now you just lied to me!" I point to my chest as I shout, then take a step towards her. "You know how I am about anything to do with my parents, and you had the nerve to go behind my back, and you never even told me about it!"

"Bryan, I was going to tell you when I knew more about it. I didn't want to hurt you," Taylor says as tears line her eyes, and normally the sight of them would crush me, but the burn of her lying overpowers that right now.

"I thought we wouldn't keep secrets! They are what almost screwed us over in the first fucking place!" I close the distance between us in a flash, so I'm looking down at her. "I'm done. Have fun in Miami. Don't call me. Don't contact me in any way."

"Bullet, don't be like that." She whispers, and I'm so angry right now that her words only bounce off my shattered heart as I storm out of her room and out of her life.

Chapter Seven

Taylor

I watch in utter shock and feeling my heart breaking apart in my chest as Bryan storms out of my room. A few seconds later, the front door slams, then I hear his truck roar to life. As I go over to the window, I watch with tears burning in my eyes as he speeds away, tires squealing on the pavement as he flies down the street. I close my eyes, allowing one tear to run down my cheek before I blink the rest away.

I hear a gentle knock on my doorjamb a moment later. I sniff, wiping my face before I turn to see Lexi standing in the doorway with Mark on her heels, confusion evident on both of their faces.

"What happened?" Lexi asks.

"We just saw Bryan flying out of here like he was on fire," Mark says.

"We just had a huge fight." I tell them, my throat burning with more unshed tears that I'm trying to not let fall from my eyes.

"About what?" Lexi asks as she walks into my room and pulls me in for a tight hug.

"About what I did with Wayne yesterday morning."

"Taylor Sparks!" Mark exclaims.

I groan. Right now, I don't want Mark to be his typical trickster self. "Mark! Get your head out of the gutter."

I go on to tell them about what Wayne wanted the other day and about the code that I broke. "Bryan found the paper I had written the code down on in my shorts from when he was doing the laundry this morning."

"He thought you were keeping it from him on purpose," Lexi says while stroking my back.

"Yeah. But I did lie to him. He asked what Wayne wanted, and I told him that he asked me to teach a shooting class." I say.

Mark comes over to me and puts his hands on my shoulders. When I look into his dark eyes, all the playfulness that was shining there when he first came in is completely gone. "Bryan will come around. He just has to cool off first."

"I've never seen him this mad before, Mark. He told me not to contact him in any way."

"Let me talk to him. I'm sure I can help him see that you were just doing what was best." Mark says. "He loves you too much to stay mad at you for long. He'll come back, just give him time to cool off and get his head back on straight."

"Okay," I say with a nod and wipe the last bit of tears from my face.

"Are we ready to go? We have a plane to catch." Lexi says an hour later.

"I'm ready." I say, after making all the last-minute checks and adding some of the freshly laundered clothes to my suitcase that Lexi helped me fold after they were done washing and drying.

"Then let's go," Mark says while picking up my suitcase for me and walking downstairs and out the front door.

When Lexi and I follow him down, I meet Dad and my ten-year-old brother, Cody, in the kitchen.

"I heard you were going on a case, Sis!" Cody exclaims.

I give him a smile that I hope he will take as genuine, even though I can feel it tremble. "Yes, I am."

"I wish I could tell everyone that my sister and her friends are the coolest! But Mom and Dad says I can't tell anyone about what you and Bryan do." He says while crossing his arms over his chest, "Why can't I?"

"Because, if you tell everyone, then we won't get the drop on the bad guys," Lexi offers in my place.

I give her a small smile of thanks before I add, "Yeah, if you tell others, the bad guys will see us coming from a mile away, and we don't want that."

"Is that why Bryan already left?" Cody asks. "He didn't even tell me bye." He adds, his face scrunching up in a pout.

Mark walks back into the kitchen, picks Cody up and hangs him upside down by both ankles, which makes Cody laugh like a hyena. "I'll make sure he tells you goodbye, little man."

I give Mark a slight nod to save me from answering my little brother, but nothing will distract my father, and I can already see him piecing together that something is not right.

"Be careful, Taylor." Dad says while hugging me. "I love you, Sweetheart. I also better hear that *he* is down there with you soon. After your mother left for work, I heard you two upstairs. I just hope that whatever that fight was about blows over and *fast*."

"I will." I say as I nod at his words. "Love you guys. I'll try to call as much as I can."

"Taylor, we gotta go," Lexi says from the front door as Mark holds it open for us.

"Gotta go, bye. I'll call Mom on the way there." I say.

"Mr. Sparks. I'll watch Taylor's back until my asshole friend comes around." I hear Mark say as he shuts the door behind him.

We walk down the sidewalk, and Mark approaches the passenger side of his blue Ford Expedition so he can open the front and rear doors for me and Lexi.

Once I get settled into the middle seat in the second row, he shuts the door before turning his attention to Lexi. He gives her a quick kiss on the lips, then shuts her door, walks around the front of the SUV, and jumps in behind the wheel. He looks at me through the rearview mirror once he's settled, the silent question rippling through the air.

"I'm ready." I tell him with a brisk nod.

Before I can even think to grab my phone out of my back pocket, it begins ringing, and I know that it's Mom already calling before I even look at the caller ID. "Hey Mom, I was just about to call you. I'm on my way out now."

"Alright. Be careful. Is Bryan with you?" Mom asks.

"You have to tell her." Lexi whispers from the front seat.

I take a breath, and I hear her utter a quick curse under her breath. "Bryan and I had a fight this morning. He won't be there for a while at least."

Mom's silent on the other end, and I know she's probably plotting his imminent death.

"It's alright, Mark and Lexi will be with me, so I'm not going by myself." I say.

"Okay." She sighs. "As soon as you get a chance, let me know when you get there."

"I'll try to call whenever I can." I say. "I love you, Mom."

We hang up, and a half hour later, Mark pulls into the airport. We're directed through a gate that leads to where the half dozen planes are parked and waiting for their passengers. As Mark pulls the SUV into a parking spot, I look through the windshield and I see a man and a woman standing near one of the smaller planes that has no markings other than the serial number on the side of the tailfin.

"That must be ours." Mark says.

"Must be." I reply as Mark kills the engine and we all get out to greet our new escorts.

"Hello, you must be Agents Stone, Smith, and Sparks. My name is Lincoln, and this is my wife Temperance." Lincoln says.

He's tall, about five-eleven, and his dirty blonde hair is styled in short waves over his head, and while his brown eyes are kind, I can tell they have seen some harsh things in life.

And his wife is just a bit shorter than him, but still taller than me. Her platinum blonde hair is pulled back into a neat bun on the top of her head, and her brown-eyed gaze flicks between us all before crinkling ever so slightly.

"Hello," Temperance says as she looks over the three of us with confusion knitting her brow. "I thought that there were supposed to be four of you?"

"He's a little under the weather." Lexi tells her while looking at me for confirmation, and I nod my head.

"Oh, okay." Temperance nods.

"I've never seen you around the agency before." Mark says while crossing his arms over his chest, silently telling the couple in front of us that he's not going to just trust them because they are supposedly part of the same team.

"We are normally stationed in Florida, so there was no way you'd know us. We were told to come up here, pick you guys up, and bring you down," Lincoln explains.

"Oh, that makes sense." I say, giving Mark a subtle side-eyed look, telling him to cool it and not be rude to these people.

"Alright, let's get going." Lincoln says. "Mark, give your keys over to this agent, and he will take your SUV to your place and lock the keys in a safe at the agency."

Another agent walks over to Mark, and he slowly hands his keys over so we can board the plane.

"Buckle up, everyone." Temperance says as she enters the cockpit behind Lincoln to assist in what I'm assuming are pre-flight checks.

I walk down the aisle a bit, take a seat beside a window, buckle my seatbelt, and wait for the plane to take off.

As the ground becomes smaller and smaller and the clouds begin to float past the glass, I wonder where Bryan is and what he's doing right now.

Chapter Eight

Taylor

After we are in the air, the sign above our seats lights up, showing we can unbuckle our seat belts and move around, but I sit in my seat for a few minutes, silently looking out the window, watching as the landscape rolls by.

"Tay, don't worry, he'll come around." Lexi says, already knowing who I'm thinking about.

"You didn't see how hurt he was, Lexi." I whisper while still looking out the window.

"He will realize that he was wrong, and he'll come down. You just have to let him cool off."

"I hope he does it soon." I sigh while finally turning to face her.

"Hey, I heard we'll have the chance to drive some wicked race cars. So why don't we see what's being offered?" Lexi says as she sits next to me, opens a small black laptop before handing it to me. "Pick your poison." She adds with a small smile.

As I look at the list of vehicles and their specifications, my stomach drops. They all have manual transmissions, and I can't drive those types of vehicles. I try to hide my uneasiness from my friend because I know she will make a big deal out of this. So, after a few minutes, I see a newer version of my Ford Focus Sport that does have an automatic transmission, and I point to that.

"I guess I'll pick the new Focus."

"Listen, babe, if you're gonna cruise with the racers, you're gonna need a hotter car than that." Lexi scoffs.

"I also need one that I can drive." I snap before I can stop myself.

"Seriously? You can't drive a stick?" Lexi scoffs and I cringe, but then her expression softens as she adds, "It's easy. I'll teach you. So let's see." She hums as she scrolls through the list of cars. "Here we go, an ice-blue Mustang. You will look *so* hot in that."

"If I get killed, I will haunt you for the rest of your life." I grumble.

"You'll be fine. Now Mark, he wants to knock on death's door. He picked a black Challenger," Lexi says while rolling her eyes.

"What about you?"

"I chose a red Lancer."

"Sounds good." I look back at the computer, eyeing the Mustang that's on the screen, and before I can think too much about it, I click on the green submit button. "There. Happy now?" I ask, and Lexi smiles triumphantly at me before closing the laptop.

"Have you two picked out your cars?" Temperance asks as she walks down the aisle from the cockpit a moment later.

"Yes, we have." Lexi beams with a wink in my direction, and I roll my eyes.

"Perfect. Would you like something to eat?" Temperance asks with a warm smile.

"Sure." Lexi nods.

"Yes, please." I say.

"Why don't you girls come with me and help me fix everyone's lunch?" Temperance suggests as she heads toward where I assume the little kitchenette is in the back of the plane.

"Okay," Lexi and I say in unison.

We follow Temperance into the little kitchen area, and she pulls out a loaf of bread while Lexi opens a small fridge to pull out a few packs of lunchmeat and cheese so the three of us can make sandwiches for everyone.

"So, Agent Sparks, how long have you been with the agency?" Temperance asks.

"Please, call me Taylor. And I have only been an official agent for a few months. But I have been in the agency before, just as a temp, but they weren't consecutive, so—" I say. "But I've been behind the badge two times before."

"Oh. Who have you worked with?"

"Well, I've worked with Lexi here and I've worked with Mark, and also my boyfriend, Bryan." I say, and I'm proud that my voice stays steady throughout the conversation. "This will officially be my first real case."

"Oh. So where is Bryan?" Temperance asks slowly.

"He needed to take care of something first; hopefully, he'll be here soon." I lie, since it seems to be the first thing I go to lately.

"Having a little trouble between you guys, huh?" Temperance says with a slight knowing smile playing at the corner of her lips.

I'm shocked that she's a total stranger, and she already knows that something is wrong between me and Bryan.

"You could say that." I say flatly as I open the cheese wrapper and slap it down on the lunchmeat before I add the top piece of bread to the plate to complete the sandwich.

"All men are stubborn, but they eventually come around." Temperance says gently as she takes the plate from me to add to the second one resting on a nearby food cart.

"Well, that doesn't help when the girlfriend is also stubborn." I mumble.

"I can see that in you." Temperance replies with a sly smile.

"Well, you just point out the obvious, don't you?" I say while giving her the side-eye.

"I try not to, but you said it first." Temperance chuckles. "How long have you been dating Bryan?"

"A little over a year."

"Yeah, a year and six months!" Lexi butts in while bumping her hip with mine.

"That's good." Temperance says. "Don't let this little fight get between you two. I can tell that you love him very much, so just be patient. I'm sure he'll come around."

"That's what I keep telling her." Lexi says, this time poking me in the side with her elbow, and I playfully swat her away.

"You have a good friend, Taylor. I can tell she has your back," Temperance says with a smile.

"I know. And I have hers."

We finish making lunch, and set it on a small table in the main area of the cabin while Temperance calls for Mark. He's disappeared somewhere in the plane, probably being nosey and getting into things he isn't supposed to.

"I'll tell ya this much; this plane is bigger than it looks." Mark says, coming from the back of the plane while giving a low whistle of the space around him. "I mean, did you see the bedroom they have on this thing?"

"No duh, it's the FBI's property; did you expect it to be small?" I ask. "And no. I'm not being nosy and walking around everywhere."

Mark just glares at me, as if saying, 'bite me'.

I walk over to him and put my hands on my hips. He's taller than me. I only come up to the middle of his chest, but I still look down my nose at him.

"Don't make me beat you up in front of these two agents." I warn and he just smiles. "Need I remind you of a few months ago? I put you on your back at least two times." I whisper with a playful smirk.

"You win, for now." Mark says.

"I always do." I say with a sly smile on my face.

Mark sits with Lexi while keeping his arm tightly wrapped around her. She gives him a small smile and I almost swear that I see a slight tremble in her lips when she looks up at him, but I don't have time to read too much into it when Temperance takes a seat next to me after she takes a plate up to the cockpit for Lincoln.

After lunch, while Temperance offers to take our trash, I sit back in my seat and look out the window again. I wish I could open the window to caress the clouds that still hang near the glass, but since this plane is moving at 550 miles per hour, it's kinda hard to do that. So, I opt to take out my phone and go through my pictures. I find one of Bryan holding me. My back pressed into his firm chest; one arm hugging me around my waist while the other is holding the phone to take the picture, bright smiles on both our faces.

As I enlarge the photo, I trail my thumb over his cheek, and my chest threatens to crack with the emotion flooding my soul. "Why do you have to be such a jerk?" I ask the picture softly.

"Is that...Bryan?" Temperance asks in a shocked tone.

I try not to jump at her voice, but I fail when I almost drop my phone. I look up to find her staring at my phone, and when I speak, my voice seems to break her focus. "Yeah, this is him."

Before she can say anything else, Lincoln and Mark emerge from the cockpit and Mark has a brilliant smile on his face and I hear him ask if he can fly the plane before the other agent laughs, kindly declining his request and turning his attention back to his wife who's still hovering over my shoulder.

"Temperance," Lincoln says, his voice tight and a touch scolding. "Come on, let her get some rest." He gently drags her away and back into the cockpit with him.

"Did you see the way she was eyeing your phone?" Lexi asks as she takes the seat next to me again.

"Yeah, I saw it. It creeped me out a little." I say.

"Well, it seems like Lincoln is a cool dude from the little bit that I talked to him while he was showing me the control panel and how he drives this thing. So don't let her get to you too much, Tay Tay." Mark says as he leads us into a seat and takes one across from me and Lexi.

A few minutes later, Temperance comes out of the cockpit with a professional smile plastered on her face. "We are getting ready to land, so please be sure you're buckled up."

After making sure my seatbelt is secure, I glance out my window and I can tell that we are descending. My ears pop with the pressure change, and the ground is getting larger while the clouds are going further away. Just as I begin to see the airport come into view, Mark breaks the silence.

"He really is peeved. He's just responding to me in short answers. You wanna see?" Mark says as he holds out his black iPhone.

I take a breath, lean over towards him, and read his message chain.

Mark: Man, u r being ridiculous. U need to call her and talk to her.

Bryan: No.

Mark: She didn't do anything wrong. I would've done the same thing if I were in her shoes.

Bryan: Don't care

Mark: Well when u r ready to be a MAN u know where we r.

"Thanks for trying, Mark." I say while trying to keep the tears at bay. I am just about to hand him his phone back when another text comes in. I turn the phone back around, and Mark looks at me, waiting for me to tell him what was said.

Bryan: Watch her

"What?" Mark asks.

"He said to watch me." I say, trying to make my voice sound indifferent rather than pissed off and hurt.

The plane lurches as it lands, and once it comes to a halt, the seatbelt light again illuminates, letting us know we are safe to unbuckle our seatbelts.

"He'll come around. I've already got him to say something meaningful." Mark says with a wink as he helps Lexi and me to our feet.

"Thank you." I take a deep breath and look between my friends. "Now let's get off this plane and get to work."

Chapter Nine

Taylor

Maybe if I get tied up in this case, I won't think about Bryan as much. I think to myself as we gather our belongings before exiting the plane.

Once our feet hits the tarmac, I see that there are three cars parked near the landing strip. Mark immediately goes to his Challenger, whooping and cheering like a kid on Christmas morning. I glance over at Lexi, and she's shaking her head while rolling her eyes.

I can't help but chuckle at her, but it fades as I stare at the blue Mustang I picked out just a few short hours earlier. Yes, I like sports cars, but I have never driven one before.

"How do you like it?" Lexi asks while bumping my shoulder.

"It's nice, but I still can't drive it." I say while waving my hand toward the vehicle.

"It's easy." Lexi says before turning around to look at the agents behind us. "Hey, could someone drive my car? I need to show her how to drive this one."

"I'll drive your car for you." Lincoln says while holding his hand out for her keys.

"I figured you knew how to drive this kind of car, Taylor." Temperance says, her brow scrunching in confusion.

"Nope. But I guess I had to learn sometime, right?" I say, trying to hide the fear in my voice.

Lexi throws me my keys, then she slides into the passenger seat. I slowly walk over to the driver's side, lower myself into the seat, and close the door before I look at Lexi.

"Okay, this part is just like any car; put the key in the ignition." Lexi instructs.

I do, and I try to turn it over, but nothing happens.

"Okay, now what?" I ask. "Is the battery dead already?"

She grins. "No. You see that extra pedal? That's the clutch. Push it in and turn the key at the same time." Lexi instructs.

I do, and the Mustang roars to life. This car has way more power than my Focus back home, so much so that it almost vibrates from the power of the engine.

"Good. Now shift into first gear. Just push the stick up one." Lexi coaches.

When I push the stick up, I see the number one light up on the dashboard.

"Now, slowly push on the gas. This has a lot more torque than you're used to." Lexi says.

"No shit." I chuckle nervously. "I can tell that with it just sitting here."

I slowly press the gas pedal, and the front of the car actually lifts up a little. When I see that happen, I slam on the brakes, causing the engine to stall out. Lexi's laughter fills the cabin, and I glare over at her, trying to get my trembling arms under control.

"You could be a little helpful here. And you laughing at me is not helping." I snap.

"Sorry. I just didn't know you would act like this," Lexi says while wiping away tears from the corners of her eyes.

"How did you think I would act!?" I exclaim.

"Okay, okay. Let's try this again." She says while waving her hand over the console of the car.

I take a deep breath, push in the clutch like last time, and start the engine again. I shift into first and push down on the gas pedal as I slowly release the clutch at the same time. This time, I at least know what to expect. When the hood of the car lifts, I just keep going.

"There, you see, you can do it."

"I don't know why, but I guess I should thank you." I tell her while trying to hide a grin at my small accomplishment.

"Oh, come on, you love it!" Lexi laughs.

"I will not answer that yet." I say as I start to hear a weird sound and see the RPM needle move higher on the dash. "See, this I don't like. What's wrong?"

"You need to shift into a higher gear." Lexi says. "Just push the clutch back in and push the stick up again."

I do what Lexi says, and a number 2 lights up on the dash.

"So all I do is listen for that sound and shift up?" I ask, and Lexi nods her head. "Now, what do I do when I slow down or need to stop?"

"Instead of pushing the stick up, you pull it down. But I'll tell you when to do that."

After a few minutes of driving around the tarmac, I look over at Lexi. "Thank you."

"Hey don't mention it. I'd do anything for my best girl." She says while smacking me on the shoulder.

Lexi rolls the window down to let the others know that we are ready to hit the road and she tells me to just take my time and, like she promised, she instructs me on what gear to shift into and when.

We pull up in front of a row of apartments about twenty minutes later, and I park the Mustang beside Mark's Challenger before shutting the engine off and stepping out of the driver's seat.

"Looks like you tamed that wild horse, Tay Tay." Mark smiles as he meets me at the rear of my car and hooks his arm around my neck.

"Yes, I did." I say, and I can't help but to match my smile with his.

Lincoln walks up to us to grab our attention before pointing his thumb over his shoulder, signaling us to follow him. "Let's all go to our place and discuss how things are going to work from here on out."

We follow him and Temperance across the street and into an end-unit apartment.

"Oh, I almost forgot, Taylor, the end apartment is yours, and the one beside that is Mark's and Lexi's," Lincoln says while pointing to another line of apartments across the street.

"Okay," I say, and I try to keep the little jolt of fear of being in a strange place by myself from showing on my face.

We walk into Lincoln's and Temperance's apartment, and it's a quaint little place. We enter right into the living room, and I see a girl sitting on the couch that is the spitting image of Temperance. She gives us all a small wave before she turns her attention back to the TV on the other side of the room.

"That's our daughter, Sophie." Temperance looks back at the three of us before turning her attention back to her daughter. "Soph, say hi to our new guests."

"Should I be talking to people that are part of your team?" She asks with a touch of an attitude.

"Sophie." Lincoln warns, and the look he shoots her is similar to what Dad would have used with me.

"What? You're the one who said you don't want me working with you until I'm eighteen."

"Which is still two years away, missy." Lincoln says while still glaring at his daughter.

"Exactly. So until then, I'm not saying anything."

I find myself smiling at her. I like the fire that I see shining in her eyes. She's going to make a great agent once she's active.

I walk in front of her and I lean into her where she has no choice but to meet my gaze. "Well, Sophie, it's nice to meet you all the same. My name's Taylor. I hope I get to see you again soon."

"I like her." Sophie says to her mother before looking back at me with a quick nod, still keeping to her guns of not talking to me, and I know it's to irritate her father.

Lincoln shakes his head before leading us into the kitchen, where we all sit around the dining table that sits in the middle of the room.

"So, in the morning, Mark will go down to the track that's a few miles north from here, and you girls will go down a little later. I want all of you to make 'friends'." He says, using air quotes. "Try to get as much info from them as you can without drawing attention."

"Is there anything else that we should know?" Mark asks.

"Like what?" Lincoln questions.

Mark looks between him and Temperance, and I can already see the gears turning in his head. "Like, what exactly is our mission here? What are we supposed to find out?"

"Honestly, I'm not so sure it's all about drugs." Lincoln sighs while leaning back in his chair. "I'm just not sure what you should be looking for yet."

"Okay, I'll try to get in tomorrow and see if I can find anything." Mark says.

I hear his tone turn serious. I'm still not used to Mark getting into agent mode. He is usually full of energy and jokes, but when it comes down to business, I know he's got our backs.

As we get ready to leave Lincoln's and Temperance's place, Lincoln stops us to give us our keys to our apartments. I am the last one to leave, and I watch as Mark and Lexi walk up to their apartment.

He unlocks the door and steps inside, turning on a light to make sure it's safe before he lets Lexi walk in. That move is so much like what Bryan would do that my eyes start to burn with unshed tears, and I take a breath to clear my emotions.

When I start to walk up to the apartment that is meant for me, I hear Lexi yelling for me.

"Taylor, come over here and stay with us. You don't need to be alone."

"I don't want to impose."

"Taylor Sparks, get your ass over here before I drag you over." Lexi scolds with her hands on her hips.

I smile as I walk through the grass and up to her porch, and we walk through the door before Lexi closes and locks it behind us.

"Where's Mark?" I ask.

"He's unpacking." Lexi groans.

"And I'm having fun while doing it!" Mark says in a sing-song voice.

"I bet you he's in your stuff." I chuckle.

"Oh, I know he is." Lexi says coolly.

I try to hide a smile as she walks away to help Mark finish unpacking. As I look around the apartment, I start to think about how Bryan is supposed to be here. I should be giving him hell for going through my stuff like Lexi is doing with Mark.

Things probably wouldn't be any different between us if I told him right off the bat. It wouldn't have mattered if I told him as soon as I broke the code; it would still be the fact that I kept something from him about his parents.

"Taylor, where is your suitcase?" Lexi asks as she walks out of the bedroom.

"I'm guessing in my apartment. I haven't seen it since I boarded the plane." I say.

"I'll go over and get it," Mark offers as he's already halfway to the door.

"Thank you."

"How are you doing?" Lexi asks when the front door shuts a moment later.

"With what?"

"Everything. Being here on your first case." She pauses. "Being here without Bryan." Lexi adds quietly.

"This being my first case is nothing. I'm used to being shot at; it's just now I have a real badge. And I don't want to talk about Bryan."

Lexi stands next to me and gives my shoulder a little squeeze. Before she can say anything, Mark comes back in with my suitcase.

"Where do you want it? In the other room?"

"Yeah, that will be fine." I say. "Thank you again, Mark."

He nods before disappearing into the other bedroom while Lexi goes into the kitchen and opens the fridge.

"Hey Tay, what do you want to eat? There is a lot of stuff in here."

"Whatever you fix is good." I say. I'm not really hungry, but I know I have to eat if I want to work this case.

"Hey girls." Mark begins as he rushes from my temporary bedroom. "Bryan said he was going to call in a minute. Taylor, do you want me to keep it private or put it on speaker?"

I don't have much time to answer because the phone is already ringing.

"Speaker."

"You got it," Mark says. He answers his phone and taps the speaker button. "Hello?"

"Hey, are you all down there?" Bryan asks, his voice soft and quiet.

I have to force myself to take a deep breath because I want to yell at him and tell him that he's supposed to be here with me.

"No, we're in the middle of a desert somewhere drinking pina coladas, dude." Mark says.

"I'm not in the mood for your jokes, Mark," Bryan says with annoyance in his voice.

"We got here about an hour ago." Mark says while taking a deep breath.

"Oh," Bryan says.

"Come on, man, ask. I know you want to." Mark says after a few moments of silence.

I get up from the couch, lean into Lexi, and whisper, "This is a waste of time. I'm going to bed." As I pass by Mark's shoulder, I hear Bryan take a breath, and I know he's heard me.

"Okay. I'll say something. When is she ready to apologize?" Bryan asks.

This time I can't keep my mouth shut.

"When *I* apologize? I think you are the one that owes me the apology." I shout, getting up to get closer to the phone.

"I'm not the one that *lied*," Bryan shoots back.

"You know what, either way, you would have been pissed. So, you just need to get over yourself and get down here. And I will tell you this much, Bryan Alexander Evans; if I get killed down here, I will come back and haunt your sorry ass." I say.

"Now break it up you two—" Mark begins, but Bryan cuts him off.

"That's right, we are breaking it up!" Bryan yells before he hangs up the phone.

I try to fight back tears, but they escape before I can even try to stop them. I run to my newly acquired room, slam the door, throw myself on the bed, and face plant into the pillow.

After a few minutes, I hear the door open, and Lexi's voice filters into the room. "Tay, can I come in?"

"I guess." I say, trying to wipe away my tears.

"Taylor, sweetie, he's just confused." Lexi coos.

"Didn't sound like that to me." I whimper. "Don't lie to me Lexi, do you think that he will come down here, or do you think that I should just move on?"

"I'm not going to tell you to give up on him." Lexi says while brushing my hair out of my face.

"He just won't shut the hell up and listen to me." I sob on the verge of ugly crying again. Lexi just stares at me and my outburst. "Sorry." I say.

"You really are that PO'd at him, huh?" Lexi asks.

"Yes, I am." I say. "If he would just hear me out, he would understand that I wasn't the one that actually found those bones in the first place."

"Well; unfortunately, we can't worry about him now; we have a case to think about. Do you want me to bunk with you?" Lexi asks.

"No, go and be with Mark. You won't be seeing a lot of him anyway until this is over. I'll be fine."

Lexi leaves my room and closes the door, and I am left alone again. I set the clock on my phone for 6 A.M. and try to go to sleep because tomorrow will be coming whether I want it to or not, and I need to be prepared for anything.

Chapter Ten

Bryan

I can't stop the growl that rips from my throat as I throw my phone across the bed. I am so furious at her and at Mark for taking up for her. I try to lie in bed to cool off, but I'm reminded of her everywhere I look.

The few paintings that I've been working on of her favorite flowers. Wild orange tiger lilies, purple hibiscus, and white roses. Her jean jacket that she wore last time she was over here for dinner a few nights ago with my grandparents, hangs off my desk chair. And I can still smell her jasmine scented perfume lingering in the air.

I release an aggravated sigh, and I pocket my phone before heading downstairs to crash on the couch for a bit and see what's on TV tonight. Thankfully, Granny is out at a church function, so it's just me and Gramps here, and I can tell he's in the kitchen fixing dinner from the smell of chicken frying on the stove. I turn on the TV and flip through the channels, but nothing finds my interest, so I tilt my head back on the couch pillow while resting the crook of my arm over my eyes.

I hear the stove knob click off a moment later, and I know Gramps is about to walk into the living room to serve dinner, but I don't move from my position on the couch. Not at first, at least. It's not until I can practically feel his stare boring into my head that I lift my arm enough to see him wiping his hands on a dishtowel.

"Somethin' on your mind, son?"

"No. I'm fine, Grandpa."

"I may be old, but I'm not senile yet, and I know you well enough to know that something is wrong."

Gramps's tone is rough, and there is a silent warning for me to quit pulling his leg.

"I just gotta work through something, Grandpa." I tell him in hopes he'll get the hell off my back.

"Well, sitting on the couch in front of the TV with your arms over your face isn't gonna work, son." He points out. "Where is Taylor?"

I try not to bristle at her name, but I fail because his chuckle crackles in the air between us as he sits down in his recliner, pulling the footrest up so he can eat.

"Well?" He says, urging me to talk.

"Grandpa, I don't mean to be disrespectful to you, but I don't want to talk about it." I can't help but snap.

"Naw, boy. I ain't letting you off that easy. What happened between you two? Besides, didn't you two have a case to go on?" At my silence, he continues, "Oh, Bryan, you damn fool. You let her go alone?"

"She's got Mark and Lexi with her." I deadpan.

"So, again. Why aren't you with her?"

I glance sideways at him. Knowing he's not gonna let up, I run my hand through my hair and I blow out a defeated sigh through my nose.

"We got into a pretty big fight. She lied to me, Gramps."

"See. Now we're getting somewhere." He grins as he takes a bite of chicken. "Go on."

"She told me she was working with Wayne on teaching a shooting class for the rookies coming in, but she was actually going behind my back about something to do with my parents."

"Do you really believe she would be that callous, Bryan?" He scoffs. "The Taylor I know would have wanted to have all the facts before she told you anything."

"Oh, my God. I don't believe it." I laugh harshly as I sit up on the couch to look at him head-on. "You feel the same way."

I was about to tell him he's nuts too, but when I look into his hardened blue eyes, I shut my mouth. No matter how old I get, that look will always stop me in my tracks. It's his Army Sargent rank coming back in full force.

"Now you listen, and you better listen well, boy. That girl has nothing but love for you, and she would never do anything to hurt you on purpose. I know you're sensitive about Paul and Cindy; hell, I would be too. But this is almost the same thing as when you got hurt and Kathy had to lie to Taylor about you being alive, so you and Taylor would be safe. Think about that for a while, Bryan." He says as he puts the footrest of his recliner down and takes his empty plate into the kitchen, leaving me alone with my thoughts.

I think back to that time not long ago when her own mother had to lie to her. When Mark had to lie to her and Lexi, all to keep the two of us safe. Now that I've had the time to calm down and think a little more clearly, I can somewhat understand where she was coming from.

"If you are done wallowing, get your ass in here and eat something, son," Grandpa gripes from the kitchen.

"Yes, sir."

When I get up from the couch and make my way to the kitchen, my phone starts ringing, and I see Wayne's name on my caller ID.

"I guess he's figured out I'm not there now." I say to the ringing phone. I take a deep breath and answer it.

"Care to tell me why the hell you're not down in Florida with your team?" Wayne's tone is stern and unforgiving. "You know what? I don't care. You better be down there within forty-eight hours, or I'm taking you off the case and giving it to another agent." He barks before hanging up.

Taylor

I feel like I've only been asleep for a few minutes when my alarm goes off, but in reality, I have been asleep for six hours. So I get up, and when I hear Lexi and Mark moving around, I come out of my room.

"So you both are awake too, huh?" I ask like it's not expected.

"Yeah, I gotta get to the track at six-thirty," Mark says. "You two can come down about eight."

I smell coffee brewing from the kitchen, so I walk over to the counter and grab myself a cup from the cabinet over-head.

"Anyone want a cup?" I ask over my shoulder as I take the carafe and pour the liquid into the mug.

"Already had one, thank you. I can't be too jittery if I'm gonna drive at two hundred miles per hour." Mark says with an eager grin.

"Mark, just stop grinding that fact in. I don't like you in that car, let alone going that fast in it," Lexi whines.

"First of all, it's not a car; it's a Challenger, and secondly," He says, his tone morphing from high energy to deathly serious so fast it almost makes my head spin at the sudden change. "I can drive that fast and do it safely. I promise I won't do anything stupid."

I watch from the edge of the kitchen as Mark gives Lexi a soft kiss on the lips before he wraps his arms protectively around her, pulling her close to his chest and his hand rubbing her back in a loving caress. I have to turn away and face the wall as tears threaten to make an appearance already.

I take a sip of the still-too-hot coffee when Lexi comes around to the kitchen, thankful the liquid helps hide my tears after scalding my tongue.

"Are you okay?" Lexi asks.

"Yeah, I burnt my tongue on the coffee. I'm gonna go and get dressed."

I walk past her, and I go to my room to actually get dressed like I claimed. When I come back out ten minutes later, I see that Lexi is also dressed, and she is looking at me with a raised eyebrow, letting me know I'm not so good at hiding from my best friend.

"Are you okay with me and Mark—"

"Lexi, just because I'm a little stressed right now does not mean that you and Mark can't be your usual selves. The only thing I ask is that you tell me to leave the room or get earplugs if things are going to get...hot."

"Oh, we did that before we left. So, we won't get *hot* anytime soon while we are here." Lexi says. "And I'll tell Mark to behave."

"Don't you dare. Bryan not being here isn't your problem; it's mine. Don't you dare stop whatever it is you do with Mark, as long as it's sensible in front of a guest," I say. "Wait, you and Mark have—" I begin to ask.

Lexi flashes a sly smile at me and looks at me out of the corner of her eye. I take her silence as my answer, and I just smile at her. "What, you and Bryan haven't hit the sheets yet?"

I shake my head.

"Why?"

"I don't know."

"What are you scared of?"

What am I scared of? I mean, before this fight, I've felt so comfortable with him. But I guess I've heard so many things of once you 'give it up to a guy', he'll drop you like last week's trash and move on to another girl. But when that thought hits me, even with the fight going on with us, Bryan is not like that. He even said it himself that he's not the screw-em and leave-em type.

"I think it's just my own fears holding me back." I say as I tell her my thoughts.

She chuckles, "Yeah. Bryan is a good guy most of the time. That is when he's not being a brooding asshole like he is now. Just trust yourself, and trust that Bryan has your best interest at heart too." Lexi says like she's speaking from experience.

"Mark treats you well in that aspect?" I ask gently, my tone letting her know that if she doesn't want to talk about her sex life with her boyfriend, she doesn't have to.

"Oh, yeah." She answers instantly with a huge smile. "He's amazing, and I trust him wholeheartedly with my body, just like he trusts me with his." She pauses as she looks at me, her face scrunching with embarrassment. "Are you sure you don't want us to even tone down what is appropriate in front of you?"

"Yes, I'm sure. Now let's go down to the track."

Chapter Eleven

Taylor

Five minutes later, Lexi and I get in my Mustang. Now that I've had a few hours behind the wheel, I can drive it fairly well. I'm no racer like Mark, but I can drive around town, and that's fine with me.

Just as I'm about to park the car, Lexi gets a text, and she shows it to me.

Mark: It's looking good Baby. I think I'm in.

"Whatever that means," Lexi says as she pockets the phone.

"Lexi, it means he's made a friend or beat someone in a race. Now, I'm not a racer, but that seems logical." I say.

I open the door of my Mustang, and I hear whistles from some of the guys cat-calling me. I try to hold myself back from rolling my eyes and keep walking.

"They thought you looked hot, and you do, by the way, in case you were wondering what that was all about," Lexi says, gesturing to my outfit.

"I guess." I say while looking at my jean shorts and a pink tank top that glides over all the right curves.

"What do you mean, you guess? You're beautiful, Taylor." Lexi beams.

I give her a small smile as we walk over to the concrete barrier that encases the race track, and Mark walks up to us with a huge grin on his face, and I'm already dreading what's about to come out of his mouth.

"There is something about a woman getting out of a nice-looking car like yours, Taylor. I wish Lexi would have driven her car down." He adds as his gaze roves over her curves, and I see them darken with desire.

"Well, maybe you could give me a few pointers in case Bryan ever gets his ass down here." I say.

If he likes watching Lexi get out of a car like this, then Bryan will too, and with the fight we are currently in, if I could torture him but ignore him at the same time, I will. It'll be a good way of paying him back for everything he's done the last few days.

"Okay. After we get back to the apartment, I'll show you some tips." Mark grins.

"No, *I* will show you some tips." Lexi butts in, eyeing Mark.

I smile at both of them. "I'm glad I have friends like you two because there is never a dull moment when I'm with either of you." I say.

"Good," Lexi says. "I love to cause chaos, you know that."

Mark's about to say something else, but he walks away when one of the guys hollers to get his attention. He gives Lexi a wink as he pushes off the wall, and I can see her cheeks warm with the slightest hint of pink at his affection.

I give her a minute to watch Mark talk with two burly racers before I'm pulling her arm so we can walk around and check this place out a bit. We take one step before a group of three girls approaches us. The bad news is that if they were to attack us, we would be outnumbered; but the only good news is that they don't look like they will.

"Hey girls, we got some new faces." One of them says while crossing her arms and glaring at us, so I glare right back. She's a tall brunette with honey-brown eyes, and she seems to be the ringleader of this group.

"Chill, we won't hurt you." One girl, a red-head, says. "We don't fight dirty like some other bitches around here."

"Yeah, we actually like to help one another out." Says another cheerfully. Her blonde hair bouncing in her ponytail as she nods her head.

"Cool. I'm Lexi, and this is Taylor," Lexi says, taking control of the discussion.

"Morgan, Roxi and Christy, it's nice to meet you." Morgan says, pointing to the redhead and the blonde in turn. "So who's dating the guy in the Challenger?" She asks as she tucks a piece of her honey-brown hair behind her ears.

"I am." Lexi says with pride.

"And you? Do you have a guy here?" Morgan asks.

"He's not here yet." I tell her.

"Lexi, is it? I would watch your back. There are things that go on here that should never be seen. If a race is called for, I would stay away from here; away from your guy," Morgan warns.

"Why, what goes on?" Lexi asks.

"Girls can be taken." Christy says while popping a piece of bubble gum.

"Christy!" Morgan snaps.

"Hold the phone. What do you mean that girls are taken?" I ask with panic rising in my chest, and I barely notice the way Lexi stiffens at her words as my own fear builds in my chest.

Morgan takes a deep breath and looks both of us directly in the eyes. "This guy, Desmond, he races our guys, and if they lose the race, they lose their cars, lives and their girlfriends. So, Desmond doesn't just race for pink slips; he races for everything." Morgan says.

"What happens to the girls?" Lexi asks, her voice trembling, and I hear her swallow nervously.

Morgan takes another deep breath. "He takes them back to his hide-out to drug up before he and his thugs rape them. Then, when he gets bored with them, he kills them. But if they fight back once the race is over, he kills them right on the spot. Either way, they're as good as dead."

I feel like I'm about to be sick. The FBI had no idea what they were sending us into.

"That is disgusting." Lexi whispers, her face even paler than mine.

"Yes, it is." Morgan agrees, but she's far away in thought when she says it.

Lexi just looks at me, and I glance past her to see if I can spot Mark, but I don't see him anywhere. Lexi then takes out her phone to text him. I don't see what she texts, but he's watching us now. His gaze is cold and hard, focusing in on our group, but his eyes never stray from Lexi.

As if feeling his gaze burning through her back, Lexi starts to walk away from my side without a word. I stand there for a moment, shocked by her demeanor, before I excuse myself from the three girls we met and catch up to her.

I reach out, grabbing her arm so she'll stop, but I see the hint of tears and panic in her eyes before she tries to school her features to look at me head on.

"Listen to me. Mark can't watch us both. He has to watch over you. If Bryan doesn't get down here within twenty-four hours, I want to have another...*person* down here to watch my back." I say.

"Tay, Mark can handle it." Lexi says, but I don't miss the wobble in her tone.

"I don't care if he can or not; I want it that way. He can't be in two places at once, and I don't want him screwing up on you. You already seem shaken up enough about this information, so I'm not moving from my decision." I say.

I look her in the eyes, and my expression is firm, telling her that I'm serious about getting someone else down here if Bryan doesn't get his shit together.

"Okay, but try telling Mark that," Lexi says.

"I will."

Later that night, Lexi and I are sitting on the couch and Mark sits on the corner of the coffee table as I tell him about what we found out this afternoon. The entire time he's listening, his hand has never left Lexi's, and she's white-knuckling his in response.

"Mark, you need to call Wayne and tell him to get another agent down here." I say.

"Taylor, I can handle this," Mark says.

"Mark, I can't have you looking after me and neglecting Lexi. What if you're somewhere because of me and she gets hurt? I won't let that happen. There is nothing you can do to change my mind, so it's just a matter of if you're calling Wayne. If not, I will."

"Alright, I'll call him. Besides, he needs to know what's going on here." Mark says as he stands to walk into the bedroom and calls Wayne.

"You know Wayne will be furious when he finds out that Bryan isn't here, right?" Lexi whispers.

"Good. He should be." I say with a mix of fear and anger in my voice.

Mark comes back out, and he sits on the sofa beside me, then throws a protective arm around Lexi, and she leans into his touch like he's a lifeline for her.

"There, your backup will be here either tomorrow or the next day. They just have to get a hold of him."

"Do you know who it will be?" I ask.

"No, when you call in backup, you never know who it will be until they show up." Mark says.

"Okay, just as long as someone's coming."

"That's what Wayne said. So if no one comes, yell at him, not me," Mark says.

I nod, but then my gaze falls to my best friend for a moment. She's just staring at nothing. I have never seen her like this. I glance at Mark, and when his dark eyes land on her, his expression is pained. He knows what's wrong with her.

"Lexi? Are you okay?" I gently touch her knee, and she jumps at my touch.

"Shhh, Baby. It's just Taylor," Mark croons.

At hearing his voice, she looks up at him, and it seems like life comes back to her eyes. She meets my concerned gaze, and tears fill her eyes.

"I never wanted you to see this side of me, Taylor." Lexi begins, her voice cracking with tears.

"What do you mean, 'this side of you'?" I ask. "What's wrong?"

"Mark, please." Lexi begs, and now my heart hurts for a completely different reason. I have never seen my friend so broken before.

Mark pulls her tightly against his chest, and she fists the fabric of his shirt.

"It was about two years ago. I know it was after your case with her, Taylor. She moved or was transferred to California, where I was at the time. Wayne had us working on a case where there was an underground skin trade and sex trafficking happening, and they were taking girls around seventeen years old and younger." Mark leans in and kisses the top of Lexi's head.

"We set Lexi up to be taken once we knew who we were looking for, and it worked. A little too fucking well." He growls. "Lexi was taken like we planned, but I had the feeling to put a tracking device in her hair tie. The lead agent told me I was stupid for that because we knew where his hideout was, but I told that asshat that something didn't feel right. And it's a good damn thing too, because the route the van usually took changed and I barely had time to get to her. But I didn't come out unscathed either. One of his thugs stabbed me in the damn back, literally."

He moves to show me the scar I remember seeing when I was in his apartment after the night I thought I lost Bryan.

"I somehow got to Lexi, but not before she was raped." He takes a breath, and I know in this moment they both are reliving that nightmare. "That bastard got one stroke in her before I ripped him off and stabbed his own blade through his chest."

Lexi finally speaks up for the first time. "Since that night, I've had PTSD episodes. For the longest time, I didn't come out of our apartment back in Cali once we were released from the hospital, but Mark stayed by my side and helped me realize that I'm safe with him. It took almost eight months before I allowed him to touch me, but we worked and still are working through it."

"Lexi." I sob. "Oh, my God. I wish I would have known." I slowly lean in, silently asking for a hug, and she opens one arm to allow me into her cocoon with Mark.

"You're the only other person who knows what happened," Lexi whispers.

"I won't tell anyone unless you want to." I promise.

"Thank you"

"Come on, girls. Let's get to bed. It's been a long day." Mark suggests, and we comply without complaint.

Mark .

After I lead Lexi into our bedroom and lay her down, she looks at me and, for the first time since that day, she doesn't have that haunted look in her eyes that would practically rip the beating heart from my chest.

"Lexi?" I ask tentatively.

"I feel better, Mark."

I sit down on the bed and push a lock of her hair behind her ear. "You do?"

She nods. "Yes. Maybe that's what I've been missing. Letting other people know what happened and talking about it out loud. When I think about it that way, I can finally comprehend it's just a memory and not the real thing still."

"Oh, Baby. I'm so happy to hear you say that." I say on the verge of tears.

"I'm sorry it took us talking to Taylor and not to you to figure it out."

"Baby, I don't give two shits who you need to talk to to be able to work through the horror of that day. I'm just glad you're feeling better. That's all I've ever wanted for you."

The trademark grin that tells me she's up to no good blooms on her lips. "But now you don't get the chance to drag me out of my own head."

"Alexis," I growl as I lean over her, caressing her through her shorts, and her gasp at my touch has me hardening to the point of pain behind my zipper. "This just means now that my entire focus is only on finding out how many times I can make you scream my name while I wring every single last orgasm out of that beautiful body of yours." I lean in to kiss her and whisper in her ear. "Once we are either alone or Taylor isn't on the other side of this flimsy wall, I am going to ravish you until you can't scream anymore."

"I'm going to make sure you keep that promise, Mark," Lexi says while she grabs me through my jeans, and I hiss out a breath.

"Alexis," I warn as I tease her clit through her shorts with my thumb. "Doesn't feel good to be teased, and you can't have the full package, huh, Baby?"

"You win!" Lexi exclaims, "For now."

I flop onto my back, and I tug her onto my chest before pulling the covers over us. I kiss the top of her head and nestle my mouth against her ear. "I love you, Alexis Smith."

"Love you too, Mark Stone."

We hold one another and as we let sleep take us, I just hope that the massive text I sent to Bryan earlier will be enough to get his ass down here.

Also, yeah, I lied to Taylor about calling Wayne. If he knew, Bryan would be pulled off the case, and he'd never get the chance to get down here.

Me: Dude. you need to grow a damn pair and get your head out of your ass and get down here. things are getting dangerous already and it's nothing like you've seen before. trust me. you want to be down here to protect Taylor.

I know you, if something happens to her, you're gonna blame yourself, (which you fucking should- you're being an ass). and you're gonna hate this, but if I knew shit that could potentially lead to more info about your parents I'd keep it from ya too until I had everything in the palm of my hand.

Oh and when you do leave, tell Cody bye. He thought you left already and he was pissed you didn't say anything to him.

Chapter Twelve

Bryan

After getting Mark's text and the conversation that I had with Gramps still echoing in my head, I make my way over to Taylor's house to pick up the suitcase that I hope is still packed for me.

As I pull my keys from the front pocket of my jeans and unlock the door, I hear Kathy's voice filling the space of the living room, and I can hear she's pissed.

"Tom, I swear, if I don't hear from Taylor that Bryan is down in Florida with her, I'm going to kill him."

"As much as I want to get in on that too, Kathy, we have to let them repair their relationship on their own terms. I doubt it would ever get to this, but the only way I'd actually kill the kid is if he'd touch my daughter to hurt her. Then he's a dead man."

"I can help you make it look like an accident if you want to get in on the killing sooner." Kathy says, her voice surprisingly cheerful.

I cringe at their words, but they have a point. I've been a complete asshole, and I deserve their wrath.

Just as I am about to announce my presence, I hear footsteps barrel down the stairs.

"Bryan!" Cody exclaims as he spots me in the foyer and runs over to stand in front of me. "I thought you left already! I was mad at you for leaving before you said goodbye!" He huffs as he crosses his little arms over his chest, his eyes throwing me tiny daggers.

Damn. How many members of this family can I piss off in two days?

"Nah. I'd never leave before saying goodbye to my best bud." I say as I pull him toward me, his head resting just under my sternum, and running my knuckles over his head.

He giggles as Tom and Kathy come into the foyer, and the look in their eyes tells me they aren't buying my bullshit like their son is.

Time to face the music. "Cody, bud. Can you give me and your parents a minute? I'll let you know when I'm getting ready to leave."

He nods as Kathy says, "Go back up to your room, Cody."

"Okay."

He gives me one last squeeze around the waist before running up the steps, sounding like a gigantic elephant, even with his small stature. When I look back to Kathy and Tom, I wish I was still having Cody's version of daggers thrown my way, 'cause the ones that I am currently getting would kill me four times over.

"Tom, Kathy. I'm—"

"I don't know what you and my daughter were fighting about, but you better get your shit together and get down there. If anything, make sure my daughter gets home safely." Kathy snaps, cutting me off.

"I will." I say because there is nothing else I can say right now. I have a lot of making up to do if I even have a *chance* of getting Taylor back.

"Your suitcase is still up in her room." Tom offers gruffly.

I nod and head up the stairs, and when I approach her door, I'm hit with her perfume. Once that jasmine scent fills my nose, I realize just how much I've missed her over the last two days. I grab my suitcase from the floor by the window, and as I turn to leave, my eyes lock on the painting I did of her back in December.

This version of Taylor is smiling back at me from the little forest behind her high school with the orange wild tiger lilies that I added in. I walk over to the painting and run my right index finger over her cheekbone, and I take a steadying breath.

"I'm sorry, Taylor. I'm coming, Baby, and I'm ready for you to rip into me. I deserve everything you can throw at me."

Taking one last look around her room, I walk out and go over to Cody's room to let him know I'm leaving like I promised him.

His room is made up of nothing but cars. I guess it comes from his father being a mechanic. He has little scale models of Mustangs, Camaros, F150s, Rams, and even a GTR from the Fast and Furious franchise—even though he hasn't watched the movies yet—he still had a good eye for the car. Even his bedsheets are covered in racecars and checkered flags.

"Knock, knock, buddy." I announce while rapping on the doorjamb.

"Hi, Bryan! Are you leaving now?"

"Yeah, I am."

"Are you scared?"

I chuckle. "Not for the case. Now your sister? Yeah. I'm terrified of her right now."

"What did you all fight about this time?"

I sigh and walk over to sit beside him on his bed. "I thought your sister lied to me about something that was really personal and important to me, and I jumped to conclusions. So remember, when you get a girlfriend one day, don't let your anger cloud your reaction."

"Ew. Girls are gross. That's why I don't have a girlfriend."

I laugh at him and shake my head. "You know, I said the same thing to my grandpa when I was your age."

"What made you change your mind?" Cody asks, his voice turning serious.

I've had two girlfriends before Taylor, and she knows that, but when I take his question and really think about it, I know in my heart what I'm about to say is one hundred percent true.

"What changed my mind is that I found someone that I knew I wanted to spend the rest of my life with. I found what true love feels like."

"Sounds too mushy to me," Cody says as he scrunches his nose up at me.

"Maybe, but it's the truth. You'll understand one day, but when you see a girl you *really* like, and every single time you see her, it feels like the world stops turning around the two of you; it's the beginning of something real. But when you want nothing more than to protect her and make her happy, that's when you know you're in it for the long haul."

"And that's how you feel about my sister?"

"Absolutely. And now that I'm not letting my anger at her keeping something from me cloud my feelings for her, I want nothing more than to go to her and protect her and help her with this case."

He nods, "Okay. Go and help my sister." He lifts himself onto his knees to throw his arms around my neck to give me a bear hug. "You go and get those bad guys, Bryan."

"I will, buddy." He releases my neck, and as I stand up to grab my suitcase, I look back at him and smile one more time before I walk out of his room and right into Tom and Kathy.

"I'm getting ready to leave." I say as I try to hide my shock at running into them.

"Why did you tell him all that?" Tom asks.

I give him a sad smile before answering, "So hopefully he'll learn early on from my mistakes."

"I knew there was a reason I liked you." Kathy says. "Be safe and bring everyone home soon."

I nod and make my way downstairs and out the front door. When I throw my suitcase into the passenger side of my truck, I take my phone out of my back pocket and shoot a quick text to Wayne to let him know I'm heading to the airport so he can ready a small plane to take me down to Florida. He already gave me the address of an apartment that I will stay at until this is all over. I just hope that it's near Taylor. That way, if she doesn't let me stay wherever she's at, at least I can see her come and go.

As I park my truck and get my suitcase to board the plane, Wayne sends me one more text.

Wayne: What car do you want to drive while you're in Fla?

I smile, and I send him the make and model of the car that I'd want to drive.

Chapter Thirteen

Taylor

Later the next morning, we arrive at the track in our respective cars. I'm in my Mustang, and Lexi is finally in her Lancer. I notice that she has a renewed sway to her step, and I know it's from her admission to what happened to her and the fact that she now has more than just Mark to confide in and protect her.

I pull her into my side and give her a slight squeeze as we walk over to the concrete wall where the other girls are standing and watching a race that's currently being run between a white Dart and a red Charger. As Lexi and I approach Morgan's side, the Charger shoots forward and wins the race by a full car length.

I hear Lexi groan, muttering curses under her breath as Mark's Challenger pulls up to the starting line. He revs the monstrous engine as the same Charger rolls up beside him, answering Mark's rev with one of their own. They are going to be the next race. Lexi looks away, covering her eyes with her hand as I notice a man we haven't met before walk in between the cars with a checkered flag.

"Taylor, tell me, who's gonna win based on the car?" Morgan asks as she leans her forearms on the concrete barrier.

"The Challenger is heavier than the Charger." I begin.

"So, you're going against your friend's boyfriend?" Christy asks.

"No, she said by the car, not the driver." I smirk.

"Then who will win by the driver?" Morgan asks.

"Should be the Challenger." I say to give Lexi a bit of confidence in Mark's driving.

"The car is only about twenty percent of what racing is about. The other eighty percent is all the driver and how they react to their opponent." Morgan says.

I turn my attention back to the track, and I have to hold back a chuckle as Lexi peeks through her fingers to watch the cars take off.

As soon as they enter the first turn, it's a sure win. Mark will take this one. He got a head start, and he fought to keep it the whole time. Blocking the Charger's every attempt to pass him at each turn and shifting at the last second to take advantage of the stronger engine to fly across the finish line.

"Eighty percent driver." I say with a smile.

Lexi grins at me. That was the first time she's actually watched Mark race, and from the look on her face, I know she wants to go and either hug him or hit him. Maybe even both.

I tug her along with me as Mark parks his car beside the Charger and both men step out of the vehicles.

Just as we approach, the guy from the Charger pulls Mark in for a bro hug, slapping him twice on the back. This guy is just as tall as Mark is, but he's even more muscled. The black tank he's wearing seems like it's on the verge of ripping across his chest, and he has tattoos dotting his skin in random places up both arms. Not a full sleeve, but it's enough to make him look menacing.

"Great job, Mark! Not everyone can beat me, and you did in the first race. How long have you been racing?"

"Thanks, dude. I've been racing for a few years. My buddy and I would find back roads and drag race our cars. Until the cops showed up, that is."

"Don't I know that." The other guy chuckles. "That's why I bought this track with two of my other teammates when it was closed down three years ago. Now we can come here and race anytime we want to without having to worry about the cops."

"Smart move, man." Mark grins as he sees us approach. "Hey, Baby." He pulls Lexi into his side and gives her a firm squeeze.

"Hi. Great job on winning your race, Baby" Lexi says, and the grin she's sporting would fool other people, but not us. She's still terrified at him racing. Mark gives her a wink as a grin pulls up the corner of his mouth.

"Hey, Baby, Tay, this is Josh. He's the main man here." Mark says, introducing us to the man before him.

"Hi, Josh." I say, extending my hand to shake his.

He takes my hand in his, and it's surprisingly gentle for a man of his size. "It's nice to meet you, ladies."

"Likewise." I say, giving Josh a smile.

"Mark, hey, can I steal you away from your girl for a bit?" Josh asks as he turns his attention from me to Mark.

"Sure. I'll meet you at home later, Lexi. You two be good." Mark gives Lexi a wink and me a smile as he lets Lexi out of his embrace.

"Being 'good'," Lexi grins while using air quotes, "is not in my vocabulary, Mark."

"Better make this quick, Josh," Mark says while giving Lexi a dark warning glare, but I notice the slight smirk on Mark's lips before he walks away.

"What was that about?" I ask Lexi once we are out of earshot and walking toward our cars.

"I gave Mark an out if he needs to cut the meeting short with Josh. It's been a thing we've done on cases before. If he thinks he needs an out, he tells me to be good, and I just act like I'm his needy little girlfriend that he needs to get back home to."

"Damn." I say, completely shocked. "You've absolutely improved on your *skills*." I say, hoping she'll catch the drift of her being a badass agent.

"Well, yeah." She says, mocking sarcasm dripping from her tone.

I just laugh at her as I open the driver's door to my Mustang. "Come on, let's go home so I can make sure you stay Markie's good girl."

Lexi cackles. "I am so gonna tell him you said that."

I flip her off as I drop into the seat, turn the engine over, while slowly making my way back to our apartment.

Mark

I watch Lexi and Taylor walk away, and I can see they are deep in conversation before I hear Lexi's cackling laughter and the roar of engines turning over.

Josh clears his throat to get my attention again.

"Sorry. I just can't tear my eyes from her sometimes." I say with a shrug of my shoulders.

"She is something to look at," Josh begins, and I can't stop my heated look at him.

"Watch it." I growl.

"Hey, I got eyes to look. Don't mean I want to touch. I have Morgan to keep my bed warm, and I'm very content with her." He takes a deep breath before letting it out. "I just wish her being with me wasn't so dangerous."

"What do you mean?" I ask, playing dumb, but knowing he's probably talking about this Desmond prick that Lexi told me about.

"You said your buddy is supposed to be coming down, right?" Josh asks, and I nod. "When will he get here?"

"Probably tonight or tomorrow." I tell him, hoping I'm right and that Bryan is finally getting his ass down here or Wayne's sending another agent.

"Okay. I'm only waiting until tomorrow for him to get here and drive his initiation race. If he misses it, then he'll have to wait on the sidelines. I need a full team to keep on deck. I've already lost two drivers to that bastard," Josh says, his voice dipping into pure anger.

"What do you mean, lost two drivers? Who's coming after your team?" I ask, playing dumb.

"This sick fuck named Desmond." He snaps. "He picks drivers seemingly at random and races them for their girls. He don't race for the cars, cause they end up destroyed during the race. All he wants is a fresh piece of ass to take back to his hideout and rape until he gets tired of them and then kills them in cold blood."

"How do you know all that?"

"The first few times, he's sent their bodies back to us," Josh whispers, rage filling his expression as he clenches his fists at his sides.

Images of what that could look like fill my mind, and I remember what it was like to actually see that happen to the one I love, and it makes my stomach roll with nausea.

"Oh, shit, man. I'm sorry to hear that. That's completely fucked up. Why don't you just race the asshole and get it over with?"

"'Cause he declines me every damn time. He knows I'll wipe the floor with him." Josh says. "He chooses people that he can easily play mind games with and make them lose."

"And the guys he chooses, they can't decline the race?" I ask.

"Yeah. If they wanna wind up dead on the asphalt with a bullet in their brain. And then their girl is still taken on default."

"Have you tried to follow him back to his hideout and rescue the girl?" I ask.

"One time, yes," Josh says as he leans against the hood of his Charger. "We almost got her out, too. But Desmond cut us off and shot her. Since then, he's changed his hideout every time, so we can't track him."

"Well, if I can do anything to help you and the team, you let me and my buddy know. We aren't afraid to fight dirty if that means we can take this sick, twisted bastard down once and for all."

"I can see that in you." Josh says while looking me up and down. "Okay. You let me know when your friend gets here, and I may just take you up on your offer. I am just tired of seeing my family torn apart like this." He gives me a hard smack on the shoulder. "Get home to your girl."

I give him a firm nod, and I slip into my Challenger while messaging Bryan.

Me: Where the hell are you??

Bryan: About an hour from landing. I'll see you tomorrow.

I just react to his message with a thumbs up emoji as I pull away from the track and get back to the girls.

Chapter Fourteen

Taylor

After Lexi and I get back to the apartment, I help her with fixing dinner. It helps me keep my mind off *things*, and Lexi knows it, too.

I am in charge of coating the chicken breast in an egg wash before handing it to Lexi so she can cover the meat with a mix of Captain Crunch cereal and cashews before placing them on a foil-lined baking sheet. Once we have all the chicken covered, Lexi washes her hands first so she can place the pan in the preheated oven.

As I empty the unused cereal and nuts into the trash and throw the egg wash down the sink, I wash my hands too. I look out over the little cutout that faces the living room and the main window of the apartment, and I notice headlights pull up in front of our building. I can't stop the little jolt in my chest that thinks, maybe it's Bryan. But that feeling is quickly squashed when I see Mark step out of his car and he walks in through the door.

"Hey, Baby, I'm home." Mark calls, and Lexi rushes out to greet him.

She throws her arms around his neck, and he places a hand on the small of her back, pulling her closer to him before pressing a loving kiss to her lips.

Damn it. I was doing so well today. I think to myself as I feel unshed tears begin to sting my eyes. *And now I've thought of* him *twice in the span of what, five minutes?*

"Something smells good." Mark says while sniffing like a dog towards the kitchen.

"God, all you think about is food." Lexi chuckles.

"Not all the time. I think about you." He says, his voice deeper as he leans in to kiss her again.

"Okay! Hey, keep it PG, or tell me to take a hike. Geez." I say while rolling my eyes, but they helped me put a smile on my face.

"I'd tell you to take a hike, but I don't think my escapades would fare well if I said that," Mark says while looking from me to Lexi with a sly grin on his face.

"Not hardly." Lexi deadpans.

We sit on the couch until the chicken is almost done, and Lexi goes back into the kitchen to finish up the side dish of mixed vegetables in the steamer.

Once we are all settled around the table, we eat among idle chatter, and when we are finished eating, Mark tells us what he and Josh talk about. I'm thankful he left it for last, because my stomach drops at the information.

"We need to tell Lincoln and Temperance about this tomorrow. I don't think they knew anything about what's really going on down here." Mark says.

"Why don't we tell them now?" I ask, my voice trembling.

"'Cause we need to let your backup know, too. And I don't want to keep saying the same damn thing over and over. It's pissing me off so much that I want to go track this son of a bitch down myself and end him." Mark growls.

Lexi places a hand on Mark's neck to get him to look at her, and her presence helps calm his racing thoughts.

"We will get to the bottom of this, Mark. I promise," Lexi says.

He nods. "I'll clean up the kitchen for you two while you go and get ready for bed. I have a feeling we'll need every ounce we can get before shit starts hitting the fan."

Lexi and I nod as we stand from the table and get our showers. Once we are dressed in our PJs, we head back into the kitchen to make sure Mark doesn't need any help, and we find that the kitchen is spotless. Every dish is cleaned and put away, the counters are wiped, and even the floor is mopped.

"Damn Babe. You in a cleaning mood?" Lexi asks.

"You know I sometimes stress clean." Mark replies. "Come on, we need to go to bed, you two."

Lexi turns off the lights, and she walks with Mark into their bedroom. I start to head toward my room, but I pause when headlights flood the living room again. I turn around and walk to the window to peek through the curtain enough where I can see them, but whoever it is won't see me. But it's so dark out that I can't see them fully either. I can only make out the shape of a yellow Camaro, and it's pulled up in the apartment that was supposed to be mine. I can tell that it's a guy by the way he walks, but that's all I can see.

"Taylor, come on. Whoever he is, he will be there in the morning." Lexi says, noticing that I didn't follow them back to my room.

"Yeah, I guess so." I say.

Bryan

I pull up to the address that Wayne sent me, and I kill the engine. I know that Mark, Lexi, and Taylor are near here, but I don't know where, and that hurts more than I care to admit right now. I'm basically breathing the same air with her, but not really.

I sigh as I get out of my Camaro and grab my suitcase from the trunk before gripping the apartment key, which was attached to the same keyring as my car key, and walk up to the little stoop. When I unlock the door, I half expect to hear Taylor come to the door to see who came in, but when I flip on the light, I am met with silence. She must be staying with Mark and Lexi, or she's not home yet.

With a sigh, I pull out my phone and send a quick text to my grandparents to let them know I made it safely before sending another to Mark to let him know the same.

> **Mark:** Thank God you're here dude. We'll take you to meet our POC's and I have some shit to spill.

> **Me:** Ok. Can't you tell me now?

> **Mark:** No man. This is something I can't keep talking about. I need everyone in the know at once.

> **Me:** Ok. see you in the morning.

I know I'm not going to get anything more out of him, but whatever it is, it has him terrified. I've only seen him this way twice. Once when I was shot, and then the other time when he and Lexi came back from their first case together.

Making my way back to the bedroom, I toss my suitcase onto a long dresser in the corner of the room before finding a pair of gray shorts and making my way to the bathroom to get a shower before turning in for the night.

Chapter Fifteen

Taylor

The next morning, when I wake up and get dressed, Mark is just heading out the door with a quick wave to Lexi.

"Had to leave early, huh?" I ask Lexi as I make myself a cup of coffee.

"Yeah, he did."

"Did you get a look at the new agent?" I ask, already nervous about who I'll be working with. I think if it was *him*, he would have messaged me last night.

"No, but I'm sure we will when we get to the track." Lexi says with a soft, reassuring smile.

"I just want to know who is going to have my back." I sigh.

"I know, and you will find out soon." Lexi says.

Once we are finished with our coffee and a quick breakfast, Lexi takes me out to my Mustang to make good on her promise of teaching me how to make myself look sexy while I get out of my car.

"Use your wedges to your advantage." She says while pointing to the sandals I have on my feet, courtesy of her loaning them to me. "Lean one leg out, then when you have it on the ground, shift your weight and poke your butt out a bit while you get out of your car."

Lexi demonstrates her instructions for me, and she's right; she looks hot. I, on the other hand, will probably look like I'm trying too hard to be noticed. Lexi urges me to try what she just showed me, and when I go through the motions, I feel like an idiot, but my friend acts like she's fanning herself when I finally shut my door and lean against the slowly warming metal.

"That was hot. See, you'll do great." She says with a grin. "Come on, let's go."

Bryan

I pull up to a stadium-sized racetrack after Mark texted me the address early this morning. As I pull in through the gates, I spot Mark leaning against a black Challenger, and I can't help the smirk on my face. I bet Lexi is giving him hell for driving that kind of car.

I pull up beside his car and step out of mine to join him.

"Hey, man. It's about damn time I see your face down here." Mark whispers in my ear as he pulls me in for a bro-hug.

"Yeah. I know." I look around the track and I see where a group of girls are gathered near a low concrete wall, but I don't see *our* girls.

"They're on their way. I had to get here early." Mark says as he notices my line of sight.

I take a breath as I nod to him. "Alright. What's going on?"

"You, my brother, need to win the initiation race."

"Against who?" I ask.

"Against Josh." Mark points to a guy next to a red Charger. He spots Mark and makes his way over to us.

"Morning man. So this is your friend?" Josh asks.

"It is." Mark beams. "This is my brother from another mother, Bryan. Bryan, this is Josh, the leader here."

I take in his form. He's the same height as Mark, but he has even more muscles and tattoos traveling up his arms.

I reach out to shake his hand, making sure my grip is firm. "Nice to meet ya, Josh."

He grins at my handshake and looks at Mark before saying, "You should have told me this guy had a death grip of a handshake, Mark. I wouldn't have given him my shifting hand."

"I can't tell you all our secrets, man." Mark chuckles darkly. "I keep telling him to take it easy, but he doesn't listen."

I have to fight to not roll my eyes. Mark knows how to fit right in with strangers. His charm wins out every time.

"Well, Bryan, you ready to race me for your chance at running with the big dogs?" Josh asks. "I hear you and your buddy would do street races a lot back home."

I shoot Mark a look. I mean, he's not really wrong, but it was on a path that we made near the cabin. Thankfully, his old man let us use his CAT to smooth out the track so we could race his SUV and my truck without totaling the suspension. So not *street racing,* but still.

"Yeah, we did." I smile, playing along.

"Alright. Get in your ride and show me what you got," Josh says while slapping me on the back and walking over to his car.

"You got any tips for me, *boss*?" I ask while giving him the side-eye.

"Boss? Wow, Bry, you're gonna give me an inflated ego."

"Well, you're acting like you're the brains here." I chuckle. "Which I guess you are at this point." I sigh.

"Nah, man. We are a team. I just made friends here first since you took your sweet ass time getting here." Mark says, and I internally groan.

He's not gonna let me live that down, and he shouldn't, to be honest.

I walk over to my Camaro, and just as I turn the engine over and pull up to the starting line, I see a red Lancer and an ice-blue Mustang pull up. My heart freezes in my chest when I notice Lexi's face behind the windshield. If she's here, then the Mustang must belong to Taylor.

As Lexi parks and steps out of her car, I can tell Mark is about to explode. Lexi's slowly stepping out, one leg at a time. And when her foot hits the pavement, she shows off her lithe body, and I look away. The other guys, however, don't until Mark shoots them a glare that should make them want to wither away. Lexi gives Mark a wink before tapping on the driver's side glass of the Mustang to get Taylor's attention.

When her door opens, I grip my steering wheel so tight that my knuckles pop and my skin turns white from the death grip I currently have on the leather. I watch as she extends one leg, setting it on the ground while pointing her sandal-clad foot, which makes her calf muscles tighten. I groan loudly when she shifts her weight onto her extended leg and pokes her butt out a little further than necessary to exit her vehicle.

"Damn it, Taylor." I growl as I squirm in my seat to try and relieve the pressure building against the zipper of my jeans while wondering if she even knows I'm here and if she does, is she flaunting herself like this on purpose to get back at me?

She walks around to the front of her Mustang, sits on the hood, and bends her right leg up enough to rest her heel on the fender while pulling her long chestnut brown hair from the hair tie. As she shakes her head to help make the strands lay softly around her shoulders, Mark starts wolf-calling her and urging the other men around him to join in.

Red fills my vision, and I am about ready to pull the e-brake, throw the transmission in neutral, jump out of the car while it's still running, and kick his ass, but Josh pulls up beside me, making my hand pause on the door.

"Fine." I sigh with defeat, but I rev the engine to get everyone's attention on me and not on my girl.

I push the clutch in and shift into first gear as a well-built, tall man with an olive skin tone walks between the cars, and he signals for us to roll our windows down. Josh rolls his front passenger window down while I do the same with my driver's side.

"We will have a clean race. One lap." He looks at me as he says, "If you are able to win in this quarter-mile sprint, then you will be initiated into the club. Lose, and you sit on the sidelines."

I nod my head as Josh shouts over the roar of the engines, "Thanks, Ian! Now, let's get this race moving!"

Ian moves in front of our cars, the checkered flag held high in the air. I hit the switch on my door to roll my window back up, and just before it closes, I hear Taylor's voice cheering over the crowd, and I can't help the smirk that blooms on my face.

"Go, Camaro!"

"Oh, Baby, would you still be cheering if you knew I was the one driving?" I ask, even though I know she can't see or hear me.

It's at that moment that, no matter what, I'm winning this damn race for more than just being initiated. I know my girl is still pissed at me, but I can't wait to see the look on her face when I get out of this car and she realizes she was cheering me on the whole time.

When Ian flings the flag down, signaling us to begin, and I floor the Camaro, quickly shifting through the gears to get up to top speed, and I let Josh stay on my bumper so he can't fling himself past me and win at the last second.

When I cross the finish line, I can hear the roar of everyone around me cheering for my win. Then, I shift into neutral, pull the e-break, and turn the wheel sharply to the left, so I can do a doughnut as a victory stunt and let the smoke from the tires conceal my form as I cut the engine and step out of the cabin.

Mark walks over to me, and I immediately grab the nape of his neck, pulling his ear close to my mouth. "I know you were trying to *fit in*, but if you ever wolf-call my girl for real, I'm gonna beat you to a pulp." I growl.

He has the damn nerve to grin wickedly at me. "I thought you two broke up? I was just trying to help her find a new man."

"Are you for freaking real?" I snap.

"Just making sure you were still willing to fight for her, man." He shrugs his shoulders like he did nothing wrong.

I smile at him as I shake my head because I know what he's trying to do. Make me jealous, and it's working like a freaking charm.

"I hate you sometimes." I grumble as the smoke finally clears and I am face-to-face with Taylor, and her expression turns from pure happiness to utter disdain in the blink of an eye.

Chapter Sixteen

Taylor

I have seen some cars take a victory lap completely around the track, but not this driver. I watch as the Camaro spins around, doing a burnout and stops right in front of me.

Once the smoke that was created from the burning rubber settles, I notice the driver is standing beside his car talking to Mark, and as I take in his form, the familiar way he moves, my jaw almost drops, but I catch myself at the last second.

"Well, look what the cat coughed up." I scoff at Lexi.

"Tay, go over and—" Lexi begins, but I cut her off.

"Don't tell me to talk to him, Lexi." I snap.

"He finally came, at least wave at him." Lexi says gently.

"No, he's going to be the one to come over to me."

Deep down I'm trying to convince myself to be mad at him, but if I'm being honest, all I want is to go to him, pull him in for a hug and kiss him. I thought he would never come down because of his anger at me for trying to keep his parents' case a secret, or that Wayne sent him on a different mission as a form of punishment. But here he is, with a genuine smile on his face.

I catch him looking at me out of the corner of my eye, like I am doing with him. When I make a complete turn toward him to look at him directly in the eye as a challenge, Mark grabs him and pulls him towards the other guys.

"You rock, man!" I hear Mark shout.

I'm not able to hear what Bryan responds with, but instead I feel an arm on mine and I turn to see Lexi looking at me with a bit of confusion lining her brow.

"What are you doing? He's finally here. Isn't that what you've wanted this whole time?" Lexi asks again.

"Well, yeah, but I'm not going to just run right back into his arms. He was the one that was wrong, and I want him to admit that." I say, still standing by what I said earlier.

"Sometimes I hate your stubbornness." Lexi says.

"Yeah, well, I'm not going to go running back. If he wants me, he'll fight for me." I say as I make my way back to my Mustang when I see the track is closing down since the races are done for the day.

Just before I get in my car, I hear Mark yell for me. "Taylor! We need to *celebrate*."

I internally groan because I somehow know he's meaning to meet with Lincoln and Temperance. Being in the same room with Bryan is not going to be easy.

"Sounds good!" I put on a fake smile as I open my door. "I'll follow you." I add as I shut my door, not giving Bryan the chance to get within earshot until I have to.

Bryan stares at me for a minute before dropping into the driver's seat of his Camaro, and the others follow suit, with Mark leading the way out.

We all park in our normal spots when we arrive at the apartment complex twenty minutes later. Lexi and I start to head over to the lead agent's unit first with the guys trailing behind us. Then I hear a noise off to my right. It sounds like a rock hitting the pavement.

I look toward the noise, but there's nothing there. When I turn my head back to question Lexi, I don't see her next to me. Instead, she's next to Mark, walking hand in hand with him, and Bryan is almost in her place, just a few paces behind me.

I glance at him, and when my gaze locks into his familiar green eyes, I can't help but feel the awkwardness between us. He tries to give me a small smile, but I quickly turn my head on him. I don't want just a small gesture of a smile to win me back. He's gotta do more.

Mark steps onto the porch, knocks on the door, and it opens a moment later.

"Mark hello. What brings—" Lincoln stops mid-sentence as he spots Bryan, but quickly recovers. "I'm assuming you're Mr. Evans?" He asks, mindful not to use 'agent' in front of his name since we are out in the open.

"Yes, sir. I am." Bryan answers in a firm and formal voice. "It's nice to meet you."

"You as well. Please, come in."

Lincoln moves to the side and Mark lets both me and Lexi enter first, which I'm thankful for. I can nab the armchair without running the risk of having Mark force Bryan to sit near me on the couch.

I see Sophie sitting in the other armchair across the room, and she gives me a small smile before tilting her head back and yelling, "Mom! You have guests!"

"Soph, I am right here in the kitchen; I can hear you just—" Temperance's eyes lock onto Bryan's, and I get the feeling that she is looking at a ghost, or the last person she ever thought she would see.

Mark and Bryan exchange a quick look at each other before Bryan extends his hand to Temperance.

"Hello. My name is Bryan Evans. It's nice to meet you."

"Temperance, please get everyone something to drink. Sophie, go help your mother." Lincoln instructs, and that seems to knock his wife out of her shocked state.

"Yes, of course. Anything in particular you all want?" She asks.

"No. Whatever you have is fine." Mark says, and we all nod our heads in agreement.

"Well, I know Dad wants coffee, so I'll get the machine filled up." Sophie says as she gets up from the armchair to follow her mother into the kitchen, and we all sit in silence and wait until the two women come back with the requested drinks of coffee, water, and a few cans of Coke.

Bryan takes the Coke, but I already know he's not going to like it. He's more of a Pepsi or a Cherry Dr. Pepper kind of guy. As he takes the first sip, he tries to hide his cringe, but I see it, and so does Sophie.

"I don't like Coke either, but Mom loves the stuff." She tells Bryan.

"It's not my favorite, but I can handle it if I need to." He says with a smile.

My chest tightens at seeing his smile in such a small space, and I have to down a few sips of my own Coke to hide the burn of tears behind my eyes.

"Okay, so what is the purpose of this meeting other than introducing us to your friend here?" Lincoln asks.

"We have news about what's going on here, and I need to tell you three all at once," Mark begins.

"Yeah, you said shit was going down here, but you wouldn't tell me what it was," Bryan says while setting his Coke can back down on the coffee table in front of him.

I notice that Temperance gives Bryan a quick look out of the corner of her eye for a moment at his words, but I brush it off as she's not used to him and how he acts like she is with the rest of us. She seems to be a bit on the paranoid side or something.

"I'm getting to it. Don't get your briefs in a twist." Mark jokes, and I know it's his way of trying to ease the tension that he's about to bring down in this living room.

"Boxers." I say and all eyes dart to mine, but Bryan's fills with mischief. He knows what I'm talking about.

"What?" Mark snorts.

"He wears boxers, not briefs." I say, and I have to fight back a smile, my first one since Bryan's been here.

"I can't do this," Temperance says suddenly and walks out of the room.

All of our laughter fades as we watch her briskly walk back toward the master bedroom.

"I'll go to her." Sophie says.

"I'm sorry about that." Lincoln says with a sigh as he runs his hands through his blonde hair. "We, uh, we lost our first child when he was about five years old in a freak accident when we were in the middle of a case, and his name was Bryan, too. So it's hard for her to hear someone with the same name and know it's not your son. He'd be about twenty or twenty-one by now."

"I'm sorry to hear that, Lincoln. Yeah, I turned twenty a few months ago. And it's kinda strange you say that. I actually lost my parents when I was that age." Bryan explains.

"What happened?" Lincoln asks, and we all stay quiet, even though we know Mark, Lexi and I have a lot to discuss, but they seem to be having a moment, and it's rude to interrupt those who still are in mourning.

"It took fifteen years; four for me personally, but I found the son of a bitch that killed my parents." Bryan growls and Lincoln grins. "And thanks to Mark, Lexi, and Taylor here, we were able to take them down." He adds, pausing when he gets to my name for a heartbeat.

"Well, I'm glad you were able to get some closure." Lincoln says.

"So am I," Temperance says as she slowly comes back out from the bedroom with Sophie on her heels. "I'm sorry. I know Lincoln told you all, but it's still hard at times."

"Well, I hope you all get closure, too. Did you catch the guy that hurt your son?" Bryan asks.

"Not us specifically. But we were told he was taken care of not too long ago. I just can't wait until I'm reunited with my baby one day." Temperance says.

"He'll be waiting for you up there in Heaven when it's your time, I'm sure." Bryan says while taking Temperance's hand in his and giving it a slight squeeze.

"Thank you." Temperance says while wiping tears from her face. "Now, why don't you tell us what's going on, Mark?"

"Okay. Sorry, I just didn't want to ruin the moment you all were having there. Cause shit's about to get depraved real damn quick." Mark looks at everyone for a moment, then takes a deep breath. "Okay, so one. This team is clean. They don't street race, like at all. All they want to do is race and go home at the end of the day. That's why they have the track that they do. That way, it's all legal and no issues with the local cops. But it's this guy that comes into their territory; he's the problem. Desmond." Mark explains.

"From what we heard, he's ruthless and doesn't mind killing people one bit," Lexi adds.

"Okay, a murdering racer. What's so special about that?" Bryan asks.

"He doesn't race for pink slips." I begin.

"He races the guys for their girlfriends, and he goes against guys that he knows he can mess with mentally. I don't know how he races, but the cars end up destroyed and the racer dies on impact or shortly after. This piece of shit takes the girls an—" Mark takes a breath as he grabs onto Lexi's hand, and I know for the first time she's the one grounding him instead of the other way around. "He takes them to a hideout that moves every, single damn time he forcefully wins a race, he drugs the girls before he and his thugs rape them, then kills them once they are bored, which who knows how long that is before that happens."

"Holy shit, Mark. Are you for real?" Bryan asks, his fists resting on his knees, and Mark nods his head.

"I wish I wasn't, man. But yeah, the girls can vouch for this, and I spoke to Josh about this yesterday. So, we need to figure out a way to stop this bastard before he takes any more of these girls." Mark says, his voice dark and determined.

"Try to figure out if there is a pattern that may tell us when this Desmond will pick his next driver. As soon as you know, keep us in the loop." Lincoln instructs.

"Yes, sir," Mark responds, while Lexi and I nod in agreement.

Mark walks out first before letting me and Lexi follow him, and Bryan gently closes the door behind him.

I grab onto Lexi's hand and pull her close to my side. "You're not leaving my side this time." I whisper into her ear.

"Who me? Never." She says, feigning innocence.

I give her a sharp look that says I'm not buying it, but she keeps her hand locked with mine while Mark and Bryan walk side by side, quietly talking to one another.

When we approach our apartment, Mark takes his keys out of his pocket to unlock the door, and we all walk in. Again, it feels so weird to have Bryan's presence here when we are still so distant emotionally.

The little blip of connection I inadvertently made over at Lincoln and Temperance's place with the boxer comment has evaporated between us, and we are back to awkward silence.

"I'm gonna get dinner started for everyone. Bryan, you're welcome to stay," Lexi says, and I shoot her a look. "Come on, Tay. Come in here and help me."

"Okay." I say, my voice quiet and somewhat thankful she's getting me out of the same room.

Lexi pulls out a box of Kraft mac and cheese to go with some chicken I laid out earlier this morning, then sets a can of green beans out on the counter.

When I see the can, I remember the time I made Bryan exercise with them after he came home from the hospital because he had issues with lifting his arm due to a bit of nerve irritation he had from the gunshot wound in his chest.

"I thought spinach made you stronger?" Bryan asks.

"Not to eat, to lift, smartass. Lift them like you're lifting a hand weight." *I replied.*

As the memory takes root, my eyes burn with tears, and I refuse to let them fall down my cheeks. I feel my knees wobble slightly from the emotion flooding my body, so I jump up onto the counter before I fall to the floor like an idiot.

Then I see Mark walk to the kitchen doorway, and Bryan is standing behind him. I look away, fixated on the boiling water in a pan on the stove for the mac and cheese, so he doesn't see the breakdown I'm trying like hell to hide.

"Come on, Babe." Mark says, his voice just a touch sad but more annoyed than anything. "Let's leave these two alone for a while."

As my best friend begins to walk away from the stove, my look towards her begs, 'don't leave', but her responding glare in my direction says, 'talk to him'.

Irritated that she would leave me here, I scowl as I look back at the pan of boiling water again. I listen as their footsteps get quieter until I hear the front door open and shut, and then I know it's only Bryan and me in the apartment. I stay where I'm at on the counter, just watching the water boil.

I hear him blow out a defeated sigh, and I flick my eyes ever so slightly in Bryan's direction.

"Taylor, I'm—" Bryan begins.

"Don't." I cut him off, hopping off the counter to stand in front of him. I don't care that he has a few inches on me and that I only come up to his collarbone; I glare up at him. "I don't want to hear your excuses." I tell him, but my damn voice breaks a bit with unshed tears.

"Annie, please." Bryan whispers, pain evident in his voice. He reaches his hand out to caress the base of my neck, and I allow that single, gentle touch.

When I hear that nickname he gave me, a part of my heart breaks a little.

"It's been terrible here without you." I sob. "I have been scared to death the past few days, and I didn't have you to hold me and tell me it was going to be alright!" My tears of sadness quickly turn into those of anger. "All I was trying to do was get as much info as I could for you. I didn't want you to have false hope if it turned out someone was playing you or if we found their message too late."

I try to take a step back and away from his hand, but he doesn't let me go. His grip on my neck is firm yet gentle, telling me we are not running away from each other anymore.

"I know that now. I am so sorry, Baby," Bryan says. "I'm sorry I blew up the way I did back home. I'm sensitive when it comes to my parents, and I took out that insecurity on you."

He wipes away the tears that are now streaming down my cheeks with the pad of his thumb as he pulls me into his chest, and I let him, no longer able to fight the distance between us. I wrap my arms around his back, curling my fingers into his shirt in an effort to pull him even closer.

"I am so sorry that I wasn't here with you sooner." Bryan says as I bury my face into his shirt and he tightens his grip on me.

We just stand in the kitchen for a few minutes, holding one another. The only sound between us is my soft crying and the bubbling of the boiling water.

I let the wall that I have been trying to build around my heart crumble as I take in everything I've missed about him. His cologne—Armani Code I got him for his birthday back in May. The feel of his strong arms around my waist and the steady beat of his heart. We melt back into one another as if we have never been apart.

He pulls away enough to look down at me. "So, are you still my partner in crime?" Bryan asks with a sly smile.

After a few minutes of silence, making him think that I'm still contemplating about forgiving him, I say, "Bullet, you know it."

His smile widens as he leans in and presses his mouth to mine. At first, it's just a chaste kiss, nothing mind-blowing, but when he lifts his left hand, his fingers digging in to grip the nape of my neck, I can't help but let my mouth fall open at his touch. His tongue tentatively grazes against my own, as if asking for permission to take this kiss deeper, and I immediately moan into his mouth, urging him on.

Tilting my head to the side, he begins to devour my mouth, our tongues dancing against each other in a desperate rhythm as he threads his fingers through my hair. I don't realize he's moved our positions until my back hits the stainless steel refrigerator in the corner of the kitchen and the shock of the cool metal makes me gasp into his mouth. Bryan growls as he runs his teeth over my bottom lip, nipping just enough to have heat pooling between my legs.

"You looked so damn sexy getting out of that Mustang. It almost made me want to say the hell with the race and come to you then." Bryan says breathlessly as he pulls back just enough to look at me with a sly smile playing on his kiss-swollen lips.

"Oh, you liked that, huh?" I tease as I run my index finger down the middle of his chest.

Bryan chuckles as he leans in and starts kissing my neck. "Yes, very much."

I bend my head back, allowing him more access to my skin, and I feel his teeth graze across my pulse point behind my ear in response.

Barely catching my breath, I say, "You have Lexi to thank for that. She taught me a thing or two."

"Oh, she did?" He questions as he places a hand on my left hip and gives it a quick squeeze before whispering in my ear, "Nah, I think she just helped you perfect what you already knew."

Chapter Seventeen

Taylor

Bryan and I are still holding one another in the kitchen when we hear the front door open. I look over his shoulder to see Mark and Lexi walking back into the living room.

"Are you two decent?" Mark yells with a hint of mischief in his voice.

"Mark, just get in here." Bryan says while rolling his eyes and letting me step away from the fridge.

"So, are we a team again?" Mark asks from the entryway to the kitchen where he finds Bryan holding me, my back pressed against his chest and his arm resting across my stomach.

"You know it," Bryan says, looking down at me with his trademark grin before giving me another quick kiss.

"Yeah, I decided to let him live. He's too cute to kill." I tease as I lick the taste of him off my bottom lip.

Mark and Lexi laughs while Bryan just looks at me for a second.

You should worry, buddy; screw with me, and I just might do you in. I say to myself. I know that's a hollow threat, but he doesn't know that.

"I'll finish up dinner while you three go sit in the living room." Lexi says.

Mark gives her a quick kiss and watches her go into the kitchen. As I pass her, I nod my head by way of a silent 'thank you' for giving Bryan and me some privacy.

"So, what's the plan?" Bryan asks as he sits on the couch while pulling me into his side.

"We don't really have one yet." I admit.

"Why?" Bryan asks.

"Because until we know when this prick makes his move, we have nothing else to go by," Mark says as he takes a seat on one of the armchairs in front of the window overlooking the street.

"So you've only heard stories of this guy? How do you know he even exists? It could be all done on the inside." Bryan asks while looking between me and Mark.

"No. This is done by someone outside. Their stories line up too much, and if someone was lying, then I'd bet good money that Christy chick would be the first to spill the beans." I say.

"Yeah, that girl is a complete blabbermouth." Lexi chimes in from the kitchen.

After a few moments of silence, Mark stands from his armchair, walks into the kitchen, then pulls four plates out of the cabinet before handing one to Lexi so she can fill the plate with the steaming, mouthwatering food.

In these few minutes of us being alone on the couch, I lean deeper into Bryan's side, letting him toy with my fingers like he always does. I hear him take a breath, and I know he's thinking about everything he's been told in the last forty-five minutes.

"I'm not backing out, Bryan. We are here to do a job, and that's what I plan to do." I tell him before he can even voice the option of me leaving and going back home.

"I didn't say anything."

"But you were thinking it." I shoot back.

He leans his head back against the couch. "Fair."

As Mark and Lexi bring out two plates apiece a minute later, he hands one to Bryan, while Lexi hands another to me, and we all eat in silence. The only noise that fills the room is the sound of rain hitting the roof and the roll of thunder from a random thunderstorm that rolls through the area.

"We are going to find this sick bastard and take him down." Lexi declares after we finish our dinner.

"I agree." I say. "And Lexi and I will be fine."

"I'm still going to worry about you." Bryan says as he brushes the back of his knuckles down my arm.

"Yeah, I don't care if we would be with you girls every second of the day; we are still going to be worried about you." Mark says as he pulls Lexi closer to him and kisses the top of her head.

"We know." Lexi whispers as she wraps her arm across his shoulder.

Mark looks between Bryan and me on the couch before glancing down at Lexi for a moment. A slight grin forms at the corner of his mouth, and I mentally brace myself for the *real* Mark to make an appearance.

"Now that you two are back together, do you think that you could go over to your place?"

"Mark! Stop being a jerk!" Lexi scolds as she lightly smacks him on the back of his head.

"Ow, Lex!" Mark rubs at the back of his head. "You're gonna pay for that later, Baby."

I groan, covering my face with my hand while Lexi scoffs and tries to call Mark's bluff.

"What do you say? You want to go over to the other apartment?" Bryan asks as he leans down to whisper in my ear.

"Yeah, let's give these two some privacy." I tease. "I'm sure they could use it."

Bryan looks at them, and Mark wiggles his eyebrows.

"Git, you two," Mark says, shooing us away.

Bryan laughs at Mark as we head towards the door to leave. He takes a black umbrella from the holder, opens the door so he can walk out first, then pops the umbrella open, and motions for me to walk under it with him.

"Mark is so weird." I chuckle softly.

"Yeah, but he's a good friend and a good partner." Bryan says.

"Yeah, he is." I say, nodding in agreement. "And I'll be honest, I think he was ready to fly back home to kick your ass if you didn't get down here."

"He would've had every right to. And you would too."

"Does that offer still stand?" I tease.

"Maybe."

"Nah, I'll leave the ass-kicking to Mark." I say with a sly smile on my face.

Bryan grins down at me before he takes a set of keys out of his front left pocket, then unlocks the front door. He flicks the living room light on and lets me go in first to get out of the rain. I turn around and watch as he shakes the rain from the umbrella and sets it in the holder by the door.

"Welcome to our home away from home, Annie," Bryan says as he spreads his arms wide to show off the living room that is a replica of Mark and Lexi's, just reversed.

"As long as you're with me, Bullet, I will always feel at home." I say as I lean into his solid body, stand on my tiptoes, and give him a sound kiss on the lips.

"I believe that with my entire soul, Annie. We are each other's home." He says as he wraps his arms around my lower back, lifting me off the floor to spin me around before setting me back down on my feet. As I slide down his muscled frame, I feel his hardened length press against my center, and I moan into his mouth at the same time my feet hit the floor.

"We should get some sleep." Bryan says, but his voice tells me he'd rather do anything but sleep.

"I forgot my suitcase at Mark and Lexi's." I say.

"Don't worry, it's here." Bryan says with a smile on his face.

"Oh, so you just took for granted that I would come over here before you asked?"

"I was hoping that you would," Bryan corrects with a smirk.

"Smart man." I deadpan.

If he had said yes, I would have kicked his ass here and now.

"And don't worry, everything is still in your suitcase. I didn't unpack it."

"Good." I say with a single nod. "Come on, let's get ready for bed."

While Bryan is getting his shower in the attached master bathroom, I unpack my things and put them in the long dresser next to his own articles of clothing, much like we did in my room back home.

"Hey, Babe, can you give me a towel?" Bryan asks as he shuts off the water a few minutes later.

I smile to myself and I think about not giving the towel to him, but for some reason, Morgan's words echo in my mind about the girls that are being killed by Desmond and that instantly kills my playful mood.

I grab the towel from the little shelf behind the door and hand it to Bryan through the shower curtain. "Here you go." I say, then walk out of the bathroom so he can get dressed.

We haven't seen the other completely naked yet, and right now, with the sadness and worry that is running rampant through my mind, I don't want tonight to be the night that we finally cross that line.

I go back to the drawer that I've claimed as my own and pull out a pair of shorts, then I open one of Bryan's drawers to take one of his t-shirts so I can get my bath.

"You okay, Babe?" Bryan asks as he walks out of the bathroom in his maroon boxers while running the towel over his dark hair to dry it. "I would've thought that you would've picked or teased about giving me my towel."

"I was going to, but I started thinking about the girls that Desmond kills, and that just kind of busted my bubble." I say softly.

"Go get a nice hot shower; maybe that will help." Bryan says gently, coaxing.

"Alright, be out in a few minutes."

He kisses my forehead, and I lean into his solid body, taking in his fresh post-shower scent.

"Go." He whispers.

And I do. I shut the bathroom door behind me, step into the shower, pull the curtain, and turn the water on. I turn around, letting the water hit my shoulders and run down my back in an effort to clear my head a bit until I feel the water start to lose its warmth.

After I get out, dry off, and get dressed, I head into the bedroom and join Bryan. He has the covers pulled up, resting mid-thigh, and he's still shirtless. His broad chest and well-defined abs are on full display for me.

"Have I ever told you that I love seeing you in my shirts?" Bryan asks as he watches me walk into the room, his eyes shining with pure desire.

His look gives me a bit of energy back, and I hold on to it like a life raft in a raging ocean. "Actually, no, you haven't." I chuckle as I pull at the hem of his shirt, teasing him with a peek of my thigh.

"Well, I do. It leaves just enough to the imagination." Bryan says with a mischievous smile.

He sits up on his right elbow, allowing half his body to shadow mine as I climb into bed beside him. With his left hand, he runs it through my still-damp hair, and I close my eyes as I lean into his touch.

Even though I'm not looking, my hand somehow always finds that little scar on his chest. The one that led me to believe he was dead for three long months. The same one that led me back to the agency for good. And I can't help but think that things are going to turn dangerous in the blink of an eye and one of us might not make it back.

"Annie, Babe, don't go there." Bryan whispers, already knowing what's going through my head.

"Sometimes I can't help it, Bryan." I say, looking into his bright green eyes.

"I know. Sometimes I can't help it either." He says, touching my side where my own scar hides under his shirt.

"Do you ever wish that you never gotten involved with the agency?" I ask.

He is quiet for a few minutes, then he looks me in the eye and smiles. "No. I have met some of the greatest people that I would have never met if it weren't for the agency." Bryan says. "I already knew Mark from when we were kids. But I met Wayne, and a few other people over the years." He smiles down at me, his voice dipping an octave lower. "And most importantly, you."

I smile as I lift my head off the pillow to kiss him. He runs his hand through my hair again as he skims his tongue across the seam of my lips, and a moan escapes my throat as I open up for him. He growls at my surrender to him as he slowly trails his hand up my side.

"Keep going." I tell him, my lips brushing against his as I speak.

"You tell me to stop," He says between kisses, "if it gets to be too much."

"Stop talking." I demand.

He chuckles darkly as his hand begins to move again, and when his fingertips brush the underside of my right breast through his shirt; I tense up. His touch, although familiar, it's foreign in this way, but Lexi's words echo in my mind.

To trust myself and to trust that Bryan has my best interest at heart.

So, I will my body to relax under his touch, and I lift my right arm above my head, gripping the corner of the pillow, letting him know I am open for him.

"Good girl." Bryan growls against my mouth.

I moan at his praise, and he begins to move his hand again. When his thumb grazes over my sensitive nipple, I arch my back into his touch, and the noise that comes out of my throat next is something I never thought I would make. It's a mix between a groan and a moan.

"I've never heard you make that noise before, Taylor." He starts to trail kisses down my neck, and I bend it to the side to allow him more access. "If I can make you sound like this just by touching you through clothes, I can't wait to hear you when there's nothing between us."

I somehow find the brain capacity to form words. "What's stopping you now?" I ask, my voice raspy with need.

He pulls back to look at me. To make sure he heard me correctly, and I smile up at him, biting my lower lip between my teeth.

Bryan smiles. "Tell me, where do you want me?"

I remember where I wanted him before Wayne's phone call interrupted us and before things went to shit between us. So, I let my legs fall open under him, and I take the hand that was just on my breast and drag it down my belly, just stopping at the waistband of my shorts.

His green eyes darken with understanding as he backs up enough where he's kneeling between my legs, and this sight alone makes fire ignite in my core.

"Can I look at you?" He asks, his voice deeper than I've ever heard it.

"Yes."

He lifts both hands, grips the elastic around my shorts, and slowly pulls them down my hips, and my legs until he pulls them completely off and I am bare before him for the first time.

"Taylor." He says on an exhale. "God, you're so beautiful."

I don't know what it feels like to have an orgasm, but I swear with his words alone I think I feel it building deep within my belly and it's all I can do not to rub my thighs together to create some kind of friction to relieve this pressure, this need that's consuming me.

Bryan smirks at me, and he sits back where his butt is on the soles of his feet. "I think I may let you lie there and get all flustered by just staring at you."

"Bryan Evans, don't you dare!" I cry out as I close my knees together and the pressure is making me feel something, but before I can figure out what it is, Bryan grips my knees and somewhat roughly rips them away from each other.

"Uh-uh." He scolds. "I am the one that is going to make you come for the first time. Not you."

He looks down at my core again before lifting his eyes to me once more. "Tap my knee with your foot if it gets to be too much."

I no longer nod in understanding, and after what feels like lifetimes have passed in the short two minutes since he's pulled my shorts off, I finally feel his touch. His thumb brushes against my clit, and my back is bowing off the bed while I try to hold my cry of pleasure in my chest.

"Let me hear you, Taylor." Bryan demands as he starts to circle his thumb around my sensitive bud, and I can't hold back my pleasurable sounds even if I wanted to. "That is music to my ears, Baby."

He continues to toy with my body for a few heartbeats before I feel his middle finger tease at my entrance.

"Do you want me here too, Annie?"

"Yes! Bryan, oh god yes!"

"Good girl." Bryan praises me again, and just as I feel the tip of his finger enter where I want him the most, the sound of a phone ringing blares over my cries of pleasure.

Chapter Eighteen

Bryan

It was amazing, beautiful, and so damn erotic to hear and see Taylor writhing under my touch. I've never had this kind of feedback with a woman, but yet, no woman has been Taylor. When I saw her naked for the first time, I was sure I was going to explode, and yes, in more ways than one.

This was such a big step for her because I know she's inexperienced and not sure if she should let herself go in that aspect and is apprehensive of her sexuality, and I felt pride swelling in my chest knowing that I was able to be the first man to ever see and touch her the way I did tonight.

So, the fact that the damn phone began ringing just as I was getting her close, I could go on a rampage and throw the damn thing through the window.

Taylor lets out a cute, aggravated moan at the phone that's still ringing on her bedside table.

I look over at the evil device—that ruined a potentially good night between us just as Taylor was finally getting into it—and make a gun with my fingers, the same ones that I was touching her sweet body with, to shoot it where it lies on the side table.

"You get that while I clean you up. It could be Wayne." I tell her as I get off the bed and stride into the bathroom to get a damp washcloth while adjusting myself, willing my blood to pool anywhere else but between my legs.

"Hi, Mom." I hear Taylor say from the bedroom.

"How does she know?" I whisper loud enough for her to hear.

I pop my head around the doorjamb while waiting for the water to warm up in the sink to hear her response, and I instantly love and regret that move.

She is still lying there, legs still where I last had them, and not even bothering to conceal any inch of her skin.

Welp, there goes any hope of easing this hard-on. I think to myself.

"She calls it mother's intuition." Taylor signs, the movement of her hands snapping me out of my daze.

"Hey, Honey. What's going on?" Kathy asks through the phone's speaker.

Just as she asks that, I bring the washcloth back over to Taylor, draping it over her core. And because I can't help it, I start to kiss her inner thigh, just past her knee but low enough to let her know where I'd want to be right now if her mother wasn't on the phone.

"Do you want us to get killed by her?" She frantically asks me in sign language.

I shake my head. *"But I couldn't help it."* I sign back.

"Hello, are you there?" Kathy asks.

"Yeah, sorry, my phone went out a sex—sec; went out for a sec!" Taylor says, and she turns several shades of red.

"Smooth babe." I sign as I finally clean her up and grab her shorts off the floor.

She gives me her middle finger, and I can't help but chuckle in response as I slide the material up her legs and settle them over her hips.

"Is everything okay?" Kathy asks, but her tone answers her own question.

"Yeah, everything's fine," Taylor says, embarrassment filling her voice.

"Is Bryan there?" Kathy asks.

Taylor takes a deep breath; no use lying to her. "Yeah, he's here."

"Are you two being adults?"

I smile, knowing her version of 'being adults' has nothing at all to do with me trying to edge Taylor into her first orgasm.

"Yes, we are," Taylor says with a slight eye roll. "But I told you that I would call you. Please, Mom, let me call you next time."

"I know, but you didn't call the last few days, and I was worried." Kathy says.

"I'm sorry. I'll try to call more. But please, Mom, we think we're ready to make a break in the case—" Taylor begins, but Kathy cuts her off.

"I understand, sweetie. I'm sorry. I love you." Kathy says.

"It's okay. I love you too, Mom. Give Dad and Cody a kiss for me."

"I will. Good night, you two," Kathy says, her tone becoming playful.

"Good night, Kathy." I say, leaning into the phone so she can hear me.

She hangs up, and my gaze drifts to Taylor. "She's good." I say, pointing to the phone. "We do need to get some sleep, though, and one brush with your mother's wrath is enough for tonight." I say while moving up the bed and lying on my back, waiting for her to snuggle up to my side.

She smiles at me, settling her head on my chest, and I know she's listening to the strong rhythm of my heart.

"Hey, does Agent Temperance worry you?" I can't help but ask.

"Kinda. What did you feel tonight?"

"She just kept looking at me like I was her son brought back from the dead. I know she explained everything, but it was still weird the way she looked at me."

"Mark, Lexi, and I picked up on that on the plane. I was looking at your picture on my phone, and she just stared at it before Lincoln had to drag her away."

"Do you think she's stable enough to be leading us?" I ask.

"Maybe. I mean, Lincoln seems to have his head on straight, so we aren't totally in the dark."

"That's the only good thing here. Lincoln seems to have this whole thing under control." I say as I pull the bedsheets up over us.

I tilt my head over enough to make sure my gun is situated in the nightstand drawer, and it's open enough for me to be able to access it but closed enough that if someone were to get in, they'd have to fully open the drawer to pull the firearm out, giving me time to attack them and gain the upper hand again.

"Well, I wouldn't worry too much about them," Taylor says. "Plus, we have each other to lean on."

"As long as they don't blow our cover, I don't care." I say as I pull her closer to my chest. "Now sleep, Annie, since we must be 'adults' and all. And 'adults' sleep." I smile as I place a kiss on her forehead.

"Yeah, being boring adults doing boring adult things." She chuckles.

I'm quiet for a minute, and just before I can tell she's relaxing to fall asleep, I ask, "Hey, are you okay with what we did tonight?"

This is the first time we've been this far, and I want to make sure she's not internally freaking out.

"Yes, Bryan. I'm fine. Lexi and I kind of talked, and she told me to trust you and that you'd have my best interest at heart, but also to trust myself too." She says sleepily.

"All I ever want is to make you happy, Baby. I want you to feel safe in every aspect with me. Whether it's a case or touching you, and eventually, when you're ready, making love to you." I tell her as I run my hand up and down her back in a soothing motion.

She's silent for a moment at my declaration of where I want this relationship to go eventually, and for a heartbeat I think I said too much too fast, but I feel her cheek pull up into a smile against my skin before she places a kiss in the center of my chest.

"And I love that you check in with me. It's totally hot," Taylor chuckles.

"Good. I'll be sure to keep doing that." I promise as I pull her closer to my side. "Now sleep, Baby. I get the feeling that we are going to have a wild ride ahead of us soon."

Chapter Nineteen

Taylor

Two days pass, and nothing really happens. Mark and Bryan just race against the other guys while Lexi and I hang out on the sidelines with the girls to cheer our guys on, and I have a feeling today will be no different.

We are all gathered around the table at Mark and Lexi's apartment eating breakfast while the guys talk about what they are going to do today.

"Dude, did you see the race lineup this morning? You're driving against Ian." Mark says as he scrolls through his phone. "He's pretty good. I can tell that from just a few runs with him."

"Yeah, I did see that. This team is so organized. Almost makes me wish we weren't here on a mission. I'd love to really hang with these guys," Bryan says.

Lexi and I can't help but groan at these two racing all the time. Mark smirks as he pulls Lexi into his side before placing a gentle kiss on the top of her head and feeding her a piece of his bacon, which she takes without protest.

"We will be fine, Taylor. Mark and I raced all the time back home." Bryan says while tangling our fingers together before lifting it to his mouth, brushing a kiss to my knuckles.

"I do. It's the car I don't trust." I say.

"Can you drive yours, okay?" Bryan asks.

"I can get from point A to B."

"Can you go faster than thirty-five miles an hour?" Bryan asks with a smile on his face.

"Can you bite me?" I ask, avoiding his question.

"Well, you and I will do something tonight." Bryan says.

"It better not be what I think is going through your mind, Bryan." I warn.

He smiles at me, and just as he leans in for a kiss, his and Mark's phones go off at the same time. Once they read it, I can feel the tension fill the room and all humor and playfulness fade from their faces.

"What's wrong?" I ask.

"We just gotta get to the track." Bryan answers as he stands and leans down for a quick kiss. "You girls should get ready and come down a bit earlier, too."

"Okay." I say while looking at Lexi, and she has the same look of trepidation on her face. She knows something is up too.

We watch in silence as both men walk out of the apartment, the front door quietly clicking shut behind them a moment before Mark turns the locks with his keys from the other side. Once we hear their engines turn over and see their vehicle's speed off, Lexi and I dart into the bathroom to get dressed in record time.

When we arrive at the track fifteen minutes later, I can tell there is a tension in the air and also pure fear. Lexi and I notice Morgan standing near a door she's holding open with her sneaker clad foot, and we quickly walk over to her.

"Get in. I'll explain when we all get in the press box." Morgan snips.

Lexi and I walk through the door and climb the long, straight staircase. I open another door to walk inside and notice that two girls are sitting in the chairs, but the others are pacing around, nervously biting their nails.

When I look to my right, I can see the whole track through the window, and there is a single vehicle sitting on the track. A blue Mitsubishi Evolution.

"What's going on?" I ask Morgan when she shuts and locks the door.

"Desmond picked his racer last night. And it's Justin." Morgan says, her voice tight, but I can see the wobble on her lips. She's trying to be strong for the girls in the room.

I hear the girls begin to whisper to one another, but what really draws my attention is the small squeak that comes from one girl. I can only guess she would be Justin's girlfriend. I look over at her and slowly take in her demeanor. She's visibly shaking and is on the brink of tears, fear coiling every muscle of her body, and her skin is so pale it's like she has no blood in her veins.

I feel a light touch on my leg, and I look over to see Lexi trying to get my attention. *"She's going to break if he loses."* She says in sign language.

"Yeah, I already thought of that." I reply, keeping my hands down and out of sight.

I then grab my phone to text Bryan and Mark.

Me: Hey, we have a girl that might break if he loses.

Mark: K thx for giving the heads up.

Bryan: Whatever happens u stay there with Lexi and the others.

Me: OK.

Bryan: Taylor I mean it.

Me: I know and I will. I love u.

Bryan: I love u 2.

I hate to stay here, but I know we need to keep a low profile unless something big happens, or unless Lexi puts herself in the line of fire; then I would follow my partner with no questions asked.

I look at Lexi, and she nods her head, already knowing what I'm thinking, and with her hand out of sight, she says, *"If something goes down, are you with me?"*

"Like your shadow." I reply.

Lexi lets a slight smile play across her lips, and then it fades when we hear an audible gasp from the girls near the window. Lexi and I walk over, and we see a matte black Charger pull in with three other vehicles: a Wrangler, a Silverado, and an old-school Challenger. All in the same matte black paint trailing behind the Charger.

"That is Desmond," Morgan says with a cold fury, and it makes a chill go up my spine.

The Charger pulls up beside Justin's Evo, and he's leaning against the hood of the car, trying to look composed, but even from here I can see the tense line of his shoulders. With that little piece of information, I can tell the car won't help. He's just as nervous as the girl in here. Right then, I realize his nerves are going to get him killed.

I text Mark and Bryan to give them a heads-up.

> **Me:** Get ready for all hell to break loose.

> **Mark:** Yeah, we know.

> **Me:** The girl up here is just as jumpy as he is.

> **Bryan:** You and Lexi just stay put.

Josh walks out on the track and stands in front of the cars, signaling the beginning of the race. The two guys get in their cars, and I watch helplessly as Justin signs his death warrant.

The girl presses closer to the window as she watches her boyfriend slam his car door while tears that are filled with fear silently stream down her cheeks.

Lexi touches my arm to get my attention. *"This is sick."* Lexi signs. *"Races are supposed to be for pinks, not this."*

"I agree. This sicko needs to be taken down, and fast." I say.

Even from the enclosed space, we can hear the engines revving, and it seems to be even louder with the eerie silence in both the press box and down on the track.

There is no cheering for this race, only somber silence, and prayers that the right driver wins.

Josh raises a checkered flag above his head a moment before he slams it down to his side and both cars take off.

Surprisingly, the Evo starts out in the lead. As I glance over at the girl, she has a huge, bright smile on her face, and she looks over at Morgan, who is now sitting beside the girl, holding onto her shoulder for support. But deep down, I have a bad feeling about this race. I have a feeling that Desmond toys with the racers. Makes them think they will win before blowing them apart in the last moments of the race.

In the second turn, the Charger begins edging up on the Evo, coming fender to bumper but still holds back, keeping Justin in the lead, and I hear the girl quietly cheer him on.

"Come on, Babe. You got this. You're better than he is."

Her voice is tear-filled and squeaky, but filled with hope that I somehow know in my heart is false, but I can't voice my thoughts to her. I can't burst her bubble like that.

In the final quarter mile, I watch as the Charger swerves to the left, and I can't help what comes out of my mouth.

"He can't ram into him going that fast!" I exclaim.

Then what I said unfolds right before our eyes. Desmond swerves away from Justin and then swerves back, hitting Justin's bumper, going 190 miles per hour. Justin's Evo plows into the concrete wall, instantly exploding on impact, but we all hear a blood-chilling scream coming from the car. The impact didn't kill instantly, but the explosion did.

"No!" Morgan screams. "Ava!"

I turn in time to see Ava fighting to get out of the press box and down to the track. Morgan, Christy, and one other girl are trying their best to keep her back, but she manages to break free, and she flies down the stairs. We all go to the window and watch helplessly as she runs towards the blazing wreckage.

I can hear her screams through the window, followed by those heartless bastards laughing maniacally. Then Desmond opens his car door and walks up to her. He grips her upper arm, and even from here, I can tell it's rough and filled with ownership. He tries to pull her away and into his car, but she fights him, hitting his arms and chest with her fists.

"No, you idiot!" Morgan sobs.

Ava pulls away from him, and I can tell she says something to Desmond before she takes a step away and heads toward the still-burning car.

A smile that is pure evil spreads across Desmond's face before he pulls a gun, aiming it at her head, and shoots her in cold blood. I know she is dead before she even hits the ground. My stomach roils at the sight, and I want to go and hurl in his face.

As I am about to look away, fearing that I may just lose what little bit of breakfast I had this morning, Lexi grabs my arm. I look back to the window with the question of what she wants on the tip of my tongue when my stomach drops past my feet.

Desmond approaches Bryan.

Holding my breath, I watch as Bryan looks this piece of shit down. Seemingly utterly cool and calm under this asshole's gaze.

He stays sitting on the hood of his Camaro with his arms crossed over his chest, trying not to pay any attention to this sicko and the scene that just played out before him. Desmond gets in Bryan's face, but he doesn't react.

"Your man's got guts," Christy whispers.

"He's just not the type to land the first punch." I say, but even I can taste my own fear as I wait to see what will unfold next.

Chapter Twenty

Bryan

I know Taylor is safe up in the press box, but I can't help but worry about her. When Mark and I got the message earlier this morning that Desmond picked his racer last night, I wanted to tell the girls to stay in the apartment. But one, I know my girl better than that, and two, we have a job to do. So, I'm thankful that they were able to get up to safety before this bastard shows up.

Justin parks his car on the racetrack and he's trying to act calm, but when I see his nervous twitches—cupping the back of his neck with his hand a moment before running his fingers through his dark hair and finally shoving his hands in the front pockets of his jeans—I glance at Mark and he gives me a subtle nod, seeing the same thing.

"When Desmond gets here, no one speaks. No one acts out of line." Josh announces to the rest of the team. We hear Ian scoff and Josh's eyes pin him with a stare that screams don't mess with him. "I'm serious, guys. Do *not* make this any worse than what it could be," Josh demands. His voice is low, but his tone makes up for the lack of volume.

We all nod our heads as we lean against the hoods of our cars just as the sound of roaring engines erupts in the air. A matte black Charger pulls in followed by a Wrangler, a Silverado, and an old-school Challenger trailing behind it, all painted the same matte black color.

"Here we go." Mark turns to whisper to me and, for the first time, I'm glad that I have my gun holstered at my hip on the inside of my jeans. My fingers are already itching to grab for it, but I keep my body still.

I look at my friend, and I know he's thinking the same thing. We automatically know that no matter what the other does, we will follow, so there is no need for that confirmation between us.

My phone vibrates with a text message, and I pull it out at the same time Mark does. I see it's from Taylor, and when she tells us, the girlfriend is just as nervous as the guy in front of me; it takes effort not to break the phone in my hand at the pulse of anger that flows through me.

Josh takes a breath and walks out on the track with the checkered flag in hand. I know I have a confused look on my face watching Josh do this. His teammate is pretty much signing his death certificate, so why wave around the flag to signal it?

The guy to my right, James, Christy's boyfriend, looks at me and says, "Desmond wants it to look like any normal race. I'm surprised that he's not bitching about the lack of cheering." His eyes, one green and the other brown, flick over to me in disgust before looking back at the track.

"Are you for real?" I ask in disbelief.

This dude is even more demented than I gave him credit for. Damn, that's all kinds of messed up.

"Yeah, man. It's true." James says.

As Josh waves the flag, both cars take off, and Justin is in the lead and keeps it until the last turn. We all watch in slow motion as Desmond swerves and rams into Justin in a perfect pit maneuver as far as a cop would be concerned, but it's going to be impossible to survive in this scenario with the enclosed walls surrounding the track.

The explosion rips through the air as the car impacts the concrete barrier, and we hear Justin's blood-curdling scream when the Evo goes up in flames.

None of us move, because we know there is no way we could even hope to get Justin out in time to save him. And I get the feeling that if the fire didn't kill us, a bullet to the brain would.

"No! Desmond! You son of a bitch!" Josh wails once the smoke begins to lift into the air.

"Fuck." Mark whispers, his voice low and tight with undiluted anger. He crosses his arms over his chest to keep them from hitting something, preferably hitting this piece of shit in the face. "That's murder right there."

"This is the last time he gets by with this." I declare with venom in my voice.

Then, a moment later, we hear shrieking and crying erupt from the press box behind us. Mark and I whip our heads around, and we see a girl running onto the track, screaming Justin's name.

Desmond gets out of his car and walks over to her. When he grips her upper arm in a rough and demanding way, I know his grip will leave bruises. Anger wells in my chest, and I uncross my ankles, almost acting on autopilot, to go over to this bastard and knock his fucking head around when Mark stops me with a quick shake of his head.

He's right; we might be able to follow them and get her back. I settle back against the hood of my car, crossing my ankles again, and wait to see what else happens.

"Don't touch me, you fucking asshole!" The girl sobs.

Desmond shockingly releases her, and I begin to wonder if maybe he won't take her.

"I won't go anywhere with you. I won't let you rape me and take away what Justin and I had together. So you'll have to kill me." She says, her tone is soft, but there is a fire in her voice.

She's going out fighting.

Desmond smiles, and it's the vilest thing I've ever seen, so much so that it makes my skin crawl. It takes everything in me not to look away, to act like his actions don't faze me.

"Desmond! Don't!" Josh screams his plea across the track as Desmond pulls a gun from the waistband of his pants and shoots the girl in the head.

"I think I'm going to be sick. This is fucked up." Mark whispers, his skin going a slight hue of green.

"Tell me about it." I whisper, swallowing hard past my own nausea.

"Thank you, Josh. Your team is always the most entertaining. You like to have fiery ones in the mix," Desmond croons, his voice carrying a slight Mexican accent.

"You had your race. Now get the fuck off my track, Desmond," Josh growls.

"But I didn't get what I really wanted, did I?" Desmond sneers.

"Not my problem. You killed her before you left," Josh snaps, venom filling his tone.

Desmond's eyes lock on mine. One is so brown that it almost looks black, but the other is pale, like a milky white. I fight to hide the shiver that races down my back, and I just hope that the goosebumps I feel exploding on my skin stays hidden under my shirt.

"I see a few new faces here." Desmond says, looking from me to Mark. "What about you?" He asks, directing his question at me. "How do you feel about all this?"

I give him a glare that says it all; I hate it. But I don't give him the honor of hearing my voice. He steps up to me, his boots coming flush with my Converses.

"I asked you a fucking question." He growls. "Are you deaf, or did you have your tongue cut out?"

My muscles tighten, fighting the urge not to punch this fucker in the face. Show him what real pain feels like. I see Ian approach my car at the same time Mark stands from his. Both readying for a fight.

Desmond glances at both of them for a moment before turning his attention back to me. "I may already know who my next racer will be. But out of the three of you, who will be first?" He asks, tilting his head from side to side. "I know you have a girl here. A pretty little brunette with a smoking hot body."

My eyes widen. Anger, fear, and a primal protectiveness blooms in my chest so fast that it makes it hard to breathe.

"I bet she would make the best sounds as I fuc—"

I don't give him the chance to finish that fucking sentence. I grab him by the back of the neck on the right side and slam him onto the hood of my Camaro, pushing the left side of his face deeper into the yellow-painted metal. I barely hear the muttered curses of those around me as my blood rushes in my ears.

I stare into his mismatched eyes, my voice low and deep. "You come near my girl and I *will* end you. You have no idea who the fuck you're messing with."

I know I should not kick the hornet's nest, but right at this moment, I don't care. I *need* to put any amount of fear, or at least worry, in this asshole's head.

I let him up a moment later, and Mark stands between us as Ian shoves at Desmond's chest to keep him walking.

"Get out of here, Desmond!" Josh orders again.

Desmond looks at him and then between me, Mark and Ian, smirking once at us before walking away. I have to force my knees to stay locked in order to keep my trembling legs from giving out. I think I'd rather go up against Phil again than this bastard. At least I knew what Phil could do. At least I knew his MO. But this guy? It's like anything I could think of that's dark and depraved, he would do with a smile on his face.

Something about the whole thing still doesn't sit right with me as we watch their vehicles drive away. He *knew* what Taylor looked like. Was he just guessing, or did he *know*? And if he does, then who told him? Does Josh have a rat on his team?

Just as the thought hits me, James and Ian rushes over to close the gates and as soon as the Wrangler hits the main road, I see Josh pull his phone out to send out a quick message and I lean against my car to keep my knees from buckling as the adrenaline fades from my veins.

"Dude—" Mark begins, but my eyes shoot to him and he stops mid-sentence.

"Don't even ask if I am okay. Hell no, I'm not fucking okay." I snap, my anger getting the better of me.

A few minutes later, we hear quick footsteps pounding on the pavement. I look up to find Taylor and Lexi making a beeline for us. Taylor crashes into my chest, and I hold her so tight against my body that I fear I'll crush her.

Her fingers fist the back of my shirt, and I place a few tender kisses on top of her head as I look over the space around me. James is to my left, holding Christy. Ian is holding his girl. I think her name is Anna. Then Josh with Morgan, and of course, Mark with Lexi.

"Go home, everyone." Josh says softly. "And we won't have the track open tomorrow. One, I need to clean this mess up, but mostly we are going to have a silent day for those we lost."

James and Ian nod as they take their girls, who are still glued to their sides, into their cars. Josh then opens the gate again so those two can drive through.

"You guys leaving next?" Josh asks.

"Yeah, man." Mark answers. "Let us know if we can do anything to help out."

"No one can do anything about him. Unless he's killed. And even after all that happened, I don't think I have it in me to do that." Josh says, and I can tell he hates that he feels helpless and weak.

"Killing is not as simple as pulling a trigger. For normal, sane people, it's life-altering." I say. "Trust me, I know from experience."

Josh looks at me in shock, and I just nod my head as I lead Taylor to the passenger side of my car. I've killed two people in my time in the agency. One Taylor knows about. Daryl. But the other was when Mark was on a case with Lexi.

I don't know the full details of their case, but I know it was the first one they worked on together in California while I was back and forth between Cali and Utah, trying to figure out more about Phil and Daryl before I knew their connections with Taylor. But something told me to go back to Cali one night, and it was a good thing I did.

After I did some digging and pinged the location on his phone, I found Mark in a run-down apartment building. He was hurt, bleeding profusely from his back, and I got to him just in time to save him from having his head bashed in by a dude with a metal baseball bat. I didn't have a choice but to shoot the guy in the chest to save my friend.

"Thanks, man." Josh says. "I just thought I was fucking weak for not being able to do the only thing I could think of to protect my family."

"You are never weak for not wanting to take a life, man. If anything, you're stronger for not being trigger-happy." I tell him.

"Take care tonight and hold your girls tight. Especially you, Bryan." Josh says and I nod.

I have a target on my back from my little stunt, but if it will bring this bastard out again where we can stop him, I'll paint it on my back for real and stand in the middle of the street.

"Yeah. I know." I say as I help Taylor into the passenger side of my car before I drop behind the wheel, turn the engine over, and drive out of the speedway.

As I drive back to our apartment, I grab Taylor's hand and I don't let it go, even when I need to shift gears. She moves with me, and I know she's just as terrified for my own safety as I am hers.

When we pull up to our apartments, Mark and I get out at the same time, and when I walk around to the passenger side to help Taylor out, he stops me for a moment.

"I need time alone with Lexi, and I know you do with Tay. So let's have tonight, and we will meet with *them* tomorrow to go over everything."

I nod my head as he walks around the back of his Challenger to help Lexi out of the car and into their apartment without another word.

I turn my attention to Taylor, and I open her door. "Come on, Annie. Let's go." I say gently.

She takes my right hand in hers, and I close the door once she's on her feet. She stays silent as I jingle my keys in my left hand to grab the one for the apartment and unlock the door.

Still holding the keys in my fist, I flip the light on in the living room before tossing them into the glass bowl that rests on top of the couch table behind the loveseat. I hear Taylor close and lock the door behind her, and I look over my shoulder to make sure the door is locked for my own mental satisfaction.

She then closes the small distance between us, wrapping her arms around the small of my back while resting her head against my chest. I pull her tighter against me as I walk backward and into one of the armchairs near the door. I sit, bringing her into my lap without breaking our hold on the other.

As I run my hand up and down her back in a soothing motion, she asks, "What did he say to you?"

I take a breath. "Asked me how I felt about what he did." My voice is flat and rough with brewing anger.

"Anything else? What made you pin him—" She begins to ask, but I cut her off.

"Nothing you need to know."

"Bryan." She asks, her tone pleading.

I sigh. "That bastard was trying to get under my skin, and it worked."

Taylor moves her body enough to look into my eyes, pleading for me to continue. I take a steadying breath. Part of me hates the 'no more secrets' pact we have, but deep down I know she deserves to know what was said.

"Okay." I tighten my hold on her, grounding myself more than any-thing. "He supposedly knows what you look like. And he told me he bet you would make the best sounds as he fucked you." My jaw clenches. "I didn't let him get that last word out, but I heard it all the same."

"Bryan," Taylor whispers, consoling me. "That's not going to happen. We are going to stop him before he can even touch anyone else."

I nod. "I know this goes without saying, but I will do anything to protect you. He will *not* get his hands on you. I will blow my whole cover wide open before that happens."

"I know you will." She says while toying with my shirt right over where my scar hides under the fabric. "You've already proven that fact." She tries to smile, but her lips wobble.

I lean into her, pressing my lips tenderly to hers. "Come on. Let's try to get some sleep. We need to take advantage of tomorrow's day off to tell Lincoln and Temperance what happened."

Taylor nods, and I ease her off my lap. "Why don't you get ready for bed first while I make sure everything's locked up?" I say while running my hand over her upper arm.

"Good idea," Taylor says as she walks back toward the master bedroom.

I watch her for a moment until she makes her way into the bathroom and out of my line of sight before I grab a kitchen chair and brace it under the front door while triple-checking the locks to make sure they are in place. I then find a metal broom to wedge into the track of the sliding glass door that leads into the small backyard.

Once I'm satisfied that I've barricaded all doors, I make my way into the bedroom where I find Taylor already in bed, wearing one of my grey shirts and a black pair of her shorts.

"I'm getting my shower real quick, Babe. I have the doors all locked up." I tell her as I pull my shirt over my head.

Even with all that's happened this afternoon, Taylor's eyes still flare with heat at seeing my bare chest.

I walk over to her and lean down, bracing my hands on either side of her hips, the mattress dipping a bit at the added weight. "You having a good look, Annie?"

She gives me a small grin at the question I always ask her when I catch her looking at me.

"I'm going to go before I say to hell with my shower and find out what sounds I can wring from your body." I say, my voice low and dripping with desire to the point where I feel my jeans tighten. "The beautiful sounds that *no other* man will ever hear."

Taylor shivers under my stare, and I can't help but smirk as I lean in to kiss her. "Not tonight, though. But soon, Annie."

"You're such a tease," Taylor quips, her tone just a bit lighter.

"You make it so easy and fun to rile you up." I say as I slip into the bathroom, shutting the door behind me.

After I step out of the shower and pull my boxers and shorts over my hips, I notice that Taylor is already dozing off. I gently climb into bed with her and tug her into my still-damp chest while pulling the bedsheets up to cover us.

I give her a light kiss on the crown of her head while I tighten my arms around her and try to let sleep come to me, but it's plagued with nightmares of what may happen if we fail this mission.

Chapter Twenty-One

Taylor

The next morning, I wake up before Bryan does. His back faces the bedroom door, and his arms are still tightly wrapped around my waist, pulling me close to his bare chest.

I turned at some point in the middle of the night so I'm facing the window, and there is just enough sunlight filtering in through the glass that it begins to push away the darkness of the room.

As I silently watch the sun rise over the horizon, I try my best to hold back the shiver as yesterday's events flicker in my memory. I can't even begin to imagine what Bryan felt hearing that. I mean, if it was me hearing a woman say that about him, I would have beaten her to a pulp; case be damned. But he knows how to bide his time, and I'm thankful for that.

Bryan's arms suddenly tighten around my waist as he throws his leg over my calf, bringing me closer to him. "I can practically hear your brain thinking a mile a minute, Annie." He says, voice deep and scratchy from sleep.

I wiggle my butt against him with a sassy comment on the tip of my tongue, but when I feel him harden behind me, all thoughts leave me in a rush.

I start to inch my body away from his, a hint of embarrassment flooding my veins as I realize I just wiggled my ass against his erection like a cat in heat.

I mean, I've felt him before, especially when we've made out back home. But now? I don't know, it's different. I feel myself wanting to respond to his actions and body more, but I'm still not sure how to really follow through.

"Don't run. Stop second-guessing your reactions. I certainly don't." Bryan whispers into my ear as he pulls my back against his chest again, and I feel his hardened length press against my short-clad center. I hear him growl at the pressure my body is creating for him.

He wants me to stop second-guessing myself? Fine. Challenge accepted. I roll over so I'm facing him. His gaze is still hazy from sleep, and he gives me a lazy smile as I kiss the center of his chest. The gesture is meant to be a distraction as I move my hand between us and press my palm against his rock-hard shaft.

"You sure that's not just morning wood?" I ask, knowing damn well it's more than that, but I can't help teasing him.

He groans as his hips rock against my hand. "Such a dirty mind for an innocent body, Baby."

His words set me alight with desire. I glance over his shoulder at the clock resting on his nightstand. Fifteen minutes before the alarm is set to go off at six.

I look back into his bright green eyes, which are now wide awake and smoldering with need.

"Touch me."

"I want all of you this time, Taylor," Bryan says as he tugs at the hem of his shirt draped over my body, signaling his intent.

I nod, and he slides his left hand up my back, lifting me off the bed enough to pull the gray fabric off with his right hand. Once the shirt is pulled over my head, I look up at him to see his expression and notice his eyes are closed.

My brow furrows in confusion for a moment, and before I can ask why he has them closed, he says, "I wanted you to see my expression when I look at you for the first time."

I chuckle and as I slide my shorts over my hips I say, "Then look at me, Bullet."

He slowly opens his eyes, staring into my face for a moment, before his gaze dips down past my chin. His green eyes darken as he takes in my breasts for the first time. With fire flooding my veins, I watch as his chest rises and falls with each sharp breath he takes.

I throw his own words back at him, my voice sultry and teasing. "You having a good look there, Babe?"

His eyes snap to mine, need shining within the green orbs. "Abso-fucking-lutly. You are breathtaking." He looks back down at me, making my nipples harden just at his heated gaze. "Can I?" Bryan begins, but I cut him off.

"Do what you want. I'll tell you if it's too much."

Bryan

At hearing Taylor say those four words, fire licks at my body. With her giving me the green light to touch her however I want, feels like I just won the damn lottery. In the soft fabric of my boxers, pain blooms between my legs as my hard-on builds, and this is from just looking at her.

She's gonna be the death of me. But what a hell of a way to go.

I lean down, pressing a kiss to the base of her neck. Her hands fist the sheets at her side, and I chuckle.

"I haven't even begun to touch you and you're already squirming?"

"Stop teasing," Taylor pleads, her breath coming out in quick pants.

"It's called edging, Baby," I growl as I trace my lips lower, stopping just before the swell of her right breast. "And yeah, you'll hate me at first," I say as I trace my tongue over her skin and flick the tip over her peaked nipple, her gasps echoing off the walls of the bedroom. "But once I let you fall over into your climax," I trace my thumb over her left nipple while continuing to lap at the right one until she's arching off the bed, begging for a release. "It's exhilarating." I say as I bite down and pinch at the same time.

"Oh, Bryan!"

She screams my name as I finally draw the first real orgasm out of her, and I am so close to following her, but I somehow hold it together.

"So how was that?" I ask once she comes down off her high. She looks at me with the most sexy smile on her face, and I can't help but chuckle as I rise higher in the bed to kiss her lips. "Did I already blow your mind, Baby?"

"Yes." She breathes, still trying to catch her breath.

"Good. Let's try for round two, shall we?" I ask, and her eyes shoot to mine.

"What?"

I ignore her as I slide my hand down her soft belly. I love the feel of her of skin against mine. I can never get enough of it.

Just as I edge closer to the apex of her thighs, I look back at her and smile. "This is going to rock your world, Baby."

She closes her eyes while letting her legs fall to the sides, giving me complete access to her body without a word. I ease the tip of my forefinger down ever so slowly, and I chuckle when she groans at my lack of touch.

"Shh, Baby. I'll give you what you want. When the time is right."

I roll my index finger over her clit, and her hips instantly buck against my touch. I smile as I pull my hand away.

"Damn it, Bryan!" She growls. "Stop messing around before we get another phone call!"

"This time, unless it rings three times in a row, I am ignoring everything but you." I tell her as I lean in to brush my lips over hers, darting my tongue inside when she opens her mouth for me.

I use that distraction, much like she did with me, to massage her clit again, pinching it between my index finger and thumb. Taylor breaks our kiss as her moans echo in my ear, and I trail kisses down her neck.

I want to bite into her flesh. Leave my marks on her. Especially for that fucker, Desmond, to know she's mine and mine alone, but I know my girl wouldn't want that. Not yet, at least. Not while on a case.

I tease at her hot and needy entrance with my middle finger, and I can't help my groan at what I feel. Taylor bucks her hips again, and I'm so caught up in how slick she feels under my touch that her movement makes the tip of my finger slide into her.

"Oh damn, Taylor. You feel so good, Baby Girl."

"More." She pants as she moves her body again.

"So eager." I croon.

I give in to her for now. I sink my finger deeper, letting her body get used to the intrusion for the first time. Once I've filled her to the knuckles on my palm, her hand shoots out to grip my arm as her nails dig into my skin.

"You okay?" I ask, my voice dripping with desire and want. "You want me to stop?" Part of me wants her to say no, but I promised her she would have the power here.

"I'm fine. Please move."

I take it slow with her. Pumping my finger in and out of her. I watch her sink into the bed, muscles relaxing under my touch.

"That's it, Baby Girl. Relax. Let me take care of you." I say as I up my tempo a bit. Testing her.

"More. I need more." Taylor pleads.

"My greedy little vixen, huh?" I ask as I withdraw to the tip of my finger and slowly ease in two more.

"Oh, shit!" She moans, and I know this time I don't have to stop.

"You take my fingers so well, Baby. You're doing such a good job for your first time." I praise.

I can tell she's getting close to another climax, so I help her build it, stone by stone. I take my time, exploring and finding where she reacts to my touch the most, and when her back begins to bow off the bed and her eyes close, I know I found her sweet spot.

I lean in, capturing her mouth with mine for a few bruising kisses, before I pull my head back enough to look down at her.

"Taylor, look at me, Baby Girl." She opens her eyes, and I see pure pleasure shining in their sky blue hue. "Come for me again, Baby."

I curl my fingers against her sweet spot, and she shatters in my hand. Screaming my name and clawing at my arm as she rides her pleasure down to the dregs.

"So damn beautiful." I kiss her again, this time tasting the saltiness of the sweat on her skin.

"That was amazing," Taylor says lazily.

"I'm glad I could make it that way for you." I tell her as I stand from the bed for a moment to look at her beautiful body. "You stay there. I'll be back."

"I couldn't go anywhere, even if I wanted to." She chuckles.

"And just think. That was with my fingers." I smirk while wiggling the digits in the air.

"You're gonna make me a boneless mess," Taylor says as she covers her face.

"Don't hide from me." I say, my voice a touch pleading. "Never hide from me. I love you in any form. Be it your no-nonsense attitude or like this. I love everything about you."

She uncovers her face and smiles at me. "I love you too, Bryan."

I return her smile as I walk into the bathroom and grab a washcloth, getting it wet with warm water under the faucet before rejoining her on the bed. I drop it over her center, gently pressing it into her soft flesh, and she sighs in pleasure.

"How do you know all this?"

"Some of it from Mark. The dude's a complete Pleasure Dom. I never thought I was until I met you." I grin. "But most ways I learned about how to treat a woman came from Gramps."

"Well, their discussions paid off." She looks at me sheepishly, the barest hint of pink blooming on her cheeks.

"What?" I chuckle.

"Is it weird to say 'thank you'?"

I laugh. I can't help it. "No Babe. It's not."

When I notice that the washcloth has cooled, I wipe her off, then stand again from the bed to toss the cloth into the hamper in the bathroom. I walk back into the bedroom, and Taylor is still lying on the mattress, but she's pulled her legs together, and I almost groan at the loss of her beautiful body on display for me.

She reaches out her hand, and I gently take it in my own, lifting her knuckles to my lips to press a tender kiss to them.

"Thank you." She says as she moves up in bed, resting her back against the headboard.

Her little quick intake of breath makes me freeze in my exploration of her hand. "Are you sore?"

"Not really. Just a bit tender. But I think I'll be okay." She says. "Thank you for taking your time with me, Bryan."

"Now that, you don't have to thank me for." I tell her. "Any type of intimate moment should be consensual for both parties involved." I grip her chin with my index finger. "I will always have your best interest at heart, Annie, and I will take it as far as you'll let me."

Just as I lean in for another kiss, the alarm clock on my side of the bed goes off, signaling six in the morning.

"Finished just in time, huh?" I ask, letting the innuendo hang in the air.

Taylor immediately picks up on it, and she smacks at my bare chest. "You are horrible."

"I know, but you like it." I stand from the bed for a final time. "Come on. Let me help you in the shower. Then let's get dressed and come up with a game plan over at Lincoln's and Temperance's place."

"Okay." She nods, and I help her to her feet and into the bathroom.

"I'll be right out here if you need me."

She nods, and I leave her alone in the master bathroom while I get ready in the hall bath.

Chapter Twenty-Two

Taylor

After I get my shower and, unfortunately, wash the feeling of Bryan's touch from my body, I get dressed and meet him in the kitchen.

"You good?" Bryan asks while standing in front of the stove, the sound of something frying filling the small space around us.

"I'm fabulous." I say as I lift up on my tiptoes to kiss him on the lips.

"Good. Breakfast will be done in five. Go and sit down." He says as he tilts his head to the small table in the middle of the kitchen.

In the time we've been together, Bryan's been in the kitchen with my dad, learning how to cook from him. I think what helps drive him to learn is that he's cooking for me and not just himself anymore.

A few minutes later, he sits a plate of scrambled eggs, toast—that is toasted to perfection—a few links of sausage, and a cup of coffee to complete the meal down on the table in front of me.

"Thank you, Bryan. This looks amazing."

"You're welcome. Now eat up. Mark and Lexi will be here in a few minutes." He says as he sits down next to me with his own plate piled high with food.

Our thighs touch under the table, and it sends fresh sparks through me. How is it that I just had two orgasms back to back and I still want more? This man is going to ruin me. But the bigger question is, would I mind it if he did? No, I wouldn't.

We just shovel the last bite into our mouths when there's a knock on the door and Mark walks in with Lexi on his heels.

"Morning, you two," Mark greets.

"Morning," Bryan says as he picks up our plates and takes them over to the kitchen sink to be washed later.

"Hey." Lexi says as she takes one look at me and a huge grin spreads across her face.

There's no way she could know.

I looked in the mirror while I was in the bathroom, and I didn't see any bruises from Bryan's kisses and nips. Which it honestly, kind of disappointed me that I, at least, didn't have something on the nipple he bit into. But I know he didn't do it hard enough to damage the skin like that. I mean, yeah, I still looked a little flushed, but I figured that was from the hot shower at that point.

"You two ready to go?" Mark asks as he leans against the wall next to the entryway to the kitchen.

"Yeah," Bryan says, then he looks at me, reaching out his hand, the same one he had inside me not fifteen minutes ago. "You coming, Taylor?"

I can't help it. I feel my cheeks heat as I take that innocent question and completely turn it into something else entirely.

Mark, thankfully, seems to be oblivious to my demeanor; but damn it, Lexi is grinning like a fool.

It takes Bryan a heartbeat to figure out the reason for my blush before he grabs my hand and pulls me to my feet.

He waves Mark on, and once he turns his back to us, Bryan leans down, his mouth next to my ear and whispers, "Was it my hand or the oh so innocent question I asked that made you blush like that, Annie?"

For a second I think about telling him it was freaking both, but I then remember he said he liked both my personalities. My pleasure-spent version and my snarky, badass version. So, I decide to let the other side out to play.

"I don't know what you're talking about." I say as I brush past him and meet Mark by the front door.

Lexi immediately pulls me to her side, and when Mark opens the door, she walks me out and down the sidewalk out of earshot of the guys.

"What the hell happened?" Lexi whisper-shouts. "And don't you dare say nothing. You have a dopy look on your face, and I saw you turn into a tomato at Bryan's words."

"We, uh," I begin, but she cuts me off with a gasp.

"Did you two have sex?"

"No. Not in the normal sense, at least."

"Oh, my god!" Lexi squeals. "What did he do? Was it mouth, fingers, or both?"

I laugh. "Are you sure Mark's giving you enough? Sounds like you're wound a little too tight."

"You're ignoring the question, Taylor," she deadpans.

So I tell her about the ways he *edged* me. I know enough from reading some spicy romance books that there are kinks out there, and I think Bryan opened my eyes to at least two.

"So edging and praising is a turn on for you. Nice! Good for you, Taylor. I'm glad that he made you feel safe. If he didn't, I would have had to kill him." Lexi shrugs her shoulder.

"I would have helped you hide his body." I chuckle.

As we make our way over to Lincoln and Temperence's apartment, I knock as Bryan and Mark stand behind us, and we wait for the door to open. A moment later, Temperance opens the door, and she steps to the side to let us in without a word.

"Linc! The teams' here." She calls out. "Please, sit down." She says with a wave over the living room furniture.

Lincoln comes out of one of the back rooms to join us a moment later. "What's going on?"

"Some shit went down yesterday." Mark begins.

"And I'm probably going to be Desmond's prime target." Bryan adds.

"Why?" Temperance asks with a touch of worry in her voice.

"I'll admit, I lost control out there yesterday. But he was talking shit about Taylor and I just reacted." He runs his hand through his hair in frustration. "I pinned the bastard to the hood of my car and had a few choice words for him."

Temperance looks scared shitless, while Lincoln looks...amused. I guess it's a macho guy thing. You know, protector of all women and shit.

"But there is one thing that keeps coming back to me," Bryan says, his voice taking on a confused tone.

"What is it?" I press.

"I don't know. There was something about his eyes. When I had him pinned to the Camaro, it's like he wasn't looking at me. It was weird."

I smack him on the shoulder, and he looks at me, confused.

"What was that for?" He asks in exasperation.

"You should have told me sooner about that." I scold.

"Well, my attention was drawn elsewhere." He smirks, and I roll my eyes while Lincoln chuckles and Temperance groans.

I am *not* taking his bait here in the middle of our leader's living room.

"Well, speaking of drawing your attention. Draw him." I snap.

Bryan looks at me before nodding his head. "Do you have any paper and a pencil or a pen for me to use?"

He directs the question to Lincoln, but it's Temperence who nods as she walks quietly back the hall and brings out a sheet of paper and a piece of charcoal for Bryan to draw with.

"Wow. Thank you. I love working with charcoal. Do you draw a lot, Temperance?" Bryan asks.

"Yes," She answers and sits on the arm of the couch to watch Bryan draw.

I silently watch them. Two artists completely engrossed in their favorite medium. I glance at Lincoln, and he has a smile on his face as he watches his wife interact with Bryan. When I slide my gaze back to them, I notice Temperence's hand reaching out for Bryan's back, like she wants to run it over his spine in a soothing gesture. I brush it off as her thinking about her own son they lost so long ago. He could have grown into an artist like her if he had lived.

After ten minutes of Bryan quietly drawing, he heaves a sigh of relief and reveals the finished product. "This is what the asshole's face looked like."

I stare at the picture. The darker eye compared to his lighter one. How it looks so vacant even in the picture.

I look at Lincoln and Temperance. "Can I send that to someone for their medical expertise?"

"Sure." Lincoln nods.

I pull out my phone and I dial Mom's number, putting it on speaker once I tap on her contact. She answers on the second ring.

"Taylor? Is everything okay?" Mom asks, her voice a bit clipped.

"Yeah, Mom. We're fine. I have something for you, though." I take a picture of Bryan's drawing and shoot it over to her in a text message. "I sent you a picture, and I want your medical input on it."

"Okay," Mom says, and I hear a door clicking shut in the background a moment before her phone pings with the incoming text. "Okay, it came through. Hang on."

We wait for what seems like years before Mom comes back on the phone.

"Okay, from this picture—which Bryan, great job, by the way."

"Thanks, Kathy," Bryan says with pride but with a hint of embarrassment mixed in his tone.

Mom continues, "I would say this guy is blind in his right eye. He had some kind of trauma to it that made him lose his sight."

"Thanks, Mom. Do me a favor and delete that pic for me?" I ask.

"You got it, Sweety," Mom says, and I hear her tapping on the screen of her phone. "Be careful. Love you two. Tell Mark and Lexi to be safe, too."

"We will, Mrs. Sparks." Mark says.

"Taylor!" Mom chastises. "You should have told me I was on speaker."

"Why is that, Kathy?" Bryan asks while moving closer to the phone. "Were you going to talk about someone behind their back?" He teases.

"Bryan Evans, you shut up. Tom is still trying to talk me out of murdering you for letting my daughter leave without you." Mom snaps, but I hear the touch of teasing in her tone.

"I'll work on getting your forgiveness when we get back home."

"Don't count on it, buddy."

Bryan smiles, "Challenge accepted, Kathy."

"Yeah, sure." Mom says. "I gotta go. Call me when you can, Taylor. Love you."

"I will. Love you too, Mom." I say, and I hang up.

I glance at Lincoln and Temperance, and before I can say anything; they are looking between me and Bryan with a look of warmth on their faces.

"What is it?" I can't help but ask.

"It's just been a while since we've seen a family that is as close to one another as you all are," Lincoln says.

"And I like your relationship with her mother." Temperance says. "Your grandparents taught you well."

"How do you know my grandparents raised me?" Bryan asks, brow arching in question.

Lincoln leans back in his chair and crosses an ankle over his knee. "You think we wouldn't look into you before assigning you to this case?" He begins by pointing at Bryan. "Your grandparents raised you after your parents' murder. Your grandfather John, from your father's side, is an Army vet and is still probably a burly mother, but he has a heart of gold. Your grandmother Gail is just an all-around sweetheart and will do anything for you. She used to be a schoolteacher before she took you in and retired to focus on raising you."

"Damn. You've done your research." Bryan chuckles.

"And you," Temperance begins, pointing to me. "Your mother is a nurse at the local hospital, and she helps out on ambulance runs, too. Your father owns his own auto shop, that Bryan just so happens to work at part-time in-between cases. You also have a little brother, Cody, who is nine, I think now. He's a cute little kid."

"Do me next. Do me!" Mark asks while waving his hand in the air like a middle schooler trying to get the teacher's attention.

"Ugh, remind me why I stay with this idiot?" Lexi grumbles.

Mark leans into her enough where only she and, unfortunately, I hear since I'm closest to them. "Because, Lex, I give you *the* best orgasms you've ever had."

"Oh, God." I groan. "I did not need to hear that."

"Well, stop eavesdropping on private conversations, you perv," Mark quips with a sly grin.

"Oh, I'm sorry. First of all, that's my job, in case you forgot." I snap back. "Plus, it would help if I weren't a foot away! You're not that quiet, Mark."

"Oh, Lexi knows that."

"Okay! That's enough." Bryan says. "We all don't need to talk about how loud we all are. It isn't a contest, although I think Taylor would beat anyone."

"Ha! I knew it. I thought you were happier than usual this morning! What'd'ya do?" Mark asks while high-fiving Bryan over my head.

"Bryan Alexander Evans!" I scold while smacking my open palm against his chest. "Don't you dare answer that!"

He laughs as my cheeks heat with utter humiliation from having our superiors know of our minute sex life. Temperance looks utterly appalled while Lincoln just laughs his ass off.

"See, I told you we liked your friendships. Not a lot of people can joke like this and during a case this dangerous." Lincoln says. "Keep that energy alive between you all."

"Don't encourage them, Linc." I grumble.

"I think it may be too late for that." He smiles as Mark pulls Bryan from his seat beside me and walks him near the door while giving me a side-eyed glare.

I sign to him with a sly smile on my face. *"I can still read lips, you know."*

He turns his back on me while flipping me off, and I burst out laughing.

"I'll just send you my therapy bill when all this is over." I joke toward Linc and Temperance.

Temperance then sits beside me, her expression suddenly all motherly for some reason. "Is he treating you well in—" She trails off, not knowing how she wants to ask her question, but I know what she's asking.

"Yes. He's been amazing. I, at least, won't go into detail, but I feel very safe and loved by him."

I don't know why I told her that. It's not like her opinion matters, but I can't help it for some reason.

"Okay, let's get these two away from one another before they talk about every single escapade we have done or have yet to do." Lexi says as she stands and heads toward Mark, grabbing him by the arm and then leading him out the door.

I look back to Linc and Temperence. "Glad to have been your entertainment for the evening. We'll be here all week."

We laugh as I take Bryan's hand and walk out of the apartment, shutting the door behind us with a soft click.

Bryan leads us to our apartment while motioning for Mark and Lexi to follow. Once inside, Mark and Lexi sit on the loveseat, and I take one of the armchairs while Bryan stands in the middle of the room with his arms crossed over his chest. The playful mood the guys had between them a few minutes ago evaporated like a cloud in the Florida breeze.

"With me pinning him on my car, I know he'll come for me for the next race." Bryan begins.

I take a sharp breath at Bryan's words. I know they are true, but I still don't want to hear them.

"We need to make a plan for when I go up against this piece of shit." Bryan says, his eyes darting over to Mark.

"I want to be able to see the race. If I have to be in the dark to other people and make them think I've run or something, that's fine. But I don't want to be completely in the dark, not again." I look Bryan in the eye as I add, "I want to be the one to...put a bullet in his head if something happens to you.

Bryan walks over to me and takes my face in his large, warm hands. "I wouldn't have it any other way, Baby."

He steps back from me and looks over at Mark. "What's your plan?"

"As soon as I think shit's gonna hit the fan, I'll call Linc and Tempe so they can assemble their infiltration team. No matter what, this son of a bitch is going down when he calls your race," Mark says with conviction.

"And Taylor and I will stick together. No matter what, we will not leave the other's side," Lexi says.

I look over at my friend, and I realize she gave us an out. We won't leave the other's side. We are not promising that we won't act if needed. Only that we will stick together. You know, power in numbers and all.

I touch her hand in what would seem like an innocent and agreeable gesture. "Yeah. We will be stuck to each other like glue."

She smiles and nods, and when I look back over at Bryan, his stance is a little more relaxed but still strung tighter than normal.

Later that night, as Bryan and I are lying in bed, I can tell his mind is still running a mile a minute. I sit up on my elbow so I can look down at him. At first, he doesn't look at me, so I trail my finger down the middle of his chest, and I can't help the smirk that blooms on my face at the goosebumps my touch causes to flare on his skin.

"Babe, don't worry, we will make it out of this. We have been in dangerous situations like this before."

"Yeah, but every situation is different. You deal with different people with different mindsets, and because of that, the whole game changes." Bryan sighs.

"Now that you put it that way, I understand it." I say.

He takes my hand and pulls it up to his mouth, brushing his lips against my skin in a tender kiss. "Can you drive the Mustang pretty well?" Bryan asks me.

"I can get from point A to point B, but not very fast." I say. "Why?"

"I want to make sure you can get out of here if you have to." Bryan says.

"Bryan, I—" I begin, but he cuts me off.

"Taylor, I have to know that when I get behind the wheel to race this bastard, you can get yourself out of here." Bryan says, looking at me in the darkness. The sliver of the moon that shines through the window makes his eyes shine a lighter shade of green.

As I stare into them, and I can see the worry reflecting back at me.

I take a deep breath, lifting my left hand and running my thumb over his lips. "Okay. You can teach me how to drive my car better."

"Thank you." Bryan says.

"How did you keep everything a secret from me before I knew who you really were?" I ask.

"It was hard. I had to ask Gramps for tips about how to keep my composure." Bryan admitted.

I try to smile at him, but I can only hold it for a few moments. I settle back down in bed and rest my head on his chest. I feel him run his hand up and down my back in soothing sweeps, trying to calm both of us.

As I close my eyes, I say a silent prayer that we make it out of this case alive, and then I drift off to sleep.

Chapter Twenty-Three

Taylor

The next morning, I'm drawn out of a blissful sleep when I hear Bryan moving around in the bathroom.

"Babe, what are you doing?" I ask groggily while sitting up in bed, rubbing the sleep from my eyes.

I look out the window and notice that it is still dark outside. I then glance over at the digital clock on Bryan's nightstand, and the red font reads 5:15 A.M.

"Bryan, are you seriously getting up at five-fifteen in the freaking morning?" I ask as I flop back down on the bed and cover my eyes with the comforter.

"I want to get you to the track before the others got there," Bryan says as he gently pulls at the covers.

"Why can't it be after hours?" I complain, holding onto the fabric in a death grip.

"Sometimes the guys stay after hours. Come on, Babe, get up and get a shower. I'll fix a nice hot cup of coffee for you." Bryan coaxes.

"Fine," I say while throwing the covers off my body and sitting up on the edge of the bed. "But you better have my coffee ready by the time I'm out of the shower."

"I will, Babe." Bryan grins as he leans in to press a quick kiss to my lips.

After I finish my shower and get dressed, I walk out of the bathroom, and just as promised, Bryan is leaning against the doorframe of the bedroom with a pink and purple thermos of coffee in his hand.

"Your coffee as I promised, ma'am." He smiles at me as I grab the thermos and take a sip, humming at the perfect combination of creamer and sweetener. "You take your Mustang and I'll follow you in the Camaro."

"Okay." I sigh. "Since you went through all the trouble of making me coffee, fine."

I follow Bryan out into the living room, and he grabs our keys from the little glass bowl near the front door, handing me the set for my car.

He opens the front door and walks out first, scanning the area before he gestures with a quick nod of his head, telling me to come on, and I walk out to join him on the stoop.

After making sure the apartment is secure, we get into our cars, and I follow him to the track. Twenty minutes later, we pull up and I notice that the gate is blocking our path. At first, I think that maybe this was all for nothing, but then Bryan rolls his window down and enters a code into a panel that sits on a pole cemented into the ground.

"Well, so much for being locked out." I grumble.

Once the gate slides open, Bryan drives onto the track and parks his car in the pit area. Just as I'm about to pull in beside him, he opens his door and puts his hand up, telling me to stop.

"Go on and pull onto the track. I'll be there in a minute."

"Okay," I say as I throw the transmission into reverse to back up enough so I can then shift into first and drive onto the track as instructed.

I pull up to the checkered starting line that's painted on the asphalt and shift the car into neutral, shaking the gearshift a few times to make sure it's in the proper gear. I then pull the parking brake and keep the car idling while I wait for Bryan.

After a few minutes, he jogs over to me, and just when I think he's going to get into the passenger seat; he comes around my side and opens my door.

"Get in the passenger seat. I want to show you how it's done." He says as butterflies flutter to life in my belly at the smirk that blooms on his face.

"Oh yes, Speed Racer, please show me how it's done." I say as I roll my eyes and step out of the car.

Bryan walks me over to the passenger side and opens the door for me so I can slide in. Once I'm buckled in, he slams the door shut before rounding the front of the car and dropping into the driver's seat.

"You ready?" He asks.

Before I can even say yes or no, he quickly releases the parking brake, throws the transmission into first, and takes off so fast that the tires squeal.

"Bryan!" I screech, one hand grabbing the part of the seatbelt strapped over my chest and the other grabbing for the 'oh shit' handle in the ceiling.

Bryan just laughs as he shifts gears again in quick succession to get up to top speed before he hits the first turn.

"Come on, Taylor! You gotta look at me!" He laughs.

I didn't realize I closed my eyes on his reckless take-off. I slowly open my eyes and I see the track flying by through the windshield.

"I thought you were gonna teach me how to drive, Bryan Evans, not scare me with a takeoff like that?!"

"I'm sorry. I'll slow down a bit." He says, and although his voice is gentle, his lips still hold a bit of a smirk.

He's in his element. A guy who honestly likes racing through and through no matter what, and he's letting me into this world of his again, just like with us and the agency.

As he slows down, so does my heart, and I can focus on what is going on around me. I glance over at him as he revs the engine enough to downshift and slow the vehicle a bit, but we are still going about 120. It's better than the 190 miles an hour he was pushing the engine to a few minutes ago.

"Okay," Bryan begins as he continues to look ahead and dips the car into the next turn. "Always keep your hand near the gearshift; you never know when you are going to have to shift at the last second. But don't keep your hand on it; that's a good way to accidentally shift too soon, and it puts extra stress on the transmission. Also, don't second guess yourself. Once you have a thought, act on it. If you hesitate in your driving or shifting, that is what can get you killed." His voice takes on a hard tone near the end, and I sit quietly for a moment.

"Mark and I have always liked to race growing up. We would mostly race go-carts at the local track down in Bluff, Utah. When we got older and got our driver's licenses, we made a dirt track out at the cabin, and we would race with my F-150 and his Suburban." Bryan says as he pulls the Mustang to a stop at the checkered line and turns the engine off. "And you know what? Sometimes he would win in that SUV of his." He grumbles as he opens his door, leaving it open for me, and I do the same with my side.

"We'll just from what I've seen here, you both seem pretty well matched."

"Yeah. We know how the other thinks, so it's kinda fun to see who can pull a fast one and win the race." He quickly pulls me against him, catching me off guard, and my hands collide with the firm muscle of his chest. "It's your turn now. Show me what you got."

Bryan steps away from the Mustang, allowing me access to the driver's seat. I sink down into the leather that's still warm from his body heat as he shuts the door behind me. I buckle my seatbelt while Bryan walks around the front of the car, drops into the passenger seat, and slams the door while smiling at me.

"Whenever you're ready, Annie." He says as he buckles in and tightens the seatbelt until it clicks once, locking him into the seat. "Oh shit, I should have brought a helmet."

"Oh, screw you." I scoff as I turn the engine over, push the clutch in, and shift into first, but I don't press the accelerator yet.

I take a breath while closing my eyes to steady myself. I can do this. I have to. I have to let Bryan know that everything will be okay and that I can handle driving at the insane speeds this machine can reach so he can focus solely on what he has to do in order to win the race against this asshole.

My eyes snap open, and I slam the accelerator down, making the wheels spin like Bryan did. I hear his sharp bark of laughter at the sound, and that makes me push the car more.

I shift when the indicator tells me to and before I know it, when I hit the first turn, I'm pushing 160.

"Is this all you have?" Bryan asks with a grin.

"Oh, you want more, huh?"

I know what he's doing. He wants me to hit 190 miles an hour. So, I fly down the straightaway, and when I hit the second turn; I shift, and when I enter the second straightaway, I'm hitting my top speed.

"This enough for you?"

"It'll do." He says while trying to hide his smile as I cross the finish line and skid to a stop.

"It'll do." I mock. "Really? I just stepped out of my comfort zone, and that's all you have to say?"

"You did amazing, Baby." He praises while leaning over the console and kissing me soundly on the lips.

He starts to open the passenger door since it's almost time for the others to get to the track, but I stop him with a hand on his forearm, the corded muscles flexing underneath my palm.

"Thank you, Bryan."

"For what?" He chuckles.

"For always pushing me to be better at things. For making me challenge myself and being there to cheer me on."

"I will always be your loudest cheerleader, Baby." He says with a bright smile, then he looks out at the track for a moment before tilting his head toward the windshield. "You wanna race against me?"

As I stare into his green eyes, they shine with a playful challenge, and I can't help my lips curving up in a slight grin.

"Okay. Sure."

"I'll be right back. Let me get the Camaro."

He exits the vehicle, slamming the passenger door, and I watch him walk away in my review mirror. His gait is smooth, confident, with just enough of a cocky swagger to make my blood heat knowing that man is all mine.

When he enters the pit area where he parked his car, I force my eyes forward and my stomach drops. The little group is standing on the bleachers, shocked looks on their faces, except for Mark and Lexi's. They must have known what Bryan was going to do.

I hear Bryan's Camaro pull up, and I glance out my driver's window to look at him. He rests his left forearm against the top of his steering wheel, looking out over the crowd that has gathered before he rolls his window down and motions for me to do the same.

"We don't have to do this if you don't want to." He yells over the sound of the engines idling.

As soon as the words are out of his mouth, I know what I want to do. If I can't race in front of those who we trust most and those who are earning our trust, how can I even think of driving when shit hits the fan?

"It's okay. Let me prove to you and to myself that I can do this."

"That's my girl." Bryan grins. "I won't go easy on you."

"Wouldn't want it any other way, Bullet."

Lexi comes over from the crowd a moment later. She has a checkered flag in her hand and a bright smile on her face.

"You know you're going to eat her dust, right?" Lexi asks as she stands beside both our cars, bending at the waist so we can hear her over the idling engines.

Bryan rolls his eyes and revs his engine while rolling up his window, telling Lexi to get the race started.

"Oh, you need to smoke his ass, Tay," Lexi grumbles.

I laugh as she walks away, and I roll my window up too. Bryan revs again, and I match him with a few of my own.

"Driver's ready?!" Lexi shouts.

Bryan edges his car forward, so the fender jumps a bit, begging her to wave the flag.

"On your mark!"

I edge forward this time, so I'm even with Bryan again.

"Get set!"

"Oh, come on, Lexi!" I shout as I shift into first, but keep my foot on the brake as I push the accelerator in so I spin my wheels a bit in agitation at her edging us on.

"GO!"

She shouts while waving the checkered flag, and I am the first one to shoot forward since I already had my tires spinning, but Bryan is quickly on my bumper. I shift into a higher gear when the indicator tells me to so I can match my speed while trying to keep some distance between us.

When we get into the first turn, I am already at my top speed and as we exit onto the straightaway, Bryan tries to use the lower side of the track to pass me, but I swerve to block him and I see his approving smile in my rearview mirror

I did something right.

"Now we're going to have some fun." I say to myself.

As we fly into the second turn, I try to anticipate Bryan's move and dip the car lower onto the track to get into a blocking position, but I hear his engine roar behind me and when I look in my side-view mirror, he shoots past me.

"Oh, you sneaky asshole."

He used my apparent arrogance to his advantage. Okay, so note to self, don't get into a blocking position until your opponent tries to pass you.

"Okay. I got you, buddy."

I shift once more, pushing my car harder, and it feels like I'm going faster than my speedometer shows. We round the final turn, and we are in the final quarter-mile stretch. I try to pass Bryan, but he blocks me at every attempt. So, I slowly edge up to the higher point of the track, and Bryan follows, keeping me from passing him.

"Hopefully, this works."

I am hoping that gravity and speed will be my allies when I spring my trap. Once we are at the very top of the track, I keep my hand hovering over the shifter, and I quickly jerk my wheel, push the clutch in, and shift in one swift motion.

I let the curve of the turn pull me away from Bryan so I'm not behind him. Then my speed catches up with me, and I pass him once we hit the straight section of the track, and I blow past the finish line first. Granted, it was only by a millisecond, but hey winning is winning.

Chapter Twenty-Four

Taylor

Through my windows, I can hear the little group cheering for my victory as they run out of the bleachers and onto the track. I skid to a halt a few feet after the finish line, and as Bryan's car speeds past me, he gives me two quick honks of his horn before entering the pit area to park his car.

The girls, Morgan, Christy, Anna and Lexi, all run after me and practically tackle me in a group hug as I exit my car.

"Oh my god, you were amazing!" Christy squeals while clapping her hands together.

"It's nothing. Bryan and I were just playing around." I say as I tuck a piece of hair behind my ear.

"Well, the bottom line is you beat him." Morgan says with a smile, like she's the proud mother hen of our little group.

Bryan then walks up, apparently hearing Morgan's comment, and I see a teasing smile playing on his lips.

"It was beginner's luck, that's all."

"You wanna second lap and get beaten again?" I challenge arching an eyebrow.

"Not today."

Morgan then speaks up again. "You girls wanna go down to the beach to celebrate?"

We all eagerly nod our heads in agreement.

Bryan chuckles as he wraps his arm possessively around my waist and pulls me close to his body while placing a chaste kiss to my lips. "You go have fun with the girls."

When I look into his eyes, I see pride blooming in their green depths. I proved to him that I can drive my car and get out of here in a rush, and if I absolutely need to, I can race and win. That was the whole point of this early morning adventure, and I aced it with flying colors.

I stand up on my tiptoes so I can whisper in his ear, "I love you. Thank you for this morning."

"Wow. It must have been fun if you've already forgiven me for getting you up as early as I did," He whispers back.

I feel his lips brush the shell of my ear, and it sends pleasurable shivers down my spine, directly into my core, and I can't help but squeeze my thighs together in response. Bryan must notice my actions because his gaze darkens.

"You better go, Annie." He begins, his voice a bit deeper than it was a moment ago. "Unless you want some help with that."

His eyes flick down my body for a heartbeat, and I can feel my cheeks heat at the simple gesture.

"Bryan, come on, man! I want you to start a race between me and Ian!" Mark yells over the roof of his car while waving Bryan over.

"Alright! Hold your ass, dude!" Bryan shouts. "Go, Taylor. Have fun and be safe."

"I will, and you be safe too." I say as I give him a quick peck on the cheek and slide back into the driver's seat, but Morgan's voice stops me from closing my door.

"Girls, go get your bathing suits, and we'll meet at the main entrance to the beach in about twenty minutes. Sound good?"

"Okay." We all say in unison as we go our separate ways to grab what we need from our respective houses.

Once we arrive at the beach, we walk down the boardwalk and into a few souvenir shops. I take advantage of our endeavor and actually do some shopping for Mom, Dad, and Cody. I buy my brother and father a shirt that says, 'Hello Florida' and I get Mom a bracelet that has sea turtles engraved into the platinum metal band.

When the others find whatever caught their eye and we get in line to check out, Lexi points to something at a nearby table.

"Tay, look at that over there."

I glance over to where she was gesturing, and there is a snow globe sitting in the middle of the table. The base is made to look like the ocean is lapping at a sandy beach, and inside of the glass globe is a blue Mustang just like mine, situated on a section of pavement that's been painted under the wheels. When I go over to pick up the globe, I give it a shake. The 'snow', which is made up of blue and white glitter, floats in the water in a mesmerizing dance back down to the bottom.

I smile as I head back in line with the others, globe in hand. "This is so pretty. I'm gonna get this for myself. Thanks for pointing it out, Lexi."

"No problem. I figured you'd like it, especially since you totally rocked the race this morning."

We check out, and after we take our bags back to our cars, we walk the rest of the way down to the beach.

Once we pick a spot and lay out our beach towels in the sand, Lexi and Morgan get to work on burying two large pink and green umbrellas while Christy and I apply sunscreen to each other. When Lexi and Morgan secure the umbrellas, Lexi sits in front of me so I can apply the sunscreen to her back, and Christy does the same to Morgan.

"Hey, I have a question." I ask when I squeeze a dollop into my hand.

"What's up?" Morgan asks.

"When did *he* start making you all race like this?"

Morgan's back stiffens and her eyes narrow at me, but of course, like I was hoping, Christy opens her mouth with ease.

"Two years ago."

"Christy!" Morgan scolds.

"What? She asked me a question, and I told her." Christy says, cowering a bit from Morgan's outburst.

Morgan shakes her head, then takes a deep breath and looks at Lexi and me.

"Two years ago is when all this started to happen. At first, it was just for pinks, like any normal race, but he would always flirt with the girlfriends of the guys he was racing just to piss them off, and because of that, they would make mistakes. But one day, I heard he couldn't get ahead of a guy, so he did that pit move that you saw the other day. I heard his girlfriend was there and was cussing him out, saying he essentially cheated his way to a win by causing an accident that resulted in a death. So, to prove how ruthless he was, and that he didn't care about death on his hands, he shot her right there on the track. From there, he made it a rule that anyone who races against him would mean losing their life, and the girl is taken and put through hell. Tortured and raped before they're killed. My sister was the second person who was a victim of his. I want him to pay so bad but there's nothing I can do. Nothing I do will bring her back, but I want him to burn in hell all the same."

We are all quiet for a little bit, and Lexi's the one who breaks the silence. "Maybe if Bryan or Mark races him, they can make this all stop."

"I don't think evil like this can ever be stopped." Morgan whispers, her voice tight with unshed tears.

"Yes, it can." I say. "I have seen evil just as bad as this, and it was stopped, so this can be too. You just have to believe it."

Lexi looks at me, and I know she understands what I'm talking about. Phil and Daryl. They were stopped by us, and this bastard will be too.

After a bit of silence, we settle down on our towels to work on our tans, with small talk filling the space around us for a while before we pack up and head back to our homes. When Lexi and I pull up to our apartments, the door to my place opens, and Bryan stands in the doorway.

"Over here, girls." He yells when we open our doors to exit the vehicles.

We walk over with our bags in hand, and Bryan holds the door open for us.

"Hey, Babe." I give him a kiss on the cheek as I pass him. "So, what happened after we left?" I ask.

"Nothing much; we had a few more races. What about you all?" Bryan asks as I pass him to set my bag down on the small table in the foyer and spot Mark leaning against the loveseat while munching on a half eaten apple.

"We got the girls to talk about Desmond. Bry, all this started two years ago." I say as I turn to face him.

"Oh damn. Are you serious?" Bryan asks, shock filling his tone.

"This bastard has got to be stopped." Mark chimes in as he dumps the apple core into the trash and pulls Lexi to his side.

"You two need to be careful. He could hurt you and say that since you can't race, he will automatically take me or Lexi because you were forced to forfeit." I say as I make my way into the living room and take a seat in one of the armchairs.

"I thought about that." Bryan sighs as he pinches the bridge of his nose in annoyance.

"Me too." Mark replies as he collapses onto the couch, with Bryan following suit.

Lexi and I notice the way that the guys are sitting on both sides of the couch. Arms crossed, heads down, staring at nothing in particular on the carpet, as if trying to figure out the best game plan but coming up with nothing.

"Hey, come on, let's fix something to eat; I'm starving." I say.

After the four of us eat a quick dinner, Mark and Lexi say their goodnights and go to their place. Once they leave, I clean up the kitchen while Bryan loads the dishwasher, and then we sit on the couch for a bit to try and unwind before bed.

"You never said. What all did you get from the boardwalk?" He asks, finally breaking the silence.

I grin at him as I stand up to grab my shopping bag and bring it back over to the couch so I can show him what I bought. "I got some shirts for Dad and Cody, and I got Mom a bracelet. Oh, and I got a snow globe." I say as I pull the globe out of the bag and unwrap it to show it to him.

"That is beautiful, Babe. It looks just like your Mustang."

"That was the main reason I got it." I say with a small smile. "Lexi actually pointed it out."

Bryan then goes quiet for a minute, and my smile fades as I feel the muscles in his body tighten from anger, fear, and anticipation.

"Hey," I say as I place my snow globe on the coffee table. "Talk to me." I urge as I rub my hand down his muscular arm.

"I wish that it could just be as simple as finding this piece of shit, forcing him on his damn knees with the muzzle of my gun shoved in his mouth while we wait for Lincoln and Temperance to come in and take him to prison. But that is just a dream that I need to get out of my head. I think it will be nothing short of a bloodbath before this asshole is taken down." Bryan says while gently brushing a piece of my chestnut brown hair from my shoulder.

"We will deal with whatever comes our way. But the main thing is, we *all* will walk away from this." I say.

"That's what I keep praying for."

"Come on, let's try to get some sleep." I say as I pull Bryan to his feet and tug him back into the bedroom, where we get comfortable in one another's arms and let the nighttime sounds of crickets chirping and the occasional honking horn lure us into sleep so we can tackle the coming days of danger and the unknown as a team.

Chapter Twenty-Five

Taylor

Three days pass and nothing out of the ordinary happens. Bryan and Mark are going to the track to race while Lexi and I hang with the girls.

Wash. Rinse. Repeat.

Which I'm glad for, but I am just waiting on the other shoe to drop. And when Bryan and I are lying in bed together, I can feel in the tense lines of his shoulders that he's just as apprehensive as I am. He thinks I don't notice them, but I do. I just don't press him on the matter.

One morning I hear Bryan's getting ready to go to the track a little earlier than he had been, and I sit up in bed while rubbing the sleep from my eyes.

"Sorry, I didn't mean to wake you, Babe." Bryan says with an apologetic smile on his face.

"It's alright. You're just lucky this is our job right now." I say, trying to lighten the mood.

"I'll make up for it once this is all said and done." He says while coming over to my side of the bed, leaning down, and pressing a kiss to my temple and then to my lips.

"I'll hold you to that, buddy." I say with a playful smile.

Since I'm awake, I go ahead and drag myself out of bed and get ready so I can head to the track later. When I'm dressed in a pair of black shorts, a pink tank top, and my Converse sneakers, I walk out into the kitchen where I see that Bryan already has coffee brewing in the coffee pot for me.

After making myself a cup, I watch as Bryan picks up his keys from the glass bowl near the front door. With a practiced movement, he slips them into his pocket, the fabric of his jeans rustling softly as he removes his Glock from the hidden holster on his right hip. He checks the firearm for ammo and makes sure the bullet loads into the chamber correctly before re-holstering the gun.

He turns around, giving me a quick smile and a wink, then he's out the door. When the door snicks shut, I can't help the feeling of dread and worry filling my veins. Like a sixth sense telling me to watch for something, but it's not telling me what.

I rush to the door, ripping it open, and I catch Bryan opening the driver's door to his Camaro.

"Be safe today. Okay?"

Bryan glances up at me with a quizzical look for a moment before he nods and gives me a confident smile. "I will, Annie. I'll see ya in a bit. Love you."

"Love you, too." I reply as he slams his car door and turns the engine over before backing out of his parking spot and drives away.

After I walk back inside, I pull out my phone and text Lexi to see if she's awake, too.

Me: Hey, u up?

> **Lexi:** Yeah, Mark just left a few minutes ago.

> **Me:** Bryan did too. I don't know y but I have a bad feeling something's going to happen. I don't like it at all.

> **Lexi:** Well, U have to think that nothing will go wrong, stay positive girl! *Winky face emoji.*

> **Me:** Ur right. I just need a good cup of coffee and it'll all be ok.

Once I finish my coffee, I make one more to go. I then grab my own keys and make sure the gun that I have hidden in a holster clipped into my specially made bra is loaded, and I head out to my car so I can drive down to the track with Lexi quick on my heels.

Once I pull up to the gate, I see a handmade sign, and the words that are painted in hot pink reads: 'Girls pull onto the starting line'.

"What the hell is this about?" I ask myself.

I pull onto the track and I pass Mark on the way in. When I roll my window down, he comes over and leans his forearms on my door, and I can see the shit-eating grin in full force on his face.

"What is going on?"

"Pull onto the track and find out."

"What hair-brained scheme have you gotten us into?" I ask while arching an eyebrow.

"Oh, Tay Tay. I'm hurt." He says, placing a hand over his heart in mock offense.

I roll my eyes and I drive onto the track, where I see four cars: a Civic, GTR, WRX and a Dart, all waiting on the starting line. I pull my car beside the blue WRX, and Morgan introduces us to a girl I haven't seen yet, Roxie, just as Bryan walks up to me.

"What's going on?" I ask as he pulls me in for a quick hello kiss.

"Well," Bryan begins as Josh, James, Ian, and a new guy I haven't seen before, Nick, according to the name tag that's stitched into his light blue mechanic's shirt, walk up behind him. "We were all talking, and we wanted to see what you girls are made of. Today is your day to hit the track."

I look between the guys, somewhat dumbfounded. The only thing that brings me back to the present is when Mark throws his arm around Bryan's neck and lets a broad grin play on his lips as Lexi walks to my side.

"I say that's a great idea. Let's show 'em that we are more than just a pretty face." Lexi beams.

I chuckle as I look back at the other girls behind me. "Okay. Let's do this."

"Alright girls. We will have pairs race first." Josh announces. "Morgan. You and Christy take the first heat. Taylor and Lexi in the next. Then, Anna and Roxie in the last."

"And the winners of those races go head-to-head in a two-lap race." Ian's deep voice booms around us as he pulls Anna against his side. "You're gonna be in the last race, Sweetheart. I know it." He adds with a quick kiss to the top of her head.

"Well yeah. I'll be in your GTR, Baby." Anna grins.

I hear Nick give Roxie some tips before he gives her a swift smack on the butt and walks away with a mischievous grin on his face while a blush colors her cheeks.

"You want some tips too, Annie?"

I jump when I hear Bryan's voice next to my ear and the heat of his body enveloping mine.

"Maybe." I say as I quickly gather my composure and give him a teasing smile over my shoulder.

"Give them hell and make them eat your dust. Trust your instincts just like you do with anything else."

He kisses me on the neck, right behind my ear, and it's a good thing he wrapped his right arm around my stomach, because that kiss was enough to make my knees wobble.

"Move your car to my garage bay. Let me check it to make sure the tires and the oil are good before it's your turn," Bryan instructs as he backs away.

I coax my legs to move so I can drive my car to the line of garages, like I was told to do. When Bryan pops my hood to inspect the oil, I watch as Morgan's Dodge Dart pulls on the track along with James' suped-up Honda Civic that Christy is going to drive.

"I'd watch that Civic," Bryan says while wiping off the oil dipstick before inserting it back into the engine to check the quality of the oil.

"Why?" I ask as I look over my shoulder and watch as he pulls the dipstick back out and slowly twirls it around, inspecting the dark golden fluid.

"It's faster than it looks. James has a turbo in the engine. So unless Morgan has the same thing under the hood of her car, she's not gonna win." Bryan says as he nods to himself after inspecting the oil and apparently being satisfied with the quality, then replaces the dipstick and shuts the hood while wiping his hands with the dark red shop rag. "But I think you can give her a run for her money."

"What makes you think I can win against the Civic?"

"'Cause you have a turbo, too. Plus, I taught you, so that's gotta count for something." He says with a sly smile.

"Oh god." I say as I roll my eyes. I give him a playful shove on his shoulder. "Go make sure my tires are good."

"As you wish, my lady."

Bryan bends at the waist as he pulls over the four blue arms of the lift that's buried in the concrete under my car and hits a button, engaging the hydraulics so it lifts my car to where my tires are now at his eye level.

I turn my attention back to the track, and James is the one to start the race between Morgan and Christy. He stands in between the cars with a checkered flag, counts them down, then he waves the flag energetically to get them started.

Both cars surge forward with a squeal of tires. Morgan is in front the whole way, and I begin to think that Bryan was wrong about the Civic being faster, but that quickly changes in the last turn.

Christy shifts at the last second, where she and Morgan are neck and neck for a heartbeat before Christy shifts again, flying by Morgan, winning that lap by a full car length.

"See? Told ya." Bryan chuckles as he lowers my car and then kicks the lift arms out of the way.

"Yeah, yeah." I say as I turn to face him.

"Now it's your turn. Don't go easy on Lexi," Bryan says as he hands me my keys with a smirk.

"Oh please. Like I would go easy on her. I didn't go easy on you, did I?"

Before he can answer, an engine revs behind me, and I see Lexi's Lancer idling in the pit lane.

"Let's go, Sparks! You ready to eat my dust?"

"In your dreams, Smith!" I shout back.

I get in my car, back out of the private garage, and I drive onto the track at the starting line. Mark is going to set us off, and he walks between our cars, tapping on the windows, telling us to roll them down.

"Alright, you two. Let's make it a fair show and no cheating."

"Um, no, Mark. You're the one who cheats. Now let's get this race started." Lexi quips as she revs her engine again.

Mark laughs as he shakes his head as he stands in front of Lexi's Lancer. "Just for that, I'm gonna give Taylor a five-second head start."

"Mark!" Lexi shouts as she gives a quick honk of her horn.

"Come on, Mark!" Nick yells from the sidelines. "My girl wants to race!"

"Fine!" Mark sighs then gives us a smirk that apparently only I catch. "Go on" He lazily waves the flag,, and I am the first to react.

"Damn—"

I barely hear Lexi's curse as I shoot forward, and by the time I'm hitting the first turn, Lexi is on my bumper and I keep her there the whole time.

In the third race, Anna and Roxie face off with Nick waving the flag. Anna, in her GTR, wins this race after a nail biting fight to the finish.

Josh then walks to the center of the track, and he takes the checkered flag from Nick.

"Alright, everyone! This is the race we've been waiting for! Christy in James' Civic. Taylor in her Mustang, and Anna in her GTR! Who will win in this two-lap race?!"

Cheering erupts around us, and I know that anyone who may be out and about at least two streets over has to hear the hoots and hollers coming from the girls and the sharp whistles from the guys.

"Let's get this started! Ladies. Start. Your. Engines!" Josh yells as he lifts the flag above his head, the black-and-white checkered fabric waving gently in the air with the movement.

We go down the line—Christy, me, and Anna. All of us revving our engines, which makes the small crowd cheer louder than I thought possible.

With all the high energy, I almost forget that we are on a case. This feels like just meeting new friends and enjoying a hobby that we all love.

"On your mark!" Josh shouts, and I shift into first, but don't let go of the clutch.

"Get set!"

 I let the clutch go enough to feel the bite point.

"GO!"

Three sets of tires squeal, and we are off. Christy, of course, is ahead of us, and Anna is fighting me for second place.

"Come on, Anna, give me an opening." I say as we roll into the first turn.

I'm trying to bide my time. See how Anna races and how reactive she is to my faux attempts at passing her. I don't intend to actually make a move until we are about halfway through the third turn. But she doesn't need to know that.

At first, she blocks me as I expected. I wait until the second turn to try again, and she blocks me. So I back off, trying to make her think I've given up, but when we are just entering the third turn, I pull the move like I did with Bryan. I let my car drift up the high outer wall, and she follows me with ease.

"Wrong move, chick."

I quickly pull my steering wheel to the left and, as soon as I have a clear shot, I shift and surge right past her. I see her hit her steering wheel in defeat, but I don't give her much of my focus. I zero in on Christy and her Civic.

"Now it's just you and me, Christy."

I quickly gain ground as we fly over the line, entering into the second lap. Christy is still in the lead as we enter the first turn, but I dip low in the track and I come out ahead into the second straightaway.

I hold that spot until the third turn, where Christy tries the same move I did with her, dipping low in the track, but I block her at the last minute.

"No, you're not. This is my win." I growl as I shift to try to put space between us.

I notice a flash of something in my left review mirror and I react, thinking that Christy is going to try to pass me on that side. But when I look in my actual rearview mirror, I see that she is on my right, and I just gave her an opening.

Before I can even think about trying to block her, she shifts, apparently using that hidden turbo and blowing past me to win the race, putting me in second place.

"Damn! That was a good tactic."

Christy takes a victory lap while Anna and I park our cars in the pit. As I climb out of my car, she comes up to me with a huge smile on her face.

"That was amazing!" She pulls me in for an energetic hug, spinning us around for two complete turns before setting me down.

"Yeah, that was fun!" I say, my voice bubbling with pure laughter.

"That was a great race! You were killing it!" Mark says as he walks over with Lexi tucked up under his arm. Both wearing smiles just as bright as mine and Anna's.

"Yeah, I thought you said you didn't know how to race. The way you were handling things out there, you didn't look like a rookie." Bryan says.

"Beginner's luck?"

"No, it was because of all of those racing movies we watch." Lexi says.

"It almost felt like I was in the movie, especially with the GTR. If the color was different, it would be spot on." I say.

I look around, and I see everyone with their partners. Sharing congratulations here and tips there. I think for once they feel like just a normal group, sharing their love for cars.

Josh and Morgan go into the middle of the group to get everyone's attention. "I just want to say that you girls did an amazing job today. Like I'm sure that your boyfriends are, I'm proud of all of you. You stepped out of your comfort zone and tried something new. And you did a damn good job at it. Maybe we need to have a ladies' race night more often." Josh says.

All the guys cheer at this, while the girls look at one another and begin to nod their heads in agreement.

"I think that's a great idea, Babe," Morgan says.

"Why don't we close up early so that we can celebrate with our girls? What do you say, guys?" Josh asks.

The guys readily agree to this idea, and they all park their cars in the pit area, pulling down the garage doors so they'll be protected while the girls drive our cars down to the beach just to hang loose a little, and take in the Florida sites.

We spend a few hours doing several things. One was just lying on the beach taking in the remaining sun and having the water splash at our toes. Then we walk the boardwalk, but we just take in the sights for the rest of the evening.

When Bryan pulls my body next to his, I finally feel him relaxing against me, and I start to wonder if that uneasy feeling was all for nothing this morning. Because nothing about today was bad. It was the best night I've had in a while.

Chapter Twenty-Six

Bryan

After the ladies have their fill in looking through a few stores, I spot a couple of people playing volleyball and notice there is a free net. Just as I'm about to point it out, I hear my phone along with Ian's ding with a text message from James' number.

He ended up staying behind since his girlfriend raced with his car, plus I heard him talking about a private celebration, and I can only imagine what that would have entailed.

Probably many of the same things I wanted to try with Taylor tonight, but with this text message, all desire I had building in my veins evaporates like lava in water.

> **James:** Bryan. Ian. Someone broke into your bays. You two need to get back to the track…now.

"Shit." I growl.

I lock eyes with Ian, and he's already taking off, Anna on his heels.

"Taylor, Mark, Lexi!" I snap as I begin jogging behind Ian and his girl.

"What's wrong, Bryan?" Taylor shouts.

"Just give me your keys." I grind out, trying to keep from yelling at her. It's not her fault, and I have a feeling I know who the hell just broke into my bay.

"Bryan—" Taylor begins to ask again, but I cut her off as I stride to her driver's door.

"Taylor. Please. Give me your keys." I say, my voice hard and just barely holding in my fear and anger.

Her eyes widen as she quickly hands over her keys and rushes to get into the passenger seat. I whip open the driver's side door, plunge the key into the ignition, and I'm backing out of the parking lot, and speeding toward the track with Ian a few hundred yards in front of me while Josh and the others follow in behind us.

"You gonna tell me what's going on?" Taylor asks.

I sigh. "James messaged me and Ian to tell us someone broke into our garage bays."

"Do you know the damage yet?"

"No."

When we pull up to the track a few minutes later, James opens the gate for Ian and me to drive through, and we immediately go for our bays, which are just three spaces away from one another.

I park Taylor's Mustang a few feet from the door and get out, not even looking back to see if she follows. When I hear her passenger door shut, I pause before I bend down to lift the garage door.

"Are you sure you want to see this, too?" I ask, not looking at her.

"Bryan."

My name falling from her lips breaks me every time. She doesn't even have to tell me to turn around; the way she just says my name is all I need. I force myself to look at her, and while I still see fear lingering in her blue eyes, I see determination shining there, too.

"We are in this together. We will face it together, and we will win together." She says.

I nod, then take a deep breath and lift the garage door. From the back of the Camaro, nothing seems to be wrong, and for a split second, I think this has all been a horrible joke. But when I notice my toolboxes are open and the various ratchets, wrenches, screwdrivers, and other tools scattered around the concrete floor, my stomach drops.

As I slowly make my way to the front of the Camaro, I notice spray paint on the driver's side door. Upon closer inspection, I see it's a red X on the side panel of the door, and on the window is a haphazardly drawn skull with white X's for eyes, telling me I'm dead before the race is even called.

I begin kicking the tools out of my way so Taylor doesn't step on them and risk falling. As I continue toward the front of my car, I notice a black tarp draped over the windshield and hood with more white spray paint covering the material. This was sprayed on a little thicker due to the drips of paint bleeding from the end of the harsh lines of what I realize are letters. When I understand what the letters spell out, my heart stops beating in my chest.

Are you next? Let's find out!

I fist my hands at my sides to keep from punching something, and I try to keep my breathing even. This is what that fucker wants. He wants me to fly off the handle so he can catch me off guard and make me easy prey. Well, I'll be damned if I let it be easy for him.

I'll just act like I'm cool and this isn't eating away at my insides like a parasite at the vandalization of my car. I'll explode in a bit behind closed doors.

"What's that?"

Taylor's soft voice brings me back to reality, and I look over at her, following the direction of her finger. She's pointing to something under the wiper blade.

It's a piece of paper.

I go to grab for the paper, but Taylor stops me with a hand on my forearm. "Wait. Put on a pair of gloves. It could be laced with something."

"You're right." I say as I turn around and pull out a pair of black latex gloves from the only tool chest where the doors are still closed.

After I snap the gloves in place, the single tinge of pain against my wrists centering my racing thoughts, I pick up the paper and read it.

My body instantly stiffens, and red-hot anger fills my blood. I can't hold it back anymore. While keeping the paper in my left hand, I pull off my other glove and stride over to the garage door, pulling on the chain that lowers the door with a loud metallic sound echoing in my ears.

Once the door's down, I spin on my heel, rearing my right arm back, and I punch the drywall that's eye level with me. Taylor's squeak of surprise is the only thing that keeps me from punching again and again to try and ease some of this anger flooding my veins.

"What did it say, Bryan?" She asks quietly.

"I—"

I'm about to tell her that I don't want her to see it, but somehow, in my raging mind, I think logically. If she knows danger is absolutely coming for her, she will know how to react in the best way possible. So I show her the note, my hands surprisingly still—not an ounce of a tremor, considering the rage burning in my chest.

You'll pay for slamming me into this piece of shit.

You're gonna lose your car, your life, and your girl! She's gonna scream so good for me when I fuck her.

I'll come get you when it's time, but remember, I'm always watching.

P.S. Your girl's a good racer...I may have some extra fun before I kill her!

"Oh, my god." Taylor whispers as I ball the paper in my gloved hand before throwing it into the metal trash bin in the corner of the garage with such force that it bounces around the container for a moment before settling into the oil-slicked bottom.

I pull off the other glove and walk away from her, moving up the other side of my car to pull the black tarp off, only to reveal even more damage.

The windshield is broken, most likely from one of the tools lying on the ground or from a baseball bat shattering the glass. The driver's side headlight is also broken and hangs loosely by a wire sticking out from the frame. I look down at the driver's tire, and it's flat. I think that's the least of my worries until I look over to the entire vehicle and all four tires have been slashed.

Taylor slowly walks over to me, stopping just past the passenger side-view mirror to look at me, but I don't meet her gaze. Not yet.

"We knew this was going to happen, but it's so much different experiencing it for real." I whisper. "I want to track this bastard down and just beat him to a pulp."

My hands clench into tight fists; the skin on my right hand splits again, reopening the wound that I don't give two shits about right now.

"I want to make him pay for all the hell he's put these people through and for threatening you. He can threaten me all damn day if he wants, but when someone threatens you, then to me, they've just signed their own fucking death warrant." I say, my voice devoid of emotion but promising so much more.

"I know, Babe. You can think of all the ways something can happen, but no amount of preparation can help when it happens for real." Taylor says softly, closing the distance between us and nestling her body into mine while placing her right hand over my heart, grounding me just a bit.

"But how did he know about the race with you girls? I didn't see his car or the cars of his goons anywhere today." I ask.

"You think an inside man?"

"I don't know. Maybe." I sigh while running my hand through my hair again.

"Come on. Let's try to get this cleaned up," Taylor says while pulling at my left hand.

"This needs more repairs than what I have available right now." I say as I look around the little garage. I need paint, headlight assembly, tires, and, most importantly, I need a windshield.

"He's making you stop practicing to repair your car," Taylor says, finally noticing all the damage.

"Exactly. Shit." I growl.

"Hey, I don't know much about cars, but I can help you with tools and things."

"Thank you, Taylor." I say while running my hand up and down her arm.

A moment later, we hear a knock on the garage door, and I hear Mark's voice filter through the metal material.

"Dude. You two okay in there?"

I sigh, letting go of Taylor, but she walks right behind me as I make my way over to the door and pull on the chain again to lift it.

"Hey, man." Mark says as he looks past me. His eyes widen when he takes in what damage he can see. "Ian's car is just as bad."

I shake my head. "Damn it."

"Come on, I heard a meeting's being called right now."

"Alright. Let's go." I say as I pull Taylor along with me, and I shut the garage door so we can follow Mark to the middle of the track where everyone is slowly gathering in the middle of the roadway.

Informant

I'm hidden in a corner of the track near the press box where no one can see me, but I have the perfect view of the pit area. I have been watching Bryan and Ian since they got back. Watching their reactions to their cars being destroyed, and from what I'm seeing, Desmond is gonna be pissed.

Just as that thought hits me, my phone begins to ring. I answer it without even saying hello.

"So, how did they take our little calling card?"

"They both are pissed, but not going off the handle like the other guys are." I say the truth of the words leaving a bad taste in my mouth.

"Damn it, J! You said this would get them riled up!" Desmond shouts. "I guess I'm gonna have to step it up a notch and put some fear in these fuckers." He adds, his voice taking on more of his native Mexican lilt than before.

"What do you mean, more fear?" I ask.

"Nothing you need to know about. Just make sure you keep me updated on the repair progress."

"You give me your word that nothing will happen to my girl. That's the only reason I'm even helping your crazy ass." I snap.

"Cuidado como me hablas o la próxima ves te caerás, pinche pendejo. Now be a good little doggie and keep bringing me info, J." Desmond says and hangs up the phone.

Watch how you talk to me or you're the next to fall, fucking dumbass. I play his words over in my head as I shove my phone back in the pocket of my jeans with an aggravated growl, hating he has this power over me, but I can't help it. I have to keep her safe.

Chapter Twenty-Seven

Taylor

Mark leads us to the middle of the track where Ian, Anna, Nick, and Roxie are already waiting for us to join the meeting that Josh called.

I find it a bit odd when Josh and Morgan aren't there to greet us, but I see him and his girl come from what must be Ian's garage a moment later. Josh shakes his head in frustration while running his hand through his hair as Morgan caresses his arm, like she's consoling him, before glancing over his shoulder when she sees James and Christy appear from behind a garage at the end.

"Josh was inspecting my car to see the damage." Ian offers, his voice rough and low with anger.

"How is the damage?" Bryan asks.

"Bad enough. Slashed tires, broken windshield, and driver's side window. I wish they would have spray-painted my car like they did with yours. The bastards keyed mine on both sides."

"Damn man. I'm sorry." Mark says while grabbing at the back of his neck and glancing over at Bryan.

I know they both are eager to discuss this more in the privacy of our apartments, but we aren't leaving for a few more minutes, so I grab onto

Bryan's arm and I feel the tension leave his muscles just a fraction and he smiles down at me, but it doesn't reach his eyes.

Josh finally approaches us, and all heads turn in his direction. "Thank you for joining me this evening, team. I wish it was under better circumstances, but you all know what we found tonight. Bryan's and Ian's cars were vandalized this evening by that shitbag, Desmond. I want us to work as a team and get these cars back on the track as fast as possible. This is his plan, to get them out of their groove and strike when they aren't prepared."

Bryan pokes my leg and in sign language says, *"Wow, he had the same thought we did about the repairs."*

I nod my head in agreement.

"Last I checked, we had everything except for the glass work we need, but they can be easily replaced at the glass shop down the road. We have the paint, tires, and other parts to take care of the other issues. Do I hear of any opposed to helping out?" Josh asks.

After a few moments of silence, he takes Morgan's hand and waves us off.

"Try to have a good night, team. I believe in us, and I refuse to lose more members in the same month. Believe me, I want this fucker taken down just as much as you all do, but we need to do it at the right time," Josh says.

I watch in silence as he receives nods of understanding from some while others go up to him to give him a handshake and a quick hug, followed by a slap on the shoulder. I can tell from the emotion flickering on his face that he wants to go after Desmond even more than Bryan does right now. This group is Josh's family, and Desmond is slowly taking them out two at a time.

We make our way back to my Mustang and Mark's Challenger and meet out front of our apartments with the unspoken thought of going over to Lincoln's and Temperance's place to tell them what happened. Mark knocks on the door and after a few beats, Lincoln answers and lets us in without a word.

"What happened? I can tell something big went down today." Lincoln asks while looking from Mark to Bryan, searching for answers.

"You can say that." I sigh as I walk in behind the guys and sit down on the loveseat while Lexi takes an armchair. Mark perches himself beside her while draping his arm around her shoulders.

I pat the space beside me on the loveseat, silently asking Bryan to sit by me, but he doesn't sit down. Instead, he begins to pace, running his hand through his hair, and just as he opens his mouth to explain what happened tonight, Sophie comes into the living room and sits by her mother on the couch. Bryan just stares at her, making him pause his pacing for a moment.

She looks between him and then to her parents. "Sorry, I can go if you don't want me to hear this." She says and begins to stand from the couch.

Bryan shakes his head. "No, it's okay. You should know this as well." He says, giving her a small smile before he starts pacing back and forth in front of the coffee table as he recounts what happened this evening.

"My car and another driver's, Ian, were vandalized tonight by Desmond. He's chosen both of us as his next racers." Bryan says while running his hand through his hair again, then pulling on the strands at the nape of his neck. "We just don't know who will be the first one to go up against him."

We are quiet for a moment, letting the information sink in again. I catch Lincoln and Temperence glancing at one another before Linc stands to go over to Bryan, once again stopping his erratic pacing.

"Hey Bryan, you need to calm down." Linc says as he places a hand on Bryan's shoulder. "You will be no good to anyone if you have a mind that's getting away from you, son."

Bryan's head whips up to meet Linc's gaze. "I'm not your son," He snaps, anger flaring in his green eyes. "You need to stop worrying about me and my team and be the lead agents we need you to be. Get whatever team you need to have on standby to make the arrest when this son of a bitch makes his move."

Lincoln takes a moment to compose himself at Bryan's backlash. He backs away a few steps before saying, "I am aware that you are not my son. If you were, I'll be honest, you'd be picking up your teeth off the floor right about now."

Bryan's growl of frustration makes me stand, but Mark gets to him first. Placing his palm flat against Bryan's chest, he shoves him back a few steps. "He's right, man. That was out of line. Linc didn't mean anything by what he said."

Lexi touches my leg to get my attention. I look down at her, noticing her hands are moving.

"He's just scared out of his mind of Desmond getting his hands on you."

I nod and look back to Bryan, but before I can even say anything to him, my phone pings with an unknown number.

> **Unknown:** You want trackers on the phones maybe?

I glance over to Sophie, and she gives me a quick smile, letting me know the message was from her. I nod my head discretely to her while updating her contact in my phone.

> **Sophie:** Give me until tomorrow. I'll bring them by while the guys and my parents are out.

I show Lexi my phone, and she smiles as she quickly signs. *"Oh, she's good."*

"Come on, guys." Mark says as he continues to push Bryan towards the door. "Nothing is going to change tonight, and we aren't getting anywhere with the current mindset. Let's regroup tomorrow with *clear minds.*" He throws that last bit at Bryan, who rolls his eyes and storms out the front door, and Mark follows behind his friend.

I give Sophie another subtle nod before turning my attention back to Linc and Tempe.

"I'm sorry about his behavior tonight. He's usually not this—" I begin, but Temperance cuts me off.

"Temperamental?" She smiles knowingly. "I have been on the same side you are now. We both have overprotective men in our lives." Linc walks over to stand beside the couch, and she takes his hand in her own while giving it a quick squeeze. "You should have seen Linc when I was pregnant with Soph. He was a *bear*." She adds with a laugh.

"I had two girls to protect." Linc grumbles.

"And exhibit number one." Temperance chuckles while poking at her husband's stomach. "Go to him and remind him that you are safe and he has the means to protect you. I have a feeling that will help him most."

She glances up at Linc, and he leans in to kiss her, like an unspoken knowledge of how they got over their own issues passing between them in that quick kiss.

"Thank you. Good night." I say as I get up off the couch and follow Lexi out the door.

As we walk across the street, Mark is standing on the stoop to his apartment, but I notice that Bryan is nowhere in sight.

"Where did he go?" I direct my question to Mark.

"He's in your all's place. You wanna crash here and let him blow off some steam?"

I give him a pointed glare. "How is me staying away going to help anything?"

Mark puts his hands up in surrender. "Okay, okay. Just text me if you need me to come over and kick his ass if he's being an asshole to you."

"I doubt that, but I'll keep that in mind." I give my two friends a small wave. "Good night."

I open the front door, and I make sure it's locked behind me before I venture deeper into the apartment. I notice the lights are on in the bedroom, so I make my way to the door and slowly push it open, thinking that maybe Bryan would be lying on the bed, but I find the mattress is empty.

Before I can call out his name, I hear the shower turn on and the glass door close a moment later. I quietly walk over to the bathroom door and peek inside, making sure to keep my eyes looking toward the ceiling in case I see him naked, but something stops me.

I need to get him out of his head like he did with me not so long ago.

So, without much thought, I pull my tank over my head, push my shorts and panties down, and walk over to the shower door, pulling it open without warning.

Bryan's head whips over to the sound, and his eyes shine with confusion for a moment before he takes in my naked body from head to foot and back again. I keep my gaze locked on his face, not allowing myself the same perusal of his own body. Not yet, at least.

"Taylor." His voice is almost a plea, but I don't even think he knows what he's asking for.

In my peripheral vision, I notice a bench built into the shower stall. I take a step toward him, pushing my hand against his water-slicked chest.

"Sit." I command.

"Taylor." He says again, this time his tone is almost one of denial.

"I said sit down, Bryan." I say, my voice not giving him any room for argument.

He sits and I step into the shower with him, angling the shower head where the stream of warm water will hit our feet.

"Tay, I'm sorry I don't have it in me to pleasure—"

I cut him off. "Who said this has anything to do with *my* pleasure?"

I kneel before him, and his eyes widen in shock as his whole body stiffens before me, and I chuckle.

"What, you don't like me on my knees for you?" I ask with a sly smile.

His body relaxes for a moment. "I just didn't expect this with every-thing that happened tonight."

"Well." I drawl, finally letting my eyes trail over the expanse of his body and taking in the appearance of his manhood for the first time.

And I swallow hard at the sight of him.

I have a feeling he's not at his full potential and yet, even with this semi-hard on, he'd rock my world.

"Annie." Bryan groans, and this reminds me of how I felt when he saw me bare for the first time, and I can't help the smirk that plays on my lips at his plea.

"Not fun, is it? To be looked at but not touched."

"I'm beginning to rethink my earlier words of not pleasuring you. I could edge you to the brink of insanity."

"Oh, like this?"

I quickly snap my hand out, gripping him at the base of his shaft. He sharply sucks in a breath between his teeth as his hips lift off the built-in shower bench in response, but I move with him; not letting my grip cause him any friction.

"Uh-uh, I get to pleasure you, not the other way around. Now, you're going to be a good boy and sit there."

I push my knees against his ankles to keep him from being able to pivot his hips against my hand.

Slowly, I glide my hand up the length of him, letting the nail of my middle finger gently scrape against the vein on the underside of his erection. With that movement, I'm rewarded with a sound that I have never heard Bryan make. It's a mix of a groan, a growl, and a hiss, and I love it. Hearing him make that sound and knowing that I am the one to drag it out of him sends a fire through my veins that makes me feel so powerful.

I look up at him so I can see his expression, and my body stills at the sight.

His chest heaves as each breath comes out in harsh, pleasure-filled pants. His head is tilted back against the tiled shower stall, while his Adam's apple bobs with each swallow and moan from his throat. I smile up at him even though he's not looking at me, but I can't help the movement my lips make all the same.

Without taking my eyes from his face, I wrap my hand around his length, my thumb teasing his crown and a breathy laugh that escapes his chest as he finally lifts his head to look at me.

"Taylor. Shit. You're gonna kill me tonight." He says as he runs his still-damp hand through his hair, making some strands gather together with the moisture.

"Well, that's not the plan." I chuckle. "I have something different in mind."

I don't give him the chance to ask what my plans are, because come on, it seems pretty obvious. I slowly glide my hand back down his length, and his head tilts back again. When I notice this, I give him a quick squeeze at the base of his shaft.

"Keep your eyes on me." I command.

He lifts his head, the lazy smile that I know and love playing on his lips.

"That's better." I say. "I want you to watch as I make you come undone."

"Fuck. I love you in control like this," Bryan whispers, his eyes closing for a moment. I dig my nails into his shaft, and they fly back open.

I give him a sly smile of approval and begin to pull and tug at him in long, slow pumps from base to tip, once, twice, three times. His growls and grunts at my touch urges me to grip him harder, make my passes faster. When a bead of liquid begins to form at the tip, I know he's just about there.

I flick my thumb over his slit, spreading the bead of pre-cum over his crown. "You are beautiful, handsome, and mine." I growl the last part and give him one final tug.

"Taylor. I'm gonna—" He breathes out as his head falls back against the shower stall again with a solid thud and his eyes close like he's trying to compose himself, denying his release.

His muscles are strung tight throughout his body, and his erection is so hard that I'm sure it's painful, but he relishes the feeling of it. I move my knees from his ankles, and his hips instantly begin to thrust into my hand, searching for the much needed friction his body is begging for.

I lean forward and whisper close to his ear, "Come for me, Bryan."

As soon as the words are out of my mouth, his release barrels out of him. He mutters curses under his breath, and I continue to stroke him through his orgasm, coaxing it to last longer and bring him even more pleasure.

When Bryan finally opens his eyes and they focus on my body, the light green color turns molten with primal desire. "I don't know what's hotter. The orgasm you just pulled out of me or the way you look right now." He says, his voice deep and breathless.

I look down, and the right side of my body, the side that is not under the water, is coated with the mess I made of him. I look back up at him, a teasing smile lifting the corner of my mouth as I gather a dollop of his release onto my index finger and I inspect it for a moment. His eyes never leave mine, and I can see the lines of his body go rigid, wondering what I'm going to do.

I lower my finger, letting my eyes travel with the movement, but I can still see he's already half hard again with anticipation, and when I swirl my index finger over my right nipple, Bryan groans.

"Did I mention you're gonna kill me tonight?"

"Maybe that was my plan." I say slyly as I continue to circle my pebbled bud, allowing my head to tip back as the sensation travels right to my core.

"Come here." Bryan growls possessively as he goes to grab my hips.

"No. Tonight was for you." I say as I push against his chest.

"No. Tonight is for *us*." He says as he grips my hips, pulling me onto his thigh and crushing his lips to mine.

His rough hand trails up my side to cup the same breast I coated his release with, and I suck in a breath as his thumb toys with my nipple.

"I love you, Taylor." He whispers into my neck. "I'm so sorry I was such an asshole tonight."

I bend my head to the side, allowing him more access to my neck. "That's why I needed you to get out of your head for a while."

"Thank you." He says as he kisses me again, his tongue skimming the seam of my lips, and I let him in. Let his touch devour me.

He leans back against the wall, pulling me up onto my knees, and his hand travels from my breast, down my stomach and ends just at the apex of my thighs.

"Time to repay the favor, Baby."

That's all the warning I get before he dips two fingers inside me. My head falls back on a cry as he starts to tease the spot that makes me see stars, and I can't help but rock my hips into his hand. Trying to find more friction, drive his touch deeper.

"That's it, Baby." Bryan praises.

Before I can let the thought get away from me, I reach down, gripping his length again.

Good lord, how can he be hard again already?

"Taylor." Bryan hisses.

"Let's come together." I pant.

Bryan chuckles darkly as he shakes his head. "Alright, but you better keep up."

He begins to pump his fingers in and out. In and out and when the sensation starts to feel too good, I forget to stroke him.

"Taylor." He sings my name on a pant.

I shake my head as I run my hand over his length again. It's rocky at first. If one of us pauses our ministration when the sensation gets too much, too distracting, we urge each other back on track until we finally get a rhythm, building one another up and up and up until we both fall over into our pleasure with shouts and cries of our names for the final time tonight.

As he tries to catch his breath, Bryan's forehead falls to mine a moment before he speaks, like he's trying to remember how to form sentences; or it could be just me that's having that issue.

"That was amazing, Taylor. Now, since we got *dirty,* " He smirks. "Let's get cleaned up."

When we finally venture out of the bathroom—after we took turns washing each other, which, as hot as it was, didn't lead to anything more tonight—we head into the bedroom. I go to the dresser and pull one of Bryan's shirts over my head while he pulls on a pair of boxers. Once we lie down, he pulls me close to his chest, his arms wrapped tightly around my shoulders. He's quiet for a minute, and I know something I don't want to hear is going to come out of his mouth.

"Baby, I will do everything I can to win in the race against this bastard. But in the event I don't—"

"No," I cut him off. "There will be no 'in the event' of nothing, Bryan Alexander. You will win, or we will bust him before the race happens."

"But you know me, and I try to plan for everything, Taylor Allison. Please give Mark, Lexi, Lincoln, and Temperance time to get to you and get you out if it's needed." Bryan says softly.

When he says my first and middle name, he is either angry at me or scared for me, and I absolutely know it's the latter right now. I take his hand in mine, bring it to my lips and gently kiss his knuckles before looking him in the eyes.

"Alright, Babe." I say, sounding a little defeated at the thought of what would need to happen for me to be taken by that creep.

This makes me want to put trackers on the phones as soon as possible, and I hope Sophie can make it over here tomorrow before I have to go down to the track in the morning.

Chapter Twenty-Eight

Taylor

The next morning, Bryan gets dressed just as we hear the engine of Mark's Challenger roar to life out front, and the sound of a honking horn follows a moment later. Bryan kisses me soundly on the lips before he makes his way toward the door.

He pauses with his hand on the doorknob and looks back over his shoulder at me with a smile on his lips. "You still coming by to help me out with the repairs today?"

"Of course. I'll be there in a bit." I say while taking a sip of my coffee.

"Alright. See ya soon. Love you, Annie," Bryan says as he walks out the door.

I head over to the main front window, and I watch as Bryan gets in the passenger seat, the smile still playing on his lips. Mark must say something to him that's well, certifiably Mark in Gutterville, because Bryan shakes his head before smacking his friend on the chest and motioning for him to drive.

Once they are out of sight, I turn back to the kitchen to put my empty coffee cup in the dishwasher so I can get ready and wait for Lexi and, hopefully, Sophie to come over.

After about thirty minutes, my front door opens, and I see both Lexi and Soph walk in with bright smiles on their faces.

"Mornin' Tay." Lexi greets.

"Hi. How are you two?" I ask.

 Lexi smiles and nods her head, and I take it that she's good.

Sophie takes a seat on the loveseat and gives me a quick grin as she says, "I'm good. I would have been over sooner, but I had to wait for my parents to leave before I came over here."

"I don't want you getting in trouble, Soph." I say.

She shakes her head. "It's okay. They'll understand, eventually. Besides, if I am ever going to do this on my own or with a team, I have to trust that my own creations will work."

"It's not all fun and games." Lexi says while taking a seat next to her, and I take one of the armchairs next to Sophie. "It's dangerous, as I'm sure you've heard from the few meetings we've had with your parents."

"I know. I've listened in more than they think I have. So I know some of the crazy shit that can happen on cases." She says as pulls a small black box from her purse and sets it on the coffee table. "I just can't wait until I turn eighteen. Then I can actually help them with cases and not hide like this."

I nod my understanding. "So, what have you brought us?" I ask, pointing to the black box.

"This is my tracking system. If you go near someone's phone with this," She holds up the black box, and it looks like a cell phone. I notice it even has a responsive screen on it too to make the simulation realistic. She waves the device over my phone, and I hear a quick beep come from the tablet that Sophie is now holding in her hand. "And now we have your cell pinged with an active tracker. It bounces off the closest cell tower, and then I can further track the signal based on that tower's location. Plus, I made it to where it's invisible to all jammers."

"So all we need to do is get close to someone's phone, and it will pick up on the device and add it to that tracking software?" Lexi asks.

"Yup," Sophie says, then her voice takes on a worried tone. "I did it so I can keep track of Mom and Dad." She says solemnly. "I almost lost them one year, and I swore that I would know where they are at all times, and if I thought something was going on, I would be able to get them help. So far, nothing like that has happened since then, but still, I want to know that I am there to help if they need me."

"Oh, Sophie, I never knew. I understand your fear. I had that happen to me personally." I say, then I tell her the short version of Bryan's gunshot wound, and she's shocked.

"Wow. That is my exact fear. That something will happen to my parents, and I would never know." Sophie says. "I'm really glad that I came up with this now. Thank you, Taylor."

"No problem. I can tell you this much, this career is not for the faint of heart. You have to be strong-willed and have complete trust in your partners or group. I trust my partners and friends with my life." I say while looking at Lexi.

"I can see that between you all. Makes me believe that I could find someone like that for me." Sophie says. "Anyway, I'll let the experts get back to it."

"Hey, if we need to track someone, you want in on the rescue?" Lexi asks, and she looks at me for my thoughts.

"Yeah. You want to help us out if we need to rescue one of these girls?" I ask her.

"Are you kidding? I'd be happy to!" Sophie says with a smile on her face.

"Keep your phone on you at all times, then. We may need you at a moment's notice." I say.

Sophie nods her head eagerly as she stands, heading out the front door and rushing back over to her parents' apartment.

"Wow, she's gonna be a good agent, I can tell." I say with a small smile on my face at her eagerness.

"Yeah, she reminds me of you once you got your head in the game with our very first mission." Lexi says.

"Oh, the one that I almost completely blew our cover on?" I ask with a skeptical look on my face.

"Yeah, okay. Bad comparison there."

Once we make our way down to the track, we slowly go about adding all the girls' phones to Sophie's program. By mid-afternoon, after I'm satisfied that we can track the girls whenever the creep of the century shows up and rescue them, I go over to help Bryan with repairs on his Camaro.

When I walk toward his garage bay, I see the car is up on the hydraulic lift, high enough where he can walk under it without bending over. Parts that look like they belong to the headlight that was broken by the baseball bat are lying on the ground in a messy heap.

I hear the sound of an impact wrench echo in the space, and I see a flash of Bryan's skin followed by a curse.

"Come out, you damn stubborn bolt."

I chuckle as I approach the driver's side, making sure to stay far enough away that I'm not going to be under the vehicle.

As I hear the tool work to get the bolt out of the frame of the fender, I notice Bryan is shirtless. Beads of sweat run down his back and chest from the heat created in the small garage, and his skin is red in a few places—the center of his chest and the tops of his shoulders—where the heat pours out of his body.

I take a clean rag off a red toolbox and take it over to the small sink in the corner, soaking it in cool water. I then walk up behind him and place the rag on his neck while bringing my mouth close to his ear.

"You should watch out in this Florida sun; you'll burn to a crisp." I whisper.

"Well, I'd really be a hot agent then, wouldn't I?" Bryan whispers back.

"Shhh, do you want them to hear you?" I ask somewhat surprised that he would say that in the open like this.

"Nah, they have too much on their minds right now. But thank you for the cool off though, Babe," Bryan says.

"You infuriate me to no end, you know that?" I ask.

"If I didn't, you'd think something was wrong."

"I guess, but still, be careful, okay?" I ask.

"Always, Babe. Hey, you wanna hand me that ratchet set on the toolbox?" Bryan asks.

I look over at the black and blue Craftsman tool chest and I pick up the ratchet and hand it to Bryan.

"Thank you, Annie." Bryan says.

I take in the surprisingly calm and focused look on his face, and I smile a little. "You look so comfortable doing this."

"Doing what? Working on cars?" Bryan asks and then shrugs his left shoulder. "I've done this for as long as I can remember. Gramps taught me a lot, and I've even learned from Mark, too. Plus, it helps when you're out on the 'road' to be able to know how to fix things in a pinch." Bryan says, making air quotes around the word road for my benefit of not saying 'while on a case.'

"True. I understand that. Now, what else can I help with?" I ask, and we get to work on the Camaro for the rest of the day.

Chapter Twenty-Nine

Bryan

By the next afternoon, I finish with the repairs on my vehicle. Mark helped me with replacing the tires and repainting my driver's side door. While the paint dried, Josh installed the windshield that he was able to get from the glass shop down the road.

I asked Ian if he needed any help, but he, along with James and Nick, were taking care of his car.

Once we got everything in order with our vehicles, we took them for a quick lap around the track to make sure the alignment felt good and to ensure the seal was airtight around the newly installed glass.

As we were testing our cars, Josh personally installed two cameras in our garages and set up the feed to be live on our individual phones as well as his own. Which I'm glad for his forethought. If someone messes with my car again, I'm gonna beat the shit out of them.

I don't care if this is really my car or not; it's the fact of someone fucking with something I'm using, and I don't like that. It's like that time with Phil all over again when he planted that kill switch in my F150 when I took Taylor out on our first date.

After I park the Camaro in the garage and make sure I see the red light showing the camera is online, I pull the door down and make my way over to the small huddle that's forming in the middle of the track.

I spot Taylor with Lexi, and the girls, and I make my way over to her. She's been such a big help since yesterday. She even helped me install the new headlight assembly, and when I needed to align my new tires, she helped me with the calibration machine.

I walk over to her, pull her into my side, and kiss the top of her head. "Thank you for all your help, Baby."

"Anytime, Bullet." She says as she stands on her tiptoes, brushing her lips against mine.

"Eyes forward, guys." Mark whispers as he walks in behind Lexi, pulling her back into his chest while his eyes dart over to Josh, who is now standing in the middle of the group.

I roll my eyes at my brother from another mother, but I pull Taylor close to my body, resting my chin on her shoulder while wrapping my arms around her stomach and her hands rest on top of mine.

"I wanted to start off by saying this was a great restoration effort for everyone. I loved seeing everyone get together, even the ladies, and work on getting these cars back on track. Thank you for all your hard work yesterday and today. Secondly, back to the main topic at hand. We don't know when the day will be, and we don't know who will be first. Bryan. Ian. I need you both on high alert and on your game. No matter how old or new you are, you both are a part of my team. I already lost two members; I'm not gonna lose another four." Josh says with determination in his voice.

Josh dismisses everyone, and I am the first one to walk off the track. I keep Taylor close to my side, our fingers interlaced as we head toward her Mustang. I open the passenger door for her to get in, and I quickly round the car so I can get behind the wheel.

We drive in silence to our apartment, and as soon as I park in our designated space, Mark pulls in beside us. I get out of the driver's seat to help Taylor to her feet, and when I look over her shoulder towards Linc and Tempe's apartment, I grimace.

"I'll be right back."

"Where are you going?" Taylor asks.

"Across the street. I need to apologize to Lincoln."

"I'll go with you."

"No, Babe. It's okay. I'll be quick." I tell her as I give her a kiss on the forehead.

She nods, and I watch as she goes inside, waiting for the lock to click into place.

I glance at Mark, and he gives me a firm nod, telling me he'll keep an ear on Taylor until I get back.

Making my way across the street, I knock on Linc's and Tempe's apartment door and wait. When the door opens, Sophie is standing in the doorway, and I give her a small smile.

"Bryan, hi. Everyone okay?"

"Oh, yeah. Everyone's fine. I just wanted to talk to your dad real quick." I say as I drag my hand over the base of my neck. "I need to apologize to him for being an asshole the other day."

"Oh yeah. He's on the phone with someone." Sophie smiles as she steps aside to let me in. "You know, you're just like my dad at times." She says. "He gets a little hot-headed and goes off too."

I chuckle. "Yeah, I get that from my grandpa. He can be hot-headed, and it doesn't help matters that he's an Army Vet either. But he's a good guy, and he's taught me a lot growing up."

"You look up to your grandpa, I can tell." Sophie says.

"Yeah. I mean, he and my grandmother raised me when my parents died. So they're like my mom and dad."

Sophie is quiet for a minute, and all I hear is the muffled voice of Linc on the phone coming from the back room. I begin to think that I'll just come back when he's free, but Sophie turns her head to look at me, and the expression on her face hurts something in me that I can't place.

"Can you miss someone you never met?"

"I'm sure you could. I mean, I don't remember my parents much at all, but I do miss them. Why do you ask?"

"It's just. I've never met my own grandparents, and I was supposed to have a big brother around your age. So, I often wonder how I can miss someone I never even got the chance to know."

I offer her a sad smile. "It's because you knew they existed at one point in time. It's normal to feel like you're missing out on something, even if you didn't get the opportunity to know them."

I glance up, and I notice Temperance standing in the kitchen with tears gathering in her eyes. She wipes them away when she notices me staring at her.

I clear my throat, suddenly feeling awkward for her listening in on me and her daughter.

"I, uh, I wanted to talk to you and Linc." I begin. "Is he off the phone yet?"

"Oh yeah. Let me get him." She says as she sniffles once and heads back the hallway.

"Thanks for talking with me, Bry." Sophie says as she leans in to give me a quick hug before bounding off to what I assume is her bedroom across the hall from the living room.

I find myself staring off in the direction she went and wondering why I have this odd sensation in my chest. Like I'm almost happy that I was able to help her understand something that no one else but me can comprehend.

Lincoln and Temperence come into the living room a few minutes later, but neither of them speak. Linc's arms are crossed over his chest, daring me to say something out of turn. I take a breath and stand before him, squaring my shoulder like Gramps has taught me over the years.

"Lincoln, I wanted to come over and apologize to you. I was a complete asshole the other night, and you didn't deserve my backlash. You were only trying to help me, and I took it personally."

"It's alright, s–" He pauses, but I give him a nod, letting him know to finish the sentence. "It's alright, son. I know emotions are high right now, and I shouldn't have responded the way I did, either."

I chuckle. "It's all good. Honestly, if my grandfather had heard me the other night, he would have told you to actually knock my teeth out, or he would have done it for you."

Lincoln smiles like he's reliving a fond memory, and I find myself smiling along with him.

"I knew someone like that too once upon a time." Linc says as he extends his hand to me. "We are good, Bryan. You can be candid with us, but just mind your tongue. Agreed?"

"Yes, sir." I say as I give his hand a firm shake.

"Good. Now get over to your girlfriend and let us know if anything changes."

"Good night, Bryan." Temperance says with a small wave.

I give her a nod and a friendly smile before I walk out their front door.

Chapter Thirty

Taylor

Two days have passed since Bryan and Ian fixed their cars, and it's been nothing but normal racing days and just hanging out while waiting for the other shoe to drop. When I arrive at the track this morning, Josh and Mark were running a race, and I caught the tail end of it where Mark won the lap by a full car length.

Lexi cheers before giving Morgan a sympathetic look. She waves Lexi off like it's all in good fun as she walks over to Josh, who is pulling his car into the pit area.

I approach my friend, and she's still beaming at Mark's win.

"You like watching him race more and more, don't you?" I ask with a smile.

"It might be growing on me," Lexi jests as she watches Mark drive a victory lap around the track before pulling into the pit area.

"There is nothing hotter than a man racing in a good-lookin' car." Christy says as she waves her hand over her face.

"Totally." I laugh as I hear the familiar sound of Bryan's Camaro drive up from the pit lane and onto the starting line of the track.

"Yo!" James calls out breathlessly. "Girls, get outta here!"

Then we all hear the sound of engines roaring in the distance. At least four of them, and they are coming in hot.

Bryan and Mark rush over to us while Josh, James and Nick gather at the entrance of the track, like their bodies will keep Desmond from entering.

"Get up in the press box and stay together." Bryan says, his voice pleading and serious at the same time.

"Yeah, we know." I say, and I quickly grab his hand as Morgan opens the door to the staircase that leads up to the press box. "Be careful. I love you." I pull him in and kiss his lips while Lexi does the same with Mark.

"Go." Mark barks his order, and we follow the others, making sure no one is left behind before shutting the door behind us.

I spot Anna already standing near the window looking down at the track, and I go over to stand beside her.

She gives me a watery smile, but she's not as jumpy as the first girl we lost. She knows better than to make it easy for Desmond to kill her. I can see it in her eyes; there's a fire in there, and she will fight tooth and nail to get away.

"Everything will be okay. Just wait." I say as Lexi leans into my right side while Morgan leans into Anna's left.

Bryan

Once I'm satisfied that the girls are safe in the press box, Mark and I march over to the main section of the track, and we stand by my car. I notice that Ian has pulled his GTR beside mine and is leaning against the trunk of the vehicle, arms folded over his chest and his jaw is so tense that I swear it would crack if it wasn't skin and bone.

We begin to hear the slimy assholes chant, 'who will it be?' over and over as they drive onto the track like they own the damn place.

I look over to Ian, and he's clenching and unclenching his fists, and I know their chants are getting under his skin.

"Hey man, don't let them get to you."

"I'm fine, Bryan." Ian begins then yells over the engines and the chanting men, "I've seen this shit before, and it just makes them look like even bigger assholes!"

Desmond's Charger pulls up a heartbeat later, and he barely puts the transmission into park before he gets out and stalks toward the two of us.

"Oh, I'm gonna have fun with you first." Desmond says while looking Ian up and down in approval. "I'll come for you another time, Slammer." He adds while looking over at me with a scowl.

"Come at me, you son of a bitch." Ian snaps, his voice full of hatred, and I realize it's to get Desmod's attention on him and away from me.

I walk backward towards my car. I don't want to turn my back on this asshole until I have to. Once I'm at my driver's door, I drop inside and I turn my engine over, pulling my car off the track so he can take my place.

When I approach the guys that are huddled near a section of bleachers, I hear Josh say, "Ian's a good driver. I just hope it will be enough to stop this fucker."

"It will be." Mark growls as he glances over at me.

James then walks out between the two cars with the checkered flag to begin the race. Just like the last time, the potential victim is in the lead, but unlike the last driver, Ian keeps Desmond just to the end of his driver's door, not letting him get behind him so Desmond can't perform his deadly pit move.

"You got this, Ian." I say, even though he can't hear me.

Ian keeps this up until the third turn, and just when I think he's going to actually win, Desmond downshifts, and my stomach drops.

"No!" I can't help but scream, and I'm moving before the wreck even happens. I know Mark is on my heels, along with Josh and the others.

Desmond moves in behind Ian and shoves him off the track, making his vehicle flip at least five times before it comes to a skidding stop on the roof. The creaking, cracking, and snapping of metal and glass filling the air around us.

"Fuck! No!" Josh screams.

Taylor

After I see that Ian was chosen as the racer, my heart is only a little lighter that it's not Bryan going up against him, but worry settles in for Ian and Anna.

As I watch the race along with Anna, she beams at how Ian's holding his own and even I think he's going to win, but when I notice Bryan start to run towards the track, we all watch in slow motion as Desmond does his dreaded pit move and causes a brutal crash for Ian that I can only hope he survives.

"No!" Anna screams, but she doesn't move from her spot.

I take that moment to grab her shoulders, forcing her attention on me.

"Anna. Please don't fight him. Give me and my friends a chance to find you."

She looks at me with tears and confusion in her eyes, and I give her what I hope seems like a determined smile.

"Trust me, okay?"

She nods her head before we hear Desmond's voice screaming through the glass of the press box.

"Where's my new bitch!?"

"Oh, I hope a car falls from a lift on that fucker like that house did on the Wicked Witch of the West." Morgan scoffs.

Anna walks down the stairs of the press box, and we all quietly follow her, gathering at the last step; an unspoken agreement among us to watch and listen to what happens, with nothing to block the sound.

She walks over to Desmond, and he grabs her by the back of the neck in such a rough way that she can't help but cry out at his touch.

"Oh, yeah." He gives Anna a dark, sadistic once over and his smile is pure evil. "You're going to be the best toy to play with, Baby. Your screams sound so sweet." Desmond turns to his group of thugs. "Let's go, boys. We have a new one to break in."

My stomach roils at his words and the crass way each of the four guys is touching Anna's body. One gripping her ass. Another fondles her breasts while Desmond drags his tongue possessively, almost like ownership over her neck, but Anna keeps walking with them.

Before she gets in Desmond's car, she glances quickly over her shoulder and we lock eyes for a heartbeat before he shoves her into the passenger side, shutting the door so hard I'm shocked the glass doesn't shatter.

"Until next time!" Desmond has the audacity to bow like he's just put on a stellar performance before he and his thugs drive off.

As soon as Josh pulls the gate and locks it, my eyes glance over at the mutilated vehicle in the center of the track, and something grabs my attention. Once I figure out what it is, I spring into action, heading toward the wreckage of Ian's car.

I turn to Lexi and whisper, "Get Sophie and wait for me at the entrance of the track." Then I give her the cover she needs to slip away as I yell, "Come on! Let's get him out!"

"He's gone!" Josh screams.

"No, he's not!"

"What?" A chorus of voices echo around me all at once.

Bryan meets me at the front of the vehicle, where the windshield is shattered, giving us total access to the interior.

"Ian?" I call out.

A heartbeat passes, and I hear a weak, wet cough.

"Help us get him out!" I scream.

Mark, Josh and James all gather around the wreckage and Bryan looks over them for a moment, then he's waving his hands toward them.

"Your shirts. Take them off. Put them over the glass on the car and the ground. Mark, you and I pull him out."

Mark and Bryan pull Ian out, and I instantly take in his appearance. He's bloody, pale, and his lips are turning blue. I put my ear to his chest, and I can hear that his right lung has collapsed.

"I need a knife, some kind of tubing, and a closed glass bottle with a hole cut into the lid and water in the bottom. Now!"

Josh and Mark rush off to gather the equipment I need as Bryan grabs a piece of glass to rip Ian's shirt down the middle so I can have full access to his chest.

As I take another quick glance over Ian's body, I notice his arm is at an odd angle. But his broken arm is secondary to his lungs. If he can't breathe and get oxygen to his organs, it's no use to reset his arm.

Josh and Mark return a few moments later. Josh hands me the hilt of a knife after he's doused with some kind of bronze liquor, whiskey from the smell, to sterilize the blade. Mark then shoves one end of a plastic tube into a hole that was cut into the cap of another large liquor bottle before placing it down on the ground, and I notice the water sloshing around in the bottom.

"Thanks, you two. You did a great job." I say as Mark pulls out a pair of gloves from his back pocket and hands them to me.

After I snap them on, I hold my hands out, silently ordering Josh to pour some of the remaining liquor on my hands to sterilize them.

"Give the rest to Ian. He's gonna need it." I order as I grip the knife in my hands.

I set my fingers along Ian's fourth and fifth rib so I can slice into his skin and slip the tubing into his chest cavity. I pause and glance up at him for a split second.

"Ian, this is gonna hurt like a bitch, but you need to stay still." I warn.

"Someone needs…to save Anna." He rasps. "Forget about me."

"We're gonna work on that." I whisper to him as I slide the knife against his skin.

Ian tenses as pain flares across his nerve endings, but his scream dies in his chest since he can't get enough air to make the sound. Once I know I'm in where I need to be, I grab the tubing and push it inside his chest cavity. I wait a moment, silently pleading for him to take a full breath.

Another heartbeat passes.

Did I do this correctly? This is the first time I've done this. Did I mess up?

Then he finally takes a breath, then another, and another. Color begins to come back to his lips as he gets the oxygen his body desperately needs.

As I was working, apparently Bryan called an ambulance because I hear the sirens blaring from down the road.

"You're gonna be okay, Ian. And so is Anna." I promise.

When the ambulance arrives and the EMTs are loading Ian onto the gurney, I use the chaos around me to slip towards the main gate where I see Lexi's Lancer waiting for me.

Chapter Thirty-One

Taylor

"I have Anna's phone pinging off an old department store near the loading docks." Sophie says as I open the passenger door of Lexi's Lancer and slip inside.

"You know we are gonna catch hell for this, right?" Lexi says as she looks at Sophie's tablet for directions to Anna's location.

"We'll ask for forgiveness later, after we save this poor girl's life." I say.

"Is he—" Lexi begins, and I know who she's asking about.

"Right now Ian's still alive. The worst of his injuries I could see at the moment was a collapsed lung. I had to rig a chest tube just to keep him alive so he could have a shot at getting to the hospital." I pause for a moment as Ian's words echo in my head. "He begged me to save her. To forget about him and to get her back. Lexi, we have to do what we can to get her back."

"And that's what we're planning on." Lexi replies with determination as she continues to follow the GPS on Sophie's tablet.

Just as we pull up to the abandoned department store, I grab Lexi's extra gun and two magazines out of her glove box and load the firearm while looking around to make sure we aren't spotted.

"Why is it that the creepy guys always hole up in something abandoned?" I whine, and Lexi nods her agreement.

"I think it's something taught in Bad Guy 101. Find the sketchiest buildings to hide in." Lexi says while rolling her eyes before turning her attention to Sophie. "Sophie, I want you to stay in the car and be our lookout. If you see anything that could give us issues, text us. We have our watches on, so we will get the notification." She says as she gestures to her Apple watch on her right wrist.

"I agree with Lexi. Plus, you can be the one to tell us if we are getting close to Anna, or if they move her." I offer.

Sophie nods her head as we all get out of the car. I gently shut my door so we don't alert anyone to our location, and Sophie picks up on my tactic, doing the same with the rear passenger door before she makes her way over to Lexi's side.

Just as Lexi is opening her door, she leans in toward Sophie. "Don't start the engine unless you have to. It's loud and will give away your location in a heartbeat."

"Okay," Sophie says before Lexi quietly closes the door and walks over to me.

I give her a small smile as she grips her gun tighter in her hands before pointing with her head, telling me to follow her.

She instantly takes point and walks up to a side door that's hidden behind a massive dried bush. We both notice it's slightly ajar, and Lexi motions for me to move ahead, since I'm the better shot.

As I nudge the door open with my shoe, I feel the muscles in my shoulder tense, waiting for the metallic creak of the hinge, but the door opens silently.

I release a breath and take a quick peek around the corner to see if we're walking into an ambush, but this part of the building, the loading dock I realize, is empty. Only bare and dusty black metal shelving units line the walls.

Lexi and I walk in, both of us taking one side of the room to clear it while making sure our backs stay close to the wall so no one sneaks up on us.

"Find anything?" Lexi whispers as we meet in the middle of the space, her eyes still scanning the room like she may be missing something.

"No," I say as I look over her shoulder and spot a set of swinging doors. "But let's look through there."

Just as I begin to walk toward the door, we hear a terror-filled scream followed by bouts of maniacal laughter that make my stomach turn with both anger and fear.

I look back at Lexi, and she's typing a message out on her watch that I know is going to Sophie, and she gives me a quick nod a moment later.

This is Anna.

"Let's go." I command as I take point with no other thought.

I swiftly approach the door on silent feet. I push one of the swinging doors open with my foot, again sending up a silent prayer of thanks that the hinge makes zero sound.

As I edge the metal door open, I poke my head out to look around the corner, and the main section of the store comes into view. White metal display units are still positioned in prime locations to grab the most views of passing shoppers, but instead of goods to buy, it's loaded up with something completely different—ammunition, knives, and guns in all sizes–from pistols to rifles. I even see bricks of what I can only assume are drugs. What kind, I have no idea, but I do know it's a shit-ton and the Feds would have a field day in here.

I notice that one of the bags is haphazardly torn open down the middle, and I hope that it's for these sick bastards need to get high and not for Anna so she can't fight back as they beat, torture, and rape her.

I hear laughter again coming further down the walkway to my right, followed by a moan. It was too low of a noise to tell if it was one of *them* or Anna, but I know we need to move all the same.

Glancing back at Lexi, she gives me a firm nod, telling me without saying the words that she has my back.

I push open the door and follow the walkway to the right, and when we hit another crossway; I peek my head around the corner, and my stomach drops. I pull back, flattening myself against the wall behind me as I squeeze my eyes shut for just a heartbeat in order to keep any sound from bubbling up from my throat.

Lexi taps my arm and, with one hand, she signs, "*What did you see?*"

"*They have her tied up between two pillars with rope.*" I take a silent, calming breath as I sign the next words. "*She's hurt. Blood on her face. I don't know where else yet.*"

Before Lexi can tell me to move in, we hear a door open and close before Desmond's voice echoes in the bare walls around us.

"We'll be back for you, Baby. We need to get nice and *energized* for you while you get relaxed for us."

"Screw you." Anna slurs.

I hear Desmond laugh, followed by the sound of his hand slapping her. My stomach clenches from her pained cry filling my ears, but I make myself stay where I am against the wall. We have to wait until he leaves. This isn't the time to go all Rambo on his ass, even though that is exactly what I want to do.

As soon as I hear the door open and close again, I ease my head around the corner to make sure no one is watching Anna. After I'm sure it's only her quietly sobbing form hanging before me, I tap Lexi on her hand and we move.

"Anna." I whisper harshly, and her head snaps up to meet my gaze.

"Taylor?" She asks in bewilderment. "How did—" I cut her off.

"No time to answer questions right now. Let's get you out of here." I reply as I focus on the door to the left of us. "Lexi, get her down. I'll hold this door."

Lexi pulls a pocketknife from the back pocket of her jean shorts and begins to cut into the ropes above her wrists.

"Did they drug you?" Lexi asks.

"They tried. I guess it's a good thing that Ian had a gut feeling this morning; so he gave me something to prevent that before we headed down to the track." Anna says, and then she looks between us as memories of what happened flood her mind. "Is he—" Her voice cracks as she refuses to ask the full question.

"Last I saw, he was still alive." I say gently, but I spare her the details of his injuries.

"We will get you back to him." Lexi says as she finally saws through both ropes, and Anna massages her wrists from the rope burn. "Let's go. Back through the docks?" Lexi directs the question to me.

"Yeah. We need to get back to your car."

Lexi takes Anna's hand and leads her back through the entryway we just walked through while I walk backward, keeping my gun trained on the opposite door. Once we make it out of this space and are back in the main section of the store, I lower my gun and look back at Lexi.

"Alright. Let's go. Maybe they're too high now to hear anything."

I get on the other side of Anna, where she's sandwiched between us, and we make our way toward the loading dock again. Lexi is the one to push the swinging door open first and makes sure the coast is clear.

"Come on. Almost there." Lexi coaxes while extending a hand towards Anna.

Just as she takes Lexi's hand, I hear a commotion behind me, followed by angry voices.

"Where the hell is my girl?!" Desmond snarls as he rushes into the main thoroughfare of the store.

His eyes lock on mine, and anger flares in them before his lips curve into an evil smirk that makes my blood turn to ice.

"Ah, the Slammer's girl has come to me, huh?" He chuckles low and menacing. "I knew you'd come begging for a real man to take that body of yours and make it sing."

He takes a step towards me, and the look of anger fades on his face.

He thinks Anna just ran from him. That she's still here and he'll get the both of us to mess with. Not in this or any other lifetime, pal.

"Oh, no." I chuckle. "My man is the only one that will *ever* touch my body. You will never get your hands on me."

His face morphs back into pure anger as he takes a step toward me while moving his right arm behind his back to grab what I can only imagine is a gun stashed in the waistband of his jeans.

But I don't give him the opportunity to draw it.

I aim at him, making him think I have the audacity to shoot him when I'm actually aiming for a shelving unit over his shoulder, and I fire.

I hear him mutter a curse under his breath as I push Lexi and Anna forward through the door that leads to the docks.

"Move now!" I scream.

Lexi grabs Anna's hand and pulls the girl behind her. Just as we get to the middle of the empty dock, a door to the right bursts open and I see Desmond, along with three other guys, rush in, all fuming with guns raised.

"Get back here, you fucking bitch!" One of them screams.

"Oh, man, boys. We hit the jackpot today. Three fine-ass girls are in our playhouse. I wonder which one can scream the loudest when I'm sliding inside her sweet body, making her come all over me?" Desmond croons darkly, his eyes scanning our bodies like he's undressing us. I see Lexi's face go from determined to pure terror as his words seem to bring her trauma back to the front of her mind. But then, just as quickly as it appeared, determined anger flashes across her face as she pulls Anna to the right and starts to run in between the black storage shelves.

"Go to hell, assholes!" She yells.

"Oh, this is hell, Baby," Desmond replies, the Mexican lilt to his voice going ominous as he lifts his rifle and begins shooting.

This sets off a chain reaction between his thugs, and gunfire erupts all around us. I duck low to the ground, walking with my knees bent and back curled over to keep myself as small as possible while I make my way to the still partially open door we entered through.

As the gunshots still ring out, I can tell they are just firing without much thought, like they don't know exactly where we are.

I spot Lexi and Anna a few feet ahead of me, trying to make a beeline for the door. I try to cover my friend as much as I can while looking over my shoulder to keep these thugs off our backs. Just when I think we may be in the clear, I see one of Desmond's thugs approaching Lexi from our left.

I don't want to shout at her and give up my location, but I realize with horror that Lexi has not one clue she's about to be ambushed, and she's about to get to the end of the shelving unit. She'll be utterly exposed if she makes a break for it and runs for the door.

"Damn it. Here goes nothing." I murmur and I push out from my hiding place while raising my gun, pointing it at the man before me.

"Hey, asshole! Did you forget about me?" I shout.

He whips his head in my direction, focusing his attention solely on me, and I take that moment to shoot him through the foot. As his screams of pain and anger fight for dominance among the hail of bullets still flying in the air, he tries to rush me, but his ruined foot fails him and he stumbles to one knee.

I then hide back in the shelves, venturing a row deeper where I'm near the back wall of the docks, trying to steady my breath so I can hear any sounds around me, before making my way towards the door again. From my position on the wall, I can see through the crack in the door, and I watch as Lexi makes it to her Lancer and helps Anna into the backseat.

Good. At least those three are safe. I think to myself.

"I know you're still in here, Baby. What's your name, by the way?" Desmond croons. "Oh, it's Taylor, isn't it?"

Some part of me had a feeling Desmond knew my name, but hearing him actually say it sends a bolt of terror through my veins. I want to tell him he's wrong. I want to throw any insult I can his way, but I know that will only give away my location if he doesn't already know where I am.

I keep my head on the swivel around me. To the left and right and even behind me, since there is one more row of shelves at my back.

I keep moving sideways toward the door, but it feels like I'm not getting any closer to it. It's like one of those nightmares where, no matter how hard you run, you never get to that safe space. I take a breath, trying to calm myself, when I hear Desmond push over a shelf a few feet to my right. With his roar of frustration, I can't keep the scream of terror from ripping from my chest.

"There you are, my pretty little slut."

"Fuck you." I growl back as I desperately try to make a break for the door.

When I am a breath away from the door handle, I reach my hand out so I can fling the door open and run to safety, but I feel fingers wrap around my right upper arm, trying to pull me back.

"Let go!" I scream and try to wrench my arm free. Try to elbow the bastard in the ribs, but nothing works.

I have the thought of turning and shooting him in the knee, but I hear a gun go off before I can even move. I know for a fact it's not mine because I don't even have my finger on the trigger. So, I wait for the pain that I am certain will follow from the bullet hitting me somewhere.

"Let go of my friend, you sick son of a bitch!"

Time begins to flow around me again as I register Desmond's screams of pain instead of my own. He's grabbing at his left arm, and I notice rivulets of blood pouring from between his fingers.

The sight has my brain rushing back into action. I turn to see Lexi standing in the doorway; gun still trained on Desmond behind me. I run past her while grabbing onto her arm to help her walk backward so she doesn't trip on anything. I gesture with my hand back and forth in a small circular motion, like I'm turning a key to signal Sophie to turn the car over.

Once I hear the engine roar to life, both Sophie and Anna open the car doors so Lexi and I can jump in once we are close enough. As soon as I put my hand on the rear passenger door, I press the switch to roll the window down so I can be ready to shoot as Sophie drives off.

Just before we get to the main road, gunshots go off and I return fire, making Desmond and his thugs scatter like the rats they are.

Chapter Thirty-Two

Taylor

As soon as we are on the highway, I roll my window up and turn to Anna before flicking my eyes up to meet Sophie's in the rearview mirror.

"Head to the hospital, Soph. We need to have Anna checked out, and I'm sure she wants updates on Ian's condition."

"Are you sure he's alive? That crash." She cuts herself short as sobs wrack her body.

"When I saw him last, he was alive. He was badly hurt, but breathing." I tell her, then I place my hand on top of hers, making her look up at me. "He wanted me to save you before him."

"That's my Ian." Anna sniffs. "Always worried about me before himself."

"I know the feeling. Bryan is the same way."

"Now we just have to hope and pray they don't lock us away for this little rescue mission." Lexi sighs from the front passenger seat.

"How did you girls find me?" Anna asks. "And who are you?" She directs that question to Sophie.

"I'm just the lookout." She answers truthfully.

"She's a friend that has very handy gadgets." I say.

"Thank you for coming to save me." Anna whispers.

"You don't need to thank us, Anna. Us girls gotta stick together, don't we?" I say while trying to pull a small smile out of her.

"Yeah, we do."

Even though her grin is wobbly, it brightens her face all the same while my smile falters when my phone begins to buzz in my pocket and I see the name flashing on the screen.

"Oh boy. Here we go. Anyone that doesn't want to hear my boyfriend yell at me, cover your ears now." I joke.

I tap the green phone icon and put it on speaker. I don't even get 'hello' out before Bryan's voice spills from the phone.

"Taylor? Oh, thank God. Where the hell are you?" Bryan asks in a huff as I hear a door closing in the background.

"Went on a rescue mission, that's all."

"That's all?" He mocks. "Do you have *any idea* what was running through my mind? Through Mark's when he figured out Lexi was missing too? And boy, shit hit the fan when we heard that Sophie was in on this. too. You three gave us all fucking panic attacks."

"I'm not sorry we did what we did, Bryan. Now, we will talk more when we aren't in mixed company." I say, my voice firm.

"You got her back?" He asks, almost shocked to hear that from me.

"Of course. What kind of girl do you think you're dating?" I try to lighten the mood.

"Right now, one that's in major trouble." He snaps back, not taking my teasing tone like I hoped he would. "You all on your way to the hospital?"

"Yeah," I reply, then I see Lexi sign something and I repeat it to Bryan, "We'll be there in ten."

"I'll meet you by the ER doors." He says before he disconnects the call.

Lexi turns in her seat as the three beeps echo in the car, telling everyone the call ended. "Would you do it again?"

"In a damn heartbeat." I reply without even thinking about it.

"That's all I need to hear. Now we just ask for forgiveness later." Lexi says.

"My parents will be just as mad at me. But I'm like Taylor; I'd help you all again if I needed to." Sophie says.

"I'll talk to Bryan, Mark, and even your parents too, Sophie. You all saved my life. And I'm forever in your debt." Anna says.

In the final stretch of the drive to the hospital, we ride in silence. When Sophie pulls under the portico in front of the ER door and, true to his word, Bryan is waiting there, arms crossed over his chest. If I knew he wasn't going to yell at me at some point, I would have found his posture cute. He looks like a bouncer at the entrance of a club.

Sophie parks the car, throwing the gearshift into neutral and setting the E-brake while pulling the keys from the ignition to hand across the console to Lexi.

As she takes the keys, she gives Sophie's shoulder a firm squeeze. "You did a good thing today. No matter what goes down, you did good."

Sophie nods as she turns her head when she sees her parent's black Escalade pull up beside the Lancer. Lincoln slides out of the driver's seat to walk in front of his vehicle and open the driver's side door of Lexi's car.

"Let's go, Soph." He says, voice firm and commanding.

I give her a sly wink, my action echoing Lexi's earlier words, and Soph flashes me a hidden smile as she slips out of the car to walk with her father to the rear passenger seat of his vehicle.

As Linc slams the door, Bryan walks over to him, exchanging some words before Linc nods and walks away. Bryan then turns his attention on the three of us still remaining in the car, motioning with his head for us to exit.

As Lexi and I open our doors, Mark walks out of the main ER doors with a wheelchair for Anna.

"I don't need—"

"Take it." I say, cutting her off. "You've been through a lot."

She nods as I help her out of the car and into the wheelchair Mark parks beside me. I can tell he's livid too, but he doesn't let it show as much as Bryan does. I can feel his eyes on me, burning into the back of my head. I can almost feel just how tight his muscles are strung as he walks behind me.

After we check Anna in with the registration nurse, she's taken right back into the ER to be examined. Once she's out of my sight, Lexi and I walk into the waiting room where we notice everyone from the track is still waiting on any news to do with Ian and now, Anna.

Josh comes over to me and Lexi, and while he looks exhausted, I see a small smile pull at the corner of his mouth.

"I don't know how you girls did it, but thank you. You both saved members of my family tonight. I will never be able to repay you."

"You don't need to repay us, Josh," Lexi whispers as Mark stands behind her, pulling her back to his chest. But I can tell the movement is from protectiveness and the need to remind himself that she's safe.

"Yeah. We were just helping out someone that we've gotten close to as well." I add.

Bryan stiffly moves to sit in an empty chair, and Josh clocks his flaring anger.

"Don't be too hard on them, Bryan. If it weren't for their selflessness, Anna would have been as good as dead."

Bryan grunts, but doesn't say more.

I sit next to him, and at least he doesn't protest or move away from me, so I take that as a good sign. Lexi takes the chair next to me, and Mark is on her other side, but we all just sit there. Not talking. Not touching. Just existing and waiting for any news to come from the medical staff on the condition of our fellow racers.

Two hours pass, and after talking with one of the nurses, Josh tells us that Anna is finally with Ian and he wanted to give them time together before we all gather in his room.

And it's in those two hours of waiting that my anger begins to flare. Both Bryan and Mark haven't said a damn word to me or Lexi. Hasn't looked at us, touched us. Hasn't done *anything*. I mean, okay, I know we messed up, but geez, pull your heads out of your protective asses and just hold us.

Unable to stand the silence any longer, I angle my head to look at Bryan. "So what, are you going to continue to give me the silent treatment for the rest of the night?"

"I am beyond pissed at you two. I can't believe you all would do something so dangerous and not even tell us where you were. And to put Sophie in danger when she's not even supposed to be in *this*," Bryan whispers harshly near the end.

"You may not believe this, but I do understand your anger. But this was a plan that Lexi, Sophie, and I had in place, and we *knew* what we were doing. Lexi and I did this kind of thing long before I knew you."

"Yeah. And that time you fucking got shot, Taylor." Bryan barks quietly.

"This is not the place to discuss this." I snap as Josh comes over to us, interrupting our quiet argument.

"Ian and Anna want to see you four first."

Bryan and Mark grumble, but they both trail behind us–like they think we are gonna run away again and they trying to prevent it–as Josh leads us to Ian's hospital room.

I open the door, and Lexi walks in behind me with Mark behind her and Bryan taking up the rear, making sure to close the door behind him.

"Taylor. Lexi!" Anna smiles as she stops running her fingers over Ian's body to walk over to us and pull us into a tight hug. "Thank you for all you did, Taylor. You really did save Ian."

"No, I—" I begin, but Ian cuts me off.

"You did, Taylor. Just ask the doctor. He said that if I didn't have that chest rig thing, I would have been dead mid-ride to the hospital." Ian says. His voice is still a little breathy from the injury to his lung, but there's a touch of strength returning by the minute.

Ian's eyes slide over to Mark and Bryan, where I finally notice both of them leaning against the wall, ankles crossed and hands in both of their pockets.

A chuckle echos in the room, and I turn back around to find Ian staring both men down while shaking his head.

"Don't be too hard on them, you two. They did a good thing today." Ian says.

I look back to Bryan and, for some reason, Ian's words seems to finally get through that thick head of his. Same with Mark. I watch as both of their expressions and body posture relax just a fraction of an inch.

Bryan sighs. "I just wish she would have told someone where she was going." He tells Ian, but I feel the words were more directed at me.

"If she would have told you what she was doing, would you have let her go?" Ian deadpans.

A muscle ticks in Bryan's jaw as I'm sure Ian's words echo in his mind. I know he wouldn't have. Or at least not without a fight that would have cost precious minutes in saving Anna.

Mark grabs at Bryan's arm and nods his head towards the door, signaling for them both to leave so Lexi and I can spend some time here without having them both breathing down our necks.

After Lexi and I spend a little more time with Ian and Anna, explaining how we saved her and talking about their recovery process, we leave after about forty-five minutes.

When Lexi and I walk back into the waiting room, we see Bryan and Mark sitting in the same chairs as before, both of their heads tipped back while looking at the ceiling.

"I swear, you'd think they were twins or something. They have been looking alike all night." Lexi whispers.

"No. They are just two guys that had their girlfriends scare them out of their minds." I reply. "They're just trying to get their reality back."

I walk over to Bryan and stand in front of him, waiting for him to look at me.

"You ready?" He asks, his voice raspy as the adrenaline seems to have finally faded from his veins, and I can tell he's trying to fight the exhaustion that's slowly weighing him down.

"Yeah." I say with a single nod.

He stands and actually places a hand on the small of my back like he normally does to lead me out of the hospital waiting room and toward his Camaro that's parked a few rows away from the entrance.

He opens the passenger door for me, and I slip in without a word. Once he shuts my door and drops into the driver's seat, he inserts the keys into the ignition, disengages the E-brake, and throws the transmission into reverse before shifting into first and drives out of the parking lot.

As he merges onto the highway, I begin to toy with the hem of my shorts, not really knowing what to say in the moment. It seems like he's slowly coming down from his rampage, and I don't want to mess things up by saying something stupid that will set him off again. So I opt for silence until he's ready to talk to me.

After about fifteen minutes, I can't take the silence anymore. I reach out to turn on his radio, but he grabs my hand. I look over at him, but he never takes his eyes off the road, even when he brings my hand to his mouth and places a gentle kiss on my knuckles.

His lips brush over my skin as he speaks. "I can't say that I'm still not pissed at what you and Lexi did, *but* after I looked at it from your point of view, I can somewhat understand what you did." He glances over at me for a heartbeat before turning back to the road. "Just promise me you won't run off like that again. Tell me what you're doing next time so I don't have insane thoughts ripping my mind and heart to shreds."

"Okay," I whisper.

He lowers our hands, placing them on the shifter, and I allow my arm to move with his hand when he needs to shift gears.

When we arrive at the apartment, I see Lincoln standing on the stoop, waiting for us. I notice Lexi's Lancer is parked beside the black Escalade, letting me know that Mark and Lexi are here, too. I sigh as I exit the car, mentally preparing for the scolding that I know is coming, and I just want to get it over with.

As I walk to the porch, I feel Bryan at my back, silently urging me forward, but I feel just a semblance of support due to our conversation in the car flowing from the way he caresses my lower back with his hand.

When I walk in, I see Sophie and Lexi already sitting on the couch with Mark in the armchair by the window while Temperance takes up another on the other side of the room.

I take my place next to the girls on the couch, giving them a small smile while Bryan takes a seat on the loveseat closer to Mark. Lincoln stands before us, only the coffee table separating him from the couch.

He crosses his arms over his chest before he speaks. "I am very disappointed in you girls. You all went into something very dangerous and didn't let any of us know."

He slowly paces back and forth in front of us as the fingers of his right hand pinch the bridge of his nose as if trying to keep a headache at bay. It's such a Bryan move that I can't help but glance at my boyfriend.

"But on another note," Lincoln says, "I'm proud of you all. You executed a rescue mission flawlessly. You saved the victim's life, and you didn't get hurt in the process." He looks over at his daughter. "And Sophie, you coming up with the technology to do this is amazing. So, I will let this slide, but just this once. Another slip-up like this and you girls." He points to Lexi and me. "Will be on the first flight home, and Sophie will go to our safe house. Also, I will recommend to Wayne that he needs to revoke your badges for reckless behavior. Do I make myself clear?" Lincoln asks.

"Yes sir. Crystal clear." We all say in unison.

"Good. Now you're dismissed." Lincoln says, but I see the hint of something like pride shining in his eyes.

Chapter Thirty-Three

Bryan

After we got back to our apartment, Taylor quietly walks into the master bedroom to get a shower and I let her have her space, for now. I know she's starting to feel a bit guilty about what she did and while it's not near as much as she should feel; it is beginning to eat at her.

So, I let her try to sort out her thoughts alone in the shower while I make sure to secure the doors in my normal routine. When I hear the water shut off and the bed creak with the weight of her body settling down on the mattress a few minutes later, I walk in to get my own shower.

I notice she's in one of my shirts, and I can't help the smirk that blooms on my face. No matter what this woman does, I can't stay mad at her for long.

"I'm getting my shower next. The doors are locked." I say, my voice somewhat hoarse, both from yelling today and now from not using it so much over the last few hours.

Taylor just silently nods, turning towards the window while pulling the covers up over her body, and I have to swallow the groan that wants to bubble up from my chest from the covers blocking my view of her.

I shake my head as I force myself to walk into the bathroom and peel my clothes off so I can get my shower. Once I get in and let the water run over me, I begin to think about what all happened today. She knew this would be dangerous, but she and Lexi did it anyway. And while she's beginning to sulk now, I know if I could get into that head of hers and see her thoughts, she'd do it again in a heartbeat.

I find myself smiling as I squeeze a dollop of body wash on my hand to wash my skin. This is the reason I love her so much. She's not afraid to do the right thing. She sees a problem, and she goes after the solution. She sees someone in trouble, and she goes in for the rescue with guns blazing, and her only focus is to help the victim get out safely.

I mean, hell, she did that when she thought I was dead after Daryl shot me. She formed a revenge plan, and she acted on it. I just wish she would let me in on her plans. Once that thought hits me, I pause in rinsing my body off.

Before today, I would have told her no. That it's not a good idea to go off by herself, into unknown territory to save a girl we didn't know. I would have fought her tooth and nail and maybe even handcuffed her to me to keep her safe. But that's not what she needs or wants.

I sigh as I continue to rinse my body and hair, then turn the water off so I can get a towel from under the sink and dry off.

I need to support her and build her up, not keep tearing her down.

I tug my black boxers up over my hips, walk into the bedroom, and crawl into bed beside my beautiful, brave, and selfless girl.

"Babe, can we talk?" I ask as I roll over on my side, pushing the comforter down that she had crammed into her neck so I can see my shirt draped over her body again.

"Why? All you're gonna do is tell me how bad it was and that I was wrong to do that. I've been told that enough already. I just want to get some sleep," Taylor snaps, pulling away from me and trying to tug the blankets back up to her neck.

"No, I'm not."

I pull the blanket back down, trailing my finger down the side of her neck, and I smirk at the goosebumps that my touch brings to life on her skin.

"Actually, I was going to tell you that no matter what, I know you did a good thing today." She flicks her eyes over her shoulder to glance at me, as if making sure I'm still the same Bryan she knows and not some stunt double. "You always put other's safety above your own." I add, as she turns her gaze back to the window.

"I know you were thinking about going to save Anna. Just please, Annie," I begin, using her nickname that I know always crumbles the walls between us as I slide my arm around her stomach to pull her closer to my chest. "Tell me that you're at least leaving my side. What if I needed you for something, or Mark did, and we had not one clue where you all were?"

When she makes no move to look at me, I lean in, pressing a gentle kiss to her temple. "You know what was going through my mind when I figured out you were missing? That I failed you. I thought that while I was distracted by Ian's accident and helping to make sure he got into the ambulance, Desmond came back to take you and Lexi. I have never been that scared in my life, Taylor. The fear of getting shot was nothing compared to the thought of losing you to someone like that."

This time she turns her head to look at me, and I can see in the light blue of her eyes that she didn't think of that part of the picture.

Tears begin to well in her eyes. "I'm so sorry. I didn't think about any of that. I didn't mean to hurt you or Mark, or even Lincoln and Temperance."

I take my hand off her stomach and I use my thumb to dry the tears that are silently streaming down her face. She looks at my hand as if she's shocked she's crying, and that makes her sob harder.

I pull her back into my chest, and I rest my chin in the curve of her neck. "Shh, Babe. I know you didn't mean it. Sometimes you get tunnel vision and you think of the big picture, but not what happens on the sidelines. Just please, I'm begging you to tell someone before you go off on a mission like that. Hell, I don't care if you tell one of the other racers. Just tell someone. Please."

"I will," Taylor sniffs, finally getting her tears back under control. "I'm sorry."

I hook my index finger under her chin, pulling her mouth to mine. When our lips touch, I can taste the saltiness of her tears on her skin. I pull back enough so I can kiss each of her eyes once before I pull back again and look down at her.

"I love you, Taylor Allison Sparks. You sometimes infuriate me to no end." I jest, and that earns me a small, tearful chuckle out of her. "But at the end of the day, you are the best thing that I could have ever asked for in a friend, a partner, and a true love."

"I love you too, Bryan," Taylor says as she lifts her head to kiss me this time, and I can't help but growl into her mouth. She laughs as she pulls back enough to speak, but her lips brush mine with each word, "I promise I'll let you know the next time I go off on some hair-brained rescue mission."

"Good." I whisper, then after a moment I ask. "Are you okay? That bastard didn't hurt you, did he?"

Taylor shakes her head. "No, he didn't. I'm fine."

"Let me be the judge of that, Baby." I croon as I lean in to kiss her neck again.

I skim my hand down her side, stopping at the hem of my shirt that rests against her thigh. I grab the fabric between my fingers and pause for just a heartbeat. Silently letting her know that she can tell me no and I'll stop. But she only smiles at me, urging me on.

I pull the shirt up, and I have to bite my lip to hold back the curse that wants to spill out as I realize she's bare underneath. After I pull my shirt completely off her frame, I am rewarded with Taylor's naked body again.

"You are absolutely beautiful, Baby Girl." I say, my voice low and filled with desire.

My upper body hovers over hers as I trail kisses down her neck and collarbone. I nip at her flesh with my teeth, and she gasps at the sensation. I pull back as the sound pours into my ears and look down to make sure I didn't hurt her, but what I see staring back at me makes me harden to the point of pain, even with only boxers on.

Her skin is red where I bit her, and I already see little traces of the bruise that I know will end up forming on her collarbone. Hidden from everyone else, but only the two of us will know it's there.

I trail my thumb over the hurt, and she sucks in a breath. "Oh, I'm gonna like seeing that on you, Baby." I look back up at her. "Do you want me to mark you up? To let every single person who looks at you know who you belong to?" I can't help the possessiveness in my voice, but the need to mark her is overwhelming. "Or do you want my marks only in places that we know about? Let them be our little secret?" I ask as I trail my lips down her chest and take her right nipple in my mouth, giving it a few quick tugs.

"Only for us." She says breathlessly.

I hum against her skin, and she writhes under my touch. "You got it, Baby. I'm going to show you just how much I love you." I growl as I continue to suck and bite at her nipple until I know she'll remember me being here.

I then slide my hand down the plane of her stomach and let it dip lower, my index finger caressing her clit and massaging the bundle of nerves in slow, tight circles.

"Oh, Bryan," Taylor moans as she shifts her hips, trying to drive me deeper into the spot, but I don't let her.

As my mouth, tongue, and teeth glide down the length of her stomach, leaving red marks in my wake, I pull my hand away for just a moment and before she can groan in frustration; I dip two fingers into her core and she cries out.

"That's it, Baby. Keep screaming out for me." I praise as I continue the slow, teasing tempo with my fingers, building her pleasure with each thrust in and out of her sweet heat.

"Don't stop, Bryan. Oh, that feels so good."

I chuckle, the sound deep and growly in my chest. "Then what I have planned next is going to blow your mind, Babe."

Her eyes snap open, and she looks down at me, where I'm nestled between her legs. At first, I think she's going to tell me to stop, but she just looks at me, waiting for my next move.

I slowly pull my fingers out of her; her arousal glistening on my digits. I have the desire to clean them. To taste her, but this is not how I want to do it for the first time. So, I gently wrap my hand around her calf, turning my head as I lift it to my mouth and place tender kisses on her flesh.

I slowly ease up to her inner thigh, and just when I let her think that I'm just going to kiss her there too, I pull her skin into my mouth and I suck on it greedily to where I know it will bruise.

"Bryan! How many more hickeys are you going to give me?" Taylor shouts as she lets her hands move down her body.

Over the various marks on her collarbone, breasts, and the two that are on her stomach. But I can hear the undertones of pleasure under her faux annoyance. She loves it; I know she does.

"As many as you and I want, Annie." I say as I kiss the bruise I left on her beautiful skin.

Trailing a few more kisses closer to her center, I pause. Looking up at her from my position, I can tell she's eager for what I'm about to do.

"Do you want me to taste you, Baby? Do you want to come on my tongue?" I ask, my voice barely audible as I flick my tongue over her clit, and she practically erupts at that single touch.

Her back bows off the bed while her hands fist the sheets next to her before she threads them through her hair. It's almost like she doesn't know what she wants to do with them, and I find it completely adorable.

"You didn't answer me, Taylor." I growl as I place a kiss on her core.

"What was...the question?" She pants and I laugh.

"I haven't even started with you, and you're already forgetting things?" I ask incredulously. "You may seriously forget your own name by the time I'm done, Baby."

She looks down at me again, and her eyes roll back in her head. "My god, seeing you that close to me is so damn hot," Taylor rasps.

"The view here isn't too bad either." My eyes flick down to look at her weeping entrance. "I'll ask once more, and this time listen to me, Taylor Allison." I chuckle, lifting my gaze back to hers. "Do you want to come on my tongue?"

"Yes!" She snaps. "Shut up and make me come."

"As you wish, my lady." I say, and I dive in.

I grip her knees, forcing them down as far as her hips will allow, and I begin with her clit again. Flicking my tongue over the nerves and when I feel her legs start trembling under my hands, I then use my teeth; grazing, nipping playfully, then biting the nub between the enamel.

"Bryan! Oh shit!" Taylor shouts, her back bowing off the bed again.

I then move lower, and I sink my tongue into her center, and I can't help the growl that bubbles out of me as the taste of her floods my mouth. I knew she would be amazing, but she tastes so much like home that I swear my heart feels like it wants to burst from my chest.

I pull my tongue back to the tip and then I plunge in again, deeper this time. Taylor must move her hand at some point, because I feel her fingers threading into my hair, pushing my head down further, and I happily oblige while my finger continues to circle over her clit at the same time.

"Bryan! Oh, that's it, don't stop. I'm so close!"

I somehow form the words around her center as I'm devouring her like a starving man looking for his first proper meal in ages. "Come for me, Taylor. Let me taste all of you."

Like the other times I've commanded that of her, she finds her release. If I thought she tasted amazing before, this is something completely different.

My body pulses with the need to follow her own release. I'm so hard behind my boxers right now that I'm seeing stars. I know that if I don't stop and get to the bathroom soon, I'm going to come in my boxers like I'm a teenager again when I found Mark's stash of magazines in his room during one of our many sleepovers. But honestly, I don't care right now. The high of showing her just what her body can do to me again is overwhelming.

With my head still between her legs, I help her ride out her orgasm until her body stops trembling in my hands. I pull away enough to look up at her, and more blood somehow rushes between my legs at the sight.

Her skin is sweat-slicked. Her chest is rising and falling in sated pants. And her hair looks like a halo around her head the way it's fanned out over the pillow.

"You did so well, Baby Girl." I praise her as I force myself away from her body.

I begin to stand up to walk to the bathroom when her hand shoots out to grab my arm.

"Where are you going?"

"To the bathroom to grab a washcloth for you." I tell her, which isn't a total lie. I would, right after I took care of mini-me.

She looks at me, her eyes darting down to my solid-as-steel hard-on, and her gaze makes my body heat even more.

"Babe, I need to—" I begin hoarsely, but she cuts me off.

"Let me help you," Taylor says as she pulls me onto the bed and my back rests against the headboard.

Once I'm settled, Taylor nestles herself between my thighs, and again the sight of her naked body makes my blood boil. Her skin is still pink and flushed from her recent climax, and the various parts of her body covered in my love bites creates a flare of desire so high that it has a heartbeat between my legs and I can't help the groan that it forces out of my mouth.

"Come on, Taylor. You can't look at me like that and not do something." I whine as I tilt my head back against the headboard with a solid thud.

"Oh, and why is that?" She asks with a mocking lilt in her voice.

Her hand then shoots out and grips my shaft through my boxers, and I can't stop the garbled moan that rips from my throat at the sensation that tears like a fire through me. I don't even think her touch is that hard. I think I'm just that sensitive.

"Taylor," I plead, and I can't stop my hips from thrusting into her hand, trying to create some kind of friction.

"That seems painful." She croons, and I breathe out an incredulous laugh. "Let me take care of you now."

She pulls the waistband of my boxers away from my body and I plant my feet into the bed next to her thighs, lifting myself off the mattress so she can pull the fabric from my hips, and the relief of not being constricted anymore hits me so hard that I know my tip is weeping at the freedom.

Taylor looks back at me, and somehow I keep my focus on her while trying desperately to hold myself together, but when her eyes take in my erection, I can't stop the pre-cum that rolls over my crown and down the side.

"You are...beautiful." She says in bewilderment.

She reaches out, her index finger grazing the underside of my shaft, and I suck in a breath at the single touch.

"Taylor, stop teasing." I demand.

"Oh, but I like it. Seems like a bit of payback for what you did to me."

"You loved it in the end." I pant.

"And you will too." She tosses back as she wraps her hand around me, tugging me from base to the tip and back again.

While she continues stroking me, she leans in, trailing tender kisses up my stomach, chest, and neck before ending on my lips. I'm sure she can taste herself there. Hell, I still can, and it's just more kindling for the fire that my body has become now.

I jerk my hips against her hand again, urging her to go faster, harder. To just push me over that blade-like edge of my own release, but she keeps me there, dangling; suspended in mid-air, it seems like.

"Do you want to come?"

My chest heaves, and I don't even have to look. I know my body is weeping for her when she flicks her thumb over my crown and I feel the extra slickness coating my skin, making her hand glide easily over my shaft.

"Bryan?" Taylor asks in a sing-song voice as her lips brush the sensitive skin behind my ear.

"What?" I pant and groan at the same time.

"Not so fun when you can't think straight, huh?" Taylor chuckles as she then places a kiss behind the same ear she's been teasing.

"You're such a brat." I breathe.

"But I'm *your* brat, Baby."

She still teases the same spot with her lips and I swear I feel her teeth graze over the skin, but I'm too wired, too sensitive to really tell apart any other sensation other than her hand wrapped around my erection and the delicious build-up she's creating that's almost to the point of pain.

"Since you're not going to answer me, then." Taylor says as she pulls away from my ear and sits back on her heels, but she never takes her hand off me. "I'm gonna talk to him."

She looks down pointedly at my erection, and I feel it twitch.

"See? He's more responsive than you are." She smiles fiendishly.

"Oh, my god." I chuckle, her words finally clicking into my brain.

I notice her touch has slowed against me. Steady enough to keep me hovering over the release I still feel coiled tight in the pit of my stomach, but not enough to give me that relief, and I finally remember she's waiting on my answer to her earlier question.

My eyes lock onto hers, and her gaze turns sultry.

"Just like I did with you, Annie. Make me come however you want."

"That's what I want to hear, Baby."

She leans in closer to me, her eyes flicking between my weeping head and my face for a moment, then looking back down again. Before I can even get my mind wrapped around what's going through her head, she moves.

Her mouth wraps around my crown, and I can't stop the way my body reacts. My head tilts back into the pillow so far that it probably looks like I'm about to break my damn neck, but I don't care. The feeling of Taylor's mouth around me is groundbreaking.

The way her tongue teases the vein that's pulsing in rhythm to my heartbeat underneath my shaft, to the way her teeth just *barely* graze over my skin, all of it makes me see stars and I know I'm just another heartbeat away from exploding.

"Taylor." I pant as I feel my orgasm race to the surface. "Breathe through your nose."

She hums against my length, and that's all it takes. I subconsciously know I'm making sounds that I didn't even make back in the shower a few days ago as my release hits me and I'm pouring down her throat, but to my surprise, she's taking everything my body gives her, and then some.

"Taylor, oh, that feels so damn good. Keep going, Baby. Take every-thing." I pant. "Take anything you want from me."

When I finally come down from my orgasm and I can finally think straight, I glance down at Taylor. At my beautiful girlfriend, who just rocked my world with her first blow-job.

She gives me one last pull with her glorious mouth before audibly popping off my crown and looking up at me with lust-filled eyes.

"That was amazing, Taylor." I say, still trying to catch my breath as I run my fingers through my hair.

"It was? I didn't know if I was doing it right. I just let instinct take over," Taylor says shyly.

"Baby, that was soul-shattering."

"Oh, come on. I'm sure one of the others you've—"

I cut her off. "First of all, while I've had two girlfriends, I only had protected sex with one. And two, neither of them gave me a blow-job. But I can guarantee you, it wouldn't have been like yours."

Her cheeks flush at my words, but it's the truth, and I let her see it in my eyes.

"Really?" She asks.

"Really." I reply.

I grab her elbow to pull her up my body, and when she's lying on top of me—while being careful to keep our lower bodies away from each other—I pull her lips to mine.

I growl when I taste the two of us on my tongue.

"What was that for?" Taylor chuckles as she traces her finger behind the ear she was teasing a few minutes ago, her eyes sparkling as she tracks her own movement.

"I never thought I would love tasting the both of us on my tongue." I tell her, and her cheeks flush a cute shade of pink. "My little naughty vixen wrapped in an innocent body. I love it."

"Oh my god, Bryan." She squeaks as she hides her face in my neck.

"It's true." I laugh. "I bet it's been coming from those spicy books I've seen in our room back home." I wrap my hand around the back of her neck, pulling her away from the safety of my body to look up at me. "Maybe I need to read some and see what you could be into. I've seen those red tabs, Baby." I arch a brow at her, and she turns beet red this time.

"Don't you dare!"

"It's that, or I see if Lexi or your other girlfriends read the same stuff and get pointers from them. Your choice, Babe."

"You are horrible." She shakes her head, but I see the smile trying to tug at the corner of her mouth.

"Come on. Let's get you cleaned up. For real this time." I say as I roll out of bed while picking her up bridal-style and walking toward the bathroom.

As I sit her down on the counter, her fingers linger on my skin as I grab a washcloth from one of the drawers in the sink and turn the water on so I can get it warm. Taylor continues to trace a vein that travels down my forearm, flexing as I wring the washcloth out; but I can tell she's already thinking.

I hook my index finger under her chin to make her look at me while I bring the damp cloth to her mouth. "What's already going on in that head of yours, Annie?"

Her eyes flick up to meet mine, and my heart always skips a beat when I see those gorgeous blue eyes staring back at me.

"I...I..." She flicks her eyes away from mine.

"Tell me, Baby." As a thought fills my head, I step in closer to her. "Did I hurt you?"

"No." She chuckles, her gaze snapping back to mine while she places a hand on my chest to ease my racing heart. "No, it's just...I *want* you. All of you."

My brow furrows, not understanding what she means, and then it clicks in my head. She wants to go all the way with me. My body lights up with the thought, but I don't act on it.

"I want nothing more than to take you back to that bed and give you what you want, Annie. *But,* and I think you would agree, when I take you for the first time, I don't want it to be while we are on a case. I want to take you somewhere nice. I want to wine and dine the hell out of you before I carry you to the bed, toss you down on it and take my sweet damn time working your body before I sink into it for the first time."

Her smile morphs from giddiness to the proposed date to desire filled hunger by the time I'm finished speaking.

"And I want it to be a private space, where we aren't sharing walls with someone, no matter who they are. Because I know we are going to be screaming the other's name, and I want that for my ears only." I growl.

"Okay. I can absolutely get behind that plan, Bryan."

She kisses me before I prompt her to lean back against the wall so I can tend to her loved core. Once I'm done, I pick her back up so I can take her to the bed. I try to grab for the t-shirt of mine she was wearing, but she shakes her head, so I instead help her into at least a pair of underwear—so I'm not tempted too much to go against what I just told her about not actually taking her yet—and hurry back to the bathroom so I can clean up, tug on a pair of boxers and pull my beautiful woman to my chest, skin to skin, as we let sleep take our sated minds and bodies.

Chapter Thirty-Four

Mark

After I shut the door to our apartment, I wait a moment, listening for any sounds of Taylor and Bryan arguing. I need to make sure he doesn't do anything stupid with her again.

When I don't hear anything from the other side of the wall, my eyes land on Lexi. She just walked into the kitchen to open the fridge so she could grab a bottle of water for herself.

Well, guess she's not offering me any.

I slowly walk toward the kitchen, but she meets me in the doorway and we both pause. I keep my hands loose at my sides, even though I want to touch her, to make sure she's okay, but I force myself to keep my arms down.

"I'm going to bed." Lexi says, and she tries to walk past me, but I snap my arm out, blocking her exit.

"No, Baby. I want to talk to you first."

"Mark, I don't want to hear it. Yes, I know it was dangerous, but you know me; I can't let something like that—" She pauses as her voice begins to crack with tears.

I give in to my need to touch her and pull her into my chest. "I know, Sweetheart. That's why I wanted to talk to you. Are you okay?" I let the question hang in the air for what it is.

Both physically and mentally.

She finally looks at me, and while her eyes are watery with unshed tears, I see *my* Lexi looking back at me and not the broken girl that would usually take over during this kind of discussion.

"Yeah. I'm okay, I think. I think it was different because I was the one in control. Plus, I had a gun in my hand, so if the son of a bitch did anything, I would have shot his dick off."

I can't help the laugh that her words draw out of me. I wrap my arms around her waist, pulling her body flush with mine.

"You are so incredibly brave, Baby. And you have a wicked mouth, too." I say as I kiss her on said mouth.

"You're not mad at me?" Lexi asks as she pulls away from my lips a moment later.

I sigh through my nose. "At first, yes, I was. I was terrified of what happened to you. But I knew we still had our little backup plan."

I pull at the chain of the little golden necklace that hides under her shirt. It's in the shape of a heart with our initials engraved on the front. I've always loved how her initials already matched mine, even though we have different last names.

M.S. & A.S.

I made this for her once we got back home from our first mission and our lives changed for the worst.

This was the only way I could convince Lexi to venture out after eight months of being cooped up in our apartment in California. As soon as my phone travels a certain distance away from the necklace, it activates one of three alarm switches.

If Lexi either presses a button located on the back of the necklace or if the chain breaks with more force than it just being caught on like the fabric of her shirt, or if the tiny heart monitor that's housed in the hollowed-out space picks up that her heart rate either suddenly spikes or dips where it's similar to being drugged or knocked out, the alarm would send me a notification on my phone, no matter if I have cell signal or not.

"But even with this, I still can't tell you that I wasn't scared out of my mind." I place the necklace back under her shirt and then push a loose strand of her blonde hair behind her ear.

"This is the first mission we've been on out of state, and look at what you do. Go in guns blazing on a rescue mission to save that girl from unimaginable hell. Even with being mad at you, I couldn't stay that way for long, Lex."

She calmly sets the water bottle down on the table behind her before turning back to me, and the look that's filling her eyes makes my blood heat in anticipation of her next words.

Hooking her arms around my neck, she slowly pulls my head down to her; and when our lips touch, we instantly meet each other, stroke for stroke. Her mouth opens for me, and I thrust my tongue in, tasting her sweet strawberry lip gloss on my tastebuds, and I growl at the flavor that explodes on my tongue.

My palms skim down her waist until I'm cupping her ass in my hands, and I lift her off her feet. She immediately wraps her legs around me, crossing her ankles at the small of my back, but she never breaks our connection. Even when she speaks, she does so in between kisses.

"Show me just how much you aren't mad at me, Mark."

"With fuckin' pleasure, Baby." I growl into her delicious mouth.

I stride towards the bedroom, toeing open the door with my shoe before walking over to the bed to drop Lexi onto it, and she shrieks with excitement. I stand at the side of the bed for a moment before lifting my right arm behind my head, grabbing a fist full of my shirt, pulling it over my head and tossing it to the side, not caring where it goes.

"God, I never get tired of seeing you do that." Lexi says breathlessly as she grabs my hand to pull me down on top of her.

"And I never get tired of this." I reply as I pull her shirt off and devour her lips again before I use one hand to unhook her bra.

Once I have her soft and supple breasts bare before me, I trail possessive kisses down her chin, her throat, over the swell of her right breast until I find her nipple with my teeth and I bite down hard enough to bruise, but not break skin.

"Mark!" Lexi moans as she threads her fingers through my dark hair.

I continue my worship of her body, making sure to appreciate her left breast before I kiss down the length of her body. I hook my finger into the waistband of her jeans and look up at her through hooded eyes.

"How do you want me to show you just how much I'm *not* angry with you?" I ask, rephrasing my usual question with her, and my heart jumps at the joy of this change for my girl.

"However you want, Mark. I'm yours."

I growl at her words as I tug her jeans down over her hips, taking her pretty hot pink panties down with them. Once I have her completely naked before me, I pull my own jeans and briefs down my hips and kick them off to settle somewhere on the floor with my discarded shirt.

Just as I'm hovering over where we both want me to be, I let my erection brush her center, but I pause, knowing this will drive her nuts, but I can't stop the question from forming on my lips.

"Where's your gun, Alexis?"

"What the hell are you talking about?" She snaps as she tries to wrap her leg around my hips to finally drive me home.

"See, I'm kinda fond of my dick, and I don't want you shooting it off since you're so trigger-happy."

"Mark Edward Stone, if you don't take me right now, I will shoot your dick off for not using it!"

"See, so trigger-happy and angry." I whisper into her ear as I use the distraction to thrust into her in one smooth move, sinking to the hilt.

"Mark! Oh! You…sneaky…asshole." She pants as I fill and stretch her sweet heat.

"You said I could take you any way I wanted. Well, I wanted you distracted and pissed." I say as I pull back and thrust into her again.

Leaning in closer, I trail my lips over her neck, biting and sucking on the spot where her shoulder connects, and I know my mark will be visible for all to see. I *want* everyone to know who she belongs to and to not fuck with me when it comes to her. I have killed for this woman, and I will do it again if I feel she's in danger, and she knows it.

"You feel so fucking good, Baby" I grab her left leg, lifting it over my hip to drive deeper, and she screams out as I continue to hit that spot I know will send her into her first of many climaxes tonight. "You take me so well."

"Yes! Only you, Mark. Don't stop."

"I didn't plan on it." I growl as I ease my hand between us and I flick her clit.

She cries out again. This time I feel her fall with her first release, and I continue to rut into her, back and forth, dragging it out as long as I can.

"That's one, Alexis."

I don't slow down as I lean over her, taking one nipple into my mouth as I tease the other between my thumb and forefinger. Lexi's fingers thread into my short hair before tightening them into fists, pulling at my scalp, and this just makes me harden even more, and I start to feel the beginnings of my own orgasm building deep in my pelvis.

"Baby, you keep that up and I'm not going to get another orgasm out of you before I come." I croon against her skin.

"I'm so close, Mark. Please." She begs.

I flip us over so I'm on my back and she's straddling me. "Then use me, Baby. Make us both come. I want to see you dripping afterward."

She leans forward, planting kisses on my chest, and I let out a breathy groan when I feel her teeth marking me.

Biting.

Sucking.

Claiming.

She increases her tempo, rocking back and forth and then from side to side as she uses me to hit every single spot that causes her walls to tighten around me, trying to milk me for the orgasm she's desperate to feel.

"That's it, Alexis. Almost there, Baby. You feel so damn good." I growl.

She leans in, looking me directly in the eye before she smiles. "Then come for me." She demands as she turns her head to bite into the middle of my neck, almost like she's a damn vampire about ready to bleed me dry and I explode, meeting her rocking movements with the upward thrust of my hips, hitting her exactly where she wants it and she shatters above me.

"Mark!"

"Such sweet music, Baby. Keep coming for me."

I think she has back-to-back orgasms the way her body is trembling above me, and I turn us where she's on her back again, riding her through the rest of her release, driving my own deeper into her.

Once we are finally spent, I pull out, collapsing onto my back, chest heaving, but the pleasant thrum of post-bliss flowing through my veins.

"You okay?" I ask, turning my head to look at Lexi.

When she lifts her head, I push a piece of damp hair off her forehead so I can place a tender kiss there.

"Yeah. I'm good." She says and then chuckles, "Don't take this wrong, and it's not that I haven't enjoyed our previous romps in the sheets, but this feels like the best one yet."

"It's just cause I'm that good, Baby." I jest, and she smacks me on the chest.

"Pompus ass."

I laugh at her while shaking my head, but then my tone goes from playful to serious in the blink of an eye.

"I think it's because this is our first time after you talked about what happened to you with Taylor and you worked through some of your trauma."

She lays her head back down on my chest while her finger traces the fresh hickey she left on the side of my neck.

"Yeah, maybe you're right. Even with what I did today, knowing what *he* and his thugs had done to girls in the past and what he had already said to Taylor, I didn't balk like I thought I would have."

"That's cause you're my bad bitch. I always told you that you were."

"You are such a dork, you know that?" She asks incredulously.

"Oh well. I'm your dork and yours alone, and you wouldn't give me back for the world."

"I don't know. Let me check my purse for the receipt. I may go in for an upgrade."

I place a hand on the other side of my chest, fingers fanning out in mock offense. "Damn, Babe. Reel the claws back a bit."

She rolls her eyes, but I grab her gently by the chin and bring her lips to mine. "I know you love me, and you'd come back and pick up the original. I'm irreplaceable."

"You're lucky you're cute, and a good ride in bed."

I bark out a laugh, and I roll out of bed before looking back at her. "I'm getting you cleaned up and then you're going to bed. You're too spicy for your own good tonight."

After I get her cleaned up, she insists on changing the sheets while I clean up, and by the time I'm done in the bathroom; she has the bed ready with fresh sheets and we climb in. I pull her head into my chest again, and I wrap my arms around her naked body, and we let sleep claim us and bring us into the uncertainty of tomorrow's troubles.

Informant

As I slide into bed with my girl later that night, I notice she's already fast asleep. I turn to face the door so I don't wake her, and just when I'm about to close my eyes, my phone lights up with a text message. Thinking it's one of the guys giving us an update on Ian's condition again, I pick the phone up off my night stand but the message that appears on the screen makes my stomach drop.

> **Desmond**: Since Slammer's bitch and her friend took my play toy away, I'm coming after their guys. I want their blood staining the pavement. Be sure everyone is at your precious track tomorrow, but I want those two newbies in my sights.

With shaking hands, I reply because I have no other choice.

> **Me:** Okay. I will have everyone there, but the girls stay out of this. Especially mine. If you don't like it, then no deal.

> **Desmond:** Just make sure the bitch's boyfriends are there and waiting. Ill call you before I move in.

I leave him on read as I turn my phone off and try to sleep with this new threat lingering over our team.

Chapter Thirty-Five

Taylor

The next morning I get up with Bryan, and I can tell he's still thinking about what we did last night. It's in the way his eyes darken when he looks at me, and the knowing smirk that plays at the corner of his lips when I meet his heated gaze and a blush flares in my cheeks. Hell, I'm still thinking about every second of last night too, and I'm shocked at what we did together. But yet with him, venturing into this part of my life feels good. Feels safe, and I love that.

When I finish off the coffee that Bryan fixed for me, I notice he's looking at his phone and I see a smile brighten his face.

"What's that smile for?" I ask playfully.

"Josh just messaged the group telling us that Ian and Anna are being released from the hospital."

"That's great news." I say.

"Yeah. Josh wants us to go down to the track and put together a welcome home party." Bryan says as he pockets his phone.

"I love that idea." I say as I trace my finger behind his ear, and I have to fight to keep from smiling at him.

"Mark and I are going down first. You and Lexi come down at your normal times."

"Okay. Love you, Bullet."

"Love you too, Annie." Bryan says as he leans in to give me a tender kiss, and I can't help but graze my teeth over his lip when he pulls away.

"Annie, you better stop that, 'cause I don't have time to kiss you properly right now."

"Oh, I'm sure you'll find the time soon." I croon.

He pulls his body closer to mine while placing his hand on my right breast, his thumb brushing over where we both know a bruise of his making hides underneath.

"Remember what happened last night, Babe? I can make it so much better." He warns, and it heats my blood.

"Okay, okay. You win for now." I step back from him, forcing him to drop his hand from my body. "Go, I'll be down in a bit."

"Good. See ya later."

As soon as I hear his Camaro start, Mark's Challenger follows, and Lexi walks over from her and Mark's apartment over to mine.

"Morning." I say, and then my eyes land on her neck where it connects to her shoulder, and I suck in an audible breath. "Alexis! Is that—" She cuts me off.

"Yes, it is, and I'm proudly wearing it." She says with a huff and a sly smile as she brushes her blonde hair away from her shoulder, flaunting her love bite.

"Okay." I sigh with a shake of my head.

"Hey, sister. Don't knock it until you try it."

I wish I had another cup of coffee to hide my smirk because I know I fail miserably at concealing my reaction to her remark.

"Taylor Allison Sparks, is that a smirk I see?" Lexi gasps.

"What? No." I scoff.

"Bullshit, girlfriend. It's written all over your face." She pauses, her eyes blowing wide. "Wait a damn minute! Did you and Bryan finally hit the sheets ?"

"No," I tell her the truth to what I know she's asking.

"Well, something happened. I can tell. You have that afterglow around you."

"I do not." I scoff.

"Stop beating around the bush and tell me! Did you and Bryan get jiggy or not?!"

I sigh, finally giving in to her, like always. "Not in the way you're thinking. But we have been fooling around a bit." I say and I lift my shirt, showing her my stomach.

She squeals at the marks Bryan left on my skin last night. After I showered this morning, I found myself staring at them in the mirror, tracing each mark and remembering everything that Bryan did to cause them.

"Oh, my god! Girl, welcome to the Hickey Committee." Lexi says while high-fiving me.

"Oh, geez." I say while shaking my head at her comment.

"I need all the deets before we head down to the track, and I *have* to tell the girls back home." Lexi says while pulling her phone out of her pocket to do just that.

"No!" I shout, placing my hand on her phone. "You know Casey. She'll blab it to everyone, and then Mom will find out and, knowing her, she'll book a flight down here and personally kill Bryan."

Lexi scrunches her nose up and nods. "Yeah, you're right. We'll keep this between ourselves. Despite that, I need the deets. So spill. I'll make another cup of coffee for us while you talk."

So I do. I tell her what all happened last night, and I swear I experience it all over again. Even with the minty toothpaste in my mouth, I can still pick up on Bryan's taste lingering on my tongue.

That was something I never thought I would do with anyone, but again, I was trusting my instincts like Lexi told me, and it was an amazing experience between us.

"Well, I'm glad you're finding your wings with him. And I promise, once you get to that last hurdle, it's amazing. I can already tell Bryan is going to make it feel perfect for you." Lexi says, "And if not, I'll shoot him where it hurts."

I laugh, but a part of it is forced because of the glint in my friend's eye. She means her words just as much as my mother would. If he hurts me, he's a dead man.

Once Lexi and I finally get down to the track, I see that the guys have been hard at work, and it reminds me of the Halloween dance that Bryan helped me and the girls set up back home.

Streamers in all different colors are hanging from the main gate, along with air-filled balloons to match, each swaying gently in the Florida breeze.

When I drive through the open gate and pass by the pit area where the garages are, I see more streamers and balloons covering them, but Ian's is the most decorated, along with 'get well soon' balloons and enough streamers to almost completely cover the metal door.

As I pull my car across the track to park in front of the press box, I notice the last piece to this party. There is a gigantic banner that spans the width of the track and in huge letters that are a mix of black and pink paint, that I know are courtesy of Bryan's painting talent, spells out:

'Welcome home, Ian and Anna.'

After I park my car and shut off the ignition, Lexi pulls up beside me, and both of our guys glance over at us. Without a word, they immediately drop what they were doing and walk over, so Lexi and I just lean against my car and wait for them to approach.

"Hey, Lexi." Mark croons as his eyes take in Lexi's body, and I know his gaze is zeroing in on her neck.

"Hey yourself." She replies as she pulls him down for a quick welcome kiss.

I turn my attention away from them when Bryan steps up to me and wraps his arms around my waist, pulling me in for a quick kiss before breathing into my neck.

"Hi."

"God, you act like we haven't seen each other in *days*. It's just been about an hour and a half." I chuckle as I brush my nose behind his ear.

"And yet here you are, rubbing your nose into me."

"Oh, bite me." I say, stepping back from him.

"What, you didn't get enough last night?" He whispers suggestively.

"Didn't get enough of what last night?" Mark quips while pulling Lexi's back to his chest and resting his chin on her shoulder.

Bryan turns his head to his friend for a moment then back to me, his eyebrow arched, daring me to answer. I just give him a smug smile in return.

"Dude!" Mark shouts, chuckling and pointing at his friend.

"What?" Bryan snaps.

"Looks like she was the one biting *you*, my brother."

Bryan's head whips around to me as things start to click into place. My actions from last night and now this morning. My lingering touches behind his ear, marveling at my apparent handiwork on his skin.

"Oh, Annie. That's not fair if that's what I think it is on my skin." Bryan growls as he bends at the waist to look in the side mirror of my driver's door.

I can't help the smile that finally blooms on my lips when he notices the bruise I left on him last night. While he was marking me, I marked him just the same. I was just sneaky about mine.

"Taylor Allison, you are in so much trouble when we get home later." Bryan says as he looks back at me.

I shrug, "Oh well. Getting to see the look on your face right now is worth it."

I glance over at Mark and Lexi, and they are both smiling like lunatics at us.

"Shut it." I tell mostly Mark because I'm sure he has some kind of witty comeback that I don't want to hear.

"I was just going to say, don't come running to me when he jumps you later. I don't swing like that."

Lexi smacks Mark on the forearm as she turns her head to look back at him. "You better shut it before Taylor and I both gang up on you two."

Mark laughs, and I see Bryan trying to hide his own smile, but fails thanks to his friend.

"Come on, Ian and Anna should be here any minute." Bryan says as he threads our fingers together and pulls me away from my car and towards the pit area.

Once we are gathered in the pit area, Bryan pulls me close to him, but before he can kiss me, James walks by us and we both notice he's in a tense conversation with someone on his phone.

James' gaze locks onto us at the same time he rolls his eyes, apparently not liking whatever is said on the other end of the call.

"Trouble in paradise, maybe?" Bryan whispers into my ear.

"I don't know." I say, but then I look at Josh and he's on an equally animated call with someone too, but I know Morgan is here and she's been smiling with the other girls, except for Christy—she's still at her apartment, apparently sick—so, I don't think they're fighting.

"I think Josh is on the phone with the body shop that has Ian's car. From what we saw, it's salvageable, and he's been trying to get it fixed without Ian knowing about it. It's going to be a later surprise once Ian's fully healed and he can get back to racing."

"That's great!" I say.

"Yo, guys! They're here!" Nick shouts from the gate and takes off running towards us to get with the welcome party we all have become.

Just as we see Anna's Civic enter the gate, both Josh and James finish with their calls and join us. When Anna pulls into the pit area, I can see Ian through the windshield shaking his head and waving his arm, which is covered in a black cast, at all the decorations, and I somehow know what he's saying, because I think Bryan would be the same way.

The decorations are too much. I just survived a car wreck; it's not anything groundbreaking.

I turn back to look at Bryan, and his attention is on the Civic. His broad smile lights up his entire face as he watches Anna park the car and Josh jogs over to open Ian's door to pull him out, bringing him into a hard, welcoming embrace. But I know what he's doing, helping him without showing Ian to be weak.

Bryan must feel me staring at him because he tilts his head down and quickly kisses me on the nose. "Caught ya staring." He teases.

"Good. I'll get caught more often." I say, smiling as I stand on my tiptoes to kiss him on the lips.

"Come on, everyone! Let's get this welcome party started!" Josh hollers as he turns on his car's radio to blast music around us while we just mingle and welcome Ian back to the group with open arms.

I see Mark cooking on a grill that's set up on the other side of the pit, away from anything flammable, and the smell of hamburgers and hot dogs fills the air.

"I didn't think Mark could cook." I say as Bryan guides me over to one of the empty garages where the food and drinks are being set up courtesy of Lexi and Morgan while Josh brings over any of the cooked food once Mark serves it on a metal cooking sheet.

"Yeah. Whenever we went to the cabin in the past and we knew we were going to be there for a while, he would pull the grill out and usually make hamburgers or steaks for the two of us."

"Huh. I didn't know that."

"Yeah. I couldn't cook for shit until I met your dad." Bryan chuckles. "I mean, you know Gramps tried to teach me, but it just didn't click for me with him. And don't tell Gramps this, but your dad made it kinda fun."

I laugh as we form a line with Ian and Anna leading the charge, and we all pile our paper plates with hamburgers, hot dogs, chips, and an assortment of other side dishes until most of the guys' plates are threatening to buckle under the weight of the food.

"Don't worry, your secrets are safe with me."

I noticed a little way down the pit area that all the guy's cars are parked in a loose semi-circle, the trunks of the vehicles all facing each other. Bryan sits his dish on top of the trunk before wrapping his hands around my waist and boosting me up to sit me on the other side. I let out a squeak at the action, and Bryan's lips pull up in a sexy smirk.

"There. Comfy?"

"Yeah. I am." I say as I take a bite of the hamburger that Bryan made for me while we were in line. "You all did a great job getting this setup."

Bryan takes a sizeable bite of his hotdog and looks over his shoulder at the surrounding decorations, then to Ian. He's leaning against Josh's car and holding his side while he laughs at a joke Mark must have told them.

"Yeah, I think we did too." Bryan swings his gaze back to mine, and a small smile tugs at the corner of his lips. "Reminded me of helping you and the girls decorate the gym back home."

"Well, this is way better." I say as I finish the last bite of my macaroni salad and set my empty plate next to Bryan's still half-full one on the trunk of his Camaro.

"Maybe, but the dance is still my favorite because I was able to spend it with the people who meant the most to me, even if I lost you for a while after that night."

As his words hit me, I can't help but look down at my hands while nervously picking at my chipping blue nail polish.

"I never apologized to you for that night." I whisper.

"Yes, you did. You left me a voicemail." Bryan chuckles as his large hand covers my smaller one.

"Yeah, but a voicemail isn't a true apology."

He moves to where he's standing in front of me while bracing his hand on either side of my hips, and his proximity makes me look up at him before he speaks.

"It's fine, Annie. Obviously, no hard feelings between us, so just let it be a part of our past that eventually brought us together in the end." He says as he leans in, pressing his lips gently to mine. "Remember what I told you? Your absence made me fight harder to get back to you, and I will be forever grateful for that, even if it hurt both of us personally for a while. I would do it all over again if it meant I would always walk away with you at my side."

I chuckle. "Gahh, how can you be this cute *and* endearing at the same time?"

Before Bryan can say anything, Mark walks over to us with his arm draped over Lexi's shoulder, and the smile that's on Mark's face is nothing but trouble.

"Yo, lovebirds, Josh and James want to race before we head out early. So move your asses off the track."

I glance over Bryan's shoulder and notice that the others have either already moved or are currently moving their cars and picking up any leftover trash from the roadway so Josh and James can get their cars out of their respective garages, and we were completely oblivious to it.

Bryan's head hangs low between his shoulders, his forehead resting on my knee, almost like he's mentally counting to ten, so he doesn't yell at his friend for interrupting our conversation.

"I really need to kick his ass one day for his antics." Bryan mumbles.

I pat him on the shoulder. "No, you don't." I glance over my right shoulder and I see Morgan waving both me and Lexi over to the press box. "I'm going to be with the other girls in the box. I have my phone on me if you need me."

"Okay. Love you, Babe."

Bryan helps me off the trunk of his Camaro, and I wrap my hands around Lexi's arm while we make our way over to Morgan.

"Hi you two. I want out of this heat while Josh and James play. Come up here where it's cooler. God, I'm sweating bullets here."

"It is hot, even with the breeze." Lexi says while fanning her face with her hand.

As we walk up the stairs, I can't help but ask about Christy. "Hey where's Christy? I haven't seen her all day. I'm assuming she's sick?"

"Yeah. She messaged me last night. She started her cycle, and the first few days are always hard on her." Morgan says as she opens the door to the press box and we all walk inside.

Bryan

Once Taylor and Lexi are in the press box, I suddenly have the thought of pulling my car into my bay.

"Hey man, I'll be right back. I'm going to pull my car into my bay." Mark nods, but he gives me an odd look. "I don't know why. Call it a gut feeling." I shrug as I pull my keys out of my pocket and walk over to my car.

After I park in my bay and pull the garage down, Josh and James are on the starting line, and Nick is waving them off while I spot Ian and Anna in the low-level bleachers watching the start of the race. Mark moves his Challenger again and pulls near the main entrance, near the gates, and I walk over to lean against the trunk of his car.

I try to enjoy the moment of silence we have between us, but this is Mark, and I know it doesn't last long when it comes to him.

"So, you are finally making moves with Tay Tay, huh?"

"Come on, man. I didn't give you hell about you and Lexi."

"No, you would just give me the side-eye and a little smug smirk after you knew I was with her for more than just our cases."

"I was waiting for you to come back after one of your little trysts and tell me she dumped your ass for not being up to her standards." I shoot back.

"Damn, man, I am not feeling the love here all of a sudden. First Lexi says she wants to trade me in for an upgrade, and now you're saying I'm not up to her standards. I'm hurt."

Just as a comeback is on the tip of my tongue, I hear the roar of an engine. At first I think it's either Josh's or James' cars as they are coming around the second turn in their two-lap race, but the tone is different. I look over my shoulder at the gates, and what I see barreling down the road sends my heart into my throat.

Desmond and his gang in two cars. His Charger and the Jeep. All with guns ready to fire.

"Mark! Watch it!" I yell as I drop low to the ground and pull my Glock out of the back of my jeans.

Then gunfire rips through the air, and I'm beyond thankful that Taylor is up in the press box right now.

"Ian! Anna! Run!" Mark yells from his position near the trunk. He returns fire, hitting the jeep twice. Once through the window and the other in the wheel well, but missing the tire.

"This is payback for your bitches taking my new plaything!" Desmond roars, firing off a few shots, which makes me and Mark duck for cover.

"This dude's a fucking lunatic!" Mark says.

"You don't say?" I reply with sarcasm dripping into my tone.

I hear tires screeching on the pavement and when I chance a look above the passenger door; the Jeep is gunning it for us.

"Move! They're gonna ram your car!" I yell to Mark.

"No! Not the car!"

"Would you rather it be your body!?" I yell as we scramble in different directions, giving them two targets to focus on.

I take off to the right, running past the Jeep, where it veers off at the last minute, missing the Challenger completely. When I realize what just happened, Mark and I lock eyes and we take off, running towards the closest building we can.

Dread fills my chest as I realize I have no Kevlar vest on and I am utterly exposed with Desmond's Charger on my left, and the closest building for me is past his car. It's no use to go back to Mark's Challenger. That would be like standing behind a paper mache wall, but I can't just stand here and wait to be shot. So, I take off running diagonally towards the building that sits behind his car. Maybe if I can circle around them, it will force them to go wider, and I can tighten my formation to the building.

I hear the engine rev and gunshots go off a moment later, bullets zipping past me and hitting the pavement just a few feet away. I push myself to run faster, and just when I think I'm about to make it around to the building; I hear another gunshot.

A roar tipped in fear tears from my throat, then fiery pain rips at my body, making me stumble and fall so hard onto the pavement that darkness rushes over me, taking my racing thoughts with it.

Chapter Thirty-Six

Taylor

I try to stay in the press box watching the chaos of the drive-by shooting happen below me, but when Bryan becomes so openly exposed against Desmond's car, I know I have to get down there.

With Lexi and, to my surprise, the other girls on my heels, we rush down the steps. Just as I swing open the door, gunfire erupts around us, and I pull out my gun that was hidden under my shirt thanks to my bra holster attachment.

When I slowly step past the safety of the door, I watch as Bryan falls after another volley of gunfire and my heart sinks.

Come on. Move.

Move.

Move.

But he doesn't.

Before I can even think about shooting back, I already hear return fire breaking out, and Mark is leading the charge, fury etched on his face. His arms are locked at the elbow, and his hands grip his weapon so hard that I can see the whites of his knuckles from my position near the press box. His long strides are purposeful, daring the people on the other end of his muzzle to try and fight back.

Then Josh, Nick, James and somehow even Ian are all gripping their guns and shooting back, forcing Desmond and his gang to leave.

"This is the last time you waltz in here, Desmond! Next time, you don't leave here alive!" Mark shouts, and I know he means it.

Lexi must know it too, because I hear her mutter a curse under her breath as his words hit her. My focus flicks back to Bryan, who still has not moved from his spot on the pavement. I hope that maybe he's playing dead so the others can draw attention away from him, but when I spot a trickle of blood coming from the left side of his body, I take off towards him.

I don't call his name. I don't scream anything. I just focus on getting to him while silently praying he's okay.

Once I'm at his side, flashbacks of that December night threaten to take me down the rabbit hole again. This is a different place and different weather, but it still feels the same.

Bryan lying face down.

Not moving.

The smell of coppery blood filling my nose.

"No. Not again. Please." I whisper as I grab onto his shoulder and turn him over. Just like I did that night eight months ago.

"Taylor!" Mark shouts just as I get Bryan onto his back. "Is he hurt!"

"I don't know!" I sob as I take in Bryan's body, my hands running over his chest first.

I prepare for them to come up bloody, but they don't, and the sob of relief that escapes my throat is loud enough for everyone that is now gathered around us to hear.

"Bryan!" Mark shouts as he checks out the gash that's on his friend's forehead. "I think he's just knocked out. Looks like he hit his head."

I reach for his face, using my left thumb to open his right eye, and while his pupil reacts to the sunlight above him, I can tell he's not there behind the green iris. When I go to check the other eye, that's when recognition flares to life, and while he looks around, dazed, his eyes land on mine for a moment before he moans in pain.

"Bryan! Where does it hurt, Baby?"

"Leg." He grunts before moaning in pain again.

I look down, and as soon as I see it, Mark is already taking off his belt. I don't know how deep it is, but Bryan's been shot in the upper thigh. Judging by the amount of blood, I don't think it's hit anything major, but until we know for sure, we need to treat it like it's a femoral artery hit.

As Mark ties off Bryan's thigh, he screams out in pain, and I stroke his cheek, making him look at me, to focus on me and not the pain.

"Hey, I'm going to help you. Just hang in there, Baby."

"Cut his jeans! We need to see how bad it is!" Josh orders. "James, close and lock the gates, but stay there so you can unlock them once we know his condition."

Nick pulls a pocketknife out of his back pocket and hands it to me as I position myself closer to Bryan's left leg. Grabbing the hem of his jeans near the seam, I begin cutting, ending just under Mark's belt that's holding pressure above the wound.

Bryan hisses out a breath as I pull the soaked fabric away from his injured muscle. Even though his skin is coated in blood, I can thankfully see it's a flesh wound, not the through-and-through injury I feared.

"I think I can take care of this." I whisper to Mark and Lexi.

"Tempe said she has a large medical kit," Lexi says while pocketing her phone after receiving an apparent text from the agent.

"Get him into my car. I'll take him and get him help. Josh, help me carry him!" Mark orders, and the leader follows.

Both men grab Bryan from under his arms, lifting him up off the ground and practically carry him to Mark's Challenger. I stand there for a moment watching them; or mainly Mark and Bryan.

Mark's face is flooding with both fear and anger, while Bryan's is pale from pain and blood loss, and with each move his body makes, his face contorts in agony.

"Taylor. Come on. We need to go," Lexi says, pulling me with her as Mark finally gets Bryan into the front passenger seat of his car.

I snap back into action, rushing with Lexi over to the driver's side of the Challenger. She opens the door and pulls the seat forward so we can sit in the back. She lets me go first so I can be closer to Bryan, and as soon as I'm in the seat, I lean forward between the console and grab his hand.

"Everything's gonna be okay. Just try to take slow breaths."

He nods just as Mark drops into the driver's seat and takes off toward the gate that James is in the middle of opening again for us. Once we're through the gates, Mark flies down the road towards Lincoln's and Tempe's apartment, quickly shifting between gears to get up to speed.

Tense silence fills the car. The only noises are the roar of the engine and Bryan's groans of pain when Mark drives over imperfections in the road. I notice Mark looking at his friend; his eyes shining with fear and worry. But being Mark, he started joking despite the tense situation.

"Oh, come on, man. You're bleeding all over my seat." He whines.

"Oh, forgive me. I'll just magically stop bleeding over your precious car." Bryan says roughly, but I can tell he's thankful for the distraction.

Bryan then tries to move in the seat so he can take some pressure off his leg, but the movement causes him to groan in pain. I place a hand on his shoulder, trying to get him to settle down, and he looks back at me once before looking over at Mark, who has just pulled up to the apartment.

"Let's get you fixed up, buddy." Mark says as he exits the car, moving his seat forward and leaving the door open so Lexi and I can follow.

"We'll get you inside, and I'll take care of you." I say.

"I know you will. Just like always." He gives me a pained smile as Mark opens his passenger door and begins to lift Bryan out of the seat.

I watch as Lincoln walks out of the apartment, ready to grab Bryan's other side once Mark has him fully out of the car. Together, the two men carry him into the apartment, making their way into a back bedroom where I see a metal table with plastic draped over it and a good section of the floor.

"Oh, shit." Sophie says as she rushes into the room, her eyes landing on the still bleeding wound on Bryan's leg and her face pales. "What happened?"

"Come on, let's get you up on the table." Lincoln's voice fills the room before I can answer Sophie's question. "Mark, get ready to lift his good leg on my count."

Mark shifts his position so his arm wraps around Bryan's thigh, right behind his knee, and waits for Linc's instruction while Temperance shows me where she's set up the large Trauma-grade medical kit. The red bag already unfolded and waiting for me.

"Does this have everything you need, Taylor?" Temperance asks, her voice tight with fear as she looks from me to Bryan and back again.

I take a quick inventory of the pack:

Gloves.

Alcohol wipes and bottles.

Sutures.

Suture needles.

Gauze and wrap.

"I think so."

"Now." Lincoln instructs Mark to lift, and they both set Bryan on the table with ease.

Lincoln steps away as Temperance walks over to Bryan with a pillow that's also covered and taped closed with plastic.

"Here you go." She says as I pull on the gloves. "A little bit of comfort goes a long way."

She brushes her palm over Bryan's forehead, moving his dark brown hair with such a motherly touch that my heartbeat freezes in my chest for a moment, and I think the same happens to him. He looks up at her, shock coloring his features more than pain for a millisecond before it all sets back in.

"Here," Lincoln says, voice tense and rough as he comes back into the room with a large bottle in his hand. "Drink this, or Taylor will never be able to touch your leg."

Bryan tears his gaze from Temperence and locks onto the bottle in Lincoln's hand.

"Jack Daniels? You sure you and my Gramps don't know each other? That's his favorite." Bryan pants, trying to distract himself with humor as he leans up on his elbow to take the whisky bottle from Lincoln.

"It's a favorite of mine that I picked up from my father." Lincoln smirks as he unscrews the cap so Bryan can drink.

I watch as he takes three long pulls from the bottle before handing it back to Linc and clearing his throat with a cough from the burn of the liquor.

I step up to Bryan's side with the bottle of isopropyl alcohol in my hand, already seeing the whisky begin to cloud his green eyes.

"I thought you told me you didn't drink?" I jest.

"I don't." Bryan begins, his voice a little raspier than it was a minute ago. "But I never said I didn't try any at one point with Mark when we were younger." A sly smile lifts the corner of his mouth as he begins to relax a bit.

"Damn, dude. Just throw me under the bus like that. It was your granddad's liquor cabinet."

"Yeah, but you dared me to unlock it and steal a half-empty bottle." Bryan says, slurring his words.

I actually find myself chuckling at Bryan's words because I can totally see Mark saying something like that and Bryan caving. Not because of peer pressure, but because he had a friend to do stupid shit with.

Once I can tell he's as relaxed as he's going to get, I turn to Temperance, who's standing behind me, nervously picking at her fingers like she doesn't know what to do with them, and Sophie's the same way. So I give them both a job to do.

"Tempe, please hand me the trauma shears. I need to cut the rest of his jeans away before I can sew him up."

Her eyes light up with a job and she rushes over to the red bag and pulls out the correct pair of scissors I need. I gently pull the already cut piece of jean material from Bryan's leg and cut through the waistband, freeing his entire left leg.

"Sophie, why don't you hold his hand? Try to distract him from what I'm doing." I say, and she walks over to Bryan's right side.

His glassy-eyed gaze tracks her movement as she takes a chair and sits down near the table. He offers her his hand with a dopey smile.

"Hi, Sophie." Bryan slurs while lazily waving at her. "I'll try to be gentle with your hand."

"It's alright. You won't hurt me too much." Sophie replies, and I notice she twists her index and middle fingers together and lets Bryan's hand wrap around them.

I know with that move, her fingers won't be broken as easily if she were just holding his hand normally.

I use this moment to clean around the wound so I can see the extent of damage I'm working with. The blood made it seem larger than I thought, but it's still deep into the muscle, so walking is going to be difficult for a while.

"You have your dad's eyes." Bryan slurs to Sophie.

"What?" She chuckles.

"You have your dad's eyes." He repeats, a bit slower this time. "I was always told by my grandparents that I had my mother's eyes."

"That's nice to know," Sophie says, smiling softly.

"Yeah. When I was younger, I would stare at myself in the mirror—at her eyes—and I swear I could feel her staring back at times."

I notice that Linc and Tempe exchange a look at Bryan's words, but I don't have time to think too much about it.

"Bryan?" I say, forcing his attention on me for a minute. "This is gonna burn, but you need to try to stay still for me. I need to clean the wound and see what I'm working with."

He nods, and I don't wait for him to say anything before I pour the alcohol onto his wound. As soon as I pour the liquid onto his damaged skin, his head tilts back against the pillow Tempe gave him, and he screams out through clenched teeth.

Then, I work quickly. I dab at his skin with a clean piece of gauze, removing any lingering bubbles of the alcohol so I can see the entirety of the wound. While it's about three, maybe four inches long, it's only about an inch or so deep.

I can do this.

I press the suture needle to his skin so I can begin stitching him up, but he cries out in pain, forcing me to pull my hand back.

"Drink." Lincoln orders, and Bryan takes another deep swig of the whisky, panting as that next dose of liquor floods his bloodstream.

"Here, see if this helps." Temperance says as she hands me a bottle.

Numbing spray.

"Thank you."

I take the bottle and I spray it over the entirety of his thigh, and after a moment I test it to make sure he's numb. Poking the needle where I did a moment ago. No reaction.

"Here we go." I tell Bryan, but I notice his eyes are closing, and when I glance over at the bottle of whisky in Linc's hand, it's about half empty.

"Boy, he's going to have a helluva hangover once he wakes up." Mark says from the corner of the room while holding Lexi close to his chest.

"Better a hangover than an open leg wound." Lincoln says while setting the bottle down on a bedside table.

I'm about halfway done with the suture, then I turn to Mark and Lexi. "Lexi, pull my keys out of my front right pocket and go over to my apartment and get a change of clothes for me and Bryan. I don't think it would be a good idea to move him across the street until he wakes up with a clear mind."

"Good point." Mark says as Lexi walks from his side and pulls my keys out.

"And get soft clothing for him. No jeans right now." I tell her, and she nods, leaving the room with Mark on her heels.

A few minutes after my two friends leave, I finish the suture and I take my bloody gloves off with a satisfied sigh. "There. All fixed."

"You are amazing, Taylor." Temperence says as she pulls out a biohaz-ard bag from the med kit. "Bryan and your friends are lucky to have you."

"Thank you." I say and I notice that Linc has left the room, apparently to put the remaining whisky back where ever he got it from, leaving Sophie to stare at Bryan's now sleeping form.

"Sophie, while your mom and I clean up, why don't you get a warm pan of water and a cloth so I can clean him up before we move him to the bed?"

She nods and gets up without a word, then returns a few minutes later with a warm pan of water, a washcloth, and a towel for me to dry him off.

"Thank you."

"We'll leave you to it," Tempe says as she walks out with her arm wrapped around Sophie.

I turn to Bryan and I begin to pull his blood splattered shirt from his body, lifting him off the table by his upper arm enough so I can lift the shirt over his head. I just finish getting the other side of his ruined jeans off when Mark walks into the room with clean clothes for Bryan.

"Figured you'd want some help in here, and I know he'd kill me if I let Lexi or some strangers in here while he's unconscious and naked." Mark says as he sits the bundle of clothes on the bed.

"Thanks, Mark." I say as I begin to pull his boxers off.

He notices me struggling with this part, so he walks over and helps lift Bryan's lower half for me so I can slide the material down his legs, still being mindful of his injury.

"So you *have* seen his—"

"Mark, if you finish that sentence, I will punch you." I look up at him as I wring the washcloth out, then begin to wipe the dried blood from

Bryan's body. "Besides, I was learning to be a nurse, so you think I haven't seen a penis before?"

"Well, yeah, maybe. But it's different when it's your boyfriend's." Mark points to the obvious.

I roll my eyes and, yeah, they may linger on *a certain* part more than they should. Damn, I hate it when Mark's right.

"You gonna help me with him or just keep spouting nonsense?"

"You hate it when I'm right, don't you?"

"Bite me." I shoot back, and he laughs, then he grabs the towel and begins drying the parts of Bryan's body that I clean.

He's abnormally quiet for a moment, and when I look over at him, I catch him staring at his friend's still sleeping form.

"Is he good to you?" I look at Mark in bewilderment, and he shakes his head, like he said the wrong thing. "I know Bryan would never hurt you, but you're like a little sister to me now, and I need to make sure he's treating you right in *all* aspects. You know?"

"Yeah. I get it." I nod. "And to answer your question, yes, he's only done what I wanted." I give him a sly smile, and I know I'm probably gonna regret this, but I ask it anyway. "I can ask the same with you and Lexi. Are you good to her and what she wants?"

"Define *good*. 'Cause Lex, oh boy." Mark begins with a sly chuckle.

"Don't. No. I don't want to know." I say, putting my hands up to stop him from talking. "Help me with his clothes so you and Linc can get him into bed."

He laughs this time, but he nods, helping me dress Bryan in a t-shirt and shorts before walking over to the door and yelling for Lincoln to help move him. And after I get cleaned and changed into fresh clothes of my own, Temperance makes me a hot bowl of soup, which I eat in the bedroom since I don't want to be away from Bryan for long.

Meanwhile, Linc leaves for a bit, saying something about getting some things for Bryan before he wakes up. And I don't know how he did it, but he comes back with mounds of gauze, tape, and even pain medication and antibiotics that I know damn well he didn't have a prescription for. But I don't press him for info. I'm just glad that there's medicine here for Bryan when he needs it.

Mark and Lexi stay for a while during the night so I can get some sleep because we all know that if I was alone with him, I wouldn't get much. I'd be too worried about checking on him to make sure he's alright. So, I turn in at 9 p.m. with the promise that Mark will wake me up at midnight so he and Lexi can get a few hours of sleep, too.

Chapter Thirty-Seven

Taylor

"Taylor, wake up." Mark's soft voice whispers in my ear for what feels like five minutes after I close my eyes, but then I remember why he's waking me up and my eyes fly open.

"What time is it?" I croak.

"Two-thirty."

"Mark!" I whisper-shout.

"What? You looked too comfortable, and Lexi was asleep on me. So I gave you both a few extra hours." Mark smiles, and I shake my head as I quietly get out of bed and make my way into the attached bathroom while he helps Lexi off the couch that he and Linc hauled into the room so they would be comfortable.

After I exit the bathroom, I notice on my bedside table are two cold bottles of water sitting on the nightstand on my side of the bed, along with the medication that Lincoln brought back last night.

"That should do until morning." Lexi says groggily, rubbing the sleep from her eyes.

"Thanks for staying, you two. Now go get some rest. I'll call you if I need anything."

I quietly walk them out the front door, making sure to lock it behind them before venturing back into the bedroom and slip into bed with Bryan.

I sit with my back against the headboard, and just when I place a pillow behind me to get comfortable, Bryan turns over, wrapping his arm around my waist and resting his head on my stomach, pulling me close to his body. He tries to throw his injured leg over mine like he usually does when he's holding me, but he doesn't make it on the first try. So, I scoot my leg closer to his, and when he moves again, our limbs wrap around one another, and he subconsciously breathes a sigh of contentment and dozes back off.

I gently run my fingers through his hair, one because I can't stop touching this man and he's mine to do what I want with, but two, it's my way of also checking to make sure he's not feverish. Once I'm happy that he's not running a fever, I gently lift the hem of his shorts and check his bandage. I don't see any blood seeping through the material, and I release a sigh of relief.

After I pull the sheets over us, I grab my phone from the bedside table to text Mom, hoping she's either awake at this time or on a shift at the hospital.

I make sure my phone is on silent, not even letting the vibrate function work so I don't wake Bryan before I send the text.

Me: Hey Mom. You awake?

Three minutes pass, and just as I begin to think she's probably asleep, I receive a response.

Mom: Hey Honey. Yeah I'm working right now. Just caught me going on break. You ok?

Me: Yeah. I'm fine. I have a question for you though

Mom: Ok? Shoot

Me: Can you send me instructions on how to care for a GSW to the upper thigh thats about an inch or so deep? Bryan is hurt and I want to make sure I did everything I could.

Mom: TAYLOR! *Screaming emoji.* Is he alright? Why didn't you call me sooner?

Me: Yes he's fine now. I was able to stitch him up, but you know me, I'm second guessing myself and I want to make sure I did everything I could. And everything happened so fast. I didn't have much time to think.

Mom: Ok. I'll send you info on it. Has the bleeding stopped? Fever?

Me: Yes and no fever. I'm with him now and he's cool as a cucumber.

I take a selfie of me and Bryan, showing her that he's asleep on my stomach with a small smile on his face. When I tap send on my phone and the picture uploads to the text feed, I see a heart emoji appear from her a moment later.

Mom: Can you take a pic of his injury?

I nod like she can see me as I send her a picture of the injury I took earlier before I wrapped the bandage around his leg.

Mom: Looks good Honey. You did well. But how did this happen?

I go on to explain what happened over the last few days. From Ian's wreck, to Anna being taken, and my little rescue mission with the girls that eventually led up to this shootout.

Mom: Geez. you always go big don't you?

Me: You told me to always do my very best. Well that includes raising hell.

Mom: *GIF of a dachshund giving a side-eyed glare*

I have to hold back my laughter so I don't wake Bryan, but I can just imagine my mother's face right now.

Me: I'm gonna let you go. Please email me any info you can on this type of wound. I appreciate it. Love you Mom

Mom: Ok I have it now and emailing over. Please be safe Taylor. And tell Bryan I wish him a quick recovery. Do you all have pain meds and stuff for him?

> **Me:** Yes. Lincoln the agent we are working down here with got them and antibiotics last night. So we are good.

> **Mom:** Ok. Let me know if you need anything else. Love you my brave girl. *Heart emoji. Kissy face emoji*

> **Me:** Love you too Mom. and tell Dad and Cody the same.

I lock my phone and as I set it on the nightstand; I notice the digital alarm clock shows it's almost 5:30am.

I slide my attention back to Bryan as he breathes in deeply, just like he usually does when he's about to wake up, and my body goes still. Maybe if he can feel I'm not moving, he'll doze back off.

Then his eyebrows furrow in discomfort, and I don't know if it's solely from his leg hurting or if he does have a hangover headache from the whisky last night.

I tenderly run my fingers through his hair, trying to soothe him back to sleep, but the action only pulls him further into consciousness. His eyes flutter open, and it takes him a minute to focus in on my face; slowly blinking again and again to clear the haze from his eyes and mind.

"Shhh. Go back to sleep, Babe." I croon, giving him a light kiss on the top of his head.

Just when Bryan is about to close his eyes, his gaze flicks to my right, taking in the unfamiliar room around him, and clarity comes rushing back to his green eyes.

"Where are we?" He asks, his voice still rough from sleep.

He tries to move from my side, which causes him to draw in a quick breath when he moves his leg and the muscles pull at the freshly stitched skin.

I can almost see his mind working, trying to push past the pain, trying to figure out where we are to keep me safe. I wrap my arms around his neck to keep him still.

"Bryan. Look at me." His body freezes under my touch, and his gaze locks onto mine. "We are safe. We're in Lincoln's and Temperance's apartment."

He looks confused for a minute before his hand comes up to his temple, rubbing the spot in small, tight circles, and I know now he's got a raging headache.

"Lie down, Bullet." I ease him onto his back, and he groans, trying to hold his leg, but his fingers come close to where the bandage covers his stitches, and I grab his wrist, stopping him. "Don't touch. Do you remember what happened?"

"Kind of. Why is my head killing me?"

"Linc got you drunk last night so you would be relaxed enough for me to stitch you up."

Bryan takes another breath, like memories are flooding back, and he pinches the bridge of his nose with his index finger and thumb.

"Jack Daniels. Yeah. I remember now."

He groans in pain, and I roll over to grab the cool bottle of water and the pain pills that Lexi left. "Here. Take these. It will help with the pain."

I sit up on my knees at his side, and he lowers his hand from his face to look at me. Pain clouds his green eyes, and my heart breaks for him. I want nothing more than to take it all away from him, but I know that this is the best I can do.

Taking the offered pills and bottle of water, he downs them before handing the bottle to me so I can sit it back on the nightstand.

His gaze locks on mine, searching my face as if trying to figure out what question to ask first. "Why are we in Lincoln's and Temperances's place?"

"It was going to be too much to move you into our apartment once I finished stitching you up and you passed out. Plus, we were all exhausted, so it made sense."

He nods in understanding, and then a grimace flares across his features, and I know it's not from the pain.

"Did I say anything last night?" Bryan asks, and he pinches the bridge of his nose again in both aggravation and embarrassment. "I did, didn't I?"

I snuggle in closer to him, and he instantly wraps his arm around my waist, just like he always does when I'm close.

"What do you remember?" I ask.

"It's hazy; I guess I was already buzzing at this point, but was Sophie there?" I nod. "Shit."

"But it was kinda cute." I say.

And it was. Maybe 'cute' isn't the right word, but what he said wasn't terrible. And that's what alcohol does. It can either make you closed up and mean, or funny and you spill every secret and thought you have.

"Me talking about whose eyes we each have is not cute." He shoots back at me, then groans when he tries to move his leg.

"Hey, don't move. You need to rest." I say.

"How bad is it?" He asks, looking down like he can see the wound through the white bandage secured around his upper thigh.

"Bad enough. The bullet just grazed you, but it was deep enough to injure the muscles."

"You stitched me up." He says it like he's just now catching that part, even though I've said it like three times now.

"Yeah, I did."

"You will never cease to amaze me. Thank you, Annie." Bryan says as he wraps his hand around the back of my neck and pulls me to him, his lips gently caressing mine.

I slide my hand up his shirt-clad chest, and when my fingers brush across his neck, I feel his other hand reach for my ass, gripping me to bring me closer to his side. While the hand splayed across my body is intimate, it's not meant to be sexual. This is just so he can feel my weight next to him, letting the both of us know we are here, safe and whole.

"I don't want to hurt you." I whisper, breaking our kiss before he bites my lower lip between his teeth, pulling me back to his mouth.

"You won't." Bryan says, his lips skimming over mine as he speaks. "Are you okay?"

"Yes, I'm—"

My breathless words are interrupted by the door swinging open, followed by the scolding voice of Temperance. "Bryan Alexander Evans! Have you no shame of where you are?"

We jump apart like we are on fire, and Bryan groans at the pain flaring in his leg at the sudden movement, and I crowd in to him again with my hand splayed across his chest, making sure he's alright.

"I would expect this shit from *your* mother, but this woman is acting like she's mine." Bryan whispers into my ear before letting me go so I can scoot away from him.

He then directs his gaze to Temperance and says. "I wasn't doing anything other than kissing my girlfriend after a hectic event and making sure she was alright." Something flashes in his green eyes, and he narrows his gaze at her. "How did you know my middle name anyway?" Bryan asks. "I didn't think it was listed on any files in the agency."

Temperance pauses, as if thinking over her words for a moment. "You don't think we wouldn't do our own background check on the agents we work with? I mean, we do have a daughter who's underage and is, as you know, close to us. So, we make sure everyone we work with is vetted."

"That makes sense." I say, verbally getting between Bryan and Tempe. "And I'm sorry that you walked in on us kissing, but I swear nothing else happened." I tell her only because we are technically in their apartment.

"If you two need anything, Mark and Lexi are here already. Lincoln went out to get you a set of crutches, Bryan, so he'll be back soon." She says quickly, then she walks out the door without another word.

"Well, that was weird." Bryan huffs as he tries to sit up to lean his back against the headboard, which causes him to suck in a sharp breath through his teeth.

"Easy," I tell him. "You don't need to rip your stitches."

"Can you get Mark and Lexi in here?" Bryan asks once he's somewhat comfortable in the bed.

"Sure."

I ease off the mattress and walk to the door, swinging it open and spotting Mark and Lexi on the love seat. I silently wave them in and shut the door behind us once they walk in. Noticing Mark's hand on the small of Lexi's back, I find myself smiling, remembering my conversation with him just a couple of hours ago.

"Yo man. How ya feel?" Mark asks while throwing his free arm out as he and Bryan does this weird handshake thing then fist bump at the end.

"It's their secret handshake, and it's annoying as hell." Lexi says, rolling her eyes.

Mark pushes the couch that's still in the room closer to the bed so he and Lexi can sit down while I take my spot beside Bryan on the bed again, waiting to see what he has to say.

"Is everyone else alright?" Bryan asks Mark.

"Yeah," Mark says, his voice tight. "What about you?"

Bryan shakes his head and swallows hard, his gaze boring into Mark's like they're having a silent conversation.

And like the hardhead my boyfriend is, he tries to move his leg again. Flexing his ankle while trying to lift it at the hip and he hisses in pain. "Shit. Not good."

"Damn it." Mark mutters under his breath.

"Care to let us know what is going through your minds?" Lexi snaps.

"I can't race." Bryan growls, his gaze still not leaving Mark's.

"Well yeah. No duh." I scoff. "Not until you're healed enough for the leg to bear weight, which will be a few weeks."

Bryan's intense green gaze meets mine finally, and the fury mixed with fear makes the breath freeze in my chest.

"No, Taylor. I can't *race* him. This was payback for you taking back what he thought was his, and for what I did to him when he first showed up."

My eyes blow wide. "He's going to make you forfeit the race because he took out your clutch leg."

"Oh, fuck, she's right." Mark growls, now noticing the real reason they shot at Bryan's left leg. "I'll race the bastard then."

"I don't think that will work." Bryan sighs. "I'd have to talk with Josh, but I seriously don't think I can have a stand in."

"What about me?" I say with little thought.

"What about you?" Bryan snaps, and I can tell he regrets his tone, but I don't let his bladed words hurt me.

"What if I race him?"

"Absolutely not." Mark and Bryan say in unison.

"Isn't that why you were teaching me to drive a manual, Bryan? So I can race?"

"No. I taught you so you could get the hell out of here for reasons like this shit right here." He says calmly, but I see the fire of protection burning in his eyes.

"I say let her do it." Lexi says, crossing her arms and looking both men down like her word is law.

"Alexis, that's not on the table." Mark grumbles.

"Don't you Alexis me." Lexi warns with a glare that I'm glad I'm not on the receiving end of. "I'm with Taylor, and think about it; this asswipe is egotistical. What if Bryan challenges him to race against Taylor in his place with the same rules applied? If the asshole wins the race, he is allowed to kill Bryan and take Taylor with no fight. If you do it that way, he won't be able to ignore the challenge. It will hurt his reputation if he declines, and it will be a sign of weakness in some people's eyes."

"Damn, Lex. I didn't know you had it in you to be so...dark." Mark smirks.

"You usually don't piss me off enough to bring out that side. But don't push your luck, Buddy."

"I still don't like it." Bryan says, and I open my mouth to argue Lexi's point, but he holds up a hand to me, forcing the words back down my throat. "But that might actually be a good plan. Play to what he thinks are his strengths and our weaknesses."

"I think that's a solid plan, too."

Our heads whip to the door, and we find Lincoln leaning his shoulder against the door frame with a pair of crutches in his hand and a serene smile on his face.

"You four work well together. I know I've probably said that, but with tensions getting higher each day, you all lean on the other more and more to look at the case from different points of view." He leans a set of crutches against the wall near the door. "Now, see if you can walk with these, and let's try to finish this case while it's still under our control."

Chapter Thirty-Eight

Bryan

We spend the afternoon still gathered in Lincoln and Temperence's apartment so I can get used to walking with crutches before Taylor allows me to leave. I catch Temperance still giving me the side-eye for what I said to her earlier, but she doesn't give me any more grief; verbally, at least.

And yeah, maybe I didn't have to grab Taylor's ass the way I did and her words *did* make it seem like something was going on, but like damn, I may be a guy but I'm not *that* hormonal to mess with my girl in a stranger's bed. But it still irks me that she yelled at us like she was my mother. I don't even think if my mom were still alive, she would have yelled the way Temperance did.

Sighing, I push those thoughts to the back of my mind and focus on getting around the apartment while trying to ignore the burning, stabbing pain in my thigh that constantly reminds me that I cannot race against this piece of shit.

The one thing I can't ignore, though, is the thought of Taylor racing against him. I don't want the images forming in my mind, but at the same time, I can't stop them. I want all the scenarios to end with her winning, but then one or two slip in of her not, and my stomach plummets through the floor.

I want nothing more than to pack her shit and get her and Lexi on the next plane out of this damn state, but I know my girl and she would probably sneak back here and raise all kinds of hell, which I would love and hate in the same breath.

So, once I'm stable on my crutches, I bite the bullet, and over the next few days, and with the lingering pain manageable, I ride with Taylor in her Mustang and make sure she can race. Help her make minor adjustments to her form, and when she second-guesses herself, I correct her as gently as I can, but I know the sharp edge of my fear still slices the air between us, but she straightens in the seat, pulls up to the starting line and does it all again.

"You did well today, Babe." I tell her when she flawlessly completes two more laps. "Pull into the bay next to mine and let me change your oil and tires."

"You sure you can do that?" Taylor asks as she pulls into the pit lane.

"Yes, Taylor. Josh found me a stool that's adjustable for me to sit my ass on while I work on the cars. Now park it." I give her a teasing smile as she does just that.

Once she pulls into the garage, I turn around towards her back seat, trying again to push the discomfort of the added pressure to my leg at the movement to get my crutches and open the passenger door.

"Pop the hood for me." I ask.

Thankfully, getting out on the passenger side allows me to use my good leg, where I'm able to hop around a bit to make room so I can get the crutches under my arms.

"You need help with anything?" Taylor asks as she pops the hood and slams her driver's door.

I pull the adjustable stool over in front of her car, and when I sit down, the pressure and pain lessen to a dull ache.

"No, Baby, I'm good. You go spend time with Lexi and the other girls." I grab her hand, pulling her in for a kiss. "I'm proud of you."

"Thanks. Love you. See ya in a bit." Taylor says as she walks out of the garage.

I watch her walk over to Lexi, both of them hugging and smiling brightly at one another. Once Taylor's out of my line of sight, I sigh and look back towards her car.

"Okay. Let's get your oil changed." I say to myself as I unlock the hood latch and push it up.

I'm thankful this car has hydraulic hood struts that automatically lock in place, so I don't have to get up to prop the hood open. Using my good leg, I push myself around the car to kick the lift plates underneath the driver's side, and just when I'm about to roll around to the front of the car to do the same to the passenger side, I find James there kicking the plates under the car for me.

"Thanks," I say as I press the button on the lift and wait for it to get to the height I need before I release the button.

"You need any help there, man?" James asks.

I glance at the tire in front of me and notice the tread has been worn down due to the driving Taylor did today with them.

"Sure. Can you swap tires for me?"

"Yeah. I can do that." James replies as he walks over to the tool chest and grabs the battery-operated impact driver and the lug nut socket.

When he comes back over to the car, I roll to the toolbox next so I can grab a ratchet along with a ten-millimeter socket so I can unscrew the oil plug.

As I slide back under the car with the dirty oil catch pan, James drops the rear passenger tire on the ground before rolling it over to the corner of the garage where the new tires sit, waiting to be mounted.

"Hey, I got a question for you." He asks as he walks behind me toward the front passenger tire.

"What's up?" I ask, looking into his mismatched brown and green eyes, waiting for the oil to drain from the engine.

"Why is Taylor racing more all of a sudden?"

I watch him for a moment. His movements seem fluid. Not in a hurry at all. He's totally in his element working on the car with me, and he just wants to know why there's a change in the group.

And it may be the way I've caught him looking at me, at my leg, out of the corner of his eye, but is that guilt flashing in his eyes?

No. It's just remorse for my injury, right?

Either way, something keeps me from stating the obvious. Keeps me from telling him that Taylor needs to be ready to race that bastard in my place. So, I trust my gut and tell him only what he needs to know.

"She's just been wanting to learn more, and I'm in no shape to race." I say, waving a hand at my leg, and his eyes blatantly zero in on the bandage that peeks out from the bottom of my jean shorts. "So, I figured I'd use this free time to teach her some things. I mean, she's not going to be as good as I am, but if it makes her feel better, then I'll do it." I scoff.

He nods, satisfied with what I know is a bullshit answer, but I need to keep eyes off her until I can't anymore, and we both continue to work in silence.

About an hour later, after the oil is changed, and I inspected the brakes, James and I install the new tires. Then, he drives her Mustang over to the alignment machine, where I roll under her car and make sure the alignment is done correctly. I don't trust anyone here to do this other than myself.

Once I'm finished and he backs the vehicle off the machine, his phone rings with an incoming call. He looks between me and the phone as if deciding whether to take the call before finally shaking his head with a look of aggravation lining his eyes.

"Sorry, man. I gotta take this."

He puts the car in park, exits the driver's seat, and leaves it running in the middle of the garage before walking off to answer the phone.

"Really, dude?" I sigh.

I hop over to the driver's side door and I slowly lower myself into the seat. My leg is starting to throb like it has its own heartbeat, and I wish I would have grabbed the pain pills from my nightstand this morning, but for the last two days, it hasn't been hurting that much. So, I know I've overdone it today with hobbling around to work on Taylor's car.

"Almost done." I grunt as I lift my leg to get it into the car.

Hopefully, I can move enough to engage the clutch slowly. I know I'm screwed when it comes to shifting for a race, but maybe just to put it into first gear won't be so bad.

I try to lift my leg at the hip, but I suck in a sharp breath when I feel the stitches and healing muscle pull at the movement.

"Oh, shit." I pant. "Damn, that hurts."

"Yo, what the hell do you think you're doing?" Josh says, then turns back to his own phone call. "Sorry, man, I gotta go. I'll talk to you later."

He jogs over to me and leans his arm against the doorframe, his brow arched in question. "What are you doing?" He asks again.

"I was just trying to drive this back to the bay." I groan, rubbing my thigh to cover the pain while trying to be mindful of the stitches under the bandage, but it does little to ease the discomfort.

"Come on, Bryan. Get out. I'll drive it back for you. Is the garage still open?"

I nod as he helps me out and parks my ass on the rolling stool in a way that makes me feel like I just got caught stealing cookies out of the cookie jar.

"I get it. You want to do things on your own, but dude, you were shot by a fucking bullet. Let us help you." Josh says as he drops behind the wheel.

"Not the first time." I mumble.

And I feel even more helpless now. When I was shot in the chest eight months ago, my body *felt* like shit, so I could handle sitting or lying around, but with the leg wound, yes it hurts like hell, but I don't *feel* like I'm still on death's door. So, it's hard for me to sit around and do practically nothing.

Josh takes Taylor's car, and I watch him drive it into her bay, and thankfully, the way it's situated, I don't lose sight of him. So I can rest a bit easier that he's not given the opportunity to be *alone* with her car.

I still feel that there is a rat among Josh's team; I just don't know who yet. So, I'm keeping my eye on everyone.

Josh picks up my crutches and waves them at me, silent question of if I want them. I nod and give him a thumbs up.

"Here you go, man. Now get your girl and go home and rest. I have a feeling you're gonna need it soon."

"Yeah. I know." I grumble, shaking my head at his tone. Then I get an idea. Test the rat infested waters. "I'll tell you one thing. That bastard better come with armored plates strapped to his body, because if he hurts my girl, I'm going to fucking kill him before he can kill me first."

"No, you won't. Like you told me, killing someone changes you. Don't stoop to his level." Josh says.

"But I have pulled the trigger on people, Josh." I snarl truthfully. "I have killed to protect what is *mine*. And I have no issues doing it again."

Granted, it's only been two people. That guy from Mark's first case with Lexi and then Daryl from my case; but despite that, Josh doesn't need to know the body count.

He stares at me, and I know he can see the fire burning in my eyes, and he actually takes a step back.

Good. If he's the rat, then he'll go running to Desmond to warn him. And James knows that Taylor is racing more, so that'll earn an update. Ian is barely here because of his still-healing injuries, and Nick is just a drifter. So I can't set them up with anything. But these two. These two feel right; I just don't know which one yet.

"There's Taylor. I'm gonna go. Thanks for helping me, Josh." I say as Taylor, along with Lexi and Mark, walk over to her garage.

"Anytime, man. Take care of yourself." Josh says gently.

I grit my teeth together as I lean on the crutches to help ease the ache in my leg so I can make it across the pit and over to the garage.

"Hey, Babe. Car's all done. Fresh oil and tires for ya." I say as I lean in to kiss her gently on the lips.

"Oh God. You two *really* need to do that in front of me?" Mark quips.

I'm about to tell him he's got a girl to do that with, but Lexi must see the comment on my tongue because she elbows me in the side.

"Ow! What was that for?" I ask, and Taylor laughs.

"Just trying to save you from more pain, buddy." Lexi smirks, and I shake my head, chuckling, but it's short-lived when my leg thumps with pain again, and I'm forced to lean against the trunk of the Mustang. Taylor's eyes immediately lock onto mine, and she gives me a scolding look that is so much like her mother.

"Let's get you home," Taylor says as she walks over to me and helps me get into the passenger seat.

As she backs out of the garage, I notice that James is standing next to the press box, like he's staring holes into the Mustang. Then, as Taylor drives behind Mark in his Challenger, we pass Josh, who's still in the main garage, leaning against the bay door with his arms crossed over his chest, just watching us leave too.

Which one of you will stab me in the back? I wonder.

Twenty minutes later, we arrive at our apartments and say good night to Mark and Lexi. Once inside, Taylor immediately goes back into the bedroom and brings out my bottle of painkillers, then walks into the kitchen to grab a bottle of water.

"Here, take these."

"Thank you." I say as I down the pills. "I knew I should have brought them today."

"No, you shouldn't have overdone it today." She scolds.

"I didn't do much." I say, and she shoots me a look that wants to call my bullshit. "Okay, okay. So maybe I was hobbling around too much."

She points to the bedroom with her index finger. "Go to the bathroom. I need to find something to cover your leg so you can get a shower."

I just make it into the bathroom, and Taylor comes in with a piece of plastic, scissors and tape, and she gives me a bright smile.

"I found a cast protector from the med kit that Tempe gave me. So I'll cut one end to slide it over your leg, and then I'll tape both ends shut with this," Taylor says as she shows me the medical tape that I know sticks to skin like glue. She helps me undress, and after she covers my bandage with the plastic; she leaves me to shower alone while she takes the main bathroom.

Once we both finish our showers, she dresses me again in my boxers and shorts and helps me into bed. Even with the pain meds flowing in my veins, it still hurts to lift my leg when she props it up on a pillow to help with swelling.

"I'm sorry, but you need to elevate it," Taylor says gently.

"I know. It still hurts to lift it, though."

"I'm sorry." She whispers again as she places a soft kiss on my skin. "Let me change your bandage and then we'll go to sleep." Taylor says as she walks out of the room.

A few minutes later, she comes back in with a handful of fresh gauze and more tape. Then, kneeling on the floor beside the bed, she slips into a pair of blue latex gloves and begins to unwrap my leg. I mentally prepare myself to see the white cloth covered with blood and gore from the wound, but it's not, and we both breathe a sigh of relief.

"It's looking good. It's just red around the stitches, which is probably coming from you walking around so much." She chastises.

"Hey, you know you can't keep me down." I chuckle. "Just ask your mother when I was in the hospital."

"Oh, I know. She's told me." Taylor smiles as she cleans and re-wraps my leg.

She takes the soiled gauze over to the bathroom to throw them, and her gloves away before washing her hands and joining me in the bed. Thankfully, our room's layout allows me to still sleep on my side of the bed that's closer to the door, unlike Linc and Temperance's apartment, where Taylor slept next to the door, which I hated once I realized it.

"Come here, Baby." I say with a small smile on my face.

Taylor gently climbs into bed, snuggling up to my side, resting her head on my bare chest while I run my fingers up and down her spine.

"Everything will work out." I tell her when I feel her dragging her index finger down the middle of my chest like she's deep in thought.

"I know. I'm just worried he won't take the bait."

"He will." I sigh. "He's too much of a greedy, attention-seeking ass-hole. He's not gonna want to ignore my challenge towards him. I'm just playing into his own ego, which will be his downfall."

"I trust you with my life, Bryan," Taylor says as she presses her lips to my chest, right over my scar.

"Good. 'Cause your life is gonna be mine for a long time, Annie. Count on it." I tenderly grab her chin, forcing her to look into my eyes so she can see the truth in them.

"I'll be sure to hold you to that, Bullet," Taylor whispers as I pull her mouth to mine, as if sealing that promise we just made between each other as we settle in for the night and prepare for tomorrow's troubles.

Chapter Thirty-Nine

Taylor

Over the next week, I'm happy that Bryan seems to be getting better each day. He's able to bear more and more weight on his leg, but he still needs to walk with a cane, which I know he absolutely hates, but he does it with my insistence.

No matter how happy I am that he's healing, I still can't shake the feeling of fear that rears its ugly head at what has now become a waiting game.

When will Desmond make his move? When will he come for Bryan that will force me to race against this prick?

I mean, I'm getting better at racing. A lot better than I ever thought I would, but the little voice in the back of my mind whispers doubts.

What if I freeze?

What if I second-guess myself even though Bryan's been forcing that action from my mind?

After I finish another practice run against Christy with Bryan in the passenger seat, and winning this race, I park my car in the garage without being told to. It's become my ritual. Race and park in the garage for Bryan to change my oil and tires.

"Good job again today, Babe," Bryan says as he kisses me on the cheek before exiting the car.

I follow him, opening my driver's side door and again popping the hood without being told.

"Thanks." I say with a small smile as he opens the hood and unscrews the oil cap.

"Could you kick those yellow arms under your car, please?" Bryan asks as he hobbles over to the passenger side, leaning more on his cane so he can use his right leg to kick the lift arms under my car on that side.

"Sure."

"Thank you." He says as he presses a button, and my car begins to rise into the air. "You gonna do anything else today?" Bryan asks as the lift locks into place and he limps over to the toolbox in the corner to get what tools he needs.

"Actually, I think I may walk down to the beach." I tell him. "I need to clear my mind."

Bryan walks under my car with a ratchet and socket in hand and glances at me before he slips the socket over the drain plug in the oil pan and then cracks the seal to unscrew the plug, letting the oil drain into the catch pan.

"You okay? Anything you want to talk about?"

"Nothing that we don't already know." I shake my head.

Bryan gives me a small smile and then nods his head toward the front gate. "Go on. Try to have fun at the beach. You deserve it anyway."

"Okay. Do you want me to meet you back here or at the apartment?"

"The apartment. As soon as I get done here, I need to get off my leg before my nurse kicks my ass." He grins and gives me a wink.

"Wow. She sounds like a nightmare." I chuckle.

"Yeah, but I'd take it, because she's dressed like a daydream." Bryan says as he shifts his weight on his right leg and hooks his cane around my waist, pulling me closer to him.

My body crashes against his, hands splayed across his firm chest, and our hips line up where I can feel the bulge slowly building between us. Heat floods my veins, and I know I can't hide the blush that's crawling up my cheeks at his touch.

"I love you." He declares with a quick kiss on my lips before releasing me and giving me a playful shove. "Go, before I second-guess letting you out that gate."

With those words, I am hightailing it out of the garage. Not that I don't want to know what Bryan's plans were for me, but I don't want others to interrupt us.

I catch Lexi's eye as Mark takes his turn on the track, and I smile at her.

"Stay here. I'm going to the beach." I sign to her, and she nods.

Once I walk past the main gates of the track, my mind immediately begins to spiral.

Bryan seems so dead-set on Desmond taking his challenge, but what if he doesn't? And with how close I know we both will be, will we have time to even draw our guns if Desmond makes a move first?

Then I start thinking about different scenarios of what could happen, and how to act in each one where we come out on top. I'm so entranced in my own thoughts I don't notice that I walk by an alley until a shadow catches the corner of my eye, making the hairs on the back of my neck stand on end.

Someone's there.

I begin to turn my body so I can face my attacker head-on, but I don't get that chance. Large, rough hands grab my right shoulder and violently pull me from the main street and into the alley, shoving me against the rough, solid brick wall.

I have the thought of grabbing my gun from my bra holster with my left hand, but he grabs my wrist, pinning my arm above my head with such force that he stumbles into me, and at the awkward angle of our bodies, he pushes me sideways a bit, making the brick scratch against the exposed skin of my shoulder and back thanks to my flimsy tank top.

As he pushes me again, the bricks rub and bite into my skin. The burn of blood rushing to the surface makes me want to scream, but I keep it locked down. I will not give this prick the satisfaction of hearing my fear.

"You're picking a fight with the wrong girl, asshole." I growl as I look up and notice he's wearing a black balaclava, only his eyes peeking through, and my heart stumbles.

I've seen those eyes.

Green and what looks to be dark brown.

"What, you think your *man's* gonna save you?" He scoffs. "He can barely walk around the fucking track without his cane."

"I know he'll save me, but I can fight just as well." I say as I lift my leg to try to knee him in the balls.

My kneecap connects, and he releases me with a grunt. While cupping his crotch with his left hand, he tries to keep my wrist pinned with his right, but his grip is weaker. I curl my hand into a fist and jab it into the crook of his elbow, breaking his remaining contact with me.

I try to bolt, to get out into the open so I can draw my gun and pop one off near him, but again he's too damn fast, and bigger than me. He grabs me by my hair and he throws me against the wall again, pressing my already injured shoulder into the rough, uneven bricks, and this time I can't stop the cry of pain that escapes my lips.

"Not so tough when you can't fight back, huh, bitch?" He says, wrapping his hand around my throat, cutting off my windpipe. "You won't be racing if I can help it. All those lessons with your man will be for nothing. Desmond will have you and get rid of Bryan all in one fell swoop, thanks to his *unfortunate* injury."

Why is he doing this? He didn't seem like this bad of a person. She's going to be devastated; that is, if she's not in on this, too.

Those thoughts run through my head as I slowly go for my gun once more. I just wrap my fingers around the grip and I'm about to pull it from the holster when I hear the metallic ringing of metal hitting something. Then my attacker crumples to the ground with groans of pain while grabbing at the back of his head.

"She doesn't always need to be tough when she's got bad bitches like us to back her up." Lexi growls as she kicks the dude in the balls with the toe of her shoe, making *him* scream.

"Serves you right, asshole." I croak while massaging my neck to ease my muscles. "Now my *man's* gonna kick your ass once I tell him who you are."

"No one will believe you." He says, voice still tight with pain.

"Keep believing that." Lexi scoffs as she gently grabs me by the elbow and leads me out of the alley.

When I look up, I notice that Sophie is standing next to Lexi's Lancer, her gun drawn and pointed down the alley, aimed right at my attacker.

"Don't worry, I have excellent aim." She smirks.

"Good." I say as Lexi helps me into the front passenger seat and Sophie moves to the rear, but she never takes her eyes off the piece of shit in the alley until Lexi is ready to hop in behind the wheel and get us out of here.

Once we all are safe inside the Lancer, adrenaline leaves my body, and it comes alive with pain. I already see a bruise forming on my wrist where he pinned it against the brick wall. My back and throat are on fire, and I can feel blood trickling down my shoulder blade.

"My dad's not home, but Mom is, and she's ready for us," Sophie says from the backseat.

"Please let Bryan know what happened." I say to no one in particular, but Sophie is the one who speaks.

"Already on it."

"What happened?" Lexi asks, never taking her eyes off the road.

"I was just walking, but I was stupid to allow myself to be lost in thought and not pay attention to things around me." I say and then explain what happened before they showed up. "How did you know to come find me?"

"I just got this gut feeling. Plus, I noticed one of the guys slipping away from the track. I couldn't tell who it was, so I just followed. Bastard gave me the slip though, but thankfully I ran into Sophie and she had the tracker on your phone, so we followed it and then came to kick ass." Lexi smirks.

We pull up to Temperance's apartment, and she's already standing on the stoop, waiting for us. As soon as Lexi parks her car, she and Sophie hop out at the same time, and Sophie opens my door before helping me to my feet.

"Come on, let's get you inside." Tempe says as she ushers us past the door.

She has the kitchen island set up with another red medical bag spread open and waiting for us. Leaning on Sophie, I walk over to the stool and ease my aching body up onto it, resting my elbows on the cool laminate surface.

"Alright. Let's see what we have." Temperance says as she pulls on a pair of opaque white medical gloves. "I tell you all this much; I'm starting to feel like I should put a sign in the window telling people this is a private medical wing. This place has become a hospital since you all have gotten here."

"Sorry." I hiss through my teeth as I feel her gloved finger brush over my irritated skin.

"It just looks like an angry abrasion. No deep cuts." Temperance says. "But cleaning it will be painful."

"I know." I pant. "But do it."

Just as she steps over to pull the antiseptic cleaner from the bag, I hear the front door burst open behind me, and I can just feel it's Mark and Bryan without even looking.

"Taylor!" Bryan says, voice full of panic and fear.

"Oh shit. What the hell happened?" Mark growls.

Lexi goes on to explain what happened while Bryan hobbles over to my side, sitting on the stool next to mine. I glance over and notice his left leg is trembling; from overuse again.

Just as I'm about to yell at him for overdoing it again, he grabs my hand. His entire body is shaking, but when I look into his green eyes, they don't shine with only fear. They also have rage swirling in them, making them the color of dark moss.

"Who did this to you?" He asks, his voice gruffer than I've ever heard it.

Then his gaze dips lower to my neck, and his eyes widen before he shuts them so tight I'm sure when he opens them again, he's going to see stars.

I feel the bruises forming under my skin, and when I lift my left hand to cup his cheek, his eyes open and zero in on the bruise on my wrist, too.

"Tell me who did this so I can beat the shit out of him." Bryan growls.

Just as I'm about to open my mouth to tell him, Temperance takes this moment to apply the antiseptic to my wound. I suck in a sharp breath, and I can't help the moan of pain that escapes my lips.

"I am so sorry, Baby. I will make him pay for hurting what is mine."

So, while Temperance treats and covers my abrasion, I tell my partners who did this and what we plan on doing about it.

Chapter Forty

Bryan

I am fuming.

This son of a bitch is lucky my leg is the only thing holding me back or I would track his ass down and just nail punch after punch after punch into his body until my knuckles were dripping in his blood. But nothing is going to stop me from confronting him with a group.

Once I know Taylor is alright, I'm coming for him.

"Alright, Taylor, you should be good to go now." Temperance says as she covers the wound with a sterile piece of gauze and tape.

"Thank you, Temperance." I say, trying like hell to keep my tone even.

"Bryan, take her over to your apartment and the both of you need to rest." Temperance's eyes drift down to my leg, which is slightly bouncing out a nervous, agitated rhythm, and the look that crosses her face is almost pained. "Stop that nervous leg tick before you rip a stitch."

I nod before turning my attention back to Taylor. "You ready to go back to our home away from home, Baby?"

"As long as you stay with me." Taylor says softly, and I know what she's asking me. If I promise not to dip out once she's asleep.

"I'm not going anywhere." I stand, hobbling on my leg a moment before grabbing my cane. "Come on."

Slowly, we both make our way to our apartment with Mark and Lexi on our heels. When we step up on the stoop, I lean the damn cane against my left hip—this thing is *really* getting on my nerves—as I fish my keys out of my pocket and unlock the door. I step inside, tugging Taylor in with me as the others follow.

"You two need anything before we leave?" Mark asks.

"Can you check the hall bath and see if there's anything for pain? Tylenol or something?" I ask.

"Bryan, I'm okay," Taylor says, but I cut her off before she can say more.

"Baby, I want to make sure you have it in case you need it."

"Okay, in that case, Lexi, can you make sure there's something easy to fix for dinner or order us some takeout that we can warm up later?" Taylor says, giving me a look like we were playing chess and she just check-mated me.

I smirk. "Bed. Now."

Mark comes out of the hall bathroom, and apparently, he heard my words because I can see him trying to hide his laughter. I distribute my weight evenly between my legs and lift my cane at him.

Maybe this thing isn't so bad now.

"Don't you even freaking dare." I warn, moving like I'm going to hit him with it.

Mark laughs this time, and lifts his hands, palms towards me in surrender. "You said it, not me."

"Get out." I growl, but I know he can see the touch of humor in my eyes.

"Mark, come on." Lexi rolls her eyes. "I ordered Chinese for us. I'll bring yours over when it gets here. Can I have your keys so I don't have to make either of you get up?"

I toss my keys in their direction, and Mark pockets them with a smile. "See ya later, you two." Then he looks down at Lexi and then back up at me. "I'm glad Lexi was able to save Taylor and that she's alright, Bryan. I know you want to go and beat his ass to a pulp, but let me in on it also, man. Tay is like a sister to me, so he hurt my family, too."

"I wouldn't have it any other way." I say with a tight smile as I watch them walk out of the apartment and making sure to lock the door behind me before I head back into the bedroom.

When I walk inside, I see Taylor sitting on the closed toilet seat, trying to untie the knot of her tank top behind her neck, but she can't get her arm behind her head.

"Here, let me." I say, walking into the room and leaning my hip against the sink, easing the pressure off my leg as I untie her tank, but she keeps the fabric close to her chest.

"I just want to wash off a bit before I get in bed."

"I'll help you since you can't get into the shower with your bandage yet." I say as I turn on the faucet to get the hot water running to fill the sink.

"You need to get off—"

"I am where I need to be." I tell her, gripping her chin lightly to make her look at me. "I'm fine. Plus, I brought the chair from the kitchen in here earlier in case I needed it when I was getting ready this morning. So sit."

She rolls her eyes, but she takes a seat anyway while I take her spot on the toilet, just to appease her.

"Better?" I ask, cocking a brow at her.

She nods. "Yes."

"Good. Now drop your tank. I think I may use this to strangle the bastard when I confront him." I say as I turn my attention to the sink, dipping the washcloth into the warm, soapy water.

When I look back at her, she's completely naked before me, her jean shorts in a puddle of fabric beside her bare feet and her torn tank tossed near the trashcan, like she tried to throw it inside and missed.

I freeze, the washcloth slowly dripping water from my hand onto my knee. The anger I was starting to feel again mixes with a possessiveness that I have never felt before.

"What?" Taylor asks, her cheeks flushing pink. "You've already seen me naked, so why are you looking at me like that?"

"I guess I'm still shocked that *I'm* the one who gets to see you like this." I chuckle.

I shake my head, clearing my thoughts and willing my slowly building erection to fade. Neither of us are in the shape to get the other off. And I *refuse* to hurt her any more than she already is.

I dip the washcloth back in the water to rewarm it before I finally wring it out and bring the soft fabric against the equally soft skin of her arm.

"I know the feeling," Taylor says and toys with the hem of my shirt.

"Taylor." I growl at her in warning. "Don't drive me any crazier than I already am. I don't want to hurt you, and I don't think my body can love yours the way I want to; the way you need it." I say, glancing down at my thigh and the exposed bandage.

"I know. I wish I had superpowers that could heal the both of us in an instant."

I force my gaze away from her and dip the washcloth into the water again before turning back and wiping her face. Her eyes, cheeks, chin, but when I get to her neck, anger flares bright and hot in my chest.

"I don't think it would be a good idea for me to have any superpowers right now. It'd be too easy to break that fucker and heal him just so I could do it all over again."

I trail the cloth over her left arm, and when I get to that bruise on her skin; I lift her wrist to my mouth and tenderly press my lips to the imperfection.

"I'm sorry I wasn't there when it was happening." I whisper.

"Bryan, you didn't know they would use today and attack me," Taylor says while cupping my cheek. "We both know that this situation is a ticking time bomb, and this dude plays dirty."

"Still doesn't make it any easier."

"I know."

Sighing, I double down on cleaning her up, making sure to take extra time on her back, ensuring it's clean. Once I finish wiping her off, even down to her feet, I help her into the bedroom and sit her on the bed.

I have to force myself to turn towards the dresser I have claimed as my own or else the sight of her naked on that bed—where we not even a few days ago were making the other come apart in those sheets—will make me prove to myself that I can figure out a way to love her body without hurting either of us in the process.

So, I find a t-shirt of mine and a pair of her shorts to slip into and help her lie down on her stomach so she's not putting pressure on her back.

"I'll be right back." I say as I kiss her on the lips and hobble out of the room.

Apparently, at some point, Lexi came by and dropped off our Chinese food according to the text on my phone. So, I warm up a small plate and bring it in for Taylor, along with a bottle of water.

"Babe, you need to sit down." Taylor says as she sees me walk in with a paper plate of pork fried rice and General Tso's chicken.

"I will; once you eat."

"Bossy butt." She grumbles, but I see the smile there, and I lightly tap her on her ass.

"Damn right. I'm bossy when it comes to the woman I am madly in love with." I say. "I'm going to get cleaned up and then join you." Then add, "With my own food."

"Okay." Taylor chuckles as she takes a bite of rice and hums at the flavors. "This is so good. Hurry up."

And I do. I put the little protective plastic sleeve over my leg and I take a quick shower, dressing in only a pair of deep green boxers before I limp into the kitchen to make my plate of Chinese and make my way back to Taylor.

After dinner, I set the empty plates on my nightstand and then turn over on my side so Taylor can use my arm as a pillow once she settled back onto her stomach for the night.

"Bryan?" She whispers.

"Yeah, Annie?" I whisper back.

"I know you're going to go after him, but please just try not to hurt yourself too much." Taylor says as she traces her finger over the curve of my shoulder and bicep.

"Do I need to remind you of what lengths I'll go to keep you safe? To avenge any wrong doing to you?"

"No. Even if I don't see it, I'm reminded every day." She says as her eyes drift down my chest to my bullet scar.

"Okay," I say. "But I will take into account that you do love my body, so I'll try not to break it too much for you."

Taylor shakes her head, and the bark of laughter that springs from her lips makes my chest swell with love and happiness.

"Oh my God, did you just channel a Mark response?"

"Yeah. I guess I did." I chuckle.

"Remind me why I keep you around?" Taylor sighs, pinching the bridge of her nose.

"Now you're channeling me?" I ask, cocking my eyebrow in mock offense.

"It would be a total you response if Mark was here." She jests.

I roll my eyes, but I lean into her to kiss her nose, then each eye before landing on her lips for a moment before I speak, my mouth brushing hers as I do.

"Because we love each other. We are *in* love with each other, and nothing will ever change that. You were meant to be with me, Taylor Allison Sparks. And I will always fight to keep you by my side."

I reach out with my right hand, encircling her left so I can gently toy with her ring finger where my promise ring still sits proudly against her skin. The pink stone shining in the semi-darkness of the room with only the milky white moonlight spilling through the window, providing enough light to see by.

I hold on to the hope that one day I can change it out for a diamond.

"I thank God every day that you are by my side. That I get to live my life with you in it."

I glance back at Taylor, and she's looking at me with a touch of bewilderment in her eyes.

"I know I don't really talk much about religion. It's not that I don't believe in God, I do. Granny took me to church when I was younger, but I always felt I had a strained relationship with Him back then. I mean, I felt like he took my parents from me, and for what?" I ask. "I was always told that God doesn't put any more on your plate than what you can handle, so why did He put the death, the murder of both parents, on a boy so young?"

Taylor is quiet, so I continue.

"And I realized over the years, it's so I can learn to handle any situation that comes my way. To lean on the people I meet so I can overcome the obstacles of life. And to be honest, without my parents dying, I never would have entered the agency when I did, and eventually met you." I brush a piece of her hair behind her ear. "So, I thank God for all my pain, sorrow and suffering if I can spend every minute of every day with the beautiful woman He created for me."

"Bryan," Taylor whispers, her voice cracking with tears.

"I'm sorry. I didn't mean to make you cry, but I just felt the need to say that."

"No. That was beautiful. Thank you for sharing." Taylor says. "And I know if your parents were here, they would be so proud of the man you've become."

"I'd like to think so too." I whisper. "They would probably smack me upside the head on some of the things I've done over the years, but yeah, you're right, I think they would mostly be proud, too."

Taylor yawns, and her eyes begin to droop, but she fights to keep them open. So, I lean in again, pressing a loving kiss to each eye, making them close, and I whisper, "Sleep, Annie. I love you."

"Love you too, Bullet." She says sleepily with a lazy smile on her face.

Chapter Forty-One

Taylor

The next morning when I wake up, I find myself on my side, tucked tightly against Bryan's body with my head on his chest and his arm wrapped around my waist, keeping me locked against him.

I glance over at the clock on his nightstand, and it reads 7:30am. We slept in. Considering we've been getting up at 5:30 or 6:00, this is sleeping in.

As if he's aware I'm awake, Bryan's deep breath rumbles against my ear before he kisses the top of my head.

"Morning beautiful. You feeling okay?"

I test my shoulder my moving my arm around, and while it hurts, it's manageable.

"It's better. Still sore, but it's not painful."

"Good. Let me change—"

Bryan's words are cut short when we hear the TV suddenly turn on in the living room, blasting the news station Bryan last left it on. We both take just a heartbeat to glance at each other before we leap from bed, Bryan not even bothering with his cane, just keeping his toes on the floor and putting most of his weight on his right leg while we both grab our guns and head out into the living room.

When Bryan moves silently down the small hallway and quickly turns the corner with his gun pointing toward the couch, his entire body freezes. I poke my head around his shoulder and at the same time, we both yell *his* name.

"Mark!"

"Wow. Do you guys always sleep in like this?" Mark asks as he lowers the volume on the TV.

"What in the hell are you doing here?" Bryan growls as he unchambers his gun and sits it down on one of the side tables near the loveseat, then runs his hands through his hair in agitation.

"What? I remember you saying not too long ago that if I walk in your all's bedroom that I'd get a bullet in my ass. Well, Lexi is kinda fond of that part of me, so I was doing the next best thing, making you two come to me."

"What do you want, Mark?" Bryan asks as he leans against the arm of the loveseat, waiting for his friend's answer.

Mark finally looks over to us and I can see the smirk forming on his face, and I brace myself for a comment that is going to be *all Mark.*

"Maybe I just felt you needed a warning to never walk in on me and Lexi unless you want Tay Tay to get an unrestricted view."

"Oh my god, dude. I'm going to kill you if you don't tell me what the hell you are doing here." Bryan says, his tone growing frustrated, but I know he's holding back his laughter too.

Mark's face falls, and in the blink of an eye, his 'agent mode' comes out to play. "Josh wants to talk to you." His gaze flicks over to me. "Both of you."

"Did he find out about Taylor?"

"Yeah. I was up at the track this morning, and a certain someone came in looking a little worse for wear." Mark says. "I have to say, I'm proud of what my girl did to that prick."

"Alright. Let us get *dressed,* since you can't text like a normal human, and we'll be ready to go in twenty." Bryan says as he limps over to me and urging me forward with his hand on the small of my back.

Bryan

After Taylor and I get dressed, she drives down to the track where we see Mark's Challenger already waiting for us near the main gate.

"Park in your bay, Baby." I tell her.

She does, and when we both exit her car, I make sure to pull the garage door down and lock it before we head over to where Mark stands near Josh's bay.

"Hey man." Mark greets as we walk up.

"Hey. Where's Josh?" I ask.

"Right here. Thanks for coming by, Bryan." Josh greets and then looks to my right where Taylor is standing, holding onto my arm. "Taylor, I heard about your attack last night; are you okay?" Josh asks as he looks her over. I can tell it's just a cursory glance to make sure she is indeed alright, so I don't get the need to punch him in the gut.

"I'll heal. It's better than it was yesterday." Taylor tells him.

"So, what did you want to talk to us about, Josh?" I ask.

He tilts his head towards his garage, and the three of us follow him, but he stops us before we can enter his bay.

"Just you and Taylor," Josh tells me, giving Mark the side eye.

"Mark is like my brother. He goes where I go and vice versa. I trust him with my life and with Taylor's. So whatever you have to say, you can say in front of him." The tone in my voice leaves no room for argument.

"Understood." Josh smiles then allows us to enter his bay, and he pulls the door down before turning on a loud fan he has set up over the door. "To keep prying ears from listening in." He adds with a smirk.

Knowing even he thinks he has a rat in his group makes me feel better about my own suspicions and makes my heart hurt for him.

"First, before we get into the nitty-gritty of this meeting, I want to make sure you have all your ducks in a row." Josh looks between me, Taylor and Mark. "How's the leg, Bryan?"

I shift uneasily on my feet and try not to lean as much on my cane. Try to show him that I'm fine, but he sees right through my charade.

"It's getting better." I grumble.

"But still not up to racing standards?" Josh guesses.

"I have a plan for that." I tell him, and he raises an eyebrow.

"And what plan would that be?"

"I'm going to give him a counteroffer. Taylor races in my place."

"That's gutsy." Josh says, then gives me a wicked smile. "I like it. Can you drive Bryan's Camaro, Taylor?"

Taylor's face pales, and my heart sinks into my stomach.

"No, but how hard can it be?" Taylor asks while looking at me, and I almost lose it.

"Damn it. Why the hell didn't I think about that?" I say mostly to myself as I pinch the bridge of my nose.

"Bryan, it's the same steps as driving my car. It'll be—"

I cut her off. "No, it won't be!" I shout, but it's mostly directed at myself and almost failing her. "My car's clutch has a different bite point than yours does. My car has a stronger engine, so it shifts at different points during a race."

"Calm down, Bryan. That's why I'm talking to you all now about this. You know *he's* going to pull any trick he can out of his damn ass to try to set her up for failure. *We* have to give her everything to set her up for success. And once we get this fucking rat out of my track, she will be safe to practice without prying eyes giving up her secrets."

"You're right." I take a breath, and I look over at Taylor. "I'm sorry for yelling."

"Don't be, I know it wasn't directed at me," Taylor says while placing a hand on my arm and giving it a reassuring squeeze.

"I have a covered tent set up behind the press box, and I have Ian schooling everyone in a game of poker. So, you ready to go exterminate our track?"

"Totally. Let's go kick some ass!" Mark says while wringing his hands together and bouncing from one foot to another.

"Let's go." I growl, and Josh nods as he turns off the fan and opens the garage door and leads us around to the tent behind the press box, just like he said.

"Taylor?" I whisper, so I'm not overheard.

"What?"

"What are the odds of me ripping my stitches out now?" I ask.

"I mean, it can still happen, but I think as long as your leg can hold your weight, you can probably get by without your cane for now." She answers, already knowing where my mind is going.

I don't want to walk into this *meeting* looking wounded, and this cane still screams that fact.

Just before we walk through the tent flap, I hand Taylor my cane, and I give her a quick peck on the lips before I turn my attention back to the men in the room. Or more like the *man* who hurt my girl.

"Oh, come on, Ian! You have to be cheating!" Nick exclaimed, throwing his cards down in an apparent losing hand.

Ian laughs, "Aw, Nick. Stop being a sore loser."

"I've always said Ian cheats, but we can never prove it." James scoffs as he chugs what looks like the last of his beer.

"Gentlemen! How goes the game?" Josh yells, his face showing full happiness as he throws his arm around Ian.

"These losers are getting pissed that they can't beat me in cards because they can't keep a poker face in place to save their life." Ian chuckles as he counts out his winnings like he won a jackpot.

"Well, you know what they say about having a bad poker face. That you can't lie worth a shit."

"Yup." Ian agrees as he looks over at me and gives me a small nod.

So he knows who the rat is too now that everything came to a head with Taylor's attack.

"You know, I often wondered if I have a liar in my team. But I go through everyone here. And even more so over the last few weeks, and I always end up at the same conclusion." Josh says as he wanders over to sling his arms around Nick and James' shoulders.

"What is that, Josh?" I ask, feeling it's the right time to interject, and Josh gives me an approving grin.

"The conclusion I've come to is that I do have a liar here. And he's in this. Very. Room." Josh says as he removes his arm from Nick's shoulder and he leans in fully on James.

I have to grind my teeth together at the wince James desperately tries to hide at the added weight to what I can only assume is a sore body thanks to Lexi's beat down. And when his green and brown eyes glance up at me and then over at Taylor, his eyes widen at her. I have to ball my hands into tight fists to keep myself planted where I am. My nails biting into the skin of my palm, the only thing keeping me grounded.

"You have anything to say for yourself, James?" Josh asks, his tone so nonchalant yet deadly that I think even Wayne would have paled at his voice.

"Me?" James squeaks like the fucking rat he is. "What do you mean?"

"What we all know to be true, *James*." I seethe, no longer able to hold back anymore. "You hurt *my girl*. Made her bleed, and I want to kill you for it."

"Josh! You can't let him attack me!" James shouts as he tries to get up and run like the damn coward he is.

"Oh, I can, and I fucking will allow it." Josh says as he shoves him back down in the chair. "See, you forget something here, James. You may be the eyes for *Desmond,* but this is my track. My *home* and I know everything that goes on here. I was just hoping I was wrong. Ever since Bryan, Mark, Taylor, and Lexi came here, you've been acting weird. So, I kept an eye on you. But the one time I take my eyes off you, you go and run out to attack an innocent girl."

"You don't understand! I was forced into working with him!" James sputters.

Josh looks up at me, and I glance over at Mark, then at Taylor. Mark knows where he's to be, holding this asshole down along with Josh so I can beat the ever-loving shit out of him.

"Don't look if you don't want to see this, Baby." I tell her as I take a step, and I let my smile play at the corner of my lips because right now, my leg is holding me. Yes, it's still shaking and there is a dull ache deep in the muscle, but I am putting my full weight on my leg.

"Bryan, please." James begs and I just chuckle, dark and low.

"I don't care what you have to say right now. You didn't have to come after my girl to save your own ass."

I walk up to him, and I don't give him time to say a word. I pull my right arm back, balling my hand into a tight fist, and I bring it down onto his cheek with a loud crack that echoes in the polyester walls around us.

His head snaps to the side, and since Mark is on the same side, he stumbles back a step so he can keep his hold on James' arm. I grab a fist full of his hair with my left hand and I punch him again, hitting the same spot. Splitting the skin, and I know I'm even making his mouth bleed inside.

"This is nothing compared to the pain you put on my girl, *but* I know my girl doesn't like violence if she can keep from it. But I need to do this selfishly for me." I growl as I send my left fist flying into his face, then a right punch to his stomach before stepping back, my hands aching from the force of my blows, and my breath coming out in controlled pants.

"You don't understand. I did it to protect my girl!" James says, almost shouting at the end.

"By what, attacking one of us?" Josh says while stepping in front of me to punch James in the stomach.

He coughs and spits a mouthful of blood onto the concrete.

"Oh my God, Josh! What the hell is going on?"

I turn at the sound of a girl's voice. She pushes past Taylor and tries to push past me, but I hold firm.

"Christy, please, Baby." James groans. "Get out of here."

"No! What is your all's problem?" Christy snaps, turning to look at us all in the eye, trying to figure out what is going on.

Josh jerks his head at me, telling me that my time is up. I walk over to Taylor, pulling her into my side, and wait to see what's going to happen next.

"Your man here, Christy, seems to be in bed with the devil." Josh says while looking over James' broken body sitting limply in his chair.

"James. What is he talking about?" Christy asks, her voice lowering in fear.

"I fucked up, Baby." James says as he sits up in his chair, looking at all of us, but his gaze lingers on mine. "Desmond somehow got my number right after you lot came here. He threatened my girl. Threatened to beat me while making me watch his thugs rape her." His gaze swings to Josh. "What was I supposed to do, Josh!? He said he'd kill her if I told anyone!"

"You take that chance and tell someone! We fight as a family or we die as a family!" Josh roars and punches James again in the face, then walks away from him and over to Christy. "You can stay if you want, but I want him out of my track, at least until all this is over."

Josh then walks up to me, and he looks me dead in the eye and speaks in a low voice, "You once said you would kill for her." He looks at Taylor. "Do you think you can take this fucker out?"

"I know I can." I say, and no matter if he lives or not, he's not going to be a problem for this group once he makes his move.

"Then be sure he leaves this world in a blaze of glory." Josh says, and he walks out of the tent.

Chapter Forty-Two

Taylor

After Josh leaves, Ian and Nick take James' broken body, and walks him out of the tent towards the main gate.

"Christy, take his keys and get his car out of the bay," Ian instructs as he reaches over to dig James' keys out of the front pocket of his jeans before throwing them to her.

She walks by me, and I expect her to be angry at us for ganging up on her man, but instead, I see sorrow filling her eyes.

"I'm sorry. If I had known, I would have said something. I'm sorry he hurt you. Please let me know if there is anything I can do." Christy says.

"It's okay. And don't stay away for my benefit. But I'm sure I know where you will be. I just hope that we can make everything right once this race is over and Desmond is gone for good." I tell her as I pull her in for a quick hug.

"You're such a good person, Taylor. Don't ever change that about yourself." Christy says while wiping at a stray tear that rolls down her cheek.

She walks away, and I watch as she backs James' Civic out of what was once his bay and drives it to the main gate, where Nick and Ian shove James into the passenger seat.

"Are you alright?" Bryan asks, his voice low and gravelly.

I look over my shoulder and slowly take in everything about him. He's leaning against some concrete blocks that are set up in the corner of the tent to keep it from blowing away if a breeze came through. His arms are crossed over his chest, and his left leg bent so he's not putting any pressure or weight on the limb.

"Yeah. I'm fine. What about you?" I look again at his body and I can't tell if the blood staining his jeans is his or James'.

"I'm okay. I think." He looks down at his hands and shakes them out twice before looking back up at me. "Let's go to my bay. You have some more racing to do."

"Bryan, that can wait." I say, but he shakes his head.

"No, Baby. We need you to be prepared. We have not a clue when Desmod will make his move now, since his inside man has been taken out."

I take a breath, nodding my head as I hand him his cane. "Can I at least look at your leg before I take your car out on the track?"

"Yeah. Once we get in my bay." He nods. "Come on."

He takes the cane in his left hand, then mine in his right, and walks toward his garage. I try to bend down to raise the door, but he beats me to it. Once the garage door is up, Bryan gestures with his head, telling me to walk inside first before he steps in and pulls it back down. I spot the rolling stool he was using when he was working on my car the other day and roll it over to him so he can sit down.

"I, uh, need to take your pants down first." I say as heat creeps up my neck and Bryan chuckles.

"You mean you're fine with undressing in front of me, but you taking my pants down makes you blush?" He asks with a raised eyebrow.

"Shut up." I shake my head. "Both times we were in the safety and privacy of our apartment when we did stuff like that. And here anyone can walk in and get the wrong idea."

"No, they won't." Bryan says as he unbuttons his jeans and pulls them down to the middle of his thighs, leaving him in his burgundy boxers. "There, better?" He asks as he sits down on the stool.

I roll my eyes and I kneel in front of him to unwrap the bandage on his thigh so I can make sure he didn't rip out a stitch, but I don't miss the way his breathing changes at me kneeling before him. So, I try to distract both of us with small talk.

"I will say, though, I've never seen you fly off the handle like that before. Never seen you actually punch a guy. And it was kinda hot."

"So you think I'm hot, huh?" Bryan says, and I can just imagine the smirk on his lips.

I smack his other knee, and he laughs out loud. "I think it's just the Florida heat making you hot." I say, just to get under his skin.

"Yeah. Whatever you say, Babe." Bryan chuckles.

I make myself remember what I'm supposed to be doing, and I actually inspect his healing wound, and I'm happy to find that no stitch is out of place.

"You're fine. You didn't rip anything." I say as I place a hand on his other leg.

"That's good." Bryan says as he reaches out with his hand and wraps it around the back of my neck to give it a reassuring squeeze.

Then, the door behind me opens.

"Bryan, are you going to...oh shit. I'm sorry, man!"

As Mark's voice fills the garage, my heart plummets in my chest, and it's the fear that I was thinking about just five minutes ago, brought to life in the garage.

"Mark, it's not what you think, you nympho." Bryan grumbles.

"Hey man, from my POV, it's lookin' a bit x-rated." Mark says as he backs up and turns his head.

"Why don't you knock the next time you enter a room?" Bryan shoots back.

"Okay. Lesson learned." Mark says as I stand up and take a step away from Bryan.

As Bryan pulls his jeans up and fastens them, he says, "You can look now. What do you want?"

"Josh wanted to know if you were taking your Camaro out."

"Yeah, I am. Taylor wanted to make sure I didn't rip anything." Bryan says. "Now get out."

Mark smirks, and he waves as he walks through the door. "I'll be here to be your flagman."

"One day I'm gonna beat him to a pulp, I just know it." Bryan sighs, but he shakes his head to hide his smile.

"He's just a child that probably still laughs at fart jokes." I say.

"He does." Bryan laughs as he pulls his keys from his pocket. "Here. Drive it like you stole it."

He walks over to the driver's door, opens it for me, and I drop in behind the wheel. As he lifts the garage, I push the clutch in to turn the ignition over, and as the car vibrates with the strength of the engine, he's right; it's stronger than my car, but I have the feeling that once I get used to it, I will be able to drive it no problem.

Bryan then opens the passenger door, and when he closes it, he gives me a smile as he fastens his seatbelt. "Let's go. Show me what you got."

I throw it in reverse, which is thankfully in the same as mine, push down then back and off to the right, and I'm backing out of the bay and then throwing it into first. I slowly release the clutch, but the transmission squeals a bit and Bryan tells me to give it a bit more gas, and I'm off.

I pull on to the track and, true to his word, Mark is there waiting for us with the checkered flag in his hand.

"You ready to drive that thing?" He yells over the roar of the engine, and I respond with a quick rev. "GO!" He laughs.

The first few times shifting is a bit rough, but with Bryan there to coach me, by the second turn, I'm shifting with no issues and pushing the engine to the limits.

"You are amazing, Baby." Bryan praises.

"It's all thanks to you." I say as I pull the Camaro back into the bay forty minutes later.

"You did great, Taylor!" Mark says as Bryan and I get out once I turn the engine off. "Bryan, you want me to take care of the oil change for you?"

"Actually, yeah. Would you?"

"Dude, I got you."

"Hey, I'm gonna have Linc and Tempe come over to my place tonight. We need to discuss a plan and have it in place." Bryan says.

"Let me know when and we'll be there." Mark says.

Later that night, after Bryan and I have dinner, he texts Lincon and Temperance, asking them to come over so we can formulate a plan of action once shit hits the fan.

It only takes fifteen minutes before the doorbell rings, and Bryan insists on answering the door so I let him.

"Hey, man! Where's the party?" Mark exclaims and offers Bryan a bottle of Jack Daniels as he walks in.

"Nice cover, dude." I mumble as Lincon, Temperance, and even Sophie follow in behind Lexi.

Bryan shuts and locks the door as he makes his way back over to the loveseat to sit beside me.

"Please, make yourselves comfortable." Bryan says as he waves his hand over the available seating throughout the living room.

Once everyone is seated, Bryan gets right to the point of this meeting. "I wanted to let you two know that we found a rat within Josh's group. The same one that attacked Taylor was someone Josh thought of as a brother. Since I exposed James, you know damn well Desmond will make his move at any time now."

All heads in the room nod.

"So, I want you two to make sure you have your teams ready. I don't know if you planned on us making the arrest or you had another team in place for that." Bryan says.

"I was thinking that once Desmond shows up, Tempe and I will be in place and waiting for the right time to move." Lincoln says.

"One of you call or text us, and we will be there once you see him." Temperance agrees.

"We just may need to arrest you guys, too. You know, to keep up the charade." Linc adds.

"At that point, I don't really care about our covers." Bryan says, and the three of us agree.

"Yeah. Josh and his team will be safe, so our ruse would have run its course by then." I say.

Lincoln nods. "Fair enough. I'm also going to order a few more Kevlar vests. Hopefully, they will be here in the morning, and if they are, I don't want any of you leaving your apartments without them on. I'm not going to lose an agent on my watch from a stray bullet."

"Let me know if you need help with anything, Linc. If you need me to meet your agent to pick up the vests, I'm your guy," Mark offers.

"Thanks, Mark. I'll let you know," Lincoln says and then looks at the four of us in turn. "Play this smart and let's go home at the end of all this."

"Yes, sir." We all say in unison and then everyone leaves for the night.

Once Bryan makes sure the apartment is locked up for the night, we make our way back into our bedroom, and when I turn on the light, the sight that burns into my eyes makes my entire body lock up.

"Babe, what's wrong?" Bryan asks as he bumps into me, his hands wrapping around my waist to steady himself.

He must finally see what I do because he stiffens behind me a moment before he grabs his gun that he still had hidden in the waistband of his jeans and walks into the room, but of course, the window is still locked, and in one piece.

Bryan looks over his shoulder at me a moment before he roughly pulls the blinds, blocking the warning that was spray painted on a cream-colored tarp. The red paint still bleeding from the letters.

TOMORROW 8PM.

Chapter Forty-Three

Taylor

"Get whatever you need for tonight. We aren't staying here." Bryan growls as he limps over to our closet, dragging out his suitcase and tossing it on the bed.

I nod numbly and pack up a set of pajamas and two sets of clothes for tomorrow while he does the same. After he closes the suitcase, I hear him on the phone with Mark.

"Mark, Taylor, and I need to crash at your place." Pause. "Because that prick knows where we are. He left me a little message on our bedroom window." Another pause. "Alright, I'm getting some shit packed up before we come over. See ya in five."

"What was that about?" I ask, taking one more look around the room to make sure I don't need anything else.

"Mark's coming over. He wants to make sure there are no cameras in here before we leave." Bryan says, then stepping closer to me, he whispers in my ear, "And to make sure we don't have tracking devices on our phones other than Sophie's."

I nod as he grabs his suitcase and rolls it out into the living room just in time for Mark to knock on the door. I let him inside along with Lexi on his heels, looking every bit the pissed-off best friend that I know and love.

"Oh, I *cannot* wait to kick this dude's ass! Ugh!" Lexi says as she pulls me in for a hug. "You okay?"

"Yeah." I nod and wait for Bryan and Mark to finish the sweep of our apartment.

"Our place is clean. No bugs or cameras anywhere. So you'll be safe with us for tonight." Lexi says.

"Good"

"Okay, girls, let's get out of here." Mark says. "I didn't find any cameras, but Bryan's phone did have a tracker on it. I just swapped sim cards into a different burner phone, and I'm gonna send the bastard on a little bit of a wild goose chase." Mark grins as he pulls a small drone out of a duffle bag that I didn't notice he was carrying.

"Strap that phone on this bad boy and send it on a little run." Bryan says, nodding approvingly to Mark. "Sometimes I love the way your mind works, man."

"Alright. Taylor, let me check your phone and make sure yours wasn't tagged too." Mark says, and I hand him my phone.

He takes it and plugs it into a tablet he has resting on one of the side tables in the living room and, after a moment of tapping at the screen, he gives it back to me with a smile.

"Only Sophie's system is on yours, and it's not being overridden by another program. So, you're good." Mark says, handing me my phone back.

"Good. Let's get out of here." Bryan says as he places his hand on the small of my back and leads me out the door with Mark in front of us and Lexi behind him.

Once we settle in the guest bedroom of Mark and Lexi's apartment, Bryan sits on the corner of the mattress to text Linc and Tempe.

"They need my new number, and I need to let them know what happened and where we are." He says, his voice short and clipped.

I walk over to sit beside him on the mattress before I wrap my arm around his broad shoulders and lean my head against him. His entire body's coiled so tight I'm shocked that with every movement of his fingers across the phone screen doesn't make him bounce around like a rubber ball.

"Talk to me." I whisper as he sends the message, the sound of the text swoosh ringing in the air around us.

"He got too close without me knowing. Why didn't I think about me having a fucking tracker on my phone?"

Bryan looks over at me, and my chest burns at the fear, anger, and sorrow shining in his green eyes.

"I should have thought about it the moment Sophie put her tracker on all the girls' phones. I put you in danger, and I didn't even know it," Bryan whispers as he drops his face into his hands.

I run my hand up and down his back in soothing motions before I lean in and kiss the exposed skin on his neck.

"Bryan, we can't think of everything that can go wrong in life. We can't prepare for every scenario, every danger. It's just not possible."

I place a hand on his cheek and urge him to look at me, and when he does, I keep my eyes locked on his.

"But what we can do is adapt. Just like we did tonight. You did the right things once we knew we were compromised. And we are safe now. *You* kept me safe." I pull him in for a sound kiss to drive that point home. "Now get out of your head and let's try to get some sleep. We both need to be rested before tomorrow gets here. Do *not* let him use sleep deprivation against us."

"You're right." Bryan says as he pulls me tightly against his chest. "I love you, Taylor. Let's end this once and for all tomorrow."

The next morning comes all too quickly, but at least we were able to get a full night's sleep. When we arrive at the track, Josh is sure to keep spirits up, but I don't see Christy among the girls, and I can tell they miss her.

When Bryan tells Josh about the race tonight, everyone jumps in to help in any way possible. Ian takes a street sweeper to make sure the track is free of debris. Nick makes sure he has all the ammo ready, which is conveniently stored in his bay, while Mark makes a secret run for Linc to get any gear that we may need for tonight.

"Thanks, everyone. While you all are doing that, I'm going to work on my car." Bryan says, then turns to me. "You wanna help?"

"Duh," I say, trying to lighten the mood, but it only helps a bit.

When we get to his bay, I wordlessly slide the lift arms under the Camaro. Once they are in place, Bryan presses the button, and we wait while the car lifts into the air enough so I can get under it.

"I'll take care of the oil, and you can do whatever else you think needs to be done." I say.

"Oh, so you can do your own oil change, huh?" Bryan smirks, but the humor doesn't reach his eyes.

"Maybe." I tease. "I can't show you all my tricks, Bullet. Where's the fun in surprising you when you least expect it?"

"You always leave me guessing, Baby," Bryan says as he sits on the rolling stool, and this time when he smiles it lights up his entire face, making the green of his eyes look like blades of fresh grass.

I lean into him, brushing my lips over his in a quick kiss before making my way over to the tool chest to grab the socket set I need to remove the oil plug. All the while, Bryan watches me. His eyes trained on every line of my body as I stretch to attach the socket to the plug.

"Are you just gonna watch me all day?" I ask while trying to keep my face covered, so he doesn't see the flush creeping into my cheeks at his intense stare. So, I busy myself with pulling over the catch pan for the oil and wait for it to drain from the engine.

"Any other time you'd be yelling at me to stay off my leg, now you're asking me to get to work?" He asks while arching an eyebrow.

Before I can say anything, he's standing from the stool and walking over to me for the first time without his cane. He still has a slight limp in his gait, but it's nothing compared to what it was a few days ago. Bryan steps behind me, wrapping one arm around my waist and using the other to brush my hair away from my neck so he can place gentle kisses along my skin.

Goosebumps flare to life on my skin, and when I hear his approving growl in my ear, it goes straight to my core.

"Bryan." I say breathlessly. He leans in closer, and I can feel the hard length of him brushing up against me. "Not here."

"I am terrified of tonight, Annie." He whispers as he continues to kiss me. "This is just a reminder to both you and me to fight like hell tonight, Baby."

"Yeah." I agree, closing my eyes as I nod and Bryan lifts his head from my neck.

I can tell he's looking above me, and I can hear the smile in his voice. "Looks like the oil is done draining. You better fill it back up."

I look at him over my shoulder, my face turned from love-struck fool to an annoyed scowl at his version of my earlier words.

"Well, if you would stop distracting me, I might be able to get some work done."

Bryan laughs as he slowly walks over to get the impact wrench so he can take the tires off.

"You distracted me first. So, it's only fair to give you a taste of your own medicine." He jests.

I shake my head and wave my hand at him, silently telling him to move. "Move so I can lower the car, you insufferable ass."

Once I fill the engine with oil, I check out what Bryan is doing. He shows me how to check the brakes and replace them and shows me what to look for in faulty tires.

We spend most of the afternoon working on his car, and when Josh and Ian walk by, they decide to also inspect the transmission to make sure the clutch plate is in good shape before refilling the transmission oil.

"Hey, Babe, you want to go start working on your car? I'll be over in a bit to check on you." Bryan says as he hands Ian a bolt to secure the transmission body to the engine block.

"Okay. I'll see ya in a bit."

He leans in for a quick kiss, but being mindful not to get his oily hands on my clothes before I walk over to my bay that is thankfully next to his. I start with the oil, and once I get it changed; it seems like time flies by and I'm hearing Bryan's voice behind me as I'm sitting on my own rolling stool, replacing my rear brake pad.

"Hey grease monkey, how ya doing?"

I look over my shoulder and catch him unfolding a metal chair that was in the corner of the garage so he can sit next to me. I take a moment to drink in his shirtless, sweat-slicked torso before I force my eyes back on what I'm doing.

"Changing my brakes. I'm shocked that I need to change them already. I've only raced what, seven times?"

"Baby, I've changed your brakes every time I've worked on your car when you've left to do other things. So this is the first time *you've* changed your brakes." Bryan says, and I don't miss the way he's rubbing at his thigh, like he's trying to cover an ache.

"You've been on your—"

"I'm okay. Yes, I was on my leg a fair amount, but I took half a pain pill, and it's already helping. I'll be fine. And I will rest all you tell me too once we are back home in Utah."

I nod, knowing there's no use in arguing with him. "Help me with this tire. I'm done with this brake."

He motions for me to get up off the rolling stool so he can roll over to where I have my tire propped up. Watching the way his muscles flex in his forearms and back when he lifts the tire makes me want to fan myself for more than just the Florida heat.

"You gonna grab the impact drill or you just going to gawk at me?" Bryan says with a knowing smirk.

"Well, you shouldn't look so damn hot at everything you do."

"Don't blame the genetics when I know you love the end results." He says with a wink.

Once we get through replacing the last brake, Bryan lowers my car and makes sure everything is tightened to spec before he pulls me into him, my back against his bare chest with his head resting on my shoulder and our hands interlaced across my stomach.

"You did a good job today, Baby. I'm so proud of you."

While his voice is steady, his body is trembling, and I know it's not from any kind of discomfort in his leg. It's fear. I turn in his arms, my hands resting on his chest, and I place a gentle kiss over his heart, not to kiss his scar like I normally do, but just to let him know that everything will work out in the end. The saltiness of his sweat-slicked skin blooms on my tongue as Bryan wraps his arms around me. One around my lower back pinning me to him, while the other grips the base of my neck.

"I'm terrified of tonight, Annie." He admits.

"Hey, you taught me everything I need to know to win against him. And I know to stay on his right side as much as possible to use his blindness against him." I lift my head and give him a quick kiss. "Everything will be fine. We will walk away from this." I tell him because that's the only scenario I will allow.

"I want you to know that I won't hesitate to protect you. No one gets to you without getting through me first."

"I know."

"I want to get this over with so badly. To put it all behind us, but yet, I want to freeze time right now and just stay in the present." Bryan whispers as he lowers his head against my neck, breathing in my sweet perfume that I know is laced with sweat, but he doesn't care.

"Well, if we froze time to stay in the present, then we wouldn't be living life, and I want to do a *lot* of things with you, Bryan Evans." I say, letting the statement hang in the air for what he wants to interpret it as. "So, let's go kick some ass, arrest the bad guy, and go home."

"Well, you drive a hard bargain when you put it that way." Bryan smirks. "Let's do this."

Chapter Forty-Four

Bryan

As I release Taylor from my hold, the sound of an engine roars behind us. I turn to see Mark's Challenger parked in front of my bay. He swings the door open and exits the car with the engine still idling.

"Hey you two. I got the vests that Linc ordered." Mark says as he opens his trunk and pulls out two solid black Kevlar vests.

"There's more in there than just for us, Mark," I say, eyeing the five remaining vests in the trunk.

"Linc never said I couldn't put my own order in. And they're blank, so no one will know they're from the agency." Mark says, and then his face goes tight with anger. "This team has done a lot for us, so to me, it's the least I can do to help them."

"That's a good idea, Mark. I'm sure they'll appreciate it," Taylor says while taking the offered vests from him.

"I'm gonna go hand these out. We have what, four hours until this bastard comes?" Mark asks as he slams his trunk closed.

"Yeah. We do." I growl as I take my vest from Taylor. "Hand those out and meet me back here. Taylor and I are going to get cleaned up before this goes down."

"Alright, I'll see you in a few," Mark says before hopping back in his car and driving to the main section of the track where everyone else is gathered.

"Come on, Taylor. There's a shower over there." I tell her as I point to a building that sets to the right of what was once a concession stand, but Josh apparently didn't restore that building when he bought the track originally.

She wordlessly takes my hand as I grab the extra set of clothes I stashed here this morning before leading her across the lot. As I'm walking, I find myself putting my weight on the ball of my left foot more than I was while in the garage. I glance at her out of the corner of my eye, and I know she's fighting with herself not to ask me if I'm okay. If I'm in pain.

I think she knows it's no use yelling at me about it unless she sees that I'm bleeding from the wound. Like I said earlier, this is the last event before we can go home, and we need to concentrate on that and nothing else.

"Girl's side is that way." I say as I point to the opening on the right.

"What? No shower together?" Taylor teases.

"Again, Annie, just reminding myself of what I can have after this is all over." I tell her as I stare into her blue eyes. I can tell mine shine so hot with need and want for her that the shade is similar to hunter green.

"And what do you want to do, Bryan?" Taylor asks, her voice low but echoing softly in the bricks around us.

I step into her, forcing her against the wall, and I brace my arms on either side of her head, caging her in.

I lean in closer to her; keeping our lips just a breath away. "I want to explore every inch of your body with my lips, tongue, teeth, and fingers. I want you to be a writhing mess underneath me and just when you think you've given me all the orgasms your body can handle, then I'm going to slide into that perfect body of yours until I'm buried to the hilt and love you until we are nothing but a limp pile of bones."

She takes a shaky breath at my words, and when I see her press her thighs together, I can't stop the approving growl from bubbling in my chest. So I close the remaining distance between us and skim my lips over her neck. When I get to the sensitive spot behind her ear, she tilts her head to the side, allowing me more access, but I pause, pulling back enough to look down at her.

"You better go, Annie, before I make those promises a reality sooner than I want to. Because once I start, I don't want to stop until my body physically gives out or you tell me to stop."

"Okay." She breathes and slowly walks away from me and into the shower room.

Once she's out of my sight, I take a breath of my own and venture into my side of the shower stalls. After the water is warm enough, I step in under the showerhead and let the water roll down my back, trying to ease the burning desire from my blood and the fear plaguing my mind.

Once we emerge from our showers fifteen minutes later, my leg feels so much better with the warm water easing my tense muscles, and I'm able to walk flat-footed again and thankfully without that damn cane. I cannot go into this meet-up with a weakness like that.

"Did you get your vest on alright?" I ask, eyeing Taylor's body and noticing the solid line of the vest that's barely visible underneath her t-shirt.

"Yeah. I'm good." She says, then she takes the back of her hand and taps her knuckles against my own vest. "What about you?"

I give her a small smile. "Yeah. I got it"

I lace my fingers with hers as we cross the parking lot and into the main drag of the track. Mark's Challenger is parked in front of Nick's bay, and

I notice all the boxes of ammunition and a variety of guns to go with them. I try to keep the shock off my face, but, like always, Mark sees right through me.

"Dude! Nick is a walking armory!" Mark exclaims.

"I'm not blind." I snap, but he only smiles.

"I just gave out the vests to all the guys, but Josh wants more for the girls." Mark says but then steps closer to me as he continues, "Apparently the girls are not going to be hiding like they usually do and Josh wants *everyone* protected."

"I bet Linc is just bursting with joy for you now." I tease.

"I'm steering clear of him until I have to pick up the other vests." Mark says while rubbing the back of his neck. "Tempe and Sophie are the only ones that thought my idea was a good one."

"Well then, that's half the battle won."

He nods just as his phone pings with an incoming text and the corner of his mouth lifts in a smile.

"And orders up. I'll be back in a bit."

He rushes to his Challenger and speeds off through the gate to get the extra supplies. I turn my attention to the armory that is Nick's bay and give him an approving look.

"Nice stash you have here." I say.

"Yeah. That's why I wasn't here when you all first arrived. I was making a run to pick these up from a friend of mine in southern Florida."

"Glad you have connections, man."

"You good on ammo?" He asks.

"If you got a magazine's worth for a Glock, I could take two more." I tell him.

I know between Taylor and me, we only have a total of four, but now with my vest, I can hide one more to my side.

"You got it, man. And Taylor, I didn't know you could shoot." Nick says, but his tone is nothing short of admiration at a girl being able to carry just as well as a man.

"Yup. I've been likened to Annie Oakley, but I wouldn't go *that* far," Taylor says, but her smirk is all for me.

"Yeah, hotshot. You can hit a stationary target. Big whoop." I tease as Nick hands us both the magazines.

His tone goes serious for a moment. "Good luck out there and play it smart, you two. Josh told me what you plan on doing. So just remember everything that you've been taught, Taylor, and put this fucker down."

"We got this. No one else is dying because of him. I promise you that." I tell him sternly, and he only nods, going back to filling various other magazines with ammo.

When I walk away from Nick's bay, I notice that Mark is already back with the additional vests, Lexi right by his side, helping the other girls with theirs.

We walk over to him as he hands the last one to Morgan, and Josh makes sure it's secure over her sports bra before pulling her shirt back down. Once he's happy with that, he turns to address everyone in our little circle.

"Tonight, we stand together as a team, and no matter what, we live or die as a team. I'm hoping the latter doesn't happen, but just know I will lay down my life for each of you if it comes down to it," Josh says. "Bryan, Taylor. You two have done all you can to prepare yourselves, and I appreciate the extra protection you provided to my team. Hopefully, they won't be needed, though. I'm assuming you have a plan in place on how you want this race to go, so trust in your plan and don't second guess on it. Action is the only thing that should be on your minds."

Damn, this dude should be in the agency. He's amazing at giving pre-mission pep talks.

"We now have about an hour before this all goes down. If you have any questions, ask them now. If not, make sure you visit Nick if you need any ammo before he closes his bay." Josh says as he finally dismisses the little meeting.

"Wow, he's good." Mark says, and I know he's thinking the same thing I was.

"You think Linc would recruit him?" I whisper.

"Maybe." Mark shrugs.

A moment later, all four of our phones ping with a text message, and Mark and I are the only ones to open the thread, since both of our girls will look over our shoulder anyway.

> **Lincoln:** We are in position and ready to arrest once this is over.

> **Me:** Good. We are all ready to go here. Armed and vests in place.

> **Temperance:** Okay. I know this goes without saying, but keep a clear mind and we will see you at the finish line.

> **Mark:** Hey! You're a poet and don't know it!
> *Winky face emoji*

"Oh my God, Mark. Really?" I grumble.

"What? You know me. I can't leave a joke untold."

Lincoln sends a GIF of a man face-palming, and Temperance sends one of a kid laughing, and I can't help but shake my head at the interaction before my chest tightens at Mark's antics.

This is not the first time I've had the thought of what my parents are missing out on with Mark, and I'm sure they would have loved him, just like I'm sure they would love Taylor.

I lift my head to the slowly darkening sky. *"Be with us tonight."* I silently pray to them and God before I turn my attention back to the situation at hand.

The hour passes by in what seems to be in the blink of an eye. I try to drive my car onto the track, but the damn stitches and the still-healing muscle won't allow me to press the clutch in enough to engage it. So Mark drives it onto the track for me while Taylor drives her Mustang and parks it beside mine.

"You ready?" Taylor asks just as she walks to my side so she can lean against the front bumper of her car.

I only get a moment to answer her when the roar of four engines fills the air.

"Ready or not, it's time." I say, leaning in close to her and cupping her cheeks with both hands. "Keep your head on straight. Do not overthink this. You get an idea, you act on it." I give her a quick, hard kiss on the lips. "You have to win. I can't lose you, Taylor." I say, allowing her to see and hear how terrified I am.

"You won't lose me, Bryan."

I don't have time to tell her more when Desmond's matte black Charger rolls up beside my Camaro. I whisper a quick *I love you* to Taylor before I stand to my full height and cross my arms over my chest. My leg protests at the movement, but I force it to the back of my mind as I stare this asshole down.

As Desmond steps out of his Charger, his smirk sends chills down my spine, and my hands itch to punch this guy square in the jaw. When I look into his eyes, my fear lessens just a touch when I notice the blindness in his right eye again.

That is gonna be your downfall, buddy.

"Desmond." Josh begins. "I see you're on time, as always."

"I'm always on time when I can get me a new play toy to use and break." Desmond says as he grins over at Taylor. The look of hunger in his good eye as he takes in her body sets my blood on fire.

I must move just half a step because I feel Taylor's hand gripping the back of my shirt. Glancing over my shoulder, I see that her face is painted with fear, but when I meet her gaze, her blue eyes are lit with the same fire burning in my blood.

Way to play the fearful girlfriend, Babe.

"Let's get this over with. I'm tired of looking at your face, Slammer," Desmond snaps, the Mexican lilt to his voice grating on my nerves. "Don't worry, Baby Doll, you'll be coming to your new home soon enough."

"She's not going anywhere with you." I say, my voice calm and lethal.

"And how are you going to stop me?" Desmond grins. "Oh wait. You can't race, can you?"

Before I can even open my mouth to offer my challenge, he kicks his leg out, his foot connecting with my left thigh, and pain explodes in my mind. The stitches I have worked like hell to not rip out tear from the skin, and I growl and groan in pain.

The next thing I know, his hand is wrapping around my throat, my back slamming into the hood of my Camaro, Desmond's body pushing me further into the metal, making it buckle a bit under our weight.

I reach up with my right arm, grabbing a fist full of his shirt, and locking my elbow to keep him from putting his full weight on my throat.

His roar of frustration fills my ears as he lifts his other hand, fingers curling into a fist, and brings it down hard against my sensitive thigh.

Pain-filled screams rip from my constricted throat at the contact.

"Bryan!"

I hear Taylor's scream, and I know I need to get this son of a bitch off me before he chokes me to death. Phil didn't get the opportunity, and I'll be damned if this fucker succeeds.

"Get. The. Fuck. Off. Me." I grunt as I pull my free arm back and send my fist flying into his face, luckily on his right side, so he has not one clue what's coming until it smacks into his cheek with a satisfied crack.

"You son of a bitch." Desmond growls as he stumbles off me and backs away a few steps.

I slide off the hood of my Camaro, but I can't make my leg hold me. The throbbing pain in my thigh makes it hard to breathe. Hard to think. But I somehow manage to hold on to the cool metal and stand on my good leg, keeping my left bent to avoid putting any pressure on what I now feel is the bleeding wound.

"Bryan!" Taylor screams again as she walks up to me.

"I'll be alright." I say through gritted teeth.

"You might as well hand her over to me," Desmond says as he pulls his gun from the waistband of his pants, and I'm staring down the muzzle of his firearm. "You forfeit the race since you can't drive. So this bitch is as good as mine to break and fuck as I want."

"No!" Taylor screams, and I tighten my grip on her, keeping her body close to mine.

"If I can't race, then you race her. You want her that badly, then let her racing skills determine her worth."

Desmond laughs. "You think that will save her? I'll still be taking her from you and killing you on the way out."

"Then you have nothing to lose then, do you? Or are you too scared to race against a woman and *lose?*" I challenge and I pray that he takes the bait.

His eyes narrow like he's thinking this through, and my knee almost buckles when he agrees.

"Fine. But when I win, you will get on your knees so I can put a bullet in your fucking brain."

"Deal. But it won't come to that cause my girl's gonna smoke your ass." I grin even with the pain throbbing with its own heartbeat in my leg.

Desmond scowls at me as he takes a step toward his Charger, and I turn back to Taylor, giving her a quick kiss on the lips.

"You got this, Annie. You smoke this asshole. Show him what my girl is made of."

Chapter Forty-Five

Taylor

As Bryan's words filter in past the fear that causes my blood to pound loudly in my ears, I give him a small nod. I begin to take a step towards my car like we planned, but Desmond blares his horn at me, making me stop in my tracks.

"Oh no, Baby Doll. You're not driving your car. You drive the one I marked. Get in the Camaro, or you're both dead."

I glare at him over my shoulder, and before I can move towards the driver's seat, Bryan grabs my hand again, and I feel something slide into my palm.

"Put this in your ear when you get behind the wheel. I'll be right there with you." Bryan says as Mark approaches his left side while throwing his arm around Bryan's shoulders.

To other people, it looks like Mark is leaning against Bryan, but I realize it's the other way around. Mark is letting his friend lean against his body to help ease the pressure on Bryan's injured leg.

Glancing down, I notice blood is starting to seep through his jeans, causing my heart to leap into my throat, but I force my eyes back up to his face.

"Take care of him until I'm finished with this." I tell Mark.

"You got it, Tay Tay. Do me a favor and school this asshat in racing." Mark grins, but it's just for show because I can see the fire in his eyes that tells me he's seconds away from ripping Desmond apart.

I take a breath as I walk away to open the driver's door of the Camaro, and I drop in behind the wheel. Once I'm in the privacy cab, I open my palm to see what Bryan gave me. A small, clear earpiece. I smile as I push it into my left ear, and I immediately hear the muffled sounds of people talking on the other end.

"I got the earpiece in, Bryan." I say, hoping he can hear me.

"Okay," Bryan says, and just hearing his voice in my ear sets my nerves at ease just a little.

I push the clutch in and turn the engine over, then shift into first gear so I can drive onto the starting line beside Desmond's Charger. I spot Bryan, Mark, and Lexi standing next to Josh while the girls are lined up behind Ian and Nick. Bryan must be able to see me looking at him because he gives me the *l love you* sign before he covers his mouth with the same hand.

"Act like you are having issues with shifting at first. Then when he least expects it, you fuckin' smoke him." Bryan whispers in my ear.

"I second that, Tay Tay. Give this asshole a taste of his own medicine." Mark agrees.

"You got it, guys."

"Good luck, Taylor. You got this. You've been taught by the best of us. You *will* win." Lexi says. "Love you, girl."

"Love you, too." I say. "I love all of you."

"Focus, Babe," Bryan says. "Josh has the flag and is walking towards the track to start you two off."

I turn my attention back to the track ahead of me, and Josh stands between our cars with the checkered flag in hand.

"One lap. No rules." Josh says, his voice full of hate for this race. "May the best driver cross the finish line first."

Josh raises the flag above his head while Desmond revs his engine. I do the same as my hand hovers over the gearshift, so I'm ready to change them at a moment's notice.

"Three." Josh counts.

"Two." I whisper.

"One." I hear Bryan say in my earpiece.

"GO!" All five of us say in unison, and I put the petal to the floor, making the tires squeal against the pavement.

I let Desmond surge ahead of me and, like Bryan said to; I shift purposefully late, where the transmission makes horrible sounds for just a moment before I slip into the right gear. It's enough to make Desmond think I can't drive the car correctly, but not enough to mess up the transmission completely.

"Good, Annie. Just like that." Bryan praises in my ear.

As we make it to the first turn, I shift again, making the transmission grind gears once more. I can see Desmond's sick, twisted smile from here, and I can't help the growl of aggravation from my voice.

"Smile at this, you sick piece of shit."

I shift into a higher gear so I'm right on his bumper, but I make sure to stay right in the middle, and when he tries to fake me out, I meet him move for move.

"What is she doing? She needs to be on his right side." Mark whispers, and I can tell Bryan or Lexi must hit him because his choked, "Sorry," fills my ears next. He must have forgotten I could hear him.

"She's waiting for the right moment," Bryan says, his voice tight with fear and anticipation.

Once we are through the second turn, I slowly start to make my way to Desmond's right side so I can end this once and for all. But just as I move, he blocks me. It's like he knows what I'm trying to do.

"Damn it." I curse. "Alright, asshole, I'm gonna have to do this fast and hard."

I hear Mark chuckle, and I roll my eyes. *Ever the child.*

"Lexi, punch him for me." I say, and I immediately hear what sounds like a solid thud against his body, and Mark coughs a moment later. "Thank you."

"You got it, girly." Lexi says.

As we enter the third and final turn, everything happens so fast it threatens to make my head spin. Desmond shifts at the last second, and slams on his brakes, forcing me to swerve out from his right side, and pulls up to my left.

This is a horrible spot for me to be in.

"No, no, no. This can't be real." Bryan says, and I can feel the pure panic laced in his words, setting my own fear into high gear.

Exiting the turn and getting onto the straightaway for the last quarter mile of the track, Desmond makes his move. Pulling away enough so he can swerve back over into his pit maneuver.

"NO!" Bryan screams in my ear.

I ignore Bryan's screams and I focus on what I need to do. I let my hand hover over the gearshift, left foot inches from the clutch, and at the last possible second, I drop several gears, making me slow down so fast that the seatbelt locks and digs into my shoulder and collarbone. But Desmond misses me by mere inches.

As Desmond passes me, I shift into a higher gear to match his speed on his right side. His blind side and I make my own move that he won't see coming.

I swerve into his bumper, and he goes flying by me in tight circles until he crashes into the opposite wall. I don't see any flames erupt from the car, but I know he's not getting out of that wreck unscathed.

When I cross the finish line, my ears explode with cheers of victory both from the earpiece and from the muffled sounds coming of the others in the stands.

"You were amazing, Baby. Oh, thank God, you're alright. I love you so much." Bryan says with a sigh of relief that I feel clean down to my toes.

I skid to a stop a few feet past the finish line, and I let the engine idle for a moment to get my bearings. Just when I'm about to turn the engine off, it stalls and sputters due to the front-end damage I now see on the left side. The hood is bent at an odd angle, and there is a bit of smoke drifting off the engine.

Opening the door with a slow creak, I step out on shaky legs and I look up when I hear Bryan calling my name. He's awkwardly and painfully hobbling over to me, holding his still bloody leg as he goes. I somehow force my legs to carry me closer to him, and when we meet in the middle of the track, he pulls me against his chest so tight that I almost can't breathe, but yet I'm doing the same thing to him.

"That was the most terrifying thing I could ever watch." Bryan whispers as he kisses the top of my head.

"I'm sure it was. It was terrifying to me, so I'm sure it was torture for you." I say softly.

"Bryan!" I hear Mark shout, his voice like a warning, then the sound that follows makes my stomach sink.

A gunshot.

I wait for Bryan to drop away from me. Wait for his eyes to register a new wave of pain, but they only flare with pure anger. I look past him as he turns on his right heel, ripping the Glock from the small of his back, chambering the first of eight bullets, and unloads the firearm into Desmond's broken body.

I look past Bryan's rampage and I find Mark on the ground, not moving, and Ian holding a screaming and crying Lexi back against his chest until Bryan's gun clicks, signaling his magazine is out of ammo. The only reason he doesn't reach for another magazine is because Desmond's body is slumped against his crumbled Charger. Unmoving.

"Mark!" Lexi cries as Ian lets her go now that the volley of bullets have stopped. "Mark, please, Baby, be okay!"

After a moment of her shaking his body in an effort to wake him up, we hear Mark chuckle in a pained and breathless voice. "I'm too stubborn to die...remember?"

"Oh, thank God." Bryan says, heaving a sigh. "Mark, are you okay?"

"Yeah." Mark groans as he sits up to pull his shirt off to reveal the Kevlar vest.

Lexi stoops down to pull at the velcro straps so she can remove the vest, and in the center of Mark's chest, I see a bruise already forming under his skin.

"Can you breathe alright?" I ask, my nursing side automatically coming out.

"I don't think I have anything broken. Just bruised." Mark says while rubbing at his chest and testing his rips to make sure nothing is awry.

"What do you know? You finally took one for the team." Bryan says, half joking.

"Screw you, man. This hurts like hell." Mark wheezes and winces in pain.

"I don't know. He didn't bleed like you and I did, Bryan. So, I don't think he loves us as much as you think he does."

Mark glares at me a moment before he bursts out laughing, even if the movement makes him grab at his chest.

"Ow! Damn it, Tay Tay, don't make me laugh." Mark groans while holding his chest.

"I'm glad you all can find the time to joke about this, but we have work to do." Lincoln says as he and Temperance step out of their SUV a moment later, red and blue lights flashing all over the vehicle.

"You brought the cops?" Josh snaps.

I just smile at him. "We are not cops. Or at least not your normal ones."

"What do you mean? Were you four playing me for a fool, too?" Josh seethes.

"No. We weren't." Bryan says as he sways on his feet. "We are with the FBI, and we came down here to *help* you. Our boss heard about something weird going on down here, and we came down to check it out."

"We were always here to help out, nothing more." I tell him.

Josh's gaze scans over us and then he turns to Lincoln, who is simply nodding his head, agreeing with us.

"So you're really with the feds?" Josh asks.

"Yeah, we are. But you all are safe. We won't turn you all in for anything." I promise him.

"Well, in that case, we are all in your debt." Josh says, and his eyes lock on Bryan. "You even kept to your word by killing him."

"I didn't want to, but you don't shoot at my brother." Bryan says, glancing down at Mark, who's still on the ground with Lexi fussing over him.

"Alright, everyone. We need you off the track so I can have my team come in here and clean up." Temperance says as she walks in with Sophie at her side.

"Let's get you two to the hospital to make sure you're alright." Lincoln says.

"Let us know if you need anything." Josh tells us as he takes Morgan's hand in his and she leans into his body, looking like they both have had a boulder removed from their souls.

"We will. Thank you." I say.

"Josh is right. Thank you all for stopping this evil that's been plaguing us for years." Morgan says with a small smile.

"It's all in a day's work." Mark grunts while he tries to stand up, but stumbles a step before Linc catches him by the arm.

"We'll get them to the hospital." I tell Linc as I take Bryan's hand and help him walk over to my Mustang while Lexi does the same with Mark.

"Okay. Keep us updated."

"I will." I reply.

Once we arrive at the hospital, I insist on Bryan staying in the car while I go in to get the nurse and a wheelchair so he can begrudgingly be wheeled inside, same with Mark.

The guys are taken back in no time when I flash our badges, and now it's just a waiting game for someone to come out and tell us we can go back with them.

Forty minutes later, our names are called, and we follow the nurse back a series of hallways towards their room. Stepping into a large room, I see the end of two beds, and I smile at the fact that the nurses roomed these two together.

"Hey, Babe." I say to Bryan as he smiles at me. While I can still see the lingering pain there, it's a lot better than what it was at the track.

"Is Lex here?" Mark asks, and I can tell from his voice that he's probably on some strong pain meds.

"I'm here, Mark," Lexi responds as she walks over to his bed.

"Lexi! Baby!" Mark shouts, eyes wide as he slurs his words a bit.

"Shhh, you loudmouth." Lexi scolds, but he ignores her.

"Ohmigod, Baby. These drugs are *amazing*." He slurs again, running his words together.

Bryan shakes his head as he pinches the bridge of his nose. "Dude could never hold his alcohol."

I give him a side-eyed glare, and he smiles again.

"Okay, neither can I. But I have pain meds too, and I'm not loopy like he is."

"And Lex, guess what? I get to keep the bullet that almost killed me."

"It didn't almost kill you, Mark. It got as far as your vest, you big dolt." Lexi rolls her eyes.

"That damn thing did crack a rib," Mark says. "So it almost could have killed me."

"Okay. Whatever you say, Baby," Lexi says in a placating manner.

"Yeah, I can look at it from now on and I can say, 'you didn't get me, you little bitch.'"

"You are so lucky you're cute." Lexi grins as she threads her fingers through his hair.

"You love me no matter what." Mark says.

"I guess you're right." She jests.

I look over at Bryan, and I take his hand in my own. "What about you? Are you okay?"

"Yeah. The nurse just restitched me and wrapped it. They put me on antibiotics again, but that's about it. We're just waiting for our discharge paperwork."

I look over to Lexi and Mark, who is, thankfully, looking a little more lucid now, and I can't help the smile that tugs at my lips.

"Looks like we have another successful case under our belts." I say.

"Yes, we do." Bryan smiles. "Even with it being as stressful as it was, it was a success in the end."

"What's a little life without some stress?" Mark says with a lazy grin.

"You are the definition of stress, dude. So, I'd shut up if I were you." Bryan says.

"Boy, you take a bullet for a brother and you still get flack from him." Mark says, rolling his eyes.

"Just you wait. Once we are both healed, watch me find you and kick your ass."

Mark extends his hand and shakes it in mock fear. "Oh, I'm so scared."

A moment later, thankfully, a nurse comes in and discusses both guys' discharge instructions. Once that's done, another nurse helps transfer them each into a wheelchair and rolls them out to the parking lot and over to our cars.

It's kinda crazy, but I'm sad about packing up and leaving this state in the next few days. I feel that these people here have become my friends, even if they were pissed at first at us lying to them, but they know now deep down that we were here to help.

After I let the nurse help Bryan into the passenger side of my Mustang, I thank her before shutting the door and driving us to our home away from home.

"Taylor?" Bryan says as I hit the interstate a few minutes later.

"Yeah?"

"I just wanted to say that you are the bravest and the smartest woman on the planet. Thank you for choosing to be mine so I can share your accomplishments with you." Bryan says as he brings my hand to his mouth for a quick kiss.

"Well, thank you for the help in making me that way. Without you teaching me how to drive this," I gesture to the gearshift. "I wouldn't have had a chance in hell at winning."

"We make a great team, don't we?" Bryan says with a genuine smile.

"Yes, we do. Like always, Bullet. Forever and always a great team." I smile, and once I pull in front of our apartment, I send a quick text to Linc, letting him know we are home and the guys are alright too.

> **Lincoln:** That's great news. We made the arrests for the remaining members of Desmond's team, so they won't be an issue anymore. We also cleaned up the track about two hours ago. So everything is all set for the others to return in the morning. Rest well, Taylor. You all deserve it. We'll see you tomorrow.

I send him a thumbs up emoji and I help Bryan inside so we can do what I was just ordered. Rest and prepare to pack in the next few days.

Mark

After Lexi helped me inside our apartment and into bed, my head no longer hit the pillow and I was out like a light. Guess that's what fear, pain and said pain medicine will do to ya.

I wake up after what I know to be a few hours later, and when I look at the clock above our bedroom door, the glowing hands reads three in the morning.

I try to turn over on my side, but the ache in my chest forces me to stay on my back. I try to reach for Lexi with my arm, but I don't find her in bed beside me. I'm about to yell out her name when I see her awkwardly leaning over in the armchair that sits in the corner of the room.

"Lexi." I whisper-shout, and she wakes up immediately.

"Mark? Are you okay?" She asks with fear lacing her tone, and it makes my chest hurt for an entirely different reason.

"Yes, Lex, I'm fine. What the hell are you doing sleeping in that hard ass chair?" I ask.

She looks down at the arm, toying with a thread that's sticking out of a seam. "I didn't want to hurt you."

"Baby, please get in bed with me. I don't want to see you on that chair anymore."

Lexi opens her mouth to argue, but I put my index finger to my lips, silently telling her to shut it and then I crook that same finger in a come hither motion and she complies, slowly walking over to her side of the bed and slips in beside me.

Yes, it hurts like hell when the mattress moves with her added body weight, but I'll take my own discomfort any day, as long as my girl is comfortable.

Once she's settled with her head resting on my shoulder, she gently traces the black and blue bruise that colors my chest, and I can tell she's starting to get in her head again.

"Lex, I'm fine." I tell her while wrapping my arm around her back, pulling her closer to me. "It's just a bruise. It will heal, and I'll be back to normal in no time." I say while kissing the top of her head.

"I never knew how Taylor felt when Bryan was shot, but I...can't get the image out of my head. This is like that one mission all over again." Lexi says, her voice cracking near the end.

"I know." I say, moving closer so I can kiss her forehead this time. "Just like that time, we will get through this, too. It will become a memory, and then you'll have me to be able to chase away the demons that haunt you."

Lexi stays quiet while I just hold her and play with her hair. Then, after a few minutes, I break the silence between us.

"You know what thoughts were going through my head when I realized what happened and what that could mean. Well, first I was thinking about Bryan, you know, gotta make sure the bro's okay." I pause to breathe through the ache in my chest, but my words cause me to get a playful smack on my other shoulder from Lexi.

"If you could be serious for once in your life, we'd be in for a big snowstorm." Lexi says, but deep down, she loves the fact that I can make her laugh in any situation.

"Okay, you want serious, well here it is." I begin. "You were the second thing on my mind. We have never talked about the 'what if's' of this job." I say as I feel Lexi snuggle closer into my side. "What if something happened to me and we had a little Alexandria, or Mark Jr. running around?"

Lexi pops up to look me in the eye at the mention of kids with a note of panic and question lingering in her eye. We've never talked about kids before.

"I saw the pregnancy test in the bathroom last week." I say gently.

Lexi drops her eyes for a second. "I was going to tell you about it, but everything was going nuts and—"

"It's okay. I know it was negative this time, but what if next time it's not? Alexis Grace, we need to have plans in place for the worse case scenario. That's what this mission has taught me. Course, you know me; I have to be shown the hardest way." I say while trying to lighten the mood again.

"I've always said you are the biggest hardhead on the face of the planet." Lexi says.

"You wouldn't have me any other way." I grin.

"You're right on both things," Lexi says slowly. "How about we talk to Taylor and Bryan once we get home? I'm sure they have had the same thoughts as we do." Lexi says.

"Deal babe. Now let's get some rest." I say while pulling Lexi close and letting sleep take us in the comfort of each other's arms.

Chapter Forty-Six

Taylor

Over the next four days, Lexi and I force the guys to relax either in our respective beds or we each take turns and hang out in the other's living room on the couch. I know both Bryan and Mark hate the sedentary lifestyle, but they know it's for their own good.

On the fifth day, while I'm in the kitchen cleaning our dirty dishes from last night, Bryan is laughing with Sophie in the living room. Since we are going to be boarding the plane later this evening to go home, she came over to say her final goodbyes in private.

As I'm drying the last dish, I lean against the doorway and watch the two of them play cards together. I smile when Sophie laughs at beating him again for the third time in a row, and Bryan shakes his head while he accuses her of cheating. I remember when he and Cody would play games back home and he would say the same thing.

It makes me think if he would have gotten the chance, he would have been a great brother to someone, and my chest hurts for his lost opportunity.

"You know you'd be a great big brother if your parents were still here and had another kid," Sophie says, as if in tune with my thoughts.

"Nah. I don't know the first thing about being a brother." Bryan says as he rubs the back of his neck like he does when he's uncomfortable.

"I don't believe that for a second." Sophie snaps. "I mean, look at you now. You're doing brotherly things. Isn't playing cards something brothers do with their little sister?"

"I guess I never thought of it that way." Bryan says.

"Yeah. I play cards, all kinds of board games, and stuff with my little brother." I offer from the kitchen, and they both turn to look at me. "Sorry, I know eavesdropping is not cool."

"No, it's okay. It's not like we were being quiet or anything." Sophie says with a smile before she turns back to Bryan. "Well, I think you'd make an awesome brother if you were given the chance."

"Thanks, Soph." Bryan says as he pulls her in for a sideways hug. "I don't think you'd be all that bad of a sister, either. Your brother would have been the luckiest guy on earth to have a sister like you if he were still here."

"Thanks, Bryan," Sophie says as she looks at him with tears welling in her eyes.

A moment later, we hear a knock on the door, and Bryan gets up to answer it, calling back over his shoulder, "Sophie, your parents are here."

"Thanks for letting me come over to say goodbye, you two," Sophie says as we meet in the middle of the living room to hug one another.

"Hey, don't be afraid to call or text either of us." I tell her. "I want to know when you go on your first official mission."

"Deal," Sophie says as she walks over to Bryan and gives him one last hug.

I glance over at Linc and Tempe, and they have this odd look on their faces. A sadness I can't quite place. I'm assuming they're having the same thought as Sophie had just minutes ago, because Bryan would be the same age as their son that they lost. So, it makes sense they would feel sad about what Sophie is missing out on.

"Let's go, Soph." Temperance says as she extends a hand for her daughter.

"Bye, Bryan." Sophie whispers, wiping away a tear from her eye.

"Like Taylor said, keep in touch." Bryan tells her while wiping at another tear that rolls down her cheeks with his thumb. She nods and goes into Tempe's awaiting arms for a loving embrace.

Linc clears his throat. "Your plane is set to leave at ten this evening. You all ready?"

"Yeah. Taylor and I are, but I need to make sure Mark is ready." Bryan says. "I tell you, that man would lose his head if one of us didn't keep him in line." He adds, shaking his head.

"He's a good guy, and he's there for you when it counts." Temperance says.

"Yeah, that's what I keep telling him, *but* sometimes Mark's antics does make you cringe." I say with a wry smile.

"I'm just glad that Lexi has to take his shit more than I do now." Bryan says while leaning against the doorframe with his arms crossed loosely over his chest.

"Oh, so push your best friend on mine, huh?" I chuckle while playfully punching him in the arm.

"I'm not pushing as much as I am sneaking away when they are together." Bryan smirks.

I roll my eyes. "You're horrible."

Bryan then walks over to me, wrapping his arm around the small of my back so he can pull me into his chest, my hands splayed against the hard lines of muscles under his shirt.

"Well, if I couldn't sneak away, then I wouldn't get to be with you, Baby." He leans in, lowering his mouth to mine in a heated kiss, and right now, I don't care that we have an audience. I just want him. His mouth, his touch, his love.

"Okay." Sophie's voice rings out, and she fakes a gagging sound as she walks away. "I don't want to see my stand-in brother make out with his girlfriend."

"I'm just living up to the temporary role, Soph!" Bryan jokes.

"Okay, role over. See ya!" Sophie tosses back over her shoulder as she walks down the steps.

Lincoln and Temperance look at Bryan like he's grown a second head.

"It's nothing. Since I'm the same age her brother would have been; I was just kind of a stand-in while we were here." Bryan says with a shrug of his shoulder before he pulls me back against his chest, wrapping an arm around my stomach and resting his head on my shoulder.

"Yeah, now I'm regretting that decision!" Sophie yells. "I need to clean my eyes with bleach to get you and Taylor kissing out of my mind!"

"I'll remember that when you get a boyfriend!" Bryan tosses back.

"Okay, Babe. Lighten up." I say, looking back at him over my shoulder, but I'm glad he's bickering like this with her. I can see it in the way his eyes appear to be a bright green, that he loves it.

"Thank you, Bryan," Temperance says with tears in her eyes. "I know this means a lot to her to have a brother figure, and it means a lot to me, too."

"You're welcome." Bryan says with a smile.

"Come on, Tempe. Let's leave them alone while they finish packing up to leave." Linc says, pulling his wife gently by the elbow.

Bryan and I watch them walk across the street, and once we see them disappear into their apartment, Bryan ushers me inside while he shuts and locks the door out of habit.

"You know, I'm gonna miss them."

"Me too. But maybe they'll come up to Utah sometime." I say with a smile.

"Yeah. Gramps will love Sophie."

"So, will Granny." I add.

Bryan nods, and just as we are about to sit on the couch, both of our phones beep with an incoming message.

Josh: Bryan and Taylor. Why don't you come by the track for a farewell feast? Mark told me you all are flying back home. So come down and we can send you off in style. :)

I look over at Bryan, and I am already nodding my head. He smiles, and I watch him reply to Josh's text.

Bryan: Okay man. We'll be down soon.

Bryan closes out of the text message app and pulls up the Uber app before turning to me.

"I'll order us an Uber and you go get ready."

"I hate that the agency already took our cars back." I pout.

"Me too." Bryan says with a sigh. "There. Our ride will be here in fifteen minutes."

I nod and go to the main bathroom to freshen up a bit, and by the time we are both standing on the porch, our Uber shows up and Bryan opens the rear passenger door for me and I slip inside.

Taking his seat beside me, he tells the driver where we want to go, and we sit in comfortable silence until we arrive at the gate of the track. When we step out, we just take a moment to look around, and I swear I can feel the peace floating around in the air.

"You ready?" Bryan asks with a smile.

"Yeah."

Just as we take a step towards the gate, we see that Mark is waiting for us, waving his arms to urge us inside faster.

"Come on! Food's gonna get cold!" Mark exclaims.

"We're coming!" Bryan shouts back.

When we reach Mark's side, we notice that everyone is gathered around a long table covered in a light blue plastic tablecloth and it's overflowing with food. Hamburgers, hot dogs, macaroni and cheese, baked beans and more side dishes.

Next to the tables are two grills. The white tendrils of smoke drift into the air from the hot coals, waiting to cook more food if needed, and three coolers filled with ice and various drinks are on the other side of the table. Most of the group here has beer bottles in hand, but the four of us only pick out cokes since we have to be flying in a few hours.

"Bryan!" Josh greets us with a bright smile as he walks over, pulling us in for a quick embrace. "Glad you came down."

"Thanks for putting this together for us," Bryan says.

"One thing though, I did invite someone here that—" Josh trails off as Bryan and I look over his shoulder and we see that James and Christy here. "After everything went down and there was no longer a threat to his or Christy's life, I talked to him. And I know James; we grew up together, so I know when he speaks if he's lying."

Bryan nods. "He wasn't telling you anything, so you didn't get a chance to hear the lie. I get it. Just as long as he doesn't come after Taylor again, I'm good."

Josh gives us an understanding smile before leading us to the table full of food. "Dig in before these heathens take it all."

As the afternoon rolls into evening, we were full of both good food and camaraderie. I'm hanging with Lexi and the girls while the guys are all playing cards for one last time, and I find myself smiling when James seems to be getting along with Mark and Bryan just as well as the other members of the team.

"We are gonna miss you two," Anna says while pulling me in for a hug.

"I'm gonna miss you all, too. You need to fly into Utah one day. We'll show ya around and have a blast." I say.

"Totally!" Lexi agrees. "And you'll get to meet our girlfriends, too."

"I'll have to talk to Josh about making that happen one day." Morgan says with a smile, but then her tone takes on an edge of seriousness. "Thank you all for doing what you did. I'm happier now that my sister can rest in peace, and I can live my life not having to worry if I would suffer her same fate."

"It's what we do. We take care of the bad guys." I say like it's the easiest thing in the world.

Morgan nods. "Keep doing that and making this world a better place for all of us."

A chorus of similar words ring out in our little group, and when we hear Mark and Bryan call our names, we give each girl a quick hug and say our final goodbyes, for now.

I check my phone when I reach Bryan's side, and I didn't realize how much time had flown by. We have an hour to get to the airport.

"Lincoln's picking us up here, then back to our apartments to get our bags before taking us to the airport."

I nod as Linc's SUV rolls up to the gate and we take one last look behind us. To the group of racers that quickly became friends waving us off.

After we arrive at our apartments, and we load our suitcases into the back of Linc's SUV, Temperance comes over once more and gives us all a quick hug to say goodbye.

"You're not coming with us to the airport?" I ask.

"No. I need to take care of some things at the agency." She says, looking at Linc for a moment before she turns her eyes back on me and Bryan. "You take care of that girl of yours, mister. Don't be letting her go off on missions alone." She adds, her voice wobbling a little near the end.

"Yes, ma'am. I learned that lesson the hard way. She's not going anywhere without me." Bryan says while pulling me closer to his side.

"Good," Temperance says while wiping a tear from her eye. "God, I'm sorry. I'm an emotional mess."

"We'll be sure to keep in touch." Bryan says, and we all agree.

Temperance nods and walks away, but Lincoln pulls her in for a quick kiss before she walks away to get into her car.

"Ya'll ready?" Linc asks, and we nod, getting into his SUV without another word.

Twenty minutes later, once we are all loaded onto the private plane and in the air, Mark and Lexi look between us and she nods her head at his silent question.

"What's going on with you two?" I ask.

"Can Lexi and I talk to you two about something?"

"Sure man. Everything okay?" Bryan asks, and I can tell by the tone of his voice he doesn't like the question, and neither do I.

"Yeah, we just gotta get some things out in the open, is all." Mark says.

"Ok, spill. What's going on with you two?" I ask.

"After I was shot, it got me thinking. Lexi and I don't have a 'what if' plan."

"A 'what if' plan? What does that mean?" I ask.

"I know." Bryan says. "I've actually thought about that, too. It's weird how getting shot makes you think about this, huh?"

"That and a pregnancy scare. That gets you in line real quick." Mark blurts out.

"What?" I shriek and look over at Lexi.

"It was negative." She shakes her head. "I'm sorry I was going to tell you too! But this is why we all need a 'what if' plan."

"Well, you know that if anything happened to either of you, Bryan and I would step in to help in any way we could. You don't ever need to worry about that." I take her hand and give it a quick squeeze. "Even Macy, Casey, and Tina would all step in and take over as aunties. You know that."

Bryan chimes in next, looking directly at Mark. "Mark, you know I would do anything for you two. Lexi is like a sister to me, and I'd do my best to be the cool uncle."

"Thanks, and I knew you all would feel this way, but—" Mark says, but Bryan cuts him off.

"But it's still good to have that out there in the universe as a kind of deterrent, right?" Bryan asks.

"You hit the nail on the head, man." Mark says. "And the same goes for you, too. If you ever need something like this from us, we're here for you."

"I know." Bryan says. "Brother's until the end, right?"

"You know it!" Mark smiles, and we all breathe a sigh of relief as we relax and enjoy the six-hour flight.

Chapter Forty-Seven

Taylor

About four hours into our flight, Mom's messaging me before I can even think of texting her first. She's sent several random celebration GIF's at hearing—no doubt from Wayne—that our case was a success.

After her last message, she calls me right afterward. "Hey, Honey. Let me know when you land so I can make sure to have dinner on the table for you all." Mom says, and I hear the rustling of plastic grocery bags in the background as she sets them on the counter.

"I will, Mom. We have about two hours left before we land."

"I am so proud of all of you." Mom praises, and I can just imagine the smile on her face right now.

"Yeah, I don't want to brag or anything, but I keep this team together." Mark says with a cocky smirk.

"You wish!" Bryan laughs. "We both know it's the girls that keep our asses in line."

"Now that's a reason I can get behind." Lexi smiles.

"I know something *I* can get behind." Mark croons, his voice dropping lower as he leans into Lexi's neck.

"Okay! I'm getting off here. You all be safe." Mom yells as she promptly hangs up her end of the call.

"Oh, my God." Bryan shakes his head. "Get a room, you two."

"What'd'ya say, Lex, you wanna join the mile-high club?"

"No!" Lexi exclaims as she smacks Mark on the chest, then pushes him away.

Bryan and I laugh at Mark's defeated look, and we allow the next two hours to pass by either talking about random things or playing cards.

When the pilot finally turns on the light, telling us to fasten our seatbelts, we do, and I hold on to Bryan's arm as the plane lands on the tarmac.

"Thank you all for flying with us." The captain's deep voice says over the speaker system. "Please exit through the door on your right and watch your step."

The guys lead us out, and I walk in the middle of our group, with Lexi trailing behind us. The sun is just starting to set here, and I breathe in the crisp mountain air that's been around me my whole life.

"Ahh, nothing like being home." Mark says as he breathes in deeply and lets out a loud exhale.

When our feet hit the pavement, we find that Mark's blue Explorer is parked on the runway and a tall agent gets out and walks over to us.

"Your keys, Agent Stone."

"Thank you." Mark says as he takes the offered keys and turns to us. "Ya'll ready to go home?"

"Beyond ready. I want a hot shower, hot food, and my own bed." I say as I stretch my arms over my head to ease my sore muscles from the flight.

"Then let's go!" Mark says as he and Bryan pick up our suitcases that just came down the luggage belt and throw them into the back of the SUV.

As soon as we're on the road, I let Mom know we're on our way, and the twenty-minute ride seems to fly by, and Mark is already pulling into the driveway of my parents' house.

Looking through the rear passenger window, I see my mom and dad standing on the porch waving at me, and Cody is standing next to them with a white cardboard sign that reads: *Welcome home, Taylor and Bryan!* Then underneath that, like it was almost forgotten, *Mark and Lexi too!*

I open my door to step out, and when my sneaker hits the grass, Cody is ditching the sign, racing towards me and Bryan, and I barely catch him when he barrels into me.

"Taylor!" He squeals.

"Hey, Cody. Oh, I missed you!" I say, holding my little brother tightly against my chest.

"I missed you too!" He says, his voice muffled from being squished.

Then he pulls back and looks to my right at Bryan, giving him a bright smile before reaching his arm out, signaling it's Bryan's turn for a hug.

"Hey, buddy. Nice to see ya again." Bryan says softly as he gathers Cody into his arms.

"Did you get the bad guys?" Cody asks, looking between the two of us with wide eyes.

"Of course." I smile over at him.

"No one can get by your sister and me." Bryan says. "Never gonna happen. We will *always* get the bad guy."

"You guys are the coolest!" Cody squeals as he wraps his arms around both our necks so he can give us a hug at the same time.

"And what am I, Cody, chopped liver?" Mark says in an exasperated tone.

"You're just the sidekick." Cody says, then bursts out laughing.

Bryan and I turn our heads as Mark dramatically clutches his chest like he's been wounded, then looks at his palm, checking for any invisible blood.

"Lexi, quick; check to see if I'm bleeding! 'Cause his words were sharp as a knife!"

"Oh, my God. Stop being dramatic, you big baby." Lexi rolls her eyes, walks up to Cody, ruffles his hair, and gives him a wink. "Hey, little man."

"Hi Lexi." Cody says.

Mark walks up and snatches Cody from Bryan's arms and tips my brother upside down, making him scream and laugh with excitement.

"You gonna say that I'm a sidekick again, twerp?" Mark asks, his voice playful.

"No!" Cody says through bouts of laughter.

"Alright then." Mark says as he flips Cody around and puts him back on his feet in the grass. "Now, how ya been, dude?"

"Good," Cody says as he follows Mark and Lexi into the house, and Bryan and I are not too far behind them. When we reach the porch, Mom immediately pulls me in for a hug.

"I'm so glad you're home, Taylor." She says as she buries her face in my neck. "Are you okay?"

"Yeah," I say, pulling back from her. "I'm okay."

Mom lets go of me, and I step over to Dad, giving him a hug while Mom pulls Bryan in for one of her own.

"I'm glad you're back, Sweetheart," Dad says and leads me inside where I smell his baked lasagna cooking in the oven.

"Dinner's about ready." Mom calls from behind me. "And we have other guests that want to meet you, too."

As we enter the dining room, Bryan rushes past us to greet his grandparents. I stand back, watching as he brings both of them in for a hug and he kisses Gail on the cheek.

"Good to have ya back, son." John's rough voice fills the dining room.

"Good to be back, Gramps." Bryan replies.

Gail looks over her shoulder at me and waves me over to them with her free hand. "Get your booty over here, Taylor. I want to say hello to you, too."

I smile and walk over, letting her pull me in between her and John.

"You keeping my grandson in line, Taylor?" John asks with a mischievous smile, and Bryan rolls his eyes.

"We've been keeping each other in line, Grandpa." I say.

After we finish saying our hello's, the four of us split bathrooms, Mark and Lexi in the main bath upstairs while Bryan and I take the bathroom attached to my room so we can clean up a bit.

Once we sit down for dinner, we talk about what all happened. Meeting Lincoln, Temperance, and Sophie. What the three of us girls did when Anna was kidnapped. And how we finally took care of Desmond and his team.

"I'm proud of you all." Mom says, and everyone nods their head in agreement.

Granny touches Bryan on the arm to get his attention. "But all injuries are doing well?"

"Yeah, Granny. Everything's healing as it should." He says as he pats her arm reassuringly.

After dinner and we talk for about two more hours, Mark and Lexi leave, and Bryan walks his grandparents back over to their house, so I decide to take a much-needed shower and get ready for bed.

When I pull one of Bryan's shirts over my head and slide into a pair of shorts, I collapse onto my bed, pulling my pillow close to my chest, letting out a sigh of relief as the familiar feel of my own bedsheets surround me.

"Was the bed down there that bad?" Mom asks with a chuckle as she sits next to me and runs her fingers through my damp hair.

"No. But there's nothing like your own bed to get snuggled up into." I say.

"Hey, I want to ask you something before Bryan gets back." Mom says, her voice morphing into her serious tone that demands all my attention.

"What's up?" I ask.

"I don't really even want to ask this, but have you and Bryan—"

I cut her off, knowing where she's taking this. "No." She looks at me skeptically, and I know I can't keep anything from her. "I'll be honest, we did *some things,* but we did not have actual sex. And Bryan's not pushing me to do it. It's on our terms and mainly when *I'm* comfortable."

"I figured, but you know me. I have to make sure you know that it's a two-way street and not to let him pressure you into anything you don't want."

"I know. And he's been amazing with me." I say with a smile.

"Just don't do anything while I'm here." Mom grumbles. "Cause I'd hate to kill 'em"

I laugh. "You got it, Mom. Love you."

"Love you too, Sweety." Mom says as Bryan walks in and she turns, standing right in front of him, and pokes a finger into his chest. He looks at me with a touch of fear in his eyes before turning them back on Mom. "You treat my girl like a queen, you got me?"

"Yes, ma'am." Bryan says with a serene smile. "Easy to promise when I already treat her like one."

Mom nods her head, satisfied with Bryan's answer, before she walks out of my room and into her own.

"What was all that about?" Bryan asks as he slips his shirt off to throw into the hamper in the corner of my room.

"Mom just being Mom." I begin. "And telling me not to let you pressure me into doing anything I don't want." I add with a smile.

"So she knows about?" He asks with a smirk while wiggling his index and middle fingers in a 'come hither' motion that makes my core pulse with need.

I hug my pillow tighter to my chest to keep myself from pouncing on him. "I mean, I didn't go into detail..." I draw out my words. "But I told her we did fool around."

"And I'm still living?" He asks skeptically.

I laugh, "Yeah."

"Good."

He stalks over to the bed and before I know it, he's pushed me onto my back, pulling the pillow from my grip and leaning over me, arms braced on either side of my head and I have to hold back my moan of pleasure as I can feel the hard bulge of him between my legs.

He trails his lips up the length of my neck and ends with his mouth on mine for what seems like years and a heartbeat all at once.

"Now I can start planning on how I can make your first time as perfect as I can for you." Bryan whispers against my mouth, his green eyes boring into my blue ones with such love I can feel it deep down in my soul.

"Just keep doing what you've been doing with me." I breathe. "Just like the other times you've touched me."

Suddenly we hear a throat clearing from the doorway and we both turn our heads to find my father standing in the doorway. Bryan sighs, leaning his forehead against my collarbone for a moment before he lifts himself off my body. Dad doesn't say anything, but he gives Bryan a fierce glare as he walks into the master bedroom.

"Your dad is still the romance killer for us," Bryan chuckles as he makes his way into the bathroom to get his shower.

"Tell me about it." I say, rolling my eyes as I settle into bed and wait for Bryan to join me.

Chapter Forty-Eight

Mark

After leaving Taylor's house, I'm eager to get back to our apartment. With finally being back in our hometown, I can't keep my hands off Lexi. She's figured out I'm being a little more handsy than usual, but she doesn't tell me to stop, nor does she let go of my hand once she takes it in her own as I drive down the highway.

When I pull up to our apartment and get her inside, Lexi stands in the middle of the living room and pins me with a glare that tells me I better start talking.

"I know. I'm being a little overly touchy right now." I say, tilting my head back and looking up at the ceiling to gather my thoughts.

"Why? What's wrong?"

"Nothing is wrong, Lex," I say, bringing my gaze back to hers. "It's just with being home now and knowing you're safe is making me realize what all happened these last few weeks."

Lexi steps closer to me, her hands gliding up over the muscles of my stomach before she rests them on my chest, toying with the fabric of my shirt.

"What have you realized?" She asks.

"Where do I start?" I chuckle. "You've gotten better with your PTSD episodes. You rescued a girl from psychotic assholes before they...could rape her. You kicked a guy's ass that attacked Taylor." I list off the many things she did as I cup her cheek, running my thumb over her bottom lip, and she leans into my touch.

"I just did what any good agent would have done. I had my teams back just like they had mine." Lexi shrugs.

"You are amazing, Baby. I love you so much it hurts." I pull her closer to me, our mouths just a breath away. "I will drown in that pain for you a thousand lifetimes over as long as I get to have you in the end."

She stands on her tip-toes, crushing our lips together in a heated kiss that I immediately deepen, spearing my tongue against hers, and when a needy moan that escapes her lips, I greedily swallow it.

Grabbing her hips, I lift her off her feet, her legs instinctively wrapping around my waist as I blindly make my way back into the bedroom, never breaking our heated kiss.

I walk through the door, not bothering to shut it since it's only the two of us in the apartment, and toss her onto the bed. She bounces once before I'm leaning over her, trailing my lips over the soft skin of her neck.

"Oh, Mark. Yes. Don't stop." Lexi pants as she bends her head, allowing me more access to her neck, which I hungrily suck, kiss, and nip at with my teeth.

"I don't plan on stopping, Baby." I growl and I trail my hand down her body, grabbing the hem of her shirt and pulling it over her head. She does the same to me, and I toss both pieces of clothing aside, not caring where they land.

Leaning back on my knees, I then arch her back enough where I can unhook her bra with one hand while using the other to pluck the lacy thing from her body, again tossing it behind me to land somewhere in the room.

I lean over her again, taking one peaked nipple into my mouth, and Lexi lets out a pleasure filled moan that shoots right between my legs, making me harden painfully against the zipper of my jeans.

I groan against her skin while trying to adjust my hips to lessen the pressure, but it doesn't help. Her sounds, her smell, her taste drives me insane.

"You are so beautiful, Lex." I whisper against her skin, then turn my attention to her other breast as her fingers thread through my hair and we both moan at each other's touch.

"I want you, Mark. Please."

I pull my mouth away from her, but I don't miss the bruises that I'm leaving behind, and I can't help the one sided smirk at knowing I'm leaving my mark on her. Tearing my gaze from her body, I look into her ocean blue eyes, so full of want and love for me that it makes my heart beat erratically in my chest. But then I remember that scare we had, and it makes me pause for a split second, and I can't help but ask the question that lingers on my tongue.

"Do you want me to wear a condom?"

She looks at me like I grew a third eyeball. "Why would you ask that?"

"It's just with the scare we had, I just wanted to make sure—" she cuts me off.

"No Mark. I want all of you. I'm still on the pill. It's just with everything that was going on; I thought I missed one, and the stress of the case messed my cycle up for a few days. That's all." Lexi says as she reaches for my jeans, flicks the button open, and I practically sigh in relief as the pressure lessens. "Besides, I kinda like the idea of the unknown. Who's stronger, the pill or you?"

I chuckle darkly as I slide my jeans and briefs down my legs, letting my rock-hard erection stand proudly between us.

"I am always up for a challenge, Baby." I say as I grab for her own jeans and yank them down over her hips before I settle between her legs, my crown teasing at her core. "How do you want it?" I ask our usual question, but it's just to know how she wants to enjoy this time between us, not because I need to chase her inner demons away.

"Soft and slow. Make it last, Baby." Lexi whispers as she hooks her right leg over my hip, edging me into her sweet body just an inch.

I groan at the sensation of her around me, and I shake with the need to sink into her in one thrust, but I hold back because that's what my girl wants.

"You got it, Baby Girl." I say as I lean in to kiss her, moving my hips enough that I sink deeper, but then pull back to the tip before I roll them again, taking more on the next thrust.

I keep that slow, gentle tempo going, pulling back almost all the way, before filling her with just a bit more than last time. I know I get to the best spot for her when her nails rake down my back, so I make sure to spend a few extra minutes caressing that spot for her before I finally sink to the hilt on my final thrust.

"Oh, you feel so damn good, Baby." I growl against her neck. "Who do you belong to?"

Lexi wraps her legs around my back, driving me even deeper as she hooks her arms around my neck, keeping my body flush with hers.

"I belong to us. To myself, just as much as I do to you. We belong to each other."

"Damn right, and don't you ever forget it." I say as my thrusts become wilder, building up her orgasm until she's trembling with her release.

"Mark!" Lexi screams as she comes around me, and I follow right behind her, my feral growl echoing off the walls as her pants and moans of pleasure fill my ears.

When her sweet body milks the last of my release out of me, I roll onto my back, pulling her with me so her head rests on my chest. Both of us are panting in rhythm, and I can't stop the elated grin curving my lips when she heaves a contented and sated sigh as she trails lazy, tender kisses along my chest.

"So?" Lexi drawls as she lifts her head to rest her chin against my chest so she can look up at me.

"What?" I ask and I run my fingers through her hair.

"Who do you think won?" She asks, giving me a smirk.

I laugh as I gently grab her by her upper arms so she's straddling me, just a breath away from where we both want me to be.

"I don't know. I think we need to try a different angle. You know, gotta test *everything*." I croon.

"Oh, you're right. We have to be *very* thorough in our scientific testing." Lexi says as she positions herself over me and lowers herself onto my already hardened length even slower than I took her, and it takes everything in me not to explode at the feeling of her walls fluttering around me.

"Oh shit, Lex." I grunt as she begins to rock her hips in all the directions that makes the both of us wild with want, and I tilt my head back against the pillow in an effort to last longer for her, but she's having none of that.

"Don't you dare hold back on me. I want everything from you," Lexi growls. Actually freaking growls in my ear before she crushes her lips to mine, and my body reacts to her provocation.

Hips pivoting up as she rocks and rolls and rides me until we are both coming apart at the seams for the second time tonight, and I'm groaning her name.

This time when we finally come down from our high, we lie in bed, just holding one another for a while, willing our souls back into our bodies.

Once I finally feel grounded in my body, I kiss the top of Lexi's head before I roll out of bed to get a washcloth from the bathroom so I can clean the mess I made of her.

As I'm cleaning Lexi off, I say, "Well, let's hope the pill is the stronger one between the two of us." I say with a smirk. "Cause that's the only thing I'll allow to be stronger than me."

She rolls her eyes, and after I finish wiping her down; I toss the dirty washcloth into the hamper that rests in the corner of the room. Leaning over her, I gently kiss her before I lie down in bed, pulling her against my chest, this time for the night.

Lexi kisses my chest once more before she whispers, "Cocky asshole, but I love you anyway," and closes her eyes, letting sleep take her.

"Damn right, Baby." I say as I pull the sheets up over our naked and exhausted bodies. "I love you, too." I add as I tighten my arms around her bare back and let sleep take me as well.

Chapter Forty-Nine

Taylor

Two and a half weeks later, Wayne insists Mark, Bryan and I follow up with the agency doctors so that we can be one hundred percent cleared for cases if he were to send another one our way. Since the three of us had to be seen, Mark and Lexi picked us up, and we all went together.

After I finish with my appointment, I take a seat in the waiting room and wait for Bryan and Mark to finish with their appointments, but I don't see Lexi in the room. I wonder if she's with Mark, but then I notice her come out of a room herself. Her gaze catches mine, and she gives me an embarrassed smile as she turns to thank the doctor before heading over to me.

"Are you okay?" I ask when she takes the seat next to me.

"Yeah. I just got some new ammunition I can use against Mark." Lexi grins as she pockets the piece of paper before I can see what's on it.

"What are you talking about?" I ask skeptically. "Do I want to know?"

"I asked Mark if he thought he was stronger than something, and I can give him his answer." She says with a smirk.

"I'm confused." I sigh, but before I can ask more, the guys come out with bright smiles on their faces.

"Got the all clear, ladies!" Mark says.

"Good to hear," Lexi replies as she gets up and walks over to Mark to give him a quick hug as he checks out with the nurse at the front counter.

I walk over to Bryan, who's waiting in line behind Mark. "Everything good with you, too, huh?" I ask.

"Yup. 'Course, I'll have a scar, but with time, it will fade a bit," Bryan says like I care about that, and I roll my eyes at him.

"I just want you to be medically sound." I tell him, sounding like my mother for a moment. "Sorry, my medical side was showing." I add with a chuckle.

"Hey, that medical side of yours saved my life."

"I bet you could do just as well if you learned a thing or two." I smile as the check-out nurse calls for Bryan.

After they are checked out, we gather into Mark's SUV so he can take us back to my house, and when we stop at a red light before entering the highway ramp, Lexi hands Mark that elusive paper from the doctor's office. He takes one look at it and bursts out laughing.

"Oh, my God," He says shaking his head. "I'm never gonna live that down, am I?"

"Nope. Bested by something that barely weighs only a few ounces." Lexi smiles as she takes the paper back and shoves it into her pocket.

"Do we want to know what you two are talking about?" Bryan asks the same question I'm thinking.

"Nope. That's between me and my girl."

When we finally make it home, since Mark and Lexi are already here, we decide to make it a day of just hanging out. So we change into our bathing suits and swim for a while. Mom and Cody join in on the fun while Dad cleans the grill so he can use it to fix steaks later for dinner.

While Mom is working on her tan, Mark, Lexi, Cody, Bryan, and I decide to toss the beach ball around, and just when I'm about to serve it to Cody, Bryan's phone starts ringing from the small side table.

"I'll get it for you, Bryan," Mom says as she picks up the phone and Bryan swims over to the side of the pool.

Mom answers it, putting it on speaker so he doesn't get the device wet. "Hello?"

"Bryan, hi." Wayne's voice filters through the phone, and the three of us swim over to see what's going on.

"Hi, Wayne. What's up?" Bryan asks as he glances over at us.

"Are you home and with Taylor?" Wayne asks.

"Yes. Mark and Lexi are here too." Bryan answers.

"Good. Good." Wayne hums. "I have something coming by Taylor's house in about twenty minutes. Think of it as the agency's reward for a job well done."

"Okay." Bryan draws out the word to where it sounds like a question, and we all look at each other, wondering what Wayne means.

"Hope you enjoy!" Wayne exclaims, and the call disconnects.

"Well, let's get out and dry off. Who knows what he's sent us." Lexi says as she lifts herself out of the water.

We follow her lead, and after we dry off and get dressed; we sit in the living room and wait for the 'surprise' the agency is sending us.

Twenty-eight minutes pass, and just as I'm about to pick up my phone and tell Wayne his *gift* is late, we all hear the roar of what I swear to be engines. Mark's eyes light up as one revs, and he's jumping to his feet and racing towards the door.

"No freaking way!" Mark shouts like Cody does on Christmas morning.

The three of us follow him out and I catch the spark of excitement that Bryan's trying to hold back in his green eyes, but once he walks through the door and his feet hit the grass, his face pulls into a bright smile at what is waiting on the street for us.

Mark is already running towards the black Challenger that he drove down in Florida, kneeling beside it once he gets to the passenger door and petting the thing like it's a long-lost pet that finally came back home.

I eye the red Lancer that was Lexi's and the blue Mustang that was mine and finally my eyes land on the yellow Camaro that was Bryan's.

"What is going on?" Bryan asks as he walks toward the vehicles with shock and confusion coloring his features.

Then the driver's doors open on all the vehicles, and we see who brought them to us. From the Camaro, Josh emerges, and from my Mustang, is Ian, then Nick from the Lancer, and finally James from the Challenger.

"What are you all doing here?" I ask as I notice the passenger doors open and the girls step out. The whole gang is here.

Josh takes Morgan's hand and walks across the yard to stand in front of us. "Your boss, uh, Wayne? He called me and asked if I wanted to help in restoring the Camaro, and I told him I would, but only if you all got to keep your cars and we could deliver them in person."

"Oh my, God. You negotiated with Wayne?" Bryan asks, chuckling.

"Yup. And he agreed with me." Josh said proudly.

"I tell you one thing." Ian begins as he and Anna walk up next to Josh. "The agency garages are something of a grease monkey's dream. All the parts you can imagine right at the tips of your fingers."

"I'm sure." I say with a smile.

"Taylor, what's going on?" Mom asks as she gathers in the doorway behind me and Bryan.

"Oh, Mom! These are the racers we met down in Florida." I tell her and introduce everyone to my parents and to my little brother.

"It's nice to meet you all." Dad says.

"Yo! You all got a track to race these bad boys on?!" James asks from further down the yard.

Mark and Bryan look at each other, and the shit-eating grins that light up their faces tell me we are in for a trip.

Chapter Fifty

Bryan

As soon as James makes that request, Mark and I instantly know where we are taking everyone.

The Cabin.

"Yeah, man. We have a place. Hope you don't mind getting dirty." I grin. "You want to tag along, Baby?" I ask, turning towards Taylor.

"Well, if you're going, so am I." She sighs, but I see the excitement lighting her blue eyes.

"Can I come?" Cody asks, his brown eyes wide and pleading.

"You have to ask your mom, little man." I say, and I give Kathy my own pleading glance. Cody is going to love flying over the humps and bumps of the track that Mark and I made a few years back.

"Don't break anything on my son, Bryan." Kathy rolls her eyes, knowing it's a losing battle to say no to two guys.

"Yes!" Cody exclaims! "I'm riding with Bryan!"

"Really, you don't want to ride with me?" Taylor asks, feigning a pain in her chest at her brother's rejection of riding with her.

"I'll ride with you on the way back!" Cody shouts as he waits impatiently next to my Camaro.

"I guess you lead the way." Josh says as he hands me the keys, and I take them with a smile on my face.

"Yeah. You'll love this place." I say and I turn to Mark. "Stay in the back, man, in case we get separated on the interstate."

"You got it," Mark says as James hands his keys over and hops in the back seat of the Challenger with Christy.

After we all get in our cars, Josh and Morgan are in my back seat with Cody calling shotgun, Taylor is taking Ian and Anna, and Lexi with Nick and Roxie with Mark following in behind everyone, we take off toward the cabin.

Once we are on the interstate, I give the engine a few revs, and Cody laughs like a hyena in the passenger seat.

"This is so cool!" He exclaims. "I want a car like this when I'm older!"

"Oh boy. I'm in so much trouble with your mother." I say, but I can't stop the smile on my face when I look at him.

"She'll be cool with it." Cody shrugs.

"Are you sure we're talking about the same woman?" I say, arching an eyebrow.

"Yup. I'll convince her. Besides, I'll have you and Dad to back me up on getting a cool car."

Josh and Morgan laugh from the backseat, and I just shake my head at him while I pay attention to the road ahead of me. Then Cody starts opening the center console like he's looking to see if there's anything hidden inside. I don't stop him because I know there won't be any guns or ammunition in the car.

When he opens the glove box, Cody gives an excited giggle, and I glance over at him. He pulls out a replica Hot Wheels version of the Camaro, and I can't stop the slight smile that curves my lips.

"Bryan, look at this! It looks like your car!"

"I see it, buddy." I tell him, and I get an idea. "You want to keep it? You know, as a placeholder until you get your own car?"

"You mean it?" He asks, excitement and longing filling his eyes.

"Totally." I smile. "You know, I had the same kind of car when I was even younger than you."

"Was that before you lost your parents?" Cody asks, his tone growing serious for the first time during this whole ride.

"Yeah," I say, my voice becoming tight with emotion I didn't realize his words would bring up. "I remember mine had a special message hidden inside from my dad. But I think I left it in Dad's car that day, and I never got it back."

Cody is quiet for a minute, as if he's thinking about something. "Then you keep this one." He says as he places the toy car in a little divot on the dash. "That way, you can always remember them." He adds, his smile back in place and joy coloring his eyes.

"You got it, bud." I say as I ruffle his hair, and he shrieks with laughter. "Thank you."

"If it makes you feel better, you can be my big brother." Cody says. "Since you didn't get the chance to have any siblings."

"Aw, that's so cute." Morgan says sweetly.

"Thanks, bud. I appreciate that." I say as I make the turn toward the off ramp and three minutes later we all arrive at the cabin.

The guys all shout and cheer at the dirt track and when I tell them that Mark and I had connections at the young age we did, they think we are pulling their legs, but Mark agrees and they look on in wonder to the track, eager looks on their faces to run it.

I take Cody through it first, at a bit of a slower pace, so I don't, as his mother put it, *break her son*, but he still has a blast at losing his stomach over the various humps in the track that make the car fly off the ground a few inches. But once I give him his fill of racing, it's on to the bigger, faster laps.

We all take turns on the course, and since this is our home turf, the guys want me and Mark to take the first lap, which I, of course, smoke him on.

"Oh, you just got lucky, is all." Mark grumbles as he pulls off to the side.

"No man. Again, I keep telling you, that thing is a heavy monster." I laugh.

"No, let a real racer try to win in it." Nick says as he and Josh take to the track in my car and Mark's, which again, my car wins.

"Damn it!" Mark sighs as Cody laughs beside Taylor.

"Mark's a sore loser!" Cody says, pointing to Mark.

"First, I'm just the sidekick, and now I'm a sore loser? Cody, you wound me."

"Well, stop being the things he accuses you of." Taylor smirks and high-fives her brother.

We spend a few more hours taking turns running the track, and when the sun is about to set, we all leave the dirt track happier and closer than we were before.

Taylor

When we leave the track, my face hurts from smiling and my throat is scratchy from laughing as much as I did. Something went down between Bryan and Cody; I just don't know what it was. But from the way both guys that I love so much were interacting with one another, made my heart swell with happiness.

I recall what Bryan told Sophie before we left—that he wouldn't be able to do the brother thing, but he's wrong. He's Cody's big brother, whether he realizes it or not.

When Ian, Anna and I get in my Mustang and after I make sure Cody is buckled up, I'm about to ask him what he did with Bryan on the way to the track, but my words die in my throat when he opens my glove box but his face falls when he pulls out a piece of folded paper.

"You don't have a Hot Wheels in your car like Bryan did with his," Cody says as he puts the paper back in the glove box.

"Bryan had what?" I ask as I shift into gear so I can be ready to drive behind Bryan when he's ready.

"He had a Hot Wheels that was the same as his car. And he told me he had one when he was little, but he lost it when his parents died, so I told him to keep it so he can remember them."

I smile at what my brother tells me, but then my mind goes back to the paper in my glove box, and something tells me to look at it. "Hey, Cody. Give me that white thing, will you?"

He reaches in and pulls out the folded piece of paper, and when I open it, I see a series of numbers on it and my stomach sinks.

"What is it?" Cody asks.

"Um." I say, at a loss for words for a moment. I stare at the code, and I know what I need to do. "It's just something I need to share with Bryan later."

"Everything okay, Taylor?" Ian asks from the backseat.

"Oh, yeah." I say, pocketing the paper to show Bryan later. "It's just something personal. No one is threatening us." I add when I see his eyebrow arch in concern.

"Okay," Ian says, although he's not fully convinced nothing is wrong. "But you let me know if you need any help."

"Ian, I'm good." I assure him.

Ten minutes later, I pull my Mustang into the driveway in behind my Focus and kill the engine as Bryan pulls his Camaro beside me. I glance out my window, and he's still all smiles and joy, and I just hope that whatever this note says will keep that emotion alive on his face, but I will not keep this from him. No matter what this paper says, we will face it together.

Later that night, after everyone has gone home, and we had a nice dinner of steaks, thanks to Dad and Bryan cooking them on the grill while Mom and I fix some side dishes, I am waiting on my bed for Bryan to finish up his shower.

When he comes out in only black boxers and towel drying his hair, I have to force myself not to look at his damp, muscular body. He must notice that I'm keeping my eyes off him, because he sits down next to me on the bed, taking my hand in his.

"Everything okay, Annie?"

"Yeah," I say as I turn to him. "But I need to show you something."

He stills, and the pulse of fear flashes in his eyes before he shakes the emotion away. "Okay. What is it?"

I pull the paper out from under my pillow, unfold it, and show it to him. This time shock, fear, and confusion fills his green eyes, and he looks at me for answers I don't have for him yet.

"When did you find this?" He asks slowly.

"Cody found it in the glove box this afternoon when we were coming back. He thought there was a car like mine in there, but he found this instead."

"You didn't crack the code?" He asks, noticing it's only the long series of numbers and no words yet.

"No." I shake my head, and I wrap my hand around his forearm. "I wanted you to help me crack it."

Bryan looks from me, then back to the paper, and he nods. "Okay. Let's crack it together.

Bryan

Another code, apparently from my parents.

My stomach is in knots with the unknown message sitting on Taylor's desk. I take a seat in her desk chair and pull her onto my lap so we can work on the code together. I need her body weight on me to keep me grounded. To keep me from pacing while I wait for her to crack the code.

I look at the series of numbers and my head spins from the amount of them. I wonder how the hell Taylor can work with something like this.

93 9268 86 6338 968 43 968 9268

86 6338 87 8398 8447 #

801-555-6987

"What do you think it means?" I ask.

"I don't know, but we'll figure it out. I promise," Taylor says.

It takes all of forty-five minutes before we crack the code, and my heart beats painfully in my chest.

We want to meet you if you want to meet us.

Text this # 801-555-6987

"How are you feeling, Bryan?" Taylor asks as she turns in my lap where she can look at me.

I just stare past her, eyes fixed on the handwritten note, trying to figure out what it is I am feeling.

"I don't know." I whisper.

Taylor looks back to the paper, and her index finger trails over the phone number, pausing over the area code.

"This is a Utah area code." She says slowly. "They are somewhere near here."

As her words click in my mind, a long forgotten memory bubbles to the surface.

I'm five years old, and Dad and I are just coming home from running errands he needed to do, and he bought me a Hot Wheels Camaro for being a good boy on our drive around town.

"Hey, Sport," Dad says later that night as he's tucking me in bed.

"Hi, Dad."

"You know, I forgot to tell you something special about this car." He pulls out the Camaro from his pocket and shows it to me. "This has a special message hidden that only you and I know about."

He pulls the body from the chassis, and when he flips the body over, he shows me the inside and reads what it says to me.

"Love you, always. Dad."

"I love it, Dad. Thank you!" I tell him as I wrap my little arms around his neck.

"Love you, Sport."

I remember the next morning; I took my Camaro with me when Mom and Dad had to run more errands, but that night when we got home; I forgot I left it in the backseat and I was about to tell Mom about it, but she picked me up as Dad ran out the front door, shouting at someone and the last thing I remember was being locked in my closet and Mom saying that everything will be alright.

As the memory fades, my whole body goes still. The area code of that strange number clicking into place and...

"Get up." I say gently to Taylor, but my voice has enough force behind it to let her know not to ask questions right now.

I jump up from the chair, and I just barely grab a pair of shorts before I'm racing down the stairs, grabbing my keys from the hook and rushing out the door.

"Bryan! What's wrong?!" Taylor calls after me, but I don't answer her.

I press the button to unlock my Camaro, and as I'm swinging open the passenger door, I am silently praying for my thoughts to be true but yet also to be a lie. I grab the Hot Wheels from the dash where Cody left it and my hands tremble as I hold it in my palm.

Stepping back from my car until I feel the grass under my bare feet, I turn the toy over in my hands until I find the little latch to pop the body off from the chassis.

When I have the two pieces in my hands, I tilt my head back and look to the sky for a moment. The twinkling stars staring back down at me as if urging me to turn the body of the car over and see if it hides something special written inside.

I notice movement out of the corner of my eye, and Taylor is standing beside me, silently waiting for me to tell her what's going on.

I look back down at the toy in my hand and, without taking my eyes off it, I say, "There should be something on the inside of this toy that only my father and I would know about. I don't think he even told Mom about what's in here."

Taylor stands beside me and holds the same hand that's still clutching the body of the toy car. "Then let's find out together."

I take a breath and turn over the die-cast Camaro in my hand. My knees give out, and I can't stop the flood of tears that pours from my eyes, and for an instant I feel like I'm five years old again, reliving that memory; like I just time traveled in the blink of an eye.

Love you always. Dad.

Chapter Fifty-One

Taylor

I have never seen Bryan cry like this. Tear up, yes. But this is like his inner child is coming back out, and they both are experiencing this possibility of being reunited with their long-lost parents.

"They're not just in the state of Utah," Bryan says through broken sobs. "They are *here*. In this town."

I stare dumbly at him for a moment, and then I look down at the toy in his hand.

"Wait. That's *your* toy." I say, putting the pieces together.

He nods. "Yeah. I lost this when I was five. The same night they...died." He pauses on the word.

I kneel beside him and run my hand up the broad expanse of his back, trying to soothe him. "Bryan?" I ask, and he turns to face me. Running my thumbs over his cheeks in the same way he's done for me so many times, I ask, "Do you want to text that number?"

He thinks for a minute, looking back at the toy in his palm before his eyes find mine again.

"Yes."

"Then let's go." I say as I help him to his feet and back into the house.

When we walk into the living room, Mom and Dad are standing next to the couch, waiting to make sure we are okay.

"We're good." I say.

"What was that all about?" Mom asks.

"I think our family is about to get bigger." I tell them, and I instantly regret the way it came out.

"Smooth, Babe." Bryan chuckles, his voice still wobbly from crying.

"Shut up." I say and playfully smack him on the back.

"What do you mean, Taylor?" Dad asks.

I quickly tell them about the code in my car and the Hot Wheels toy from Bryan's, and they both pull him in for a quick hug.

"I'm happy for you, Bryan. I know your parents would be proud of the man you've become." Mom says.

"Thank you, Kathy," Bryan says, his voice a little stronger now.

"Come on. Let's go and send that text." I coax, and Bryan leads me up to our room.

As we get into bed, I grab my phone and copy the number that was on the paper into a new message while Bryan pulls me against his chest and looks over my shoulder to watch what I type and what may come back as a response.

"You ready for this?" I ask.

"Yes, and no," Bryan answers.

"Bryan, they are going to love you. I know it." I say as I take his hand in mine, bringing it to my lips to kiss his knuckles. "And if they don't, then they will have me to answer to. Plus, you know Mark is going to rip them a new one."

Bryan laughs, "I know he would. Alright, let's do this."

I type out a quick message, and the reply is almost instant.

Me: Hi. We figured out your code and Bryan does want to meet you.

Unknown: We knew you were smart Taylor. And we are so happy that my baby- well not so much a baby anymore- wants to meet us.

I hear Bryan's sharp intake of breath as he reads the words, and I lean back into him, allowing my body weight to ground him.

Me: When do you want to meet and where?

Unknown : How about on Friday? We still have a few things to take care of from the area we just moved from. But we will be free then. How does 2:00 sound? I think there's a little walking path with pavilions in Bryant's Park. Is that close to you all?

"That's fine." Bryan whispers, voice cracking from tears again.

Me: Yes! That's great! We will be there. He's so excited to meet you.

Unknown: We are too. See you two Friday.

Me: Ok. see ya.

Unknown: Also, bring your grandparents, Sport. I know Mom and Dad would love to see us too.

When Bryan reads that message, he breaks down in sobs again, and I turn in his arms to just hold him. He buries his face into my neck, and I just let him release any and all emotions that have been locked away for fifteen years.

"I'm sorry. I just never thought I'd read that nickname again."

"Hey, don't ever apologize for you having emotions." I tell him as I again wipe the tears away.

"I don't know if I can sleep for two more nights." Bryan says as he pulls back to look at me, and I run my fingers through his hair.

"It will fly by before you know it." I tell him. "Let's tell your grand-parents tomorrow, and then it will be one more night; then you will be meeting them the next day."

"And we gotta tell Mark. I want them to meet him and Lexi, too." Bryan beams.

"Yeah. I agree." I say as I lean in and give him a sound kiss on the lips before pulling back and giving him a bright smile. "I am so happy for you, Baby. I know this is something you've been wanting for a while, and all your prayers are paying off."

Bryan moves down in bed where he's lying on his back before he pulls my upper body partially across his chest. "I have been talking to them up in Heaven for all these years, and they've been here on this earth the whole time." He shakes his head in disbelief. "I wonder where they've been this whole time?"

"Well, we will have to ask them when we meet them on Friday. Deal?" I ask.

"Totally."

I snuggle my face into his neck and just as I'm about to ask how he would feel if he had a sibling; I notice he's fallen asleep already. I guess from all the crying he's done, it's exhausted him more than I thought.

Tucking myself back into his side, I allow sleep to take me as well, bringing us one day closer to meeting Bryan's mystery parents.

Chapter Fifty-Two

Bryan

Taylor's alarm wakes me the next morning, and she stirs on my chest, reaching over to hit the snooze button on her phone. As the feel of her body brings me more and more into consciousness, last night comes flooding back into my mind.

My parents are alive, and I'm meeting them tomorrow.

My heart feels lighter now without the weight of their loss plaguing me every day. The void that was in my chest is gradually filling up, and a smile tugs at my lips with the thought.

Taylor runs her hand across my bare chest and toys with the few pieces of hair that trail down my sternum. "Morning, Baby." She yawns and then kisses my chest.

"Good morning." I say as I kiss the top of her head.

"So, who do you want to tell first?" She asks, already knowing where my mind is.

"If I don't tell Mark first, he'll kick my ass." I chuckle. "Hell, he still might kick my ass for not calling him last night."

"Nah. I won't let that happen."

We sit up in bed, and I lean over to grab my phone, opening my contact list and tapping on Mark's name. When the phone starts ringing, I put it on speaker so Taylor can hear too as I lean my back against the headboard.

He answers on the third ring. "Hello? Bryan? What time is it?" He groans as he apparently looks at a clock. "Dude, it's six in the morning on a Thursday; this better be good."

"Oh, it is, man. Believe me." I say with a smile in my voice.

"Oh my God, did you and Taylor finally have sex and you're telling me all the juicy deets?" Mark says, now fully awake. "Do you need tips on how to make it better for next time?"

"What? No," I say. "Plus, I don't need *tips* from you." I roll my eyes. "I can take care of my girl just fine in that department, thank you, once I get to that point with her. But no, man. It's about my parents."

"What do you mean? I thought we closed their case? Did we miss something?" Mark asks question after question.

"They are alive, man." I say, letting the truth linger in the air.

"What do you mean?" Mark asks again, this time slower.

"Just what I said. They are alive."

"How do you know this is real and not someone playing a trick on you?" Mark asks, his tone growing firm and challenging.

"Because there were things that were said and something physical that only my parents would have known about." I say, and I go on to tell him about the toy car and the message that was found in Taylor's Mustang.

"So they knew that you would understand the meaning of the car and that Taylor would be the one that could break the code. Damn, your parents are scary smart."

"Yeah, they are."

"And you're meeting them tomorrow?" Mark asks.

"Yeah, and I wanted to know if you wanted to come along."

"Hell yes, I'm coming along!" Mark exclaims. "I'm not going to miss meeting my brother's long-lost family."

We hear Lexi say something in the background about Mark being overly dramatic, but when he tells her what's going on, she's instantly hopping on the line.

"Oh my God, Bryan, that's amazing!" Lexi says. "I'm so happy for you."

"Thanks," I say. "You better be there, too."

"Oh, you got it! I can't wait."

After we hang up, Taylor kisses me again, and I pull her on top of me, where she's straddling my hips. And right now, I don't care if Taylor's parents catch us; I am too far gone with happiness that I want to share everything I'm feeling with my girl as long as she'll let me.

Threading my fingers through her long chestnut brown hair, I gather a fist full of it in my palm so I can hold her head where I want, and she obliges with no complaints.

I deepen the kiss, teasing her lips with my tongue; a silent request for her to open up for me, and she does. I almost groan as her taste explodes in my mouth, and I keep up the punishing tempo of my lips claiming hers.

She rocks her hips against mine, and this time, I do groan at the friction she creates; making me hard only for her.

I break the kiss before I really throw caution to the wind and take her right now, but the smirk on her lips tells me she's about to push my buttons and my restraint.

"So you don't need any *tips*, huh?" She teases.

I knew it.

"Well, I might need a few." I begin as I buck my hips so I can get the angle I need to flip us around where she is on her back and I'm nestled between her legs, arms braced on either side of her head. "From you. You need to tell me what you like and what you don't."

I lean down, crushing my lips to hers again, tongues dueling, teeth dragging across lips, and ragged breaths filling the intimate space between us. Then I pull back, and just as she starts to moan at the loss of my touch, I trail kisses, nips, and even quick little flicks of my tongue across her neck, and she bends to allow me more access to her soft skin.

My teasing little touches are just enough to get her skin flushed, but not where there'll be any lingering proof that I've been here.

My eyes drift lower down her beautiful body, and I see her nipples are practically poking through the fabric of my shirt she wore last night, just begging me to turn my attention to them next. I slowly lift the fabric, exposing her perfect breasts, and Taylor squirms under my stare.

"Any tips yet, Annie?" I ask as I take her right nipple in my mouth, teasing it with my tongue, and her quiet moan sends shockwaves right between my legs to the point of pain.

I rock my hips into hers, and I want to lie to myself and say it's on instinct, but I really want her to feel just how much I want to take this to the next level. How much I want to love her thoroughly and have her screaming my name each time I bottom out inside her.

"Annie." I ask in a sing-song voice as I turn my head to nip and suck at her other breast, this time hard enough to leave a bruise on her delicate skin.

"Don't stop." Taylor whispers breathlessly.

"Don't stop what?" I tease. "This?" I bite at her flesh again, and her hands shoot into my hair, pinning my lips against her body, but I push back enough that I can still speak around her skin. "Or this?" I roll my hips against hers again, and I wish she was bare for me like she was down in Florida, but I'll take what I can get here.

"Any of it! I'm so close." She cries softly, like she knows deep down she needs to be quiet so her parents won't hear, and I like the challenge.

"Alright, I won't stop until you come for me, but you need to stay quiet. We don't need your mother barging in here to kill me just yet." I say with a smirk.

I get back to working her body up to that breaking point. Nipping, kissing, caressing, and biting her breast, stomach, and neck until she's vibrating with need under me, and with one final roll of my boxer-clad hard-on against her clit, she's shattering for me and I have to crush my lips to hers to keep her from screaming out.

This is the first and only time that will happen.

"You are so gorgeous and sound so sexy when you come for me, Taylor." I whisper against her ear.

"I want you. All of you, Bryan." She says, voice barely audible.

"I know, Baby. Just give me a bit more time. I want things to be perfect for your first time." I tell her as I force myself to pull away from her body, but when I look down, I have to immediately tilt my head back, staring at the ceiling to keep my desire locked firmly away for now.

"What?" Taylor asks, and I feel the bed move under me as she sits up to look down at the marks I left in my wake on her breasts and stomach. "Whelp, I won't be wearing a bikini anytime soon." She tries to sound annoyed but fails.

"You love it." I smirk as I coax myself off the bed so I can go into the bathroom and get a quick shower.

Thirty minutes later, after we both finish our showers and eat a quick breakfast with Tom and Kathy—who don't give me the knowing stink eye or outright try to kill me for making their daughter orgasm practically under their nose—Taylor and I head over to my grandparents' house to drop the news on them.

I lead Taylor up the steps and knock twice before testing the doorknob and finding it unlocked; then we step inside.

"Oh, Bryan! Taylor! Good morning, you two." Granny greets us near the door. "Kathy called John and told him you two were coming over with some news." Granny looks between us; her brown eyes sparkle for a moment before they harden into a look that over the years has warned me I'm in for a scolding of my life. "What's going on, you two?"

Grandpa then walks in from the kitchen with two cups of coffee, and he hands one to Granny before he takes a seat, giving me and Taylor a once over.

"Well, Gail. If I'd have to guess, I would say our grandson here is going to tell us to expect that great-grandbaby you've always wanted."

"Oh my! Is that true, Bryan?" Granny asks, but then, in the same breath, she smacks me on the back of the head. "Your grandfather and I taught you to wear a condom, boy! You two aren't even married yet to be thinking about having babies!"

"What, Granny? No!" I say, but she smacks me again for good measure, and Taylor is no help in the situation. "No, Taylor is not pregnant. Hell, we haven't even gotten that far." I cringe as the words slip out, but I quickly add. "No, this right now is even bigger than that."

"How can anything be bigger than you becoming a father, Bryan?" Grandpa asks.

I sigh and I just blurt it out. "Because *my* father is alive. So is my mother."

They both go still as a statue, and I swear I think they stop breathing for a minute.

"How do you know for sure?" Granny asks softly.

"Because we found some things yesterday that only Bryan and his dad would know, and I found another code hidden in my car. Plus, we texted them last night." Taylor offers.

"But it could still be a setup, Bryan," Grandpa says gruffly.

"I know. But you remember the nickname Dad called me?" I ask.

"Oh, God," Grandpa whispers. "Sport. Oh, I haven't heard that in so long."

"Yeah." I chuckle wetly as tears prick the corners of my eyes. "Neither have I. But he called me that last night through text."

"When are you meeting them?" Granny asks tearfully.

"Tomorrow afternoon, at two." I say. "In their text, they said they had to finalize some things from the previous state they were in."

"We will absolutely be there for you if you want us to be, Bryan," Grandpa says.

"What do you mean, *if I want you?* Yes, you're coming along. He also wants to see his parents." I say. It's still weird to actually think of them as Mom and Dad. It's not natural to want to call them that. I've always talked about them in the past tense, so to me, it's weird still to talk about them in the present. "Plus, I want you both there. *You've* been my parents for practically my whole life, and I want to share in this experience with you, too."

"I will make sure we are both ready tomorrow. You can pick us up in that fancy new car of yours, Bryan." Granny wiggles her eyebrows as she glances out the window to look at the Camaro in Taylor's driveway.

Chuckling, I nod my head. "Deal."

After we say our goodbyes, I walk Taylor back over to her house and wait for tomorrow to arrive.

Chapter Fifty-Three

Bryan

Today is the day.

I meet my parents for the first time in fifteen years.

I've just loaded Granny and Grandpa into the backseat of the Camaro, and Granny is all smiles and full of laughter sitting there, but I also see a bit of glee in my Grandfather's eyes too.

Mark and Lexi arrived at Taylor's place about ten minutes ago, and Mark is urging me to hurry up, but I know he's doing it as a distraction mechanism. Trying to get me pissed at him, so I'm not freaking the hell out like I want to.

Taylor's parents decided to stay home and let this be a meet-up between what they said was my 'immediate family'. I wanted to tell them they were included in that, but Tom agreed, and insisted that once I met my parents and if I still wanted to include them, they would be invited to dinner.

Once we are finally on the road and heading to Bryant's Park, I'm practically vibrating with nervous energy. Taylor reaches out and gives my bicep a quick, loving squeeze, and her touch calms me a bit.

"I am so happy and excited for you."

"I've never been so nervous about anything in my life. I think I'd rather go on a case and get shot at." I chuckle.

"It will all be just fine. Once you see them, I'm sure you'll feel less nervous."

I nod my head as I pull into the parking lot, and I already see a dark-haired couple gathered at a picnic table with their backs toward us, and I wonder if it's them.

"Well, here goes nothing." I say as I get out and try to help my grand-parents first, but Grandpa shakes his head at me.

"You get your girl out, then get us."

"Yes, sir."

I go over to the passenger side and I help Taylor out of her seat, and Mark comes over to help Gramps and Granny.

"Thanks, Mark." I say as we all meet in front of the Camaro and we stare at the pavilion a few hundred feet away.

"You think that's them?" Mark asks.

I take a deep breath. "I don't know, man. Maybe."

"Come on, let's go meet them," Taylor urges.

"You two go on ahead; we'll catch up. Besides, you should meet them first, Bryan," Granny says.

I nod and I take Taylor's hand in mine and make myself take the first step towards meeting my parents.

As we approach, they must not hear us, because the woman, my mother, says, "They're late. Oh, what if he doesn't want to see us? I mean, we've been lying to him all this time."

"It's okay. Even if he doesn't show up, he knows that we're alive now and how to find us when he's ready."

Their voices sound so familiar to me, and I feel tears want to prick the corner of my eyes, but when I see something move out of the corner of my eye, the tears dry up instantly and utter confusion floods my body.

"Sophie?" I whisper.

The man and the woman who I thought were my parents turns to us, and I lock eyes with Lincoln and Temperance.

"Bryan!" Sophie exclaims as she runs over to me, throwing her arms around my waist.

"Hey," I say. "It hasn't been that long since we've seen one another, only a few weeks, and you act like I've been gone for years."

"I know. I'm sorry. It's just I'm excited."

"Why?" I ask.

"Well, apparently, Mom and Dad's been holding out on me, and I *do* actually have a brother out there. So we're supposed to meet here soon, but he's not here yet."

"Geez, and your brother's here in Utah, too?"

She nods her head. "Yeah."

"Well, it's an extremely small world because Bryan is meeting his parents. News flash, they're not dead like he thought they were." Mark adds helpfully from my left.

"Seriously?" Sophie says, shock filling her tone as she looks back to Linc and Tempe.

My gaze follows hers as I take in the two agents for the first time, and my heart begins to stutter in my chest.

When we were in Florida, their hair was blonde, and now both of them are sporting a dark brown hue, like Sophie's. And while Lincoln's eyes are the same brown they've always been, when I look into Temperance's eyes, I have to take a step back when her gaze locks onto mine, and the world seems like it's going underwater, where I barely hear Taylor's question as I stare into my own green irises.

"Well, we can wait on our families together." Taylor says, and as she takes a step away from me, Grandpa's shout brings me back into focus.

"Oh my God, is that you, Paul?"

Paul? Paul, not Lincoln. But then, as if I have a television screen behind my eyes, I see their names before me.

Paul Lincoln Evans and Cindy Temperance Evans.

Lincoln and Temperance. Paul and Cindy. They are one in the same.

I've been with my parents for *two and a half months* and I didn't even know.

"Yeah, Dad. It's me," Lincoln–Paul says, and I take a step back.

They lied to me. They've *been* lying to me. They lied right to my damn face down in Florida and didn't have the decency to tell me a single thing.

All the nervous energy I felt on the way here morphs into hot anger deep in my chest.

I take another step back, and this time I can feel all eyes on me, but that doesn't stop my backward momentum.

Temperance–Cindy, reaches a hand out to me, trying to stop me. "Bryan, let's talk about this."

As her soft words hit my eardrums, I can't help the scoff that bubbles from my chest, and anger takes over.

"Talk? You want to talk now? You both had over two damn months to talk, and you didn't say a thing! Even after I inadvertently told you that Phil and Daryl were dead and in the ground, you didn't say a fucking thing!"

"We didn't want to jeopardize the case you were on at the time, Bryan." Paul says, his voice gentle but stern, but I don't care.

"The hell with the case! You left me for fifteen years! Were you both just going to live your life like I never existed? Change your appearance, your name, have another kid, and live a different life?" I say, and I just can't stop the word vomit that's coming out of my mouth. I never imagined meeting my parents would go like this.

"I got into the agency at sixteen to try and find you, to try and get answers because no matter where I looked, people *lied* to me. Told me the case went cold. Told me they had no evidence when it was screaming at them in the face, but Phil was too dirty for anyone to fight back! I *begged* Wayne to let me in and I worked my ass off on this, and I was almost killed trying to find you or the true answers!"

I storm a few steps away before I hear Paul's voice behind me.

"We didn't know Phil and Daryl were truly dead until you came down to Florida!"

"Now even that I have a hard time believing, Paul. Unless you changed in the last fifteen years, you would never leave a cold case alone. You would always keep an eye on it in case something changed or caught your eye that you missed before." Grandpa says.

"Seems to me like you gave up on your son," Mark says darkly, arms crossing over his chest.

"No. It's not that." Paul says, shaking his head and pinching the bridge of his nose. It's the same damn thing I do when I'm stressed.

"I'm not listening to this anymore. I'm out." I say.

"I thought you wanted to see us, Bryan. We're still the parents you lost," Cindy cries.

I whip around, staring both of them down. "I would rather my *parents* have been complete strangers off the street than someone who, again, has been lying to my face." I growl and storm out of the pavilion and towards my Camaro.

"Bryan!" Taylor runs after me and stops just before she reaches the hood.

"Annie, please, I need to be alone right now. I don't want my angry words to hurt you when it's not directed toward you. I can't lose you too because of this messed up situation." I say, trying to lighten my voice, but I still hear the hard tone inflected there.

"Okay. Just don't keep me out for too long. I love you."

"Love you, too." I say as I get in my car and drive to the one place that always gives me peace.

Chapter Fifty-Four

Taylor

I watch helplessly as Bryan speeds away in his Camaro, tires squealing on the pavement as he hits the main road, and I have a feeling I know where he's going to end up.

I can't imagine the pain and confusion he's feeling, and that is the only reason I am giving him space right now. Plus, I want to go into this with a clear head and get the answers he needs when I finally go back to him.

"Are you gonna be okay to get yourself and his grandparents' home?" Mark asks, his voice rough, and I know he's just as pissed.

"Yeah. I'll figure something out. Go to him; he needs you to keep him together." I say. "I'll get answers for him and meet you all there either later today or tomorrow."

"I'll smack him around a bit. I'm sure he needs a punching bag right now," Mark says, trying to lighten the mood, then places his hand on my shoulder before giving it a quick squeeze, his voice going hard again. "I'll let you know how he is."

I nod, watching Mark drive away in his Challenger and bury the emotion that threatens to bubble to the surface. I need to face this crazy ass situation head-on and with a cool head.

After I take a calming breath, I turn and walk across the grass, stepping right up to the table, bracing my hands on the weather-worn wood.

"You better start talking." I say, my voice calm but firm. "This is the exact shit that almost cost me my relationship with him when you two planted those bones in the warehouse."

Paul sighs, and he looks me in the eye as he speaks. "We heard rumors that Phil and Daryl were scrambling in a panic because of apparently what you and Bryan were doing with the case, and I knew that eventually, they would go back to that warehouse for their intel meetings. So I drove up, and I planted those skeletons in there, but when four and a half months passed, we figured Bryan didn't want to see us."

Paul looks over at his father with a smirk.

"And you're right, Dad; I could never leave a cold case alone. So, thankfully, when Wayne updated the case file, and we knew you had *just* broken the code, we had high hopes that Bryan would want to meet us again, but Phil and Daryl's deaths were not added to the report."

"We seriously didn't know about that until Bryan told us himself." Cindy adds.

"Why didn't you tell him all this as soon as you knew that?" I ask.

"I was telling the truth when I said I didn't want it to jeopardize the case. Just hearing about the fight that apparently we caused between you two, we didn't want to make things worse or make him lose his focus and you all get seriously hurt in the process." Paul says.

"So when you all finally finished the case and went home, Paul and I talked and we decided to try once more. I knew Bryan's car was being shipped somewhere to get fixed and just as I was going to the agency to tell them to ship it to the Utah garage, your friends from the track offered to fly there and work on it and they would make sure you got the cars back."

"That's when we drove up here, and as soon as the cars were done and ready for delivery, I slipped in and planted the Hot Wheels while Tempe—uh—Cindy planted the code for Taylor." Paul says.

"We never meant for all this to happen the way it did. If we had even an inkling of how he would react, we would have stayed away." Cindy says, tears pooling in her eyes. "I never wanted to hurt my baby boy, but Phil forced us to make an impossible decision."

"What happened that night?" I ask gently.

"Phil came by the house because I left a little calling card on his desk. A photo proving he and Daryl had been in the warehouse selling FBI secrets to the mafia overseas. When he pulled up to the house, I barely made it out the front door before his gun went off. He shot me low in the stomach." Paul chuckles. "Bastard thought he had a kill shot, but his aim was shit. Yes, it took me a while to heal, but I knew that Phil would not stop until I was dead or he would go after my family."

"We made the decision, actually on the way to the ER, that I would falsify the report, saying that Paul died on the table and that I was shot while on scene, but didn't know it at the time and I died there in the woods next to the hospital. That way, when they went looking for the body and they couldn't find it, they would just chalk it up to me being torn apart by scavengers."

"Now I know why everything felt so convenient, but I didn't know where the hell you two would have disappeared to." John says while rubbing the back of his head.

"You two even kept me in the dark. Lied to me too. You told me I had a brother, but he was killed when he was five. What, did you falsify that report too?" Sophie says, her brown eyes welling with tears.

"I'm sorry, Honey. We were only doing what we thought was best for everyone. We wanted to keep both of our kids safe, and not letting the other know you existed was best, at the time." Paul says.

As I stare at her, I can tell that while Sophie is angry that her parents lied to her, she has her mother's temperament and tries to see things from every angle, while Bryan is like a copy of Paul. He lets his anger boil to the surface before cooling down and looking at it from another angle.

"I can't promise anything." I begin. "But I will talk to Bryan either later this evening or tomorrow once he's cooled off. I'll tell him everything you told me and see if he wants to try this again."

I look at the three of them but I turn my attention to Sophie since she's had the most real relationship with him as a stand-in-turned-real-brother.

"Sophie, let me ask you something. Let's say this all hadn't gone to shit, and if Bryan was still here, what would you say to him?"

She sniffs and looks me in the eye. "I would tell him that no matter how badly our parents messed up, he's *really* my brother and I want to get to know him. That is, if he wants to know the 'other kid.'"

"That's fair to say." I give her an understanding smile. "Like I said, I am not going to guarantee anything, but I will try."

She smiles, and I step back as I look over at Paul and Cindy. "Do I still use the same number that I texted you on?"

"Yeah. Just let us know either way." Paul says.

I nod and I look at Granny and Grandpa John. "You two want to stay for a while?"

"You're more than welcome to." Cindy says.

"I think we will." Granny smiles.

"We'll bring them home later." Paul agrees.

I kiss both Gail and John on the cheeks, and I walk away with Lexi on my heels. I'm tired, angry, sad, but also a little hopeful that I can get through Bryan's thick skull and help him see things from my perspective.

Chapter Fifty-Five

Bryan

As I'm driving towards the Cabin I stop at an ammunition shop and buy six boxes of twenty-five-count training ammunition. I know I need to let off some steam, and this is the best way to do that. By letting my gun do the exploding for me.

After I pulled up to the cabin fifteen minutes later, I don't even bother with going inside. Grabbing the bag of ammunition, I head around back where Mark and I built a dirt berm near the line of trees a few hundred feet away from the cabin.

Setting the ammunition down on a nearby table I walk over to a small shed that I built and take out several white 8-inch round metal targets then get to work on setting them up around the area in front of the berm in an offset pattern that will force me to move as I aim at the target.

Once I have the targets in place, I walk back to the shed and grab a can of red spray paint, giving it a few rough shakes as I make my way over to the targets. And instead of painting the whole thing like I normally do, I paint a simple tight circle where I want my bullet to go.

I need a focused point to shoot at, not just the whole 8-inch target to hit.

Unloading the boxes of ammo from the bag, I fill as many magazines as we have so I can keep swapping them out as I go. Because once I start, I don't want to stop until every last bullet is gone.

As I load my first of fifteen magazines into my gun, I step up to the 10-yard line we had marked in the dirt and brace my feet into a comfortable shooting position while gripping my gun in a two-handed hold before I raise my arms so the first target is in my sights. Then, I take one centering breath before I let this raging inferno of anger, hurt, and confusion take over my trigger finger.

Bullets fly, as do the chaotic thoughts in my head.

My parents are alive, but yet at the same time, they're still dead.

They lied to me. All this damn time, they've been lying to me, and I didn't know it.

My gun clicks. I grab another magazine, load it, rack the slider back, and get back to obliterating the same spots on the targets. Back and forth. Back and forth between the six I have set up.

They almost ripped apart my relationship with Taylor. Twice.

Once when I was shot, then when they planted those damn skeletons, and I forced her to go to Florida without me.

The gun clicks, and I load another magazine.

They had another kid. They forgot about me and had another damn kid. They moved on with their life and left me behind in their fucked up dust.

My mind goes blank as I unload the rest of the bullets. Several of the casings fly back and hit my arms and shirt-clad chest, but I don't care about the singe of the hot copper; I'm too numb to the pain in my heart.

When my gun clicks again, I reach for another magazine, but I pause when I notice a hand offering it to me. I look up to find Mark leaning against the table, one hand braced on the smooth surface while his other hand is still offering me the magazine. When I go to reach for it, he snatches it back with a smirk, and for a heartbeat, I want to punch him for it.

"What are you doing here, Mark?" I snap.

"Making sure you're not destroying shit." He looks over at the targets and winces. "Looks like we may need a few new targets."

"I am not in the mood for your antics." I warn.

"Well, let me check and see if I care." He taps his chin thoughtfully while looking up at the sky before turning back to me. "Nope, don't care."

"Give me the magazine, Mark." I snap, holding my hand out to him.

He does, but not without a question following with it. "So, what? Is everything we've worked for over the last four years for nothing?"

I load the magazine but don't chamber the round as his words echo around me.

"I don't know, man." I sigh. "I am so damn angry and confused."

"I can understand the anger. Yes, they were alive for all these years, but maybe there was something bigger going on that we don't know about," Mark says.

"Sure," I scoff. "What's bigger than abandoning their son?"

"I don't know; what if they thought Phil would just come back for them when he figured out he didn't get the job done?"

"Maybe. But I mean, leave me little things like I did with Taylor." I say as I remove the magazine from my gun and set them both down on the table in front of me.

"Fair." Mark nods his head while folding his arms over his chest to look at me. "Now, what's confusing you? Or should I say, what are you afraid of?"

"I'm not—" I start but he cuts me off.

"Yes, you are. You're doing that little foot wobble thing you do when you're scared of something."

I look down and growl when I see the toe of my Converse shoe rolling side to side in nervous energy.

"Okay, fine." I say as I step away from him. "What if I let them back into my life and they run off again? What if I let them back in my life and—" The words catch in my throat, and I didn't even know these fears existed until I got past the anger, and now I don't want to voice them.

"And what, Bryan?" Mark asks softly. "It's just you, me, and the trees here. Talk to me."

I turn and walk a few steps away while running my hands through my hair, and when I face him again, I can't stop the tears that well in my eyes.

"What if I let them back into my life and I'm not what they expected? What if, just like I did when I was growing up, I had an image of how they would be in my head, and what if they have that with me and I don't measure up?"

The tears are flowing down my face now.

"And, God, Sophie." I chuckle wetly. "I don't know the first thing about being a big brother, and with what I said about her being *the other kid,* she's liable to tell me to fuck off than want me in her life now."

"That's better." Mark says with a smile, "Now, we're getting somewhere."

"Screw you." I say as I roughly wipe the tears from my face.

"As far as you measuring up, dude, come on. You are a badass agent. I mean, look at what just you and I have accomplished in our four years. Plus, when you met Taylor, and now the case we just got off of. Dude, you are the perfect son. And if they think otherwise, well, screw them. You don't need their approval on a damn thing. That is between you, your grandparents *who raised you,* and Taylor."

I take a breath and let his words sink in and I nod my head, letting him know I understand them.

"And with Sophie, if you want to be that for her, then just take it one day at a time. I mean, you're my brother, so to me, it's not that different. Plus, I know Cody thinks of you as a big brother. So, you just have the flesh and blood match for it, that's all."

"God, I hate it when you're right." I shake my head.

"Really? 'Cause I love it." Mark laughs as he hooks his arm around my neck and pulls me toward the cabin. "Why don't you get a shower and I'll clean up out here? But let me ask you something. You up for talking to Taylor to see what she's found out?"

"Yeah. Does she already know where I am?"

"Yes, she was just giving you space until you were ready." Mark says as he opens the sliding door and shoves me into the kitchen. "Get a shower and I'll text your girl."

"Thanks, Mark. For everything." I say, and he waves me off like I'm thanking him for something as simple as breathing. So, I get a shower and wait for Taylor to come and fill in the blanks that are my parents.

Chapter Fifty-Six

Taylor

With a quick text to Dad, he arrives at the park in ten minutes and takes Lexi and me home.

"So I'm guessing things didn't go well." Dad says.

"You could say that." I sigh and tell him what all happened, and where I think Bryan and Mark are now.

"I know that if anything can get through to Bryan, it's you, Taylor." Dad says with a soft smile.

"Thanks, Dad."

Once we get home, it's waiting for Mark's text that is the worst. Two hours pass, and just as I'm about to text Mark, my phone finally lights up with his own.

> **Mark:** He's good to talk now. We're still at the cabin.

> **Me:** Thanks, Mark. And Lexi is here at my place, so I'll bring her with me.

> **Mark:** Thanks.

"Let's go, Lexi." I say as I interrupt her game of *Sorry* with Cody.

Lexi nods before turning her attention back to Cody. "Good game, kiddo. You learn how to cheat from Bryan?" She asks teasingly. She's lost two games in a row, and I know she's actually trying to beat him. Lexi doesn't pull her punches one bit.

"No!" Cody giggles. "I beat him all the time on my own!"

"Sure." Lexi arches an eyebrow as she ruffles Cody's hair before joining me by the door. "Let's go."

I grab my keys from the hook near the garage, hop into my Mustang, and we drive to the cabin in silence.

When I pull up, Mark is already heading out the front door to meet us.

"Hey, Baby," Mark greets Lexi first, pulling her into his side before turning his attention to me. "He's inside in the master bedroom in the back."

"Thank you, Mark. For everything." I say.

"I don't need to be thanked for being there for my brother when he's hurting."

I nod and give them both a small smile before I make my way to the door, gently easing it open to walk into the living room. Once I shut the door behind me, I find the space to be quiet. No sign of life at all. Then I recall Mark saying that Bryan was in the master bedroom, so I walk down a hallway off to the right and I find an open bedroom door.

I stand in the doorway for a moment as my eyes glance over to the bed and I find Bryan lying on his back on top of the rustic red and navy comforter, in nothing other than a pair of black shorts.

I can't help but smile when I notice he's sound asleep. And I can tell he didn't plan on falling asleep because his shirt is still clutched in the hand that's resting on his chest. This whole ordeal was a lot for him to take in, so it's no surprise for me to find him passed out.

I slowly ease out of my sneakers, my socked feet just a whisper over the hardwood floors as I walk over to the opposite side of the bed, pulling a cream-colored blanket from a chair sitting in the corner of the room before crawling into the bed and cocooning the both of us in the soft warmth.

Once I get settled, I brush my fingers through his just barely damp hair, and his eyes flutter open, looking confused for a moment of why I'm here, before understanding floods them a heartbeat later.

"Hey," I say softly.

"Hi," Bryan says, his voice deep from sleep. "Sorry, I didn't mean to fall asleep before you got here."

"It's okay. You probably would have still been asleep if I could keep my hands off you."

"Don't ever keep your hands to yourself." Bryan smiles, "I love being woken up by your touches."

"Okay. Good to know."

Bryan moves to sit up in bed, putting his back on the headboard, and I sit cross-legged beside him, both of us trying to ignore the elephant in the room that we both know we need to talk about.

After a few more minutes of silence, I reach out and run my hand over his knee in a gentle caress, "You have to ask, Bryan. I'm not going to just start talking. You have to want to hear what they told me."

He lets out a defeated sigh while pinching the bridge of his nose for a moment before removing his hands and looks at it like it's not attached to his body.

"What's wrong?" I ask.

"He, uh, Paul, does that too. I guess it's a trait I picked up without even knowing it."

"Stop stalling, Bryan."

"Okay, fine. What did you find out?"

"First, just so you know, they do feel terrible for what they've done. I mean, even Sophie was angry at them for lying to her too." I begin, and I take a breath before I get into the nitty-gritty of the story I was told.

"Paul caught Phil on camera selling the information to the mafia, and he left it on his desk at the agency. Well, you should know Phil, he got pissed, and he showed up at your all's house that night. Your dad—"

"Please don't call him that yet," Bryan cuts me off. "Please, just Paul and Cindy for now."

"Okay." I nod. "Paul rushed out the door, I guess, as Cindy was taking you upstairs. Paul no longer got out the front door, and Phil shot him."

As I say the words, it's like Bryan is reliving that night again, and his body jumps like he's heard the gunshot that he thought took his father's life.

"When Cindy knew Paul was going to be alright, she hacked into the system and falsified the report to show they both died. Paul on the table, and when she learned of his fate, she took off into the woods and died from her own gunshot wound that she didn't realize she had."

Bryan chuckles lightly. "So they couldn't find the body."

"Yeah," I agree. "So after that, your da—uh—Paul, just kept an eye on the case file, and when he noticed that Phil was acting strange due to the pressure we had on him, Paul planted those skeletons in the warehouse because he knew Phil was going back to the same place he was selling his info and was hoping we would follow."

"Why didn't they tell me this down in Florida?" Bryan says.

"I think they were telling the truth that they didn't want to distract you with that info bomb, plus they truly didn't know about their deaths until we told them in person. Remember, those skeletons were sitting in the FBI lab for four months before I ever got the chance to look at them.

So, Paul and Cindy thought you didn't want to see them. And they were going to let you live your life, but when Wayne sent us on the case, that's when they figured out that you didn't know anything."

I scoot in closer to him. "Cindy said she never meant to hurt you or Sophie. She only wanted to protect both of her children from the threat she thought was still out there. She said that if she knew you would have reacted like that, she would have just left everything as it was."

"What should I do, Taylor?" Bryan asks as tears pool in his eyes.

"I can't tell you that, Bryan. Only you can figure it out." I reach out, caressing his cheek with my hand while running my thumb over his cheekbone like he's done with me so many times before. "But just know that whatever you choose, I'll be by your side."

"They've missed out on so much." He begins. "They've missed out on fifteen years' worth of birthdays, Christmases, and every game of baseball that Grandpa signed me up for when I was younger."

"While that may be true, they have so much more to experience with you, Bryan. They have *this* Christmas and your next birthday. And you turn twenty-one, so that's a big one. And if you want, as long as we have some downtime again, you can sign up for a few games of men's softball and have either Paul play on the same team or just watch you from the bleachers."

Bryan shakes his head, but I can tell the movement is mostly for him and his narrow line of thought. "How you're able to find the silver lining in almost every situation I'll never know."

"It's a gift." I jest.

"What about Sophie? Did I mess things up between us?"

"She's pissed at you, yes. But she wants to get to know her brother, that is, if you want to get to know her."

"Yes, I do; I just don't know where to start."

"How about we start by meeting with them again? This time hearing what everyone has to say before making any final decisions."

Bryan nods, and a true smile finally pulls at the corners of his mouth. "Okay, deal."

"Good." I say before leaning against him, pulling him in for a hug.

"I don't know how I'll ever thank you for trying to fix this impossible situation." Bryan says. "I love you so much, Annie."

"Oh, I can think of a few things if you're up for it." I say as I trail my finger down his neck, "Show me just how much you love me."

"I wanted our first time to be special and perfect."

"Life isn't perfect, Bryan. You should know that better than anyone. I mean, look at what just happened a few hours ago." I tell him as I pull the blanket away from the rest of his body and I move between his legs before looking up at him again. "I want you. All of you."

It takes him all of a heartbeat to answer. "Then you'll have all of me."

I lean over his body, pressing my mouth to his for a moment before I trail my lips across his chest, then his stomach, and down to the solid V at the top of his shorts.

"Taylor." Bryan pants as I hook my fingers into the fabric. He lifts his hips so I can pull his shorts and boxers down at the same time.

My breath catches in my throat as I take in his naked form before me. His erection standing proudly between us, and his whole body is expanding and contracting with each and every breath. And he is all mine.

"I get to make you feel good before you have your way with me." I say, and before he can protest, I take him into my mouth, making his head tilt back into the pillow with a growl. But I want more.

I release his length with a pop, and he looks up at me. "I want to hear you scream my name. Now let's try this again." I say with a smirk.

I take his crown into my mouth again, this time working him deeper, and I'm rewarded with him not just screaming my name, but words of encouragement too.

"Taylor, oh Baby, that feels good." Bryan groans as he bucks his hips, driving himself even further down my throat. "Breathe through your nose, Babe. You're doing so well."

I smile around his length and moan my approval against him; the vibrations making him shudder under my hands.

"Oh, shit, Taylor. Don't do that, or I'm gonna lose it."

But I want him to lose himself. I want him to come undone for me, so I moan again, driving him higher and his breathy laughter fills the air around us.

"Oh, you are in so much trouble when it's my turn." He growls as he fists the bedsheets at his hips, again trying to stave off his orgasm.

Without breaking my connection with him, I lift my hand and sign, *"Stop holding back on me."*

"But it's so much fun." He smirks.

"I'll show you fun." I warn.

As I suck on him again, I place two of my fingers behind his testes, pressing in and up. I know I have the right pressure point when his back literally bows off the bed like a man possessed, and I can't help the chuckle knowing that he's possessed by me.

"Taylor, what the hell are you doing?" Bryan asks with an almost whiney quality to his voice, and I love it.

I release the pressure I had against him, and he glances down at me like he wants to ask me again just what the hell I'm doing. So I press into him again with a wicked grin playing on my lips. He gasps while closing his eyes and biting his fist in response.

I release him with an audible pop and ask with innocence dripping into my tone, "What do you mean?"

"You know what the hell I mean!" He shouts as I press in again and this time hold the pressure there.

"Oh, you mean this?" I ask as I get into position again. "This is *your* magic button. Now come for me, Bryan." I demand as I take him into my mouth as far as I can in one go as I press on his prostrate again.

"Oh, shit! Taylor!" Bryan cries out as his orgasm races through him and I swallow every last drop.

After what seems like forever, Bryan finally looks down at me, his green eyes brighter from post-release bliss. "How did you know to do that?"

"I was studying to be a nurse, so knowing the male anatomy was a requirement." I smirk.

"Alright, smartass," Bryan says as he leans up to grab me by the back of my neck and he flips us where I am the one on my back and he's hovering over top of me. "You have too many clothes on. Let's fix that."

He lifts the hem of my shirt, and I raise my arms, allowing him to take the shirt from my body and throw it over his shoulder. Bryan then crashes his mouth to mine while he slips his hand behind my back to unclasp my bra with his deft fingers.

"So fucking beautiful." He growls as he takes in my bare breasts.

I gasp when Bryan takes one of my peaked nipples into his mouth while he caresses and teases the other with his hand, then pinching the tender bud between his thumb and index finger.

"I love the little sounds you make when I'm touching you like this," Bryan coos next to my skin.

"I want you." I plead as I hook my leg around his hip, making his crown brush against my short-covered center, but the implication is enough.

Pulling away from my leg, he gently hooks his arm around my back, lifting my hips where he can slip my shorts down my thighs, exposing my body to him fully. Bryan takes my calf in his hand, lips trailing tender kisses across my skin, and stops just short of the apex of my thighs.

"Bryan, please." I beg, and he has the nerve to smile.

"Are you sure?"

"I wouldn't say it if I wasn't. Now stop stalling!"

He leans over me, and just as I'm about to grab him and pull him back to where I want him, he pulls something from the bedside table and brings it in front of me.

His wallet.

"Why do you need—?" I stop short when I see him pull the silver foil packet from the leather.

"What? You heard I was raised to use condoms." He says with a smirk as he tosses his wallet back on the nightstand.

"How long have you had that in there?" I ask in shock.

"About two weeks. But I change it out once a month." Then his lips lift into a smirk. "Been carrying them for a while now."

"Seriously?"

"Yes. Always gotta be prepared when you're around a pretty girl." He coos.

I smile as I shake my head at him, but I love that the man I fell for is back with me at this moment. His eyes are not the haunted and confused version he was a few minutes ago. My eyes travel again to the foil packet in his hands, and he lifts it to his mouth, tearing it open with his teeth, and I shudder. That was sexy as hell.

"You alright there?" He teases.

"No, I'm not. You're taking your good ole time on purpose to drive me nuts."

"That was the plan, Baby," Bryan says as he rolls the condom down over his erection, and I almost combust, but his dark chuckle keeps me from exploding.

He leans over me, pressing a few quick, hard kisses to my mouth, but he keeps our hips away from each other. I open my mouth to protest, to beg that he finally take me, but he uses that opportunity to deepen our kiss; tongues and teeth merging and scraping together.

I moan when he pulls my swollen bottom lip between his teeth, and I don't realize I hooked my calf around his back until I feel his covered crown brush against my clit, making us both growl and gasp at the sensation.

"You tell me if I hurt you." Bryan pants.

"It's going to hurt the first time."

"Tell me if it gets to be too much, Taylor Allison." He demands.

"Okay." I say with a nod.

He kisses me again, threading one hand through my hair while his other skims down past my breasts, stomach, and hip where he finally settles between our bodies, notching himself at my entrance and I moan at the feeling of him so close to where I'm desperate for him to be.

I arch my back as if on instinct, forcing him to slide in just a half-inch, and I can't help the hiss of pain/pleasure at the sensation.

"Shhhh, pretty girl," Bryan whispers as he presses his thumb against my clit, giving me another sensation as he sinks deeper. "Damn, you feel so good, Taylor."

"So do you. Don't stop. Please." I pant.

"Didn't plan on it, Baby," Bryan says as he pulls back to the tip, then pivots his hips, driving deeper still, and I bite my bottom lip between my teeth to keep from screaming out.

He withdraws again, slower this time, and just before he thrusts back into me, he grabs my hip, and then slams his mouth into mine, forcing me to let go of my bottom lip. Once my mouth is his to control for a moment, he breaks our kiss to look down at me, and the green hue of his eyes is a shade darker than I've ever seen before.

"I want you screaming *my name,* Taylor. It's not fair that only you get to hear me and I don't get the same treatment." Bryan growls. "Now, let's take advantage of the privacy of this cabin."

Keeping my hip at an angle, he slowly moves, taking his time sinking into me inch by glorious inch, and true to what he demanded of me, I wrap my arms around his neck, burying my face into the curve of his shoulder and I scream with pleasure coursing through me.

"That's it, Baby. Oh, you're doing so well." Bryan praises. "Just a little bit more for me." He adds with a grunt.

"It feels like you're everywhere." I groan.

"Does it hurt?" He asks.

"God, no. It feels so freaking good." I pant, and my hips buck on instinct again, and that forces him the last inch inside, and we both freeze at the realization.

I hook my legs around his waist, locking them at the ankle, keeping him pinned against me as we both allow my body to stretch around his length. Bryan begins kissing, nipping, licking at my neck, all the while whispering praises and telling me how much he loves me in my ear.

Even without him moving inside me, I can feel my orgasm building, my walls fluttering around him, causing him to growl and groan with each contraction.

"Move, please." I beg him.

And he does. The gentle, slow, and languid thrusts send waves of pleasure rippling through me, and I claw at his back in response. This only spurs him on, making each movement quicker, harder, and impossibly deeper until I can't tell where he ends and I begin.

"Yes, Bryan. Don't stop. Please don't." I beg as my orgasm builds to the breaking point, and he knows it.

"Not until you come for me, Baby," He growls, his thrusts becoming even wilder than before, and I shatter underneath him with his name pouring from my lips.

"That's it, Baby. Fall apart for me. I'll put you back together again." He praises as he falls behind me with his own shudder of pleasure.

His pace slows, drawing our orgasms out as long as he can until we both come down from our high. When he pulls out, I hiss at the slight discomfort, but Bryan is right there, kissing me. His green eyes are wide with fear that he hurt me, and I can't help but smile up at him.

"I'm fine, Bullet. I promise."

"Alright. Let me get rid of this condom and clean you up with a warm washcloth."

I nod and I watch him ease off me; the bed moving a bit from the loss of his weight causes a glorious ache to throb in my core, but I keep the moan buried in my chest. When Bryan comes back into the room a few minutes later, he has a washcloth in one hand and a small plastic bowl in the other.

"Hopefully, the warm water will help with your soreness." Bryan says as he gently places the bowl on the bedside table, then wrings out the washcloth and drapes it over my center.

"Oh, that feels so good." I sigh. "Thank you."

Bryan leans over my body, gently kissing my forehead before lowering his mouth to mine, his words a whisper against my lips. "You're welcome, Baby Girl."

Then he turns his attention back to the task at hand, wetting the washcloth again to finish cleaning me up. Once he's satisfied, he takes the bowl back into the bathroom and joins me in the bed a few minutes later, pulling me close to his chest while absentmindedly running his hand up and down my back.

I kiss his chest before looking up at him, and he still has that sated look in his eyes, and my chest fills with pride and contentment, knowing that I was the cause of that look.

"That was amazing. Ten out of ten would do again."

Bryan bursts out laughing as he pulls me closer against him. "I'm glad to hear that, Babe."

After a few minutes of silence between us, Bryan is the first to speak.

"I want to meet them again."

"If you're sure, then I'm with you all the way." I tell him. "Just let me know when you want to meet and we'll text them."

He nods. "Okay. Let's take the night for us. Then tomorrow we'll call and see if they want to meet me. Do you seriously think they'll still want to after my outburst?"

"Yes, they do. I promise you, they want to get to know the man you've become, Bryan."

"Alright. Tomorrow then." He says with a smile.

"Tomorrow." I agree.

Chapter Fifty-Seven

Bryan

Once Taylor and I finally let sleep take us, we slept through the night in the cabin. I'm up before her, like usual, and I honestly wanted to be alone for a few minutes to gather my thoughts about everything that's happened over the last seventeen hours.

So here I am on the back porch, just off the kitchen, sipping on a cup of coffee, listening to the birds chirping their morning song in the trees around me.

My parents are alive and, at least according to Taylor, they do want to see me again. And I have a little sister. I just hope I can smooth things over with her and be her friend first and then, if I can fall into the brotherly role, then great.

But even after all that, the thing that I keep coming back to is how amazing last night was between Taylor and me. And it's not just because I had sex with a girl. No, it's because I made *love* to an amazing, beautiful, caring, fearless, and strong woman that I get the privilege to call mine.

I love Taylor with every single cell of my body, and nothing will ever change that.

As I finish my coffee, I set the cup in the sink and make Taylor a cup before I go in and wake her. She's still sound asleep as I walk into the bedroom, but she's rolled over partially on my side of the bed, and she's hugging my pillow close to her chest while snoring slightly. I have to cover my mouth with my hand to keep the laughter that wants to bubble up my chest at the sight of her.

I know she's going to kill me if she ever finds this, but it will be a worthwhile death. So, I pull my phone out of the back pocket of my jeans and, after ensuring it's on silent; I pull up the camera app and take a picture of her.

I look at it for a moment, and I can't stop the smile that pulls at the corner of my mouth. I don't think Taylor knows just how beautiful she is. I could just stare at her for hours, and it still wouldn't be enough.

She then takes a deep breath, and the smell of coffee must hit her nose because her eyes flutter open, and they land on me first. I give her a lazy grin as I discreetly pocket my phone and gesture to the coffee cup on the bedside table.

"Morning, Baby. I made you a cup of coffee just the way you like it."

"Morning." She yawns while stretching out over the mattress, and I catch a glimpse of her still-naked body from under the covers, which instantly makes me hard behind the zipper of my jeans.

I take a breath to center myself. Now is not the time to think about that.

"What are you doing up already?" Taylor asks as she fortunately or unfortunately, pulls the covers up over her body and leans against the headboard to take the cup as I offer it to her.

"Really? I'm always up before you." I chuckle.

"Bite me." She quips as she takes a sip and hums at the taste. "Perfect."

"Good." I say as I sit on the bed, facing her direction. "But actually, I was just thinking about everything that happened yesterday."

"And?" Taylor asks.

"I still want this to happen. I haven't changed my mind."

"Okay. Find my phone and let's call them." She says, but I don't miss the lingering question in her eyes, if that's all I thought about this morning.

"*But* I also was replaying what we did last night over and *over* in my mind." I smirk, and the adorable flush to her cheeks has nothing to do with the coffee. "And I'm counting down the minutes until I can lose myself inside you again."

"Bryan," Taylor whispers, her breathing kicking up a notch.

"But I'm sure you need a day or so to work out the tenderness, so I'll wait." I tell her. "But as soon as you're ready and willing, I want to love you again and again until we get absolutely lost in each other."

I get up off the bed to leave her with that revelation between us. Just as I hit the doorway, I turn back to her, and she's still sitting there in shock.

"Once you're done with your coffee, get dressed for me so we can make that call to Paul and Cindy."

She comes out fifteen minutes later and sits beside me on the couch before she hands me her phone and I see the number that belongs to Paul and Cindy sitting on the screen, waiting for me to press the green dial button.

"Whenever you're ready, Babe," Taylor smiles as she takes my hand in hers, threading our fingers together.

"Okay," I say, my voice tight with apprehension, as I press the call button.

The phone rings three times before Paul picks up. His voice light, and friendly. "Good morning, Taylor."

"No, it's me." I say, my voice cracking like a teenager.

"Bryan," Paul says with shock coloring his tone. "Good morning."

"Morning." I say, my voice a bit stronger this time. "Listen, I uh, I want to try this again." I begin lamely.

"We do too, Sport."

I heave out a tear-filled sigh, and I hear the same thing from his end. We both thought we would never say or hear that nickname again.

"You want to meet up at the same park?" I ask, voice thick with emotion and tears filling my eyes, threatening to spill over and down my cheeks.

"Yeah, that sounds good." Paul agrees. "When do you want to meet up?"

"Is in about an hour good for you all?" I ask.

"Yeah, we can make that work." Paul says, and I can hear Cindy say something in the background, and it almost sounds like she said *my baby* something, but it's enough to make the dam burst on my tears, and they spill down my face.

I sniff and chuckle wetly at them through the phone. "Alright, see you all soon. And please make sure Sophie is there with you, too."

"You got it, Bryan. See you soon," Paul says, and he disconnects the line.

I stare at the phone for a minute before I hear Taylor sniff beside me and I see tears flowing down her own cheeks, and that just makes me smile and cry harder.

"We are both a mess." I say wetly.

"Yeah, but I don't care. This is a big thing for you."

"I'm glad I have you by my side to be a mess right along with me." I tell her as I wipe her tears away with the pad of my thumb. "Let's go. I know we'll be crying more once we get there."

I stand first, helping her to her feet, then we walk out the door and over to my Camaro, where I open the passenger door for her to slip inside.

I know from where the cabin is we will get to the park in about forty-five minutes, but I don't care. I'm not running from this anymore.

When we arrive at the park and I help Taylor out of her seat, we walk toward the same pavilion and wait for...my family—if I can even call them that—to arrive.

Fifteen minutes later, we hear a radio blaring a Taylor Swift song, and I look over my shoulder to see the same black SUV that Linc—Paul—was driving down in Florida pull up beside my Camaro. I can't help but smile when I hear Sophie and Cindy singing about 'haters gonna hate' and to 'shake it off' and both of them doing the dance that I guess goes along with the song.

"At least they have good taste in music." Taylor says from my side.

I roll my eyes and I see Cindy and Sophie exit the SUV, still singing and dancing, even though Paul has shut the radio off.

"What did I tell you girls about getting out of this SUV?" Paul shouts as he stomps over to Cindy and grabs her by the waist, and what I see makes me instantly flush with embarrassment.

Paul gives Cindy a quick smack on her ass before pulling her flush against his body to press a quick, hard kiss to her mouth. It's so much like what I would do with Taylor that it's weird to see it happen with someone that's not me.

"Oh my God, you two! Get a room!" Sophie exclaims while making a gagging motion and turning away from her parents.

"I feel ya," I whisper, even though she can't hear me from this far away.

"He reminds me of you," Taylor quips from my side, apparently seeing the same thing I do.

"Gee, that really helps right now, Taylor." I groan.

"What? I think it's romantic. You both just like to show that you can take care of your girl." She teases.

"Oh, you do, huh?" I ask as I back her against the nearby support beam, resting my knee between her legs; not enough to set her off, but enough where she'll feel me there. "Do you need a reminder of how I can take care of you, Baby?"

"I already see that trait had been passed on. These Evans men don't know how to act in public, do they, Taylor?" Cindy asks, with a hint of humor in her voice.

"No, they don't. But I can't say I'm too embarrassed about it," Taylor says with a smirk.

I step back from her while shaking my head toward Cindy and Paul. "I just got caught up in the moment with her."

"It's okay. I can tell you both have great chemistry together." Cindy says. "It's the same thing I picked up on while we were down in Florida."

"Why don't we all sit down and talk?" Taylor offers, waving at the picnic table behind her.

Paul and Cindy nod, but as I look over their shoulder, I see Sophie walking under a nearby weeping willow tree, picking up sticks and batting at the overhead branches.

"I'll be right back. I want to talk to Sophie first." I say, and I get three nods of understanding before they sit and wait for me to talk to my sister.

As I head over in her direction, I realize I have not a clue what I'm going to say. I mean, how do I begin to apologize for being the biggest asshole to her? When I step up to her side, I stuff my hands in the front pockets of my jeans and just watch her swat her stick at a low-hanging branch.

"You know, you don't have to make this awkward. You've been around me before; it's just with the knowledge of what I really am to you," Sophie says.

I can't help but chuckle at her no-nonsense tone, and I rub the back of my neck with my right hand as I step closer to her. "My God, you are just like your grandfather, you know that?"

"So I've been told. By him directly, too." Sophie says.

I take a deep breath, and I gently turn her so she's facing me. "I'm sorry for what I said yesterday. For calling you the other kid. That was very selfish on my part, and I hurt you."

"I do understand where you were coming from. You just never want to think about your parents woohooing after they had you. I get it." Sophie says.

This time, I outright laugh at her words. "Woohooing? Really?" I shake my head as I turn and lean my back against the trunk of the tree, bending my right leg to rest my foot against the bark. "You played too many Sim's games, if you know that term."

"You've played the Sims game before?" Sophie asks. "I didn't think you were *that* cool."

"Mark and I played it a fair amount when we were younger." I say.

Then, after a few minutes of awkward silence between us, I sigh and say. "You want to know something? I've always wanted a sibling. Someone I could confide in, and to help our father protect from anyone who wanted to hurt them. And my fear of not living up to your expectations is what made me make very poor word choices."

She nods in understanding. "Well, you know I've always thought about what my big brother would have been like if he were here." She shakes her head and glances over at her parents. "That will take some time still getting used to. I have to keep reminding myself that story is not true anymore."

"You're smarter than I am, so I'm sure you'll work it out." I give her a small smile. "Sophie, I want to be that brother for you. That is, if you'll give me the chance."

"I'll do it, but on one condition." Sophie says, and my heart freezes in my chest. "If you promise not to be as lame as my dad. Don't threaten bodily harm to any boyfriend I meet."

I laugh and push off the tree, closing the distance between us. "I'll do my best to be the cool one. But if he hurts you, I will step in along with Paul. Sister or not, you were my friend first, and no one hurts my friends and gets by with it."

"Okay, that's fair, I guess," Sophie says, then she drops her eyes to the ground while still toying with the stick in her hand, almost like she wants to ask something, but she's afraid of my answer.

"What is it, Soph?" I ask.

"Can I hug you?"

"Sure. I'd love that." I say, opening my arms to her, and she drops her stick and practically flings herself into my arms.

"You feel so good. It's a little like Dad, but different. Dad's a little taller, but you have more muscle than he does. You still feel similar, though." Sophie whispers into my chest.

"Well, I have to be strong to keep you and Taylor out of trouble. I think now, between the two of you, you're going to give me a run for my money." I say with a smile.

"Okay, buddy, keep telling yourself that. We did just fine without you." Sophie says, sarcasm dripping in her tone while backing out of my embrace.

"Race ya over to Mom and Dad!" Sophie giggles as she takes off at a dead sprint towards the pavilion.

"Oh, it's on!" I shout and chase after her.

She ends up winning, but only because she picked up a freaking pinecone and threw it at my head.

"Cheater." I mumble as we take our respective seats at the picnic table. She's next to her parents, and I'm by Taylor.

"Oh, so you're the sore loser sibling."

"Play fair and I wouldn't be." I toss back as I reach over the picnic table and gently shove her shoulder.

Taylor grabs my hand and gives it a reassuring squeeze, and I automatically bring her knuckles to my lips and place a loving kiss on her skin, which Sophie instantly groans at.

"Oh God, now I'm gonna have you two *and* my parents being all lovey-dovey around me."

"You'll find your person, Sophie." I say as I look over at Taylor and give her a quick wink that makes her cheeks flush.

I turn my attention to Paul and Cindy, and my smile falters a bit when I notice them looking between me and Sophie, but I see a hint of fear lingering in their eyes. I know I have to be the one to start this conversation, so I take a breath and rest my arms across the picnic table between the four of us.

"I don't really know where to start here." I begin. "I want to tell you all so many things. But I want to get to know the two of you. I want to fill in the fifteen years worth of missing time with good memories instead of the ones I've been haunted with."

Cindy takes my hand from across the table and looks me in the eye. "One thing I want to tell you is I am so proud of the man you have become, Bryan. I know that John has instilled all the same great qualities that I fell in love with in Paul. I can see them in you and how you treat Taylor. Tell me, how did you all meet?"

I smile as I look over at my girlfriend and I tell my parents of how I met her and the secrets she was hiding herself.

"Once we both found out we were agents, things took a turn for the worst. We fought, of course, after Taylor found out I was lying about being undercover, and during that time Daryl kidnapped her and took her back to the warehouse. I was able to find her, thankfully, but it almost cost me my life."

The three of them look at me in confusion, and I pull down the collar of my shirt to show them the bullet-shaped scar on my chest.

Cindy walks around the table to sit beside me and lifts her hand like she wants to touch me, but pauses just before her index finger connects with my skin. I give her a firm nod, and she closes the distance between us, running the pad of her finger over the flawed skin.

"I'm sorry. I am so sorry you had to go through this. I'm sorry you both had to. We almost lost you and we never would have known." Cindy says, her voice breaking near the end.

"I'm not. This just made me realize how much I loved Taylor, and it helped me fight to get back to her. Even if for three months she thought I was dead because of this." I say, pointing to my scar.

"What?" Paul growls.

I nod and tell them about what happened over the last eight months and about how I got into the agency in the first place. How Mark and I teamed up to help find any answers we could about their murder.

"I'm gonna kill Wayne for letting you in that young," Paul grumbles. "Sixteen, really?"

"What do you expect from someone who was raised by an ex-Army vet? Of course, I was going to know more about gun and war tactics better than a normal teenager." I toss back.

"I know. You're like me," Paul says as he looks over at Taylor. "Sorry, Taylor, his actions of always feeling the need to be a protector comes from me."

"Sometimes that's good, to an extent. But I honestly think it's an agent thing. Mark is the same exact way. He thought he could take care of me and Lexi when we were down in Florida before Bryan got down there."

"By the way." Cindy says and smacks me on the side of the head. Not hard, but enough to get my attention, and I'm genuinely shell-shocked by her actions.

"That is for letting Taylor come down to Florida on a mission alone, just because you were upset at her for finding the code we planted." Cindy says. "You should know, with getting shot the way you did, that nothing is off limits in a mission. You never would have been able to forgive yourself if she got hurt and you weren't there with her."

"Yes, ma'am. You are one hundred percent right. And I had to learn that the hard way, but yes, I will never let Taylor leave my side again."

"Good man. Now how about we go and say hello to an old friend, shall we?" Paul asks with a sly smile on his face.

"Oh yes, let's go see how Wayne Anderson is doing these days." Cindy says as she smiles at her husband. "I have a few bones to pick with him."

"Oh, you are about to see a show, Bryan. Mom is scary when she's mad." Sophie chuckles as she stands to join her parents at the end of the pavilion.

"I'm ready for the show." I say with a smile. "Let's go."

Chapter Fifty-Eight

Taylor

After we are in the privacy of Bryan's Camaro, I find him watching Paul and Cindy's SUV drive away with a smile on his face. I grab his hand to get his attention on me.

"Are you alright?"

"Yeah." He nods. "This feels like a dream. That went a lot better than I thought it would."

"Yeah, it did."

Bryan leans over the console towards me to give me a quick kiss before resting his forehead on mine. "Thank you for being my rock through all this."

I wrap my hand around his neck, tugging him even closer. "You're welcome. You'd do the same for me if the roles were switched. Now you want to call Mark and Lexi and let them in on the fun?"

"Hell, yes." Bryan smiles as he starts the engine and backs out of the parking space.

I press Lexi's contact on my phone, and she picks up on the second ring.

"Hello?"

"Hey, Lexi. We just left the park after meeting with Paul and Cindy again."

"Oh, how'd that go?" Lexi asks.

"It was great. We are actually on our way to the agency now to meet with Wayne. You know, gotta share the reunion with him too."

"Oh my God, we are totally there." Lexi exclaims. "Mark, get pants and a shirt on; we are going to see a hell of a show!"

"Damn, are you two always naked?" I ask, chuckling.

"You should try it. It's always a great time when clothes aren't involved." Lexi says playfully.

"I'm slowly learning that." I say while looking over at Bryan, and he gives me a wink that heats my blood.

"Wait, what?" Lexi asks quickly. "Did you and Bryan finally hit the sheets and go all the way?!"

"I'll see you at the agency." I say and immediately disconnect the call.

"You know that's just going to come back and bite you in the ass, right?" Bryan asks.

I shrug. "It'll be fun to see how she'll react."

Bryan shakes his head, and we ride in comfortable silence for the next fifteen minutes until we pull into the FBI parking lot.

Paul has already parked, and he, Cindy, and Sophie are waiting for us. Just as we pull in and Bryan is helping me out of the seat, Mark's Challenger pulls up beside us, and he immediately gets out of the car and heads toward Bryan.

"Everything good, man?"

"Yeah." Bryan nods. "Just doing a little meet and greet here." He adds with a smile.

The four of us walk toward the door, but Paul stops us, looking over Mark for a moment before he speaks.

"Mark, I wanted to thank you for being there for my son. I can tell you both mean a lot to one another. That is a brotherly bond I haven't seen for a while."

"Bryan's my best friend. So, it's a no-brainer that I would be there for him." Mark says.

"Of course, it would be a no-brainer since you don't have a brain." Bryan says with a sly smile.

"Hey! Take that back man!" Mark says while running after Bryan.

Bryan takes off, running in between cars in the parking lot before they circle back toward us. Bryan slides across the hood of Mark's Challenger like one of the guys from the Dukes of Hazzard and then runs behind me.

"Hey, oh no. I'm not gonna protect you." I say as I step away from him, leaving him open for Mark's attack.

"Hey, man! You better not have scratched my paint!" Mark says.

Paul, Cindy, and Sophie all watch the banter between those two, and it brings a smile to their faces as well. What they saw in Florida is the exact same here.

"Alright, you two, let's get inside and get this over with." Paul says to Bryan and Mark before looking over at me and Lexi. "You girls have to deal with this all the time?"

Lexi and I both nod, but we smile at the two guys that are roughly pushing each other around while laughing like they don't have a care in the world.

"Yeah, we do. But it's us. It's normal." I say, and Lexi agrees.

Once Bryan and Mark are at our sides again, we all walk inside and up the cream marble staircase that leads to Wayne's office.

"You three stay here." I tell them before I knock on Wayne's door.

"Come in." His booming voice commands.

I open the door and as the four of us walk inside, his face morphs from the serious set that he usually wears it in to a friendly smile at the sight of us.

"Hey, Wayne. It's the fantastic four!" Mark exclaims.

"I can see that, Stone. I'm not blind." Wayne says, but I see the laughter he's trying to hide. "What do I owe the pleasure of your company? Do you all want a case again already?"

"Not yet." I begin. "We actually want you to meet someone." I nod toward Bryan, and he pokes his head out the door and waves his hand.

"Who do you want me to—"

His words are cut short when he sees Paul and Cindy filling the doorway. For a second he just sits there behind his desk, mouth open and eyes wide, but then he chuckles like he's just caught something that he should have figured out a long time ago.

"Lincoln and Temperance? God, I should have figured that out a lot sooner." Wayne shakes his head. "Paul, Cindy, how have you all been? We need to catch up."

"Yes, we do, but one thing first." Cindy begins.

"Oh boy, here it comes." Sophie says from between me and Bryan.

"How dare you let Bryan into the agency at sixteen!?"

"Well, it was either letting him in or letting him run free with that one by his side." Wayne says while pointing to Mark. "So I figured picking the lesser of two evils by letting him in where I could keep an eye on him was better than no one having his back." Wayne then looks between me and Bryan, his eyes locking on Sophie. "Who's this?"

"This is our daughter, Sophie." Paul says.

"She's going to be a pretty good agent herself one day. She made an amazing tracking system for us down in Florida," Bryan says while knocking his shoulder with his sister.

"Stop it. You're embarrassing me." Sophie says while looking down at her shoes.

"Well, that's what brothers do; they embarrass the shit out of their little sisters. Just be lucky that I don't know all the crazy things I'm sure you did when you were younger." Bryan teases.

"Oh, I'll be sure to tell him all about that kind of thing." Paul jests.

"Dad! No!" Sophie cries, and Paul just laughs and pulls his daughter into his side. "No, I won't, Sweety. Unless he asks, then all bets are off."

Wayne laughs as he sits back in his chair. "Well, I'm glad to see the Evans family back in one piece after all these years apart. And Sophie, once you are ready, let me know and I'll give you a case to work on your own." Wayne then waves his hand toward the door. "Now get out of here. I have a meeting to get to. But, Paul, Cindy. It's so good to have you all back with us."

"It's good to be back." Paul agrees as he leads his family out of Wayne's office, and we follow behind them.

Chapter Fifty-Nine

Taylor

As the seven of us walk out of the agency, I turn toward Paul and Cindy just as Paul is getting ready to open the door for his wife.

"Hey, you guys want to come by my place for dinner? I want you all to meet my family too, and I'm sure that John and Gail would love more time with you all." I ask and look at Bryan to make sure he's okay with this, too.

Bryan nods. "I would love that. Would you all be free later?"

"Yeah, we will be there. Send me your address, Taylor, and what time dinner will be," Paul says as he smiles at the four of us before helping his girls into the SUV.

"Deal."

Later that night, after I told Dad we were going to have a full house for dinner, I texted Paul to let him know that dinner was going to be at six and sent him the address.

Mark and Lexi are already here, sitting on the couch, and Bryan just came in the door with his grandparents on his heels. They are talking animately about something, and the broad smile on Bryan's face warms my heart.

"So you gonna tell me if you're hitting that or not?" Lexi says from my side, and I jump at her sudden appearance.

"Why do you want to know? It's not like you tell me every time you and Mark hook up."

"Oh, I can, if you want," Lexi says, but before she can say more, thankfully the doorbell rings and I watch as Bryan's face morphs from happiness to hesitation for a heartbeat before he smiles at his grandmother.

"I'm going to go over with Bryan." I tell my friend.

God, I hope she doesn't say something off the wall tonight.

I meet Bryan in the middle of the living room, and I walk to the door with him. He gives me the briefest of smiles before he's opening the door.

"Good evening." Paul greets. "I didn't know if we should bring anything, so I got some Jack Daniels to share."

"That's great for everyone else," Bryan chuckles. "Gramps is gonna love it."

We both move to the side and show the three of them in, so I can introduce them to my parents.

"Mom, Dad, Cody, this is Paul, Cindy and Sophie."

"So these are the same agents you worked with down in Florida?" Dad asks.

"Yes."

"Well, it's nice to meet you all." Dad greets them while shaking Paul's hand.

"Dinner is on the table if you all are ready to eat," Mom says. "And you better get in there; Mark is already filling his and Lexi's plates." She adds with a slight laugh.

"Yeah, we better go or Mark will eat the table clean." Bryan says.

After a wonderful dinner of roast beef with the choice of carrots and potatoes or a mix of vegetables, we all settle down to eat among idle chatter of different tales of our lives.

Paul tells everyone what happened after he was shot and his long recovery in a private hospital, and I tell them how I got mixed up in Paul and Daryl's mess because of Lexi and her case.

Once the main course is over, I notice that Bryan gets up and walks out back. Finding it odd that he would just walk out on us, I follow him and find him sitting on one of the lounge chairs with his head in his hands.

"Hey, what's wrong?" I ask as I take a seat beside him.

He looks up at me and with tears in his eyes again. "God, I feel like such a crybaby lately."

"Hey, don't feel bad. You've had a lot thrown at you in the last few weeks. I mean Mark getting hurt, then having the parent bombshell dropped. It's a lot for one person to take in. So, I say cry away if you need to. I don't care because I will always be here to dry your eyes." I say as I wipe a few away from his cheek. "And don't think that crying makes you any less of a man."

"Thank you. I love you so much. I am beyond blessed to have such a wonderful woman like you by my side. And like always, I will fight like hell to get back to you," Bryan says.

That phrase makes me think back to the first time he told me he loved me on the couch at his grandparents' house a little over a year ago.

"I love you too, Bryan Alexander Evans, and I will fight like hell to always come back to *you*." I say.

"I'll make sure we hold each other accountable to that promise, Taylor. Because I want to spend every minute of every day with you." Bryan says as he presses his lips to mine like he's sealing that promise between us.

"I love that idea." I say as I stand and offer my hand to him. "Let's spend some time with your new family before they leave, because I want to spend the rest of my night with you."

"Oh, you do, huh?" Bryan says, his voice dipping an octave lower as he pulls me flush against him, and I can feel just how ready and willing he is for me. "Well, we'll have to see how quiet you can be, then. I don't want your mother killing me just yet. I want the chance to at least get to know my parents and sister first."

"Fair. But I would get in there soon, because Mark's been staring at us with a look that spells nothing but trouble." I tease.

"I swear, if he opens his big mouth, I'm gonna *kill him*." Bryan says as he steps away from me and walks inside.

I take a moment to look up at the sky, at the full moon that hangs above me, and I wonder what case will come our way next that will top this one.

The End

Epilogue 1

Taylor

TWO MONTHS LATER

"Come on, you two. You're killing me here!"

I'm in the kitchen with Dad packing lunches for our little baseball game this afternoon, while Bryan is in the living room with Cody and Sophie playing Mario Kart on the PS5.

"Is my brother this much of a whiner when he's losing?!" Sophie asks Cody as she throws another puka shell at Bryan's car.

"Always!" Cody shouts.

I can't help but smile at the three of them. Over these last two months, Paul, Cindy and Sophie have been coming over to either my parents' house or we've been meeting over at Bryan's grandparents' house for dinner once every week or two. And I've slowly seen the walls begin to crumble between Bryan and his parents.

Now he still doesn't call them mom and dad, but he's been bonding with Paul while they work on either the F150 or the Camaro at Dad's garage or if Bryan's helping my dad fix dinner, he shows his parents how good he's gotten in the kitchen.

And just like today, we are going to have a small baseball game between our friends. Mark and Lexi are picking up Josh and his team from the airport and will meet us at the field. That way we can have a guys vs girls game and see who can play better.

"Bryan! How dare you throw that banana at me?!" Sophie yells in offense.

"Now who's the whiner, Soph?" Bryan bites back. "I'm coming for you next, Cody."

"No!" Cody wails as he tries to throw a banana at Bryan's character, but misses.

I watch as Bryan smiles wickedly, throws a puka shell at Cody's car before flying over the finish line.

"I am victorious!" Bryan says in a mocking English accent, and I can't help but laugh.

"You are such a dork. It's only a video game."

"Hey, I take sibling rivalry very seriously now." Bryan says as he places the PS5 controller back onto the TV stand.

"Oh, you do, huh?" Sophie challenges as Bryan begins to get to his feet, then looks at Cody. "Commence Operation Pounce?"

My brother gives Sophie a mischievous smile before nodding once. Then they move. Cody wraps his little arms around Bryan's ankles while Sophie wraps hers around his neck, and she pulls down while my brother trips him.

"What the—" Bryan begins, but he doesn't finish as he face plants into the carpet, Sophie then straddling his back while Cody moves to Bryan's right side and begins tickling him.

"How's this for sibling rivalry?" Sophie asks while trying to give Bryan a noogie, but even I see when her center of gravity goes off balance, and I know her brother feels it too, when his lips curve into a smirk.

"I don't know, you tell me?" Bryan asks as he places his palms flat on the carpet, doing a push up that knocks Sophie from his back where she falls flat on her butt just as Bryan spins on his knees, grabbing both my brother and his sister into his arms and pinning both of them to his chest.

Just then the front door opens and my mother along with Granny, Gramps, Paul and Cindy walk in and they just stare at the three of them. My mother is the only one who rolls her eyes while the others blatantly smile, but I see her trying to hide her own behind her attitude.

"If you are all done with your wrestling match, we need to get Paul's SUV loaded up." Mom says.

"Okay. Okay." Bryan says, still smiling. "Let's go play some ball."

Bryan lets my brother and his sister go, and they all walk into the kitchen to grab the three coolers that are filled with water, Dr. Pepper, Gatorade, and sandwiches and takes them out to Paul's SUV, setting them in the hatch.

I grab the three bats and four balls that Dad found in the attic the other evening from his days of playing baseball when he was younger from beside the front door, and I walk them out to the open trunk of Bryan's Camaro. I shut the trunk, and when I turn, I find Bryan waiting for me by the wide open passenger door.

He wraps his hand around my waist, pulling me into him before kissing me tenderly on the lips, and when he pulls away, I catch the smirk on his face.

"You ready for me to beat you at baseball?"

I shake my head with a laugh. "Oh, I think it's going to be me who's beating you."

"Alright. You better bring your A game, Baby."

"Don't go crying to Mark when I win." I say as I drop into the seat, ignoring him to look through the windshield.

Bryan leans down, but before he can utter a single word, we hear Sophie yelling at us as she hangs out the rear passenger window of her father's SUV.

"Let's go! Do your mushy mushy kissy shit after the game!"

"If it's not your mother or a phone stopping us, it's my sister." Bryan grumbles.

"You regret having a sibling yet?"

"Not in a million years." Bryan says with no hesitation before closing my door.

"Bryan! Come on. I want to see Taylor kick your ass."

"Geez, you're not rooting for me to win?"

"Hell no!" Sophie grins as she slips into the SUV and rolls the window up.

Bryan opens the driver's side door and drops into the seat with a smile lighting up his entire face.

"Now I may regret the sibling thing."

I smack him on the shoulder. "You're horrible."

Bryan's phone pings with a text message, and it's Mark telling us he's picked up Josh and the others and are on their way to the ball field.

"Let's go. I wanna play ball!" I say while swinging an invisible bat towards him.

We arrive at the ball field thirty minutes later, and when we park, we see that Mark is already on the field tossing balls back and forth to the girls while Josh hits balls into the outfield for either Ian, Nick, or James to catch.

Mark looks over his shoulder, spotting us getting out of our vehicles, and I see the wild smirk on his face, and I know a Mark response is moments from erupting from his mouth.

"'Bout time ya'll got here. I wanna get this game started and show my girl that I know my way around a bat and balls."

"Oh, my God! Mark!" Lexi scolds while throwing said ball at his head, and he just cackles at her.

"Ugh, let's get on the field before Mark makes you guys lose by getting himself hurt. I don't want to win on a forfeit." I say.

"Let me help Paul and your dad with the coolers, and I'll be there." Bryan says while opening the gate for me so I can walk onto the field.

Josh gives me a glove as Mark tosses me a ball, the smile still bright on his face.

"One word from you and I'll make sure you guys lose." I warn.

Mark holds up his arms in surrender. "I didn't say a thing out of line. Your and Lexi's little brains took it wrong."

"Uh huh, sure." I say as I throw the ball to Lexi, who looks like she's about to kill Mark.

"Hey, can I play too?" Sophie asks from the gate.

"Me too!" Cody exclaimed. "Bryan said it's gonna be a girls against guys and I wanna beat my two sisters!"

My heart swells with happiness when Cody thinks of Sophie as his sister too, and before I can even say anything, Mark is grinning and pulling another two gloves from his duffle bag he has hanging on the fence near the visitor dugout.

"Sure thing, little man. Let's kick those girls' butts." He turns to Sophie. "And you can join the girls and try to beat us."

"Oh, we will win. Girls rule, and boys drool."

This gets all the guys laughing at us, and just as Bryan gets on the field and is getting down on the catcher's mound to catch some of Mark's warm-up pitches, I push Mark aside.

"This is why we will win." I wind up like the pitchers I've seen on TV, and I send the ball flying into Bryan's mitt. The solid thwack of leather hitting leather echoing in the air. "Girls, let's go. I think we will be up at bat first. Show these guys what we got. I say the first team to four and can close out that inning, wins."

"What if we shut you all out in the first inning?" Mark taunts.

"Then it's the best out of two." I say.

Bryan smiles at me, and it makes my blood heat. Just like any other time, he's silently daring me to show him how badass I am. And I intend to do just that.

As the guys take their spots on the field, Mark yells for Cody to be his catcher, or ball chaser for a more accurate job. Well away from the batter's box, but close enough that he can grab the balls once they roll on the ground and throw them back.

The girls and I decide to go in alphabetical order for our at bat line up, with Anna being first up. She misses the first two pitches Mark tosses underhanded her way, but on the last pitch, her bat connects with the ball and it flies past Josh, who is covering shortstop, bouncing once before Nick can catch it.

"Run!" The girls and I scream from the dugout as she races to first base.

Nick throws the ball across the field to James, but not quick enough. Anna's shoe touches first base. She's safe.

Christy is the next up to bat, and she unfortunately strikes out, just swinging at anything Mark throws at her. While Lexi is heading to bat, we show Christy what to look for in good pitches which, Mark is intentionally trying to make Lexi swing at his attempts, and on his last pitch she nails the ball clean over Mark's and Bryan's head where the field is empty.

Nick and Ian scramble to reach the ground ball, allowing Anna to run all the way to third while Lexi takes second just as the ball is thrown to Bryan. Both are safe.

Our families, which fill two bleachers on the home team side, erupt in a fit of cheers at Lexi's hit. And when I look at Bryan through the dugout fence, I can tell that while Paul and Cindy are cheering for the opposing team, he loves hearing them all the same, from the sly smile he has on his face.

Morgan is the next to take to the plate, and she knocks the ball towards the right field after two pitches. The ball sails past James and Bryan, giving Anna time to run home and for Lexi to make a break for third, but out in the right field, Ian grabs the ball and puts heat behind the pitch to Josh who taps Lexi out just before her shoe can touch the base. Anna is home, Lexi is out, and Morgan is safe on first. One point to us.

Roxie decides to let Sophie up next to bat so she can keep explaining to Christy what's going on with the game, and I can already see the teasing look on Bryan's face at his sister taking the field.

"Hey, Soph. Send the ball towards Bryan if you can." I tell her before she walks out of the dugout.

She looks in his direction, taking note of his down and ready stance and the smirk on his face. "Oh, he's gonna eat dirt."

Sophie takes the batter's box, checks her bat at the plate and aims her bat right at Bryan. "You better be ready, big bro. It's coming for ya."

"That is if you can make contact, little sis." He taunts.

Paul and Cindy's cheers for their daughter mingle with Granny and Grandpa's, and Bryan gives his grandparents a playful 'what the hell' look before focusing on the game again.

Mark makes the pitch, and Sophie cracks it on the first attempt. And like she promised it flies at Mark, making him drop to his stomach, while rocketing towards Bryan, where he tries to run backwards before trying to jump and catch it, but he ends up missing and falls backwards, tumbling onto his back, before rolling onto his knees and watching Nick run to pick up the ground ball, taking a moment to figure out a play before throwing it to third, tapping Morgan out.

This is our third out of the game, and now it's our turn to play the field, and Sophie takes over Cody's job of going after the balls and throwing them back. Roxie is our pitcher, while I'm covering first base, and I smile when Cody is the first up to bat.

"Come on, Cody! You got this!" Bryan hollers while the other guys cheer him on.

Roxi sends him the pitch, Mark screams at him to swing, and my brother does. I stand in shock when the ball soars high in the air, flying over Roxie's and Morgan's—who is covering second base—heads. Christy scrambles to catch the ball, so Anna races over, scooping the ball up before looking to see where Cody is and launching the ball towards Lexi who is running alongside my brother to try and catch the ball to tag him out as he rounds third, but even she misses the ball and Cody runs home.

Tied one to one.

Nick takes to the field next, and the freaker hits a home run on Roxi's first pitch. Two to one.

James takes the plate, and thankfully, Roxi is able to make him strike out. Josh is on the field next, and while he hits the ball, it's a pop up and Morgan is able to easily catch it in the air for a second out.

"Come on, girls!" I shout. "One more and we go next!"

Mark is next to bat, and he gives Lexi a smirk before pointing the bat at her. "My ball is coming for ya."

"Nice try. You're not getting me with implied dirty talk again, Stone!" Lexi barks.

He laughs as he gets into a ready stance, bat hovering over his shoulder. "Already did!"

Lexi groans, and just as she's about to hang her head, Roxi sends the pitch and Mark hits it. Over to my side of the field.

We were unprepared, given Mark's warning of where he was going to send it, and the ball flies past me. Thankfully, Christy catches the ground ball, but instead of throwing it to Morgan on second, she's throwing it to me.

I catch the ball, and as soon as I look at Morgan, Mark is rounding second and coming in hot at third, so I fling the ball at Lexi.

And she catches it just as Mark dives for third, sliding through the dried dirt. Her glove comes down, smacking him on the back just before his fingers brush the plate.

Third out. Still two to one. Our turn.

"Come on, girls. We got this!" I say, urging the girls on.

Roxi takes the plate first, and she hits the ball clean into the unmanned center field, and by the time Nick picks up the ball and throws it to Josh, she's sliding into third base–safe.

I breathe out a calming breath as I take the next at bat, especially since while I'm hearing cheers coming from my teammates and my parents in the stands, I'm also getting chewed out by my little brother from the foul line and Bryan, who's staring at me from second base, driving his fist into his mitt, telling me he's going to be catching my ball.

I circle the barrel of the bat over my shoulder, letting Mark know I'm ready for his pitch, and he delivers.

Crack.

The bat echoes in the air, and the ball soars, passing over the fence. I just hit a freaking home run!

I take my time running around the bases, soaking in the easy score. When I pass second, I give Bryan a little smirk.

"Can't catch the ball when it flies over your head and the fence."

"That was a lucky hit. I'll get a homer when I get up to bat next and win this game." He taunts.

"Sure. Keep dreaming!" I say as I run past him, tapping my foot on third before coming home to the group of girls screaming in my ear.

Three to two.

Lexi decides to go next, and she, amazingly, also gets a home run too. Making her ball fly over Josh and Nick's heads, and into the treeline to be lost forever among the pines.

Four to two. We only need to keep the guys from scoring when they take the bat at the end of this inning. Mark must know it too, because when Anna, Christy and Morgan are the next ones to bat, he easily strikes each of them out.

"Alright, girls, we need to play this hard if we want to win this. We need to keep the guys from making any runs. Just don't hold on to the ball. It's better to make a play than not do anything at all."

"Yeah! Let's go!"

We all take our positions on the field, and Cody is again the first at bat. He hits the ball between me and Morgan, but I'm able to scoop it off the ground, tagging him before he can touch first base. His little head hangs as he drags the bat behind him, and I give him a smile.

"Hey little man. You were great." I say as I look over his reddened cheeks. "Go get some water from the coolers."

"Okay," He says pitifully as he walks off the field, and I see Mom intercept him at the gate to give him a bottle of water.

James comes up next, and he hits a ball into center field, and by the time we get the ball into our hands, he's on second, and the same thing happens with Ian. He hits the ball towards Anna, and when she gets it to Lexi, we only stop the guys enough where James and Ian are on third and second base.

Josh is up next, and he hits the ball over Morgan's head, and she races to catch it. James slides home, and when Ian is just about to hit third, somehow Morgan launches the ball to Lexi and she catches it, but not before both guys safely touch the bases.

It's now four to three, and we still need two more outs to win.

"Come on, Roxi. Shut him down!" I cheer as Nick takes the plate, and she manages to get him out, even with pitching him three balls to start with.

"Time!" Roxi calls from the pitcher's mound as Bryan takes to the batter's box and does some practice swings.

The four of us from the bases gather around the dugout to try and formulate a game plan, when Paul catches my attention, waving me over.

"What's up?" I ask.

"Do you think it would be alright if I pitch for this play?"

I glance over my shoulder towards Bryan, who's still warming up with practice swings to notice us at the dugout.

I turn to Roxi, and motion for her to hand over her mitt.

Epilogue 2

Bryan

I hear the girls clap their hands behind me and run to take their positions back on the field. Taylor passes me on her way to first base with a sly grin on her face. I reach out, swatting her on the ass, and she spins around, using her mitt to cover her beautiful curves.

"Bryan!" She scolds, her face turning bright red. "Not in front of Paul!"

"He's in the stands—" I begin, but I'm cut short when I hear his voice call out to me, but it's a lot closer than I realized.

"Let's go, Sport. You can flirt with your girlfriend after the game."

My heart leaps at the teasing tone in his voice, and even with them being in my life for two months, I can't lie and say that I don't get a strange fluttering in my chest when he calls me Sport.

At first, I think about letting his comment slide, and go to the plate, but he told me one day while we were working on my F150 to be myself around him. Not to hold back on any snarky, teasing comments. So I'm not gonna hold back now.

"You sure you can throw a ball, old man?"

"Get your ass on the plate and let's find out."

And I told him that snarky comments go both ways with us, and he doesn't disappoint.

With a smirk, I step up to the plate, balancing the bat over my shoulder, trying to figure out what kind of pitch he's going to send my way.

He throws me a fastball. Ball one.

Then a slider. Strike one.

He throws a curveball that almost makes me want to swing, but I don't. Ball two.

Then a sinker that's a strike.

"Come on, old man, give me something to swing at!"

"Alright, you asked for it."

He throws me what looks like a curveball, and it's right in the sweet zone to send it flying, but then as I swing, it sinks, and I strike out.

"Damn it!" I hear Mark and a few other guys utter curses under their breath, but the girls are squealing with their victory.

Paul walks from the pitcher's mound while rolling his shoulder as if easing the ache out of the joint, and I can't help but smile at him.

"See? This old man still has tricks up his sleeve."

"Nah, you just got lucky." I say while shaking my head at him.

He smacks me on the back before squeezing the soft spot between my neck and shoulder. The movement is something that I've always dreamed of having my father do since I was a boy, that it makes my eyes burn with tears.

"That was still a helluva game, Sport. Good job."

"Thanks." I say, my voice tight with emotion.

Then Sophie comes running over to us, throwing herself at her father...at *our* father.

"Daddy! We won!" Then she turns to me. "I told you girls rule."

I laugh, rolling my eyes at her. "We'll get you next time. Don't let this win go to your head."

"Sore loser." She says, then blows a raspberry at me before bounding off to the girls' dugout to help gather the equipment.

I can't help but shake my head again as I follow Paul off the pitcher's mound and lend a hand in raking the field along with Josh and Mark. As my best friend and I rake around the dirt of second base, he taps me on the shoulder.

"Hey, that was cool of Paul pitching to you."

"Yeah, it was."

"I just know that was important to you, and I wanted to let you know I was happy for you two," Mark says. "But, I'm not gonna let your dad cramp our games. Old man couldn't pitch and cost us what should have been an easy win."

"That's what I thought! I think the girls planned it."

"Totally." Mark grins as he finishes raking his spot of the dirt.

Then, once the field is put back in order, we all wash up in the public bathrooms before piling into a nearby pavilion to eat lunch. Josh and his team need to catch an evening flight back down to Florida, so we offered them lunch after the game.

As I'm getting a sandwich and a bottle of Dr. Pepper from the cooler, Grandpa stops me, and I notice the sly grin on his face.

"What are you up to?" I ask with a raised brow.

"Nothing at all. I've just heard that the girls want to have a nice dinner from you guys tonight to celebrate their win, and I may or may not have a half a bottle of wine that I'd hate to see go missing from my liquor cabinet."

I look at him in shock. I didn't think he knew about Mark and I taking that bottle when we were younger.

"What? You think I didn't notice that bottle missing from my cabinet? I just didn't say anything because I knew you and that damn heathen were in the house, and I kept an eye on ya'll. Figured it'd be better for you two to learn about your alcohol tolerance in a safe environment than out on the street where god only knew what was in the shit."

"Well, at least thanks for making me think we got by with something." I say sarcastically, but his words do give me an idea.

I spot Mark over at a table with Nick and Ian, so I walk over to him, making sure to pull him aside before I ask him my question.

"Hey man. Are you planning on going to the cabin tonight?"

"No. I'm just taking Lexi back to our apartment to celebrate. Why?" His eyebrows shoot up to his hairline, figuring out already why I'm asking. "Ohhh, you wanna get cray cray with Tay Tay?" He asks while rolling his hips suggestively.

"I'm not going to tell you—okay, yes. We tried it two weeks ago, and I thought Taylor was quiet enough, but the next morning Kathy was shooting daggers at me over her scrambled eggs, and frankly the way she was stabbing them with her fork scared me."

All Mark does is laugh.

"And the way Tom was throwing tires around the shop that afternoon didn't help. So, Taylor and I haven't done much since then."

"So you have blue balls and it's getting to ya, huh?" Mark asks while patting my shoulder in mock consolation.

"Screw you, man!" I groan, as said balls ache as a reminder of when I last came for Taylor.

"Nah. I don't swing that way. But if you do, more power to ya."

"Mark, shut the hell up." I say as I shove him away from me.

"Hey you better be nice or I'll tell your grandpa about the alcohol we took from his cabinet!"

"Jokes on you, asshole, he knows. Has the whole time!" I pull him closer with an elbow around his neck. "But, I bet he doesn't know about you copying a picture of him and cutting his head off to put on the swimsuit models in your Playboy magazines when we were in junior high."

"You wouldn't!"

"Keep saying stupid shit and let's find out."

He growls under his breath before shoving my arm from his shoulders. "You always fight dirty, man."

I laugh as he walks away, joining Lexi at the picnic table, and his frown instantly turns into a smile for her. I'm still chuckling when I take my spot next to Taylor, and she looks between me and Mark with amused concern in her eyes.

"Do I want to know what you all were talking about?"

"No, you don't." I say as I open my Dr. Pepper and take a drink. "Hey, tell your parents you aren't going to be home tonight."

"Oh! Are you taking me out to celebrate?" Taylor asks. "But why don't you tell them?"

"I kinda want to live to see tonight."

"My parents are not gonna kill you."

"Well, I'm not gonna press my luck." I say, then take a bite of my sandwich. "I'll pick you up at, say, seven?"

"What do you have planned, Bryan Evans?" Taylor asks as she trails a finger up my forearm, making goosebumps come alive in her wake.

"You'll have to wait and find out." I tease with a playful wink and then turn my head to join in the conversations happening around us.

After making sure that Josh and his team get safely on the plane later that afternoon, I prepare the cabin for Taylor and, as promised, I'm pulling up to her house at seven sharp in my Camaro. She must have been waiting for me by the window, because she's flinging open the front door, runs across the yard and into my arms.

I catch her, spinning her around before setting her feet on the ground and giving her a quick kiss.

"You ready to go?" I ask.

"Beyond ready for my celebration adventure."

Before I can turn around and open my car door, I hear Kathy's voice ring out from the stoop.

"Be *safe,* you two."

She gives me the evil-eye gesture, and I know what she means. I give her a firm nod as I say, "She's in good hands, Kathy. Don't worry."

"She better be." She says as she crosses her arms over her chest, but I see the slight smile on her face at my words, and I'm beginning to think that maybe she won't kill me for our escapades. "If you hurt her, I'll kill you."

Welp, so much for that thought.

"Mom! Come on! Be nice," Taylor says as she grabs my hand. "Let's go."

I give her another kiss, not caring that it's in front of her mother, and I lead her to my car and help her inside. When I drop in behind the wheel, Taylor turns on the radio, and she sings her head off on every Taylor Swift, Maroon 5, Daugherty, and Pink song that comes across her Spotify list, and I end up singing along to some too.

When we pull up to the cabin, the soft glow of the lights shines through the windows, and I help Taylor out of the car and onto the steps. Her soft gasp hits my ears as she takes in the pink and red rose petals I sprinkled across the wooden porch.

"Bryan, what did you do?" She asks breathlessly.

I stay quiet as I open the door, and as we step in, the table comes into view first. It's draped with an ivory tablecloth that I got from Granny, along with battery-operated taper candles sitting in the middle. I have Taylor's favorite dish, lobster and rice, to go with the white wine I have resting in a bucket of ice.

"Bryan, this is amazing." She says, still in awe as she takes in the different size roses strewn about the room.

"I told you I wanted to wine and dine the hell out of you before we made love." I whisper next to her ear, and she shivers against me.

"Yes, you did say that." She turns to look at me over her shoulder, pressing her ass against my hips, and making me already needy for her. "Let's eat."

"What if I wanted to change the menu?"

"And waste this lobster? No way!" Taylor says, but I see the teasing light in her eyes. "Besides, there's always dessert." She adds with a wink.

So we sit down to eat, and it's both the longest and shortest meal we've ever had, and we didn't even eat half of the food.

I no longer down my remaining gulp of wine from my glass and I'm pulling her into my arms, kissing her deeply, skimming my tongue over her lips to beg for entry. When our tongues meet, her hands shoot into my hair, tugging at my scalp, and I break.

"Bedroom, now."

"Good thing Mark wasn't around to hear that, or he'd really be cackling now."

"The only man's name I want on your lips is mine, Annie." I growl as I pick her up by her thighs, making her wrap them around my waist as I carry her to the master bedroom.

I drop her onto the bed, and I rip my shirt over my head before I reach for hers, letting them both fall to the floor to be completely forgotten. I take in her lavender bra softly cupping her perfect breasts together, and I harden painfully against the zipper of my jeans.

"You drive me absolutely crazy, Taylor. You know that?" I ask as I let my gaze travel over her body before letting my fingers unbutton her jeans, which give me a little peek of her matching panties.

"The feelings mutual," Taylor pants as she rakes her nails down my chest and stomach, stopping just at the top of my pants.

"How are we gonna fix that?" I wonder as I remove her jeans, throwing them to the opposite side of the bedroom, leaving her in only her bra and panties.

"You're a smart man. I trust you to figure that out."

"Oh, you do, huh?" I ask as I lean in, bracing my arms on either side of her head, my lips just a breath away from hers. "Well, then I'll need to ask some questions first. You know, to help me figure things out."

I turn my head, kissing her neck then I travel down her throat until I reach the dip between her collarbones.

"Where do you want me first?"

Taylor slides her hand down her body, her thumb pulling at the fabric of her lavender panties. "Here. I want you to start here."

"Are you already weeping for me, Baby?" I ask as my own blood pulses and rushes between my legs, making me hard as steel.

"Bryan, please."

"Well, since you asked so nicely." I croon as I glide my hand down her belly, hooking my index and middle fingers into her panties and slide them from her hips. "Fuck, Taylor." I groan this time when I see she's completely soaked for me. "This is going to be the best dessert I'm ever gonna find."

I don't give her time to think through my response. I grab her calves in each hand, throw them over my shoulder and I dive in. My tongue travels up her core before I use the tip to tease her clit, and she's already panting, moaning and chanting my name, and it's music to my ears.

"See? Told you. Best thing ever, Baby."

I drive my tongue deep inside only to pull it out before diving back for seconds, and thirds.

"Bryan! I'm gonna come!" Taylor screams.

"That's it, Annie. Give it to me. Let me taste the cherry on top." I give her clit a flick with my finger as I dive into her core with my tongue, and she shatters, her legs pulling me closer so I can taste every last drop of her climax.

Once she comes down off her high, she looks up at me, pleasure written all over her beautiful face. "That was amazing."

I chuckle darkly at her as I slide off the bed, pulling her down to the end with me. "And I'm not even done with you yet, Baby."

"What?"

I pull the foil packet from my front pocket before taking my time in pushing my jeans and boxers down my hips, letting my erection free from the painful confines of my pants.

"Turn over on your hands and knees." I order as I tear the condom package with my teeth the way I know she loves to see and roll the latex over my hard-on.

"Bryan." Taylor pants, and I can hear the note of apprehension along with wonder about what I'm going to do as she turns over to rest on her hands and knees.

"You ready for this?" I ask as I step behind her, unhooking her bra, and as her breasts hang free, I'm barely able to keep my crown from brushing against her clit.

"Yes," She whispers.

I grab her hips with my hands, fingers digging into her flesh. "Good. Because I'm tired of waiting."

I make myself take my time pushing into her, relishing in the way her walls flutter and squeeze around me, and in this position, she somehow feels even better, and I have to fight to keep from already coming. Just as I bottom out in her Taylor sways back on her knees, pushing me even deeper, making her moan the most erotic sound and forcing a growl from my throat.

"Oh my god, Bryan! Yes! More, please."

I can't form words; I can only act. I pull my hips back, loving the feeling of her this way just as much, and when I have just the tip remaining inside, I slide back in, easier but no less pleasurable. And I keep going, her moans, pants and gasps urging me on. Harder, deeper, faster until I'm lost in her feel, her sound.

I somehow float back down the earth, and I lean into her back so I can whisper in her ear. "You're taking me so well, Baby. You feel amazing around me."

Her inner walls begin to flutter and contract at my words, and I know she's close to another climax, just like I can feel my own building low in my back.

"Don't hold back from me, Taylor. I can feel you wanting to come. Give it to me, Baby." I urge as I pick up my tempo, pounding into her.

Her head tilts back as the loudest cry of the night tears from her throat, and she comes around me to the point she's shaking on the bed, and that does me in. With my arm around her stomach, I pull her to my chest; the angle making me somehow drive even deeper, immediately igniting another climax for her while mine also barrels down my spine, making my thrusts become erratic and growls leave my throat.

"You're so beautiful when you come for me, Taylor." I kiss the side of her neck before biting into it, not even caring that I just left my mark for anyone to see. I want people to know she's mine.

"And you're so handsome and strong when you come for me, Bryan," Taylor says, and she turns her head, kissing me on the lips where I know she can taste herself on my tongue.

Feeling a bit more grounded in my body again, I slowly loosen my hold on her, and she rests her hands back on the bed. When I ease out of her, she softly moans, but I know it's just from the loss of my body from hers and not from me hurting her.

"Let me take care of this condom and get you a warm washcloth."

"I know I always say this, but I love the way you care for me."

"Always, Baby"

After I take care of the condom and tend to her well-loved core, we slide into bed together. Her head resting on my chest while I trace idle lines up and down her back.

"Tonight was amazing, Bryan. Thank you. For everything."

"Anything for you, Annie."

We are quiet for a few minutes, just taking the other in, but I'm tossing around an idea in my head and I decide I'm just gonna ask her and hope for the best.

"Hey, Taylor?"

"Yeah?" She answers, tilting her head up to look at me.

I brush my fingers through her hair, and I take a breath before I speak. "What do you think about getting our own place?"

"What?" Taylor asks, and for a split second I think she'll say no. I mean we are only twenty and nineteen.

"Bryan I—"

"If you're not—" She cuts me off next.

"Where would we live? Here?" She asks, looking around the cabin.

"We can get our own apartment. I've seen a few for rent around town. This can be our home away from home." I tell her. "What do you say?"

"I would love to move in with you, Bryan. Then we wouldn't have to sneak off for nights like these. I can have you to myself whenever I want to," Taylor says as she trails her nails down the center of my chest.

"Are you already wanting more, my little vixen?"

"Are you up for more?"

"Baby, I could live inside you, and I could never get enough."

"Let's put that to the test then, shall we." She teases as she pulls another condom from the nightstand, straddling my hips while rolling the latex over my erection and then takes her time riding me, building our climaxes to the breaking point until we both explode for the second time tonight.

Acknowledgements

I'd like to give a heartfelt shout-out to my beta readers for this book!

Kaaidth

Natacsha

Dice

Thank you all for taking the time to read this and help me make it even better with your tips and insights!

Also, a big thank you to my ARC reader, Sabrena L.

OX- B.M. Light

Other Works

Thank you for reading, *Secrets in Miami.*

If you liked this story, please consider leaving a review on Goodreads or wherever you purchased this story. I would greatly appreciate it!

Also, if you want to see where Bryan, Taylor, Mark and Lexi's story started, read the first book in the series *Everyone Has Secrets.*

Other works:

The Wolf Within- Paranormal Werewolf Romance -Fated Mates- Protective MMC's

Fire and Water- Elemental Power System- Friends to Lovers- Enemies to Lovers- Side Character MM Romance

See you in the next book, Readers!!

X.O. B. M. Light

9 798990 255487